Lions of the Grunewald

Aidan Higgins was born in 1927. His books include the novels *Langrishe, Go Down* (1966), which won the James Tait Black Memorial Prize and the Irish Academy of Letters Award and was filmed for television with a screenplay by Harold Pinter, and *Balcony of Europe* (1972). His selected shorter fiction, *Helsingør Station & Other Departures*, and travel writing, *Ronda Gorge & Other Precipices*, were published in 1989.

Aidan Higgins

Lions of
the Grunewald

Minerva

A Minerva Paperback

LIONS OF THE GRUNEWALD

First published in Great Britain in 1993
by Martin Secker & Warburg Ltd
This Minerva edition published 1995
by Mandarin Paperbacks
an imprint of Reed Consumer Books Ltd
Michelin House, 81 Fulham Road, London SW3 6RB
and Auckland, Melbourne, Singapore and Toronto

Copyright © 1993 by Aidan Higgins
The author has asserted his moral rights

A CIP catalogue record for this title
is available from the British Library
ISBN 0 7493 9718 7

Photoset by Deltatype Ltd, Ellesmere Port, Cheshire
Printed and bound in Great Britain
by Cox & Wyman Ltd, Reading, Berkshire

For Paris and Yanika
of the Finca Fuente de la Vieja

Apologia

We have incorporated material previously published in fugitive *Ur*-fiction, notably from *Ronda Gorge & Other Precipices* (1989), as stages in the process of *yolking* together the massacre at Sharpeville (21 March 1960) and *Schwarzer September* (Munich 1972) via a nightmare in Schwabing, an archery contest, a river flowing backwards, some pseudo-gangsters, and the broken eggshells from a blackbird's nest fallen into a Munich fountain; now all set in their proper context, relocated from embryonic themes.

Other local Berlin references are lifted from *Zoo Station*, an earplay commissioned by BBC Radio 3.

Nico's yarns are wrung from *Colossal Gongorr & the Turkes of Mars* (Jonathan Cape, 1979), written by my three sons in their days of innocence; since remaindered, as also *Ronda Gorge*.

A.H.

Contents

Part II Fugacity of Pleasure, Fragility of Beauty

Part III Injuries of Time and Nature

Dallan Weaver (TCD*, DILDO**), an Irish author
Nancy (née Els), his South African wife
Nico, their only son

Franz Born, head of DILDO
Titania ('Titty'), his wife
Bertha Busse, his secretary

Mando Demotropoulos (DILDO), Greek poet
Baron Bogdana Kuguar (DILDO), Polish poet
Baroness Kasia, his Polish wife

Professor Paul Pflücker
Libgart, his wife

William ('Winky') Prendergast (DILDO), Irish sculptor
Nelly (née Ebert), his Berliner wife

Bart ('Murt') Murnane, poet and honorary Irishman
Sasha (née Barathea), his Jewish-Russian-American wife

Dr Wieland Weissenborn, former Gestapo officer, banker
Margarete (née Taut), his wife
Randall ('Randy') Loftus, Pan Am pilot

*TCD: Trinity College, Dublin, Weaver's Alma Mater
**DILDO: Deutsche-Internationale Literatur-Dienst Organisation

Dora ('Dot') (née Deck), a Vermont milkmaid; his wife
Dixie, their golden retriever

Peter Handke (DILDO), Austrian dramatist
Wolfgang Bauer (DILDO), as above
Günter Grass, German novelist and librettist
Max Frisch, Swiss novelist and dramatist

Volker Schlöndorff, Munich film director
Margarethe von Trotta, his wife

Arland Ussher, Irish sage
Emily (née Lysaght), his wife
A Sandycove seer

Betty Buzzard, Nancy's South African friend
Martin Lindemann, Weaver's Berlin friend
Toby ('Trimmer') Tyrrell, Winky's friend
Mad Mick, another
Fat George, another
Rex Gamble, Nancy's admirer
Varna Anders, Weaver's Munich friend
Ulrike Noyes, Varna's friend

Luis Nkose, African in a dream
Sir Delves Digby Bullpitt of the British Council
Meyric Mellor, his no. 2
Vernon Hoare, their harpist
Sir Kenneth Clark, patrician aesthete
Herr Otto von Bismarck, Munich tailor
Takahashi-san, sculptor and pornographer
Rudolf Hess, the last Nazi in Spandau Prison
Arno von Rajinski, Polish-German, of Crown Mines
Rita (née Power), his Irish-South African wife
Colonel Hans Spengler, Vereeniging Police Chief
Colonel Piet Schreiber, Munich Police Chief
Abu Daoud, Al Fatah terrorist

Jack Lynch, Irish Taoiseach

Heinz Otto Walser, Lore's chief

Sepp Walser, his son

Papa (Axel) Schröder, Berliner

Mama Schröder (née Axmann), his wife Magda Anneliese

Hannelore (Lore), their only daughter

I see the Berlin Wall, flowers, graves,
H. speaks of the last days here, the
streets on fire, the lions loose, the
world that has outstripped our nightmares,
our subconscious.

John Cheever, *Journals*

Marriage knots aren't going to slip apart
painlessly, with the pull of distance.
There's got to be some wrenching
and slashing.

Alice Munro, *The Progress of Love*

In the evening there, in little cul de
sacs, the soul seems to dissolve.

Vladimir Nabokov, *Speak, Memory*

Prologue:
Herr Hasenclever Calls

One evening at dusk a small-sized man in a tubular tweed overcoat rang the bell and stood on the mat in the unlit porch.

Weaver threw open the door and saw the luminous low snow-covered roof of the *Fleischermeister*'s bungalow, across the ridge of which a chimney-sweep in fulginous work-clothes with face blackened under a tall top hat made his slow way with the extreme caution of a diver weighted down by pressure on the seabed.

Weaver shook the small damp simian hand as the low voice whispered that he was Walter Hasenclever and had moreover the honour of being moderator at Weaver's reading at the Akademie der Künste scheduled for early March; even if he was no relation to the famous German dramatist of the same name, teehee.

'Come in anyway,' said Weaver, motioning him in.

'Thank you.'

The diminutive visitor removed a beaver cap with woolly earflaps; under one arm a box of Milk Tray, and in one gloved hand a red rose, presumably presents for Nancy, but nothing for Weaver.

Khukov's men, the advanced spearheads, entered Berlin through the northern suburbs, screeching as they ran. The infantry went in first over the minefields and tank traps, to be blown to glory; but others came on, screeching, wave after wave. Then the tanks went in.

The sneery sculptor who had fluent Spanish asked Weaver what was his astrological sign. When told Pisces he scowled, muttered '*Kalt blut*'. A month later Weaver heard that he had died of a heart attack, crawling downstairs from his walk-up apartment on Krumme Strasse to expire naked on the pavement below. Near there Weaver and Lore drank glasses of superior red wine at Hardy's by the Opera in a darkened room where they were alone and she told him that in Bastia the black bucks had displayed themselves shamelessly, hung like horses.

The Black Cells, sometimes called Anarchists, ran through the passive resisters as hyenas among wildebeest and the police bulls watched from behind wired glass in their paddywagons parked in side streets, at times drenching both parties impartially with water-cannons or running them with fierce baton-charges.

Insistence on the particular and unique (The Singular Me) had spawned the microbe Duplication. The Face was on the screen, on the high hoardings, in the street; and violence let loose there in the open, the dream gone mad. For the individual as such was disappearing and the world's capitals had become *pissoirs*.

Schlagermusik throbbed from underground rock cellars along the Ku'damm; one gaudy entrance led down into an inflamed red throat out of which rose the whiff of perdition.

I

*Fugacious Nature
of Life and Time*

1
Wannseebad

The *Motorschiff Vaterland* steamed by the *Dampfer Siegfried*, one outward-bound for Spandau, the other inward-bound for the Wannsee landing-stage. Soon their wakes joined up to become one, sending a shiver over the broad reaches of the Havel.

Presently dirty waves were slapping against the Wannseebad shore where ill-tempered swans waded through the shallows, hissing, choking on the slops of bread floating there; whole sodden loaves were bobbing half-submerged along the shoreline stained a brownish tinge.

Basketweave beach-huts with fleecy linings and coy marine motifs of sprat, anchor and shell were up-ended like coffins with open fronts averted from the wind; set along the fine sand shifted years before in containers from the Nordsee shore. Married couples of companionable middle age sprawled asleep on this white sand that got into food and clothing and ruined picnics; *his* balding head beaded with perspiration and strands of tow-coloured hair stuck to the hot scalp, *her* dentures askew. Their loyal *Hunde* snored next to them, all three snorting and twitching in identical key, *ein hübsches Lied*!

The warm air was rising off the lakes.

Weaver watched the people below, the perambulating citizens, how complacently and solidly they passed, seldom alone but with a dog or two in tow, going clockwise or anti-clockwise about the two little lakes, breast out, seeking Nature's embrace, putting in time before *Kaffee und Kuchen* again. Their days revolved around good solid square meals; they looked mightily determined, these stoutly complacent bottom-feeders, full of – well, themselves; gorged with life.

Weaver descended a flight of steps onto which sand had blown and drifted and was among tall trees that grew near the water's edge and the grey Schlachtensee that reflected them back again and the clouds that passed over and the jet trails in the sky that went drifting as the wind shifted them along as the jets came and went on the Tempelhof air corridor.

As if newly risen in a dream or a condemned spirit moving in free space, Weaver went down there, the balmy air off the Schlachtensee rising to meet him. To see a great lion and lioness coming down from the Grunewald to drink in the golden light of those sandy shores would scarcely have surprised him.

2
Vampyr Model

The Weavers were on the lookout for quiet and secluded accommodation through the academic year in Berlin (West), with most of their outlayings covered by the Deutsche-Internationale Literatur-Dienst Organisation *stipendium* from Bonn. Herr Franz Born, head of DILDO, had put his Mercedes and his time at their disposal. The DILDO people also were keeping a sharp lookout. Bertha Busse showed them over a number of apartments, but none were suitable. The right place would be found in time, it was only a matter of looking. A number of apartments and houses were considered in the Charlottenburg and Dahlemdorf areas, then as far afield as Nikolassee, where at last a suitable house was found with a secluded back garden sown with fruit, a fenced lawn out front. The honorary title of Professor was Franz Born's idea, for it would create a good impression on the Berlin landladies.

Berlin landladies, *ach*, what a breed!

The *Hauswirtins* – Franz Born called them 'professional landladies' – had themselves worked out a graded scale of rents based not on good or bad character but on nationality, for dealing with DILDO's foreign guests. First on the scale came the small quiet Japanese who appeared to be so obliging – Ishi the composer (would he require stereophonic equipment; Franz Born was worried). Then came the Americans bursting with dollars.

Then wily French and phlegmatic English, these two already part of the occupational force; they were all right. But not so all right were the Italians; Greeks were suspect; Slavs more so. And as for the Turks, Bulgars and Balks, the messy Balkan races, forget them; they were not welcome.

The Irish were an unknown breed, 'Professor' Weaver being the first such representative on the Bonn payroll.

No. 51 Beskidenstrasse was situated in nookshotten Nikolassee near the Jochen-Klepper-Weg – a narrow woodland walk that led to the Little Squirrel Inn hard by the student village. The house itself would not have looked amiss beside the grander mansions that fringed the Rehweise and the meadows below. The present owner, Frau Ursula Meinhardt, was a war widow. A month after the first viewing, by which time the present American tenants would have departed, the Weavers could move in. Terms were agreed upon and a contract drawn up, with an awkward proviso that left the attic at the disposal of the landlady, should she at any time care to visit Berlin, which she thought was mostly unlikely; which proved to be nothing less than a barefaced lie.

She arrived one afternoon from Wiesbaden, haunt of four-square *Hausfraus*, with two tall Airedales on the back seat of the green Karman Ghia, to view the 'Veevers' and their little boy, Nico. She had not long left off her widow's weeds but would never refer to her late husband, no doubt one of the many officers killed before frozen Stalingrad, or at Kursk, or in the butchery of the Caucasus, or in the Kuban in the death-struggle to open a way to Tiflis; not a word.

She liked to flirt discreetly over the fence with the retired *Fleischermeister* who lived alone in the bungalow opposite between the Dutch people from the Berlin Symphony Orchestra and the Pan Am pilot and his family. Beyond the silent Dutch pair lived the former Gestapo man from the death-camp who now worked as a political adviser at the Dresdener Bank on the Bundesallee.

Out of the ex-butcher's squat chimney belched thick black smoke. Perhaps he was destroying thick incriminating archives and tabulated files of evidence? Wieland Weissenborn of the Dresdener Bank and Maidanek camp had a charming wife, Margarete Weissenborn, and the two brats Fritz and Klaus who spent much time quarrelling in the sandpit. Twice every morning at postal delivery time, weekends excluded, the Americans' pedigree retriever Dixie went for the stout delivery woman who arrived punctually and flustered at 10.30 a.m. on an old-style bike and Dixie would have eaten the leather patch off her broad bum were it not for the protective mesh of the ten-foot-high cyclone fencing.

Dr Weissenborn admitted to having machine-gunned Jews in the camp; he should have turned the gun against his companions in the SS. He was not getting on too well with his nice wife and was to spend much time bending the Professor's ear on this touchy subject, over many Italian white wines, beers and steins in the Weissenborn home, in the dark recesses of the sinister Gambe Stube, a place for indiscretions. Or al fresco at the Rönisch Kiosk on the Argentinische Allee, when not at the old bar before Nikolassee S-Bahn, or the platform service that sold drink, conveniently situated *en route* to and from work; not to mention a couple of bars in Mexikoplatz stop-over, or the remoter Eichhörnchen on the fringe of the wood, where one evening the Professor sat opposite a sleeping Weissenborn, a limp fag dangled between tobacco-stained index and middle finger, his weary head supported on his chest. In a church not far away both Goebbels and Heydrich had been married, though not to each other, thank God.

Two other slumberers snored over their unfinished steins. Weaver waited for Weissenborn to wake up, which he did presently, dipping his lips into the beer. Wieland Weissenborn was not his real name, he had confided once, but Pavel Jerusalem; his father came from Slutsk in Belorussia.

9

If it was hard to deflect him off the subject of the marital tedium and frustration he suffered, it was impossible to divert him from the no less tiresome subject of Marxism and World Socialism that would one day arrive; once fairly started he droned away for hours.

The Pan Am pilot and his wife, Randall and Dora, played relentless games of incompetent tennis on the hard courts near the Lutheran church where the Nazis had once plighted their troth; while the silent Dutch couple, being tinged with that slightly ceremonial Dutch reserve, played no games. They did not mix but kept themselves to themselves and spoke only to their two children, a boy and a girl as Dutch as Delft. In a month's time these good people would be the neighbours of the Weavers.

The Meinhardt mansion had all that one could wish for in the way of home comforts. A glassed-in sunroom overlooked the garden stocked with vines and strawberry; a hammock was slung between two cherry trees; the veranda above led into the low-ceilinged master bedroom, a broad double bed covered in scarlet damask.

The house immediately left of the Meinhardt spread belonged to a seedy weatherbeaten bachelor who passed no. 51 daily with head lowered, carrying an empty string shopping-bag, looking furtive, heading for the store at the corner near the bakery. Half an hour later he would slink back with the bag still empty. This lugubrious shopper was caretaker for no. 51 when it was unoccupied; looking after the boiler-room in the basement and airing out the house.

The neighbours to the right were the Winds. Hans Wind was Dutch and deaf as a post, seldom spoke – as if he were dumb – and liked to take his little son Günter out on a rubber dinghy on Krumme Lanke. Dutch mother Hilde was a dead ringer for Queen Juliana of the Netherlands. Their pretty daughter had long auburn hair, ran a green Karman Ghia (a lighter shade of green than Frau Meinhardt's), and was attended by an adoring boyfriend, rendered speechless by her beauty. The Winds were model neighbours. An odd sapling with luminous lemon-yellow leaves grew in their garden and was fed with milk.

Weaver, a great walker, took to rambling about the Rehweise or took the path that traversed the Jochen-Klepper-Weg; for could you find anything pleasanter than emerging from the shadowy wood to espy just ahead the blue neon sign for Schultheiss Bier welcoming the drinkers in, and Wieland far away in the vaults of the bank on the Bundesallee!

At weekends the convivial Weissenborns would have friends in for drinks and invited the Weavers, new guests in Berlin, across to meet Horst Busch and Ulli Udet and horrible Hans Hund the killer of hares in the Harz Mountains. And there too, sometimes, alas, Freddi the sop to the host's passionate socialism – the part-time gardener and full-time alcoholic Freddi in a catatonic state of inebriation and no little embarrassment. Freddi stank to high heaven, but the genial host threw his arms about his shoulders and led him to the drinks.

'Man, the only animal that can remain on friendly terms with the victims he intends to eat, until he eats them!' Wieland dumbfounded Freddi, now cross-eyed with puzzled feelings, *zicke-zacke*.

Balancing precariously on the balls of his feet, Wieland stoutly declared: 'Espionage has become another branch of industry in modern Germany! Have you read Heinrich Böll, Professor?'

Indeed he had; and furthermore had met Günter Grass, at a *Bücherfest* in Amsterdam.

'He is our greatest writer.'

Much Schultheiss beer and Italian white wine were dispatched and cigars and cigarettes offered around and Busch sang hoarsely out of tune

> 'A'hmm dreeheemen uvva Red Chrissmass
> Yuss lack the vons vee ussa know, ho, ho, ho!'

Otherwise those Nikolassee nights were silent as the grave. Apart from the sound of distant trains, so disturbing to any Jewish ears that might be listening, or the footsteps of Dr Weissenborn, sprightly when going forth (sober), stumbling when unsoberly returning on one of his regular sorties to and from the Rönisch kiosk a kilometre away on the Argentinische Allee.

The Weavers in their commodious bed were to become very familiar with the hard slam of the back door. The high-pitched screech of wifely rage, the manly drone of urgent pacification (before leaving), the frantic yelping of disturbed housebound dog, the screams of alarmed spoilt children, little Klaus at it again, egging on Fritz; then the resounding slam, the manly footsteps stumbling into the night (Margarete's '*Acchscheissemensscch!*' hurled like a javelin after the departing figure), Wieland on his way back to drink the Rönisch dry.

This, to be sure, is all premature; an overture of droning woodwind and p*ff*-pp*ffff*ing of octave flute sunk in the orchestra pit awaiting curtain-rise.

That half of Berlin at that time – *circa* 1970 – is a place difficult to imagine; but once seen never forgotten, impossible to forget. The truncated metropolis hereinafter designated *Nullgrab* is of course very much our own invention and figures and descriptions may be more aromatic than exact. An odour of pines pervades all.

But for the most part the nights were peaceful, the house silent, only the surrounding woods crepitated with its unseen nightlife. Strange birds made their odd calls at unusual hours and the squirrels flitted across the roof in their passage from one part of the wood to another.

Thereinafter, the dawn chorus. Then the barking of Dixie signalling mail-time again, the garden loud with birdsong and the deaf man next door mowing his lawn, the queer fellow passing with his string bag, Queen Juliana feeding milk to the strange tree, all in one dry summer.

Professor Weaver did not exactly hit it off with Frau Meinhardt. Particularly when she took to spending long weekends in the attic with her two Airedales. On sunny mornings she currycombed the two spindly bitches on the veranda and curly doghair floated into Weaver's morning coffee on the terrace below.

One of the bitches was called Aya, a classical allusion. Frau Meinhardt took them on vacation with her to Malta, but the island was unsuitable for dogs – no shade.

The Professor, unshaven and surly, never at his best in the morning, sat smoking a twisty black cigar like a stick of liquorice, in a mood as black, not creating a good impression. Frau Meinhardt seemed to be spying from above; then she was in the kitchen, then passing through the living-room, clicking her tongue. Then she was in the hall, then out the front door; then she was around the house, examining things; now she was tiptoeing onto the patio again, the two Airedales following on spindle legs. She seemed to be checking up on her new tenants (the Irish were known to be dirty), her eyes fixed on the place where valuable household effects had been shifted or, far worse, removed, perhaps (oh horror!) broken, all her lovely effects vandalized by barbarians. *Ach!*

She had no English, and since the Professor's command of German was negligible the polite exchanges were left to his wife Nancy (old father Wolfgang Els came from Wuppertal) who had a smattering of German. These unwelcome weekend visitations became a refined torture. 'Should we ask her down?' Why yes, she would be delighted to join them.

She descended in a tight dress of shot green taffeta with a purple floral motif, the thin lips daubed with a dark lipstick and set in a severely forbidding line. Sat herself in one of her own comfortable armchairs, angular legs crossed stiffly as nutcrackers, one practised claw holding up a vile blue concoction (Curaçao) removed from the back of the cocktail cabinet, sipped from a long-stemmed green wine glass.

'*Ja, richtig!*'

Shooting venomous glances at the sprawling Professor (at pains to prove that he was the lawful sub-tenant) who was assuredly no gentleman.

German sentence constructions were not easy, Frau Ursula agreed, re-crossing her nutcrackers and nodding her head, sipping her blue poison. All nouns began with a capital letter and all the sentences ended with a verb, while the definite article had innumerable forms and could also be used as a pronoun. Berliners of course spoke the purest German. The long German sentence was a form of grammatical warfare and no fun at all for beginners, Frau Meinhardt said, sipping Curaçao, a thin smile fixed on her thin lips, observing the Professor.

Berlin of course had changed much; the old heart of the city was dead. Two of her oldest friends had been obliged to give up apartments they had lived in for years, both in good areas with eight or nine rooms in each, which they could no longer afford. Now they shared one flat near the Opera. One lady worked late; when she went to bed her friend got up. They would manage somehow. But it was hard; housework had to be done and the place kept clean.

Flushed with her blue tipple, Frau Ursula demonstrated how to operate the vacuum cleaner, a *Vampyr* model. The snout could burrow into awkward corners of armchairs and sofa, setting up a high-pitched whine when it discovered dirt; the bag became inflated with crumbs, hair, dust, swelling up in a self-satisfied way. It could manage a specific number of tasks, when properly set to it. German efficiency!

'*Berliner Schnauze*,' said Weaver when Frau Ursula had again retired to her attic with the dogs. 'A truly German machine – all snout and stomach. Do you suppose we will see much more of her, or will we ever get her out?'

Nancy was slicing lemon for two stiff gins.

'Consider how much strength the bourgeoisie derive from the lumber of the world,' Weaver said, accepting a gin and tonic. 'The security that environmental reliability gives. But how long can this go on? Could she not perhaps take a hint?'

'What had you in mind, Professor?'

'Boarding up the attic, when she's in there. Poisoning those bloody Airedales. Did you see the blue poison?'

Frau Ursula Meinhardt had clicked her dentures in a censorial way and flushed with possessive pride when Nancy ran the *Vampyr* over the risen pile of the Bukhara rug; her rug, her *Vampyr*, in her house! *Ach!*

3
Mando Demotropoulos (The Dark Prune)

Mando Demotropoulos had a commanding port and the bearing of a great operatic diva. Add to this the physique of swarthy opulence, flashful darksome eyes and a massive Géricault rump. She took short fussy steps, dispensed with headgear and carried about with her the tools of her trade, wrapped-up volumes from Marga Schoeller's bookshop, folders and folio notebooks, a string bag bursting with accessories. She had fluent French, adequate English, some Spanish and Italian, and of course her native Greek.

The face was very odd when seen close to – and Mando liked to stand close – the fierce shiny dark mask of the Bogey Man; an overwhelming and possibly dangerous presence – The Dark Prune. Her vocal delivery was sibilant and splashy. She had published poetry, but away from Greece she was a political activist with two undercover names. The working conditions of the Greek *Gastarbeiters* concerned her; for they made no effort to learn the language of their employers, were unable to read the danger signs and *Verbotens* and suffered injuries at work. These were the lost bands of low-sized, sallow-faced, dark-skinned men with great mustachios who wandered about West Berlin, window-shopping, lost and miserable in the rich city, before hastening back to their wretched compounds. Spaniards, Algerians, Bulgarians, Croats, Turks, Armenians and Balts were there too; but their fate did not concern her. She listened to the grievances of her fellow countrymen, translated for them, gave them good advice. Feeling the claustrophobia of the divided city, Mando Demotropoulos swiftly packed an overnight bag and took the next train to Paris where friends waited; she did this in order to stay sane.

As blindness cuts blind persons off from seeing-people and the things of the world in all their multiplicity, or deafness cuts deaf people off from the hearing ones and the multiple sounds and cries of the world, so it was with Weaver and the German language. He could neither speak it nor understand it, when spoken fluently by Germans, who seemed (to Weaver) to be making it up as they went along.

Only through Lore (who will presently appear on stage) could he begin to understand what Berlin had to offer him and what for her it was to be a Berliner, a Prussian. They were to meet 'by hazard', as Lore charmingly put it. A few digits awry in the phone number and out went an alternative left-handed invitation to Professor Weaver, who found himself accepting a call intended for Baron Bogdana Kuguar, the Polish poet who had an apartment at the end of Beskidenstrasse. The invitation was to Sepp Walser's afternoon tea party, an *English* tea party with muffins; which Lore under normal circumstances would never have attended, for she *never* accepted afternoon invitations, least of all on Saturday afternoons. The meddling goddess *Schnicksal* was operating here.

For lo and behold a Berlin autumn tea party was laid on with Earl Grey tea from Jackson's of Piccadilly with imported muffins and all the right people invited. Some *interesting* people were coming, the wavery voice assured Weaver, the brilliant Pole – later discovered pole-axed by eighty-proof vodka – regrettably not among them.

'I'm in a darkened room with the curtains drawn . . . wearing

17

dark glasses like Mr Hamm,' the wavery voice said mysteriously. 'There will be someone there who wishes to meet you. A Greek lady, a poetess from Athens, very famous. You will come?'

Deathly pale Sepp Walser wearing blind man's glasses was preparing to go mad again; he knew when the madness was coming upon him and voluntarily committed himself. This was the last party before he went in.

'You mustn't disappoint the lady,' the reedy voice said. 'She has translated *Ulysses* and, I understand, parts of *Finnegans Wake* into modern Greek. She is, ah, one smart cookie.'

'Honoured,' said Weaver feebly, already regretting his over-hasty acceptance. This might turn out to be a recurring social obligation: afternoon tea with muffins at Sepp Walser's place to meet Professor Weaver fresh from Dublin and TCD.

'Who was that?' Nancy called from the kitchen.

'An invitation to tea, solo.'

'You must go; it will be expected.'

It was the year when the Social Democrats first came to office, led by Willy Brandt as Chancellor, to the great satisfaction of all right-thinking Germans. It was a year unlike any other year for Weaver, as every year must be.

The false Professor, feeling every inch the impostor, his nerves frayed by much hand-wringing, found himself in a large quiet empty room free of tobacco-smoke and away from the hand-wringers and garrulous tea-imbibers and passing over into a narrow brightly lit kitchen came upon a further group of sallow Germans engaged in confabulation while drinking Scotch. The Glenfiddich was by the breadboard and polished glasses neatly lined up.

'May I?' Weaver asked, was ignored, helping himself to a generous dram.

The sofa in the large room – an area which had shrunk in his absence – was now occupied by a broad swarthy foreign lady who was leaning forward and smiling pleasantly in his direction.

'You are DILDO?' Weaver hazarded, advancing with hand outstretched. 'You must be the Greek lady!'

With much ruffling of gorgeous phosphorescent plumes and amber beads the swarthy presence with sudden dexterity extended a be-ringed and chubby brown hand – she might have been levelling a pistol.

'I am indeed – Mandodemotropoulos! And you are . . . the *Irish Professor*! Professor Beaver, I am enchanted!' She shook all over.

'The pleasure is all mine,' murmured Weaver shiftily in what was intended to be Old World gallantry, taking her brown and warmly palpitating paw and giving it a delicate squeeze.

'The title is honorary. Clever Franz Born's idea to flummox the Berlin landladies. A Professor would make a better impression, preferential treatment, you know.'

'The DILDO people were helpful?'

'Oh most helpful – Born could not do enough for us.'

'And they found a place for you and your wife . . . and I understand a small son?'

'They found a very grand place in Nikolassee.'

'Nikolassee! Why then we are practically neighbours. They found me a place in Wildpfad. You and your wife must come around. In the meantime,' said Mando Demotropoulos, patting the sofa, 'you could sit here. I won't *eat* you.'

Weaver sat himself circumspectly at some remove, holding the dram in both hands, smiling weakly.

The massive bowsprit bosom was barely contained in a tufted plum yak-skin bolero that exuded a heady aura of the Levant and the secretions exuded by Mando's pores. Determined wrestler's legs were set on the carpet as positively as the boles of great trees; about her throat were disposed several twists of amber beads the size of medlars; her overwhelming perfume sang of Paris, *Mystère de Rochas*, agreeable womanliness, *quadrille naturaliste*, ripeness and opulent fullness; it sang of copious Byzantine-Greek largesse.

Who had said teasingly that a stranger is always exciting? Opening wide her darkly cavernous nostrils and inhaling herself deeply, Mando now turned her great heavy fullness sideways-on to the quailing Weaver. The grave dark eyes fixed upon his, devouring him.

'Do you happen to know the workers' bar in Friedenau?' Mando inquired, looking 'off', and coughed delicately behind a barbarously ringed hand.

Weaver sprang to his feet.

'No, but we can offer a very good Scotch from the kitchen.'

'Why now that might be nice,' Mando twinkled up at him. 'A neat Skotsshh.'

'Speak to no one. I shall return directly.'

'Okeydoke!' cried Mando brightly.

Fired up with Glenfiddich Mando confided that it was her intention to interview the famous trio resident in Berlin: Grass, Hans Magnus Enzensberger and Frau Ingeborg Bachmann when they made themselves available; she had already spoken to Hans Magnus on the phone.

'What will you talk about?' asked the pseudo-Professor, smiling archly into his Scotch.

Looking flushed and belligerent Mando threw out one stout arm, giving Weaver a blast of armpit that no deodorant could subdue.

'Oh the usual *Mauermalaise*. What else is there to talk about in Berlin? As apartheid in South Africa or leprosy in . . . *the swamps*!' Whereupon Mando let out a great squawk of dark pruny laughter.

This abrupt outburst caused those within earshot to shift uneasily about, as a herd of gnu alarmed by lioness-roar in the long grass.

'This is a city of frightened people. *Very* frightened citizens carrying about rings of keys. Everything shut up by eight in the evening. Leave your apartment and try to get back in – maybe you forget something – no, you *cannot*! The gate is locked, the front door bolted and barred and on its safety-catch, the guard dog howling. You cannot *get back in*! They quite positively won't let you!'

This was killing Mando. Some of the more sober tea-imbibers had meanwhile wandered in and were standing about and talking and smoking and sending cutting looks at Mando. Lowering her voice and fixing Weaver with her bold brown eye, Mando utilized her free hand as a fan.

'They fear the Reds are coming. They're at the very door for Berliners. Communism begins for them just outside the Brandenburg Gate, and that's not so far away. Not even all their padlocks can keep the fear out and this really puts the wind up.'

Another storm of guffaws left Mando temporarily speechless. Excited multilingual voices in the kitchen indicated that the sober tea-drinkers had found the Glenfiddich and bottles of wine and beer were broken into.

'Some of the Berlin Wall, so called, isn't wall at all; some of it is the Havel, some the *Spreee*!' Mando spat out, splashing the Professor with dynamic sibilants. She couldn't keep it bottled up: *Spppphh-ray!*

'The Berlin Wall is like Dr Kafka's Great Wall of China, with missing parts that won't join up. But enough of those mundane matters,' said Mando clutching the Professor's arm. 'You must tell me what the Irish think of their Mr Joyce.'

'They have mixed feelings about him,' Weaver said. 'As a general rule they don't think about him very much or bother to read him.'

'They don't read *Ulysses*?'

'Least of all that.'

'My goodness me.' Mando said raising a stiff straight Scotch to eye-level in the grasp of her determined brown hand. 'They really don't? Now you *do* astonish me.'

The noisy drinkers had by now infiltrated the room and the

atmosphere was fast becoming steamy. Mando Demotropoulos began a true story concerning Mr Beckett which had happened in his Boulevard St-Jacques apartment near the Santé Prison. The story also involved 'your clever Mr John Jameson', and had been told to her by a friend from Mykonos, Zographos. They spoke of Dublin. Then Zographos asked Mr Beckett if he had ever felt home-sick for Ireland, did he ever think of it or miss his own country, as a Greek certainly would out of Greece. Mr Beckett threw one of his fierce looks out over his granny-glasses and said sharply, 'No . . . never,' frowning . . . or as if taken aback by such impertinence, you see, for it was a personal question that would only have occurred to a Greek. Zographos however said nothing, lit up a cheroot and sent a sly look around the room, then back at Mr Beckett and snickered. For all but himself (Zog) were Dubliners all drinking Jameson out of Waterford cut glass. Whereupon Mr Beckett permitted himself a quiet hollow laugh, in a guarded way.

Here Mando barked out *her* laugh, folded her brown hands and rattled bangles, dark eyes fixed once more on the Professor who rose straight up, saying 'Very good . . . that sounds like him all right. Now if I may refresh . . . ?' Mando crossed massive legs and lit up a cheroot which she had extracted from a commodious holdall.

The Professor presently returned with a tray on which were arranged refills of straight Scotch given with an unwavering hand and a decanter of water.

'Water here,' Weaver said, 'just in case we set ourselves alight.' The Professor seated himself, saying: 'You know he was in the French Resistance through the war, and was decorated after it by de Gaulle. This he dismissed as "Boy Scout stuff". Boy Scout stuff against the Gestapo.'

'I saw some very bad things in my country during the war,' Mando said soberly. At break of day the Greek hostages were rounded up, taken from their town and marched to an execution wall where the SS machine-gunned them and Mando as a child had to watch, holding her mother's hand. Professor Pflücker had watched the execution from the safety of the Luftwaffe tower. Mando had written a poem about it in Greek, as had Professor Pflücker in German, two quite different poems.

Now the room was a-swirl with cigarette and cigar smoke and crowded with merrymakers who had discovered the Scotch, with beer for the boozers and wine for the discerning, while the amiable young host entertained the merry company by pulling terrible faces while laughing like a hyena. Weaver's interior was scorched with the fine Scotch and had Satan himself cared to join them on the sofa, that would have been quite all right, the Dark Sovereign would have been made welcome.

'Now you have tickled me pink,' Mando admitted, all flushed, throwing one powerful stubby leg over the other, within their warm casement of covering cloth.

'Oddly enough,' Weaver said, 'I had a dream myself the other night about Mr Joyce.'

In the dream, in the dream! Snowbound climbers – little Chinamen, by God – were trapped in a deep defile or ravine while attempting to climb Mount Everest. Shivering among them but a little apart from them stood Mr Joyce. He had just caught up with them and now they were all trapped in this ravine. Above, off a narrow shelf of exposed rock, snow swirled in a great turbulence of disturbed air and then, by Jove, came a sudden smart crack of thunder, sending Mr Joyce, already speechless with the cold, into a deep blue funk – for being superstitious he did dread thunder. The petrified Chinamen were covered in snow like on the fells, a line of them roped together and a very white Mr Joyce, all staring fixedly into the blinding snowstorm, while above the thunder rumbled away.

'Poor Mr Joyce,' Mando sighed.

'Poor Chinamen,' amended Weaver.

Now the lovely dancer who had twice passed by the open door

with an eye on the carousing within took her courage in both hands and resolutely entered the crowded room and made her way through the press and hubbub until she stood before Mando and the Professor, inquiring vivaciously, 'What language do we speak?'

'Here we seem to be speaking a sort of English but drinking Skotssh,' Mando said.

'Can I get you something?' Weaver asked, springing to his feet. 'This is Mando of Mykonos and I am your most humble servant Beaver or Weaver late of Dublin and always delighted to oblige.'

'You are German?' Mando asked steamily from below.

'*Ja*, I'm a true Berliner.'

'Come and sit with us then,' Mando said briskly, looking most fondly up as though she *would* eat her.

Weaver fixed his eyes on this glittering black-and-white apparition in model's white supple boots.

'May I have a Scotch?' asked Lore Schröder, lowering herself into the place just vacated by Satan, while catching the Professor's eye and sending a glistening shaft that would take some extracting.

'I'm Lore Schröder,' the dancer told Mando. 'Heinz Walser is my boss and his son Sepp is your host.'

'Actually I myself am from Athens, not Mykonos,' Mando said.

The party went on, the noise increasing, the pitch of the voices rising, Sepp Walser levitating between his guests. Weaver sat between the ladies; the newcomer spoke excellent unaccented English.

'Where did you learn your English?'

'In Harrogate.'

'Ah,' Mando said, as if this explained all.

So the party went on, the fumes thickening, Weaver's charges insatiable for Glenfiddich. At last the host succeeded in intercepting him on his trips to and from the kitchen and drawing him aside intimated that a lady in homespuns by the door was most anxious to meet him and would consider it an honour if he would speak to her, if he had a moment to spare. And really how pleased he, the host, was that the Professor had met Fräulein Schröder at last; for he knew her quite well and had thought they would 'hit it off'. And so they had.

'She is a professional dancer?'

'Well no,' Walser said, 'but she dances.'

The homespun lady seemed a little demented. Fixing the wilting Professor with her basilisk eye (grey steel) she laid into him; the Irish were a shiftless race known for their duplicity and bigotry and now murderous proclivities. Weaver sagged against the ropes, took the blows; she was *unhinged*.

The thin lips exuded venom; it was nothing personal, she just couldn't stand the Irish.

Weaver found himself talking to strangers in parts of the room far removed from the sofa, catching sight of Mando with legs widely parted, reaching down for her reticule, or her black cheroots. The lovely Lore was engaged in animated conversation with a swarthy fellow in a red tie (like a long tongue protruded) who was draped all over the back of the sofa.

Later when the party was breaking up and street clothes being collected and handed out by Walser, active as a cricket, he was at Weaver's elbow to murmur that Fräulein Schröder would be happy to give the Professor a lift to the nearest station; and there she was smiling by the door.

They stepped out together into dead leaves. Parked not far away was her wasp-yellow Karman Ghia, which Lore drove like the wind down the Kurfürstendamm to an all-night bar. After the vision of rounded knees in white nainsook, the one for the road, to which the driver seemed quite amenable, she led him to a table by the window and ordered a carafe of red house wine. Seen close to, she had remarkable dark eyes, the chestnut hair combed down to the eyebrows in the siren manner of Louise Brooks. She said she did not give out her telephone number to every Tom, Dick and Harry (Horst, Wolfgang, Dieter), but she would give it to the Professor. It was not her home number but Heinz Walser's office; she could be reached there.

'How did your party go?' Nancy murmured into the darkness of the bedroom where her husband was struggling to unobtrusively remove his trousers at four o'clock in the morning.

Nancy, already asleep again, received a garbled account of the proceedings at Walser's where an offensive woman in homespuns featured, as did the host in blind man's glasses, and a swarthy Greek poetess; but no mention was made of a lovely linguist.

A day or two later Nancy admitted to having dreams of her own. The air was extraordinary, and most conducive to dreams. It was the renowned *Berliner Luft*. One needed two hours less sleep than in Bonn, Franz Born believed.

4
Ye Sated Baste

The Kaiser-Wilhelm-Gedächtniskirche or Memorial Church was indeed a smelly place with a pool of piss in front of the plaque and bums and hippies having a good exhibition time on the steps during the warm months, pissing merrily away in the ruins next to embarrassed tourists. It is every Berliner girl's secret wish to be married there.

However, Weaver saw no brides in white leaving in a white coach drawn by white palfrey pelted with confetti. Most of them were brunettes with darkly inviting Latin eyes; a new species, the *Schlüsselkind* of the war become ripe *Weib*.

The old clock still functioned, the good old Prussian heart still sound. Hear those heavy resonant chimes! The ruins are the stump of a great tree struck by lightning a quarter of a century ago. No bride-to-be holding white roses to her palely anaemic face, hiding her blushes in a white veil, amid the roses, ever plays in the ruins of this quartered city of widows in sad hats (who believe the heart is dead), hard vertical rain, serious men attacking thick steaks, ghosts in broad daylight. Its population dropped to 2.2 million after the war and the cultural heart shifted west, away from Unter den Linden to the Kurfürstendamm and the Opera, Schiller-Theater, IBM Centre.

City of legendary Teutonic over-eating, burnished boscage of the Tiergarten and the Grunewald (it must be something in the soil, unless it's something in the air). Rabbits burrow for roots in the Tiergarten, moles are digging in the Rehweise, a hawk flies down Schlüterstrasse in the rain. Now that the country is being poisoned by chemicals, the birds and animals have moved into the city; Megapolis is coming.

Built in the late nineteenth century, gutted in the Second World War, but for the bell tower, and with a great hole over the nave, it stands there in all its glory, in a very permanent manner, its blind eye looking crookedly down the Kurfürstendamm. A turret of blue stained glass has been grafted on: a modern church, Mies's fancy. There may be no more grandiose cathedrals built in our times, Gaudí's the last. Stand in the once-holy place, in the piss, study the plaque!

ZUR ERINNERUNG AN WILHELM I, KÖNIG VON
PREUSSEN UND DEUTSCHER KAISER, WURDE IN
DEN JAHREN 1891–95 UNTER DER
REGIERUNG WILHELM II AUS SPENDEN DES
GANZEN DEUTSCHEN VOLKES DIE ERSTE
KAISER-WILHELM-GEDÄCHTNISKIRCHE ERBAUT.
WÄHREND DES II. WELTKRIEGES IN DER NACHT
ZUM 23. NOVEMBER 1943 WURDE SIE BEIM
LUFTANGRIFF ZERSTÖRT. DER TURM DER ALTEN
KIRCHE SOLL AN DAS GERICHT GOTTES
ERINNERN, DAS IN DEN JAHREN DES KRIEGES
ÜBER UNSER VOLK HEREINBRACH.

Hard by, over the way, in Wittenbergplatz, another more sinister monument proclaims:

ORT DES SCHRECKENS, DIE WIR NIEMALS
VERGESSEN DÜRFEN: AUSCHWITZ, STUTTHOF,
MAIDANEK, TREBLINKA, BUCHENWALD,
DACHAU, SACHSENHAUSEN, RAVENSBRÜCK,
BERGEN, BELSEN. ERINNERN UND VERGESSEN.

As darkness falls over *Nullgrab* – the empty grave of West Berlin – the heavy winged creatures issue forth from the belfry and the great dark hole above the nave. *Ganzen, Erinnerung, Nacht, Turm, Krieg, Kaiser, Vergessen* and *Volk* fly out over the Europa-Center as the bells toll and a male-voice choir intones a Bach motet.

The vendors in their kiosks do not bother to peer out, with all summer about them in the glow of concupiscent female flesh; as freezing air from the Baltic streams in a perishing fog crawls along the whole length of the Kurfürstendamm.

Step out of the Bahnhof Zoo, cross under the arched flyover, pass along the colonnade, experience the brassy clarity of evening ever-invigorating oxygenated air from the woods around. Draw this lusty Berlin air deep into your lungs. Hear the heavy, resonant chimes!

In Spandau Rudolf Hess walks in the prison garden planted by Speer who has been released and is four years now a free man. A long pretence of insanity has worn away his shattered nerves and Hess himself wonders if he can survive much longer alone, for he has all his life-sentence still to serve.

Over the wall someone is whispering in German. He hears the cries of children at play carried on the breeze that blows through the chestnut trees near the gates and his spirits sink still further. Someone is still whispering outside. He misses Albert Speer. Outside, a blue evening has fallen.

Ah, something offered, then withdrawn; offered again, refused again; then lifted away, lost beyond retrieval now.

And everywhere, to be sure, the jaundiced features of the pseudo-Saviour, the wirrasthrew Jesus, a tortured combination of Ernesto ('Che') Guevara, the wanderer-in-the-forest, and Charlie Manson, the insane murderer-by-proxy. The street style tended to be both haphazard and predictable, a baffling mixture of Occident and Orient. Hindu priests in sandals paced gravely along with their hands up their sleeves as if wrapped in deepest thought; mendicant friars shuffled by with begging bowls amid

Reb stragglers lost after Vicksberg and Bull Run. The sad procession shuffled down Schlüterstrasse, 'Jesus' holding aloft an olive branch, with many Mary Magdalenes in tow.

Rousseau wrote from the confusions of a previous century: 'Perfect beings do not exist; the lessons which they give us are too remote from us.' And crusty Saul Bellow, familiar with *our* predicament and time, amended it thus: 'Paranoia is perhaps the normal state of mind in savages. The psychotic mind is all deep melancholia and distrust.' In the clutches of the obscene, Hell is noise, and noise means home. They do not seek a new Saviour but look for their totems – idolatrous animism. The Gnostics believed that the angels put the same question to every newly arriving dead person: 'Where do you come from?' From Berlin-Spandau, *natürlich*!

In the rock cellars they were reverting to savages. The asinine cacophony was deafening, amplified howling and drumming went on relentlessly in the stink of sulphur. It had to stink enough to drive the angels out of Heaven. The rockers preferred to be stupefied by such tumult, exulting in din as bluebottles in dung.

Meanwhile, in a small neat garden in Lichtenrade, close to the Wall, the air is permeated with noxious fumes from the paper factory next door. An old white-haired lady sits in the garden and polishes some well-worn garden gnomes who smile all the year, and all the years will go on smiling. She is afflicted with *morbus pictus*. In Lichtenrade, in Lichtenrade!

The quartered city is wedged between two great rivers, Oder and Elbe to east and west; into one tributary, fouling up the filthy river Ine, in a few days of June 1969 an overflow from a chemical works manufacturing a product classified as organo-chlorine compound of persistent nature (capable of destroying four hundred different types of insect) wiped out twenty-five million fish. Lethal against insects, *Hoechst Endosu* caught them below Bingen-Luch and they never made it to the Nordsee. Man comes in and turns the fishes out!

Imagine a city sans head, its limbs lopped off, as in a fairy tale (German, naturally). Its true symbol should be the Wild Boar; *Berliner Schnauze*, they say of themselves with intense self-satisfaction and just a pardonable touch of conceit.

When fishes die they begin to stink from the head. Talk about the inner organs of beasts and fowl, of nutty gizzards and urine-tainted breath! Capitalism's true function is: to gorge itself and grow, becoming monstrous in the process.

Your true Berliners were ever peerless trenchermen and stuffers of the gut, and may be observed doing it with much gusto behind treble-glazed restaurant windows along either side of the Ku'damm at lunchtime and again by night in every one of over five thousand such eating-places, on a graduated scale of prices, but offering something hot and tempting to suit every taste. Try *Rinderbrust* or *Schlachtplatte* if you can stomach their butcher-abattoir-meatcleaverblood associations. Try, if you dare, *Brathering* or *Eisbein oder Kassler Rippenspeer mit Bier* or boiled ham hocks served up with heavy garnishings of soggy sauerkraut washed down with pints of that highly carbonated green beer with its distinctive poisonous colour and no less distinctive after-taste so suggestive of just-upchucked vomit. *Ach!*

With heart hammering, palms sweaty, dog-collar reversed, and holding his breath (in sight of prey), Father Con Condon, curate of Ballyferriter, was getting an eyeful of the porno display in a nearby sex shop – lusty lad playing truant or Rumpelstilzchen dancing around his secret fire?

As an innocent child, fresh from the hills of Andalucía, Nico had been astonished by all this rampantly lewd display. '*¡Mira!*' he called, pointing up at haunches on a hoarding. '*¡Culos!*'

The human originals of these healthy nude strumpets walked around Berlin and Munich, Hamburg and Frankfurt, when they were not appearing on the high hoardings of these cities, blown up ten times lifesize and presented in ambiguous proximity to stables and horses, grooms with rough hands and randy stable-boys with vigorous erections. They (the strumpets) looked ripe enough for ready eating, succulent morsels already undressed: erect nipples and sets of white teeth were the salt and pepper; axillary and pubic hair the garnishings. Some breasts were excessive in dimension, with sore-looking roundels; and below all that splendour, the unshaven Mount of Venus!

But marvel once more, the 'PoPo look' had just arrived from Japan, where golf bags are manufactured from the prepuces of whales. PoPo! – the clever Orientals imitating the primitive African, ever-devoted admirers of outsize female posteriors suggestive of flesh-pots and stewing missionaries. But observe how the timeless erotic zones have been switched about, arsy-versy; and lo, now it is the receding form that is most admired. Denim slacks were stone-washed and cut to cling; and cling they certainly did, as though avid hands were convulsively clutching. Bosom uplift and cleavage had been supplanted on a grander scale by braced buttocks and cleft accentuated by the flimsiest of thin covering, or nothing at all.

Laforgue was on the razzle, frequenting all the lowest dives, recording in his diary: 'A Jewess with black armpits, a blonde made of wood, the red-faced English girl . . .' From the cover of *Time* the shocked pinched features of Nabokov stared insolently. With weight inclined on one hip a young whore solicited near the Hotel Bogotá. Along the Kurfürstendamm the kiosks reeled under their burden of soft winter porn; the nude photo models with all imperfections such as pimples and rashes and love-bites airbrushed away now lewdly glowed like veritable beds of begonias. Bare flesh was burning lushly through the long winter months when the thoughts and fancies of chilled citizens turned longingly towards the sun, the nudist camp of Bastia. Bared flesh and wipe-open mouth stood for repleteness in the great consumer society, the sick society; cleavage and cleft and wetted hair and smiling mouth were cheekily, cheesily perpetuated a thousand times, ten thousand times in Axel Springer's magazines and did not differ greatly from the movie displays set up in the foyers where blue movies were shown, one with the come-ons for the strip joints.

In the arcade by Bilka a bronzed middle-aged woman bought the new issue of *Spontan* and around Bahnhof Zoo the colour magazines *Bunte* and *Marie Claire* were invitingly laid out and blowing open on the wide pavement, the wind tantalizingly lifted a page and lo and behold we are into a *Wald und Wiese* situation – a pretty blonde strumpet smiles nudely at the camera and her grinning young male companion with *Knorpel* erect grins back at her in the country, deep in Bavaria, as raucous car horns blare and the Uhlandstrasse traffic rages by. Bonnet to bonnet the cars take off, wild beasts stampeding towards a water-hole in the dry season. A tall Negro in cowboy boots, wearing one earring, strides past the bullet-riddled Amerika Haus. *Herbst, du bist chic!*

The same feature film was showing in all the big cities. With identical poster and plug, the high hoardings identified McQueen and Dustin Hoffman in *Papillon* and in *My Name is Nobody* (*sic*); while at the Palast Kino the naked back of a brunette, long and sleek as a destroyer, with rapt look and damply parting lips, is offering a pressurized dream in a lurid glow, perpetuating the great damned lie: 'Ye Sated Baste'.

And where had the brainy Prof read that all whales have syphilis?

5
Merlin's Hoardings

Road-hippies on endless round trips to the 'way-out' regions sold their blood in Kuwait, took overdoses, 'split', 'crashed-out' in sleeping-bags, one with the teeming poor of the deprived nations. Lost ones blew their brains out, the only way to admit some sense at last. A huge organ played at noon in a department store. Alcoholic professors taught their own versions of history; how progress and civilization had come up against a dead wall in a world gone mad.

Students were apprehensive to leave the campus. In the surrounding woods maniacs prowled whistling all night. The young debated much on their 'development', drawing up endless schemes; schedules were considered, debated, abandoned. Leaders sprang up, spoke torrentially, were listened to, went out of favour, were gunned down. They seemed to be exclusively concerned with drugs of one sort or another, *gris-gris* and voodoo, crack, Indian Buddha teachings highly corrupted; claptrap about 'freedom'.

High above the savage growl of the fast traffic a cut-out of the murdered actress Sharon Tate gazes as if indifferently on the human clotting below, the beard-plucking hippies on the prowl with beads and bangles, the hurdy-gurdy man cranking out an old Berliner tune, the sandwichboardman trailing along advertising the strip joints.

'PIGS', her murderers painted on the Polanski home. Disordered thoughts, unchaste desires, drugs, lewdness, hallucinations, *Chaos oder Anarchie* in the here-and-now: Manson's tribe. Karl Kraus had defined German girls: 'Long legs, obedience.' Not any more. Only dreaming, lost in an ideal dream, does the German dare to give his opinion, which he has kept deep in his loyal German heart, Heine thought. Germany would last forever, because it was a *thoroughly healthy land*; with its oaks and lindens, its fine women.

But clever Nietzsche thought: 'We know that the destruction of an illusion does not necessarily lead to a truth.' Well spake, Friedrich! *Woher kommen wir? Wohin gehen wir? Sollten wir Geld mitnehmen?*

Bahnhof Zoo is an eerie place – a sort of Lido for German inverts. At seven in the morning some poorly dressed cleaners are sweeping dirt away with heavy brooms. The American Army is still plugging away, engaged in sporadic sharpshooting in the Grunewald by the GDR border, the Forbidden Ground. In the Berlin Zoo the snow-owls screw their heads about 180 degrees to stare fixedly upwards, the predatory eye unblinkingly fixed in its socket. The young fledglings float down from a low perch to pick out the eyes of dead white mice thrown in by the keepers. It is difficult to guess the mood of the snow-owls, whiter than snow here, a brilliant Arctic whiteness that reminded Weaver of the flavour of Polar Bear Mints sucked in convalescence as a child recovering from measles. The dead eyes of the white mice are brilliant as rubies, or the last drops of heart's blood. They say, wrote Saul Bellow, that you go to the zoo to see yourself in the animals; but there aren't enough animals in the world to see ourselves in.

The screech of the Madagascar vari in the night is said to stop the heart, twice.

In this year of grace there were 63,705 dogs registered in Berlin West; or one dog to every 32.8 inhabitants. Berlin – a grey

35

steel-engraving set down on the edge of the Prussian Plain. Phantasmagorias of snow, light, and glittering void. The winters are protracted and severe. The Havel lakes freeze over and the skaters appear, among them Klopstock, Jules Laforgue and Vladimir Nabokov as a boy. Industrial salt is laid along the verges of the *Allee*s at Dahlem, Im Dol, Potsdamer Chaussee and Kronprinzessinnenweg, Podbielskiallee, Lohengrin-, Nibelungen-, Tristan- and Isolde-, Von-Luck- and Lückhoffstrassen, killing the overhang, mostly chestnut, all the way to Rittergut Düppel and the *Waserwerk*.

The fringes of this half-city have a distinctive atmosphere. Lowly Lichtenrade, Teltowkanal, Marienfelde, the wheatfields around the village of Lübars (somewhere in an inn there Weaver and his friend Lindemann the welterweight boxer are sharing a flagon of good Franconian red wine, puffing at Danemann cigars, enjoying the cool breeze that sometimes blows from Arcadia).

Blind Borges called it the ugliest city on earth. It had been a railroad centre in the nineteenth century; a city of the Hanseatic League, a centre of the garment industry. Today it's an industrial centre processing partially finished materials which are then made up and exported as finished products. The half-city (341 square miles, 250 acres of agriculture and gardens, 19,000 forested, 6 per cent made up of lakes and waterways) is as said before situated between two rivers, a hundred miles inside the GDR.

Berlin is a city of the old. Every second citizen is over forty years of age, and more than 25 per cent over sixty-five years of age, with 13,000 more dying than are being born each year, as another 37,000 expire. The place is a veritable warren of graveyards, with extensive ones below Rudow and Buckow and another great necropolis between Britz and Steglitz below the Südring. *Klinikum*s and *Krankenhaus*es abound, and the *Kurgarten*s so popular with the old ladies.

City of war widows, blinded veterans, corpulent short-tempered nightwatchmen and their Alsatian guard dogs on short leads. The face on the high hoarding, stiff and forbidding, stalks through the streets.

6

The Old Admirer

The Old Admirer was at times more persistent than Sweaty Petersen, for he was always there; the lecherous old romantic Prussian octogenarian with whom she shared the office was always pressing gifts on her. Orchids with fond dedications, fresh flowers for her vase, boxes of chocolates, tickets for the opera and so on; nor would he be gainsaid – he was the Old Admirer.

He arrived at the Walser office with cheeks on fire and a gleam in his eye, bearing gifts as homage to her beauty. The doting rheumy old eyes of washed-out blue followed her every move: her visits to the toilet, he knew her periods, he adored her mesial groove, the tautness and correctness of her curvy rump, her 'seat' on the swivel chair, as if she was horse-riding. He bought her meringues to go with the office coffee, stayed on himself when she stayed late, to 'protect' her; offering his card, his undying love, if only she would, if only (but he quite understood if she couldn't) he could see her safely home.

'But, dear Helmut, I have a car,' she protested, laughing.

'I am too young for you,' she told him diplomatically; never the hurtful corollary: 'You are too old for *me*, old prankster! *Quatsch!* I want to be enjoyed by a bounding lover like Weaver my mad Harz Mountain Hare.' But, being well brought up, she would never say that.

Nor were there great distinctions to be made between her Old Admirer and Sweaty Petersen, or between him and the Platonic Lover; all were very sweet and attentive, with fifty years' difference between two of them; all had this in common; they were boringly dull and she didn't want them.

'What use is his undying love to me?' she asked Weaver. 'He can keep it.'

The Old Admier groaned (quite audibly) to himself when she moved, when she passed him; he breathed in her perfume (his present). *Ach, Gott!* the fleshly presence, the port, the seat, the flow. Cruel Enchantress, take pity! But she swept past, leaving her wake behind, making him suffer. She could not tell him: 'But, *lieber* Helmut, I am not free; there is Weaver!' Did he guess anything of the Weaverish presence in her soft cheese? Not a thing. Did he suspect that there might be somebody out there – some young buck? Certainly he did. Only too well did he know that glow and what it fairly sang of, what it purported to say to those who knew (he had not been a bachelor for nothing, he had his conquests, in his time).

Was he jealous?

Sick with it.

Would he persist?

Yes.

Was that in vain?

Yes.

Could he do otherwise?

No.

As though she, the Cruel Enchantress, wished to clean out this Augean stable (or stinking hen-coop) of frustrated affection and thwarted lustylove a-tremble in the balance (for the old man desired her), Lore suggested that Weaver call on her formally after working hours, when she could receive him alone. He was to phone from a nearby call box and come up if the coast was clear. A coded message was arranged in the event of her boss staying late; she could get rid of the Old Admirer.

This bold Weaver did.

He came into a part of Berlin that was strange to him, walking there as if on air that had become a colour, so dense it was, so suggestive, looking for a new Lorelove, a more humble one, the working Lore Schröder, the one who earned the rent. It was like beginning their courtship all over again.

This humbler version of the proud couturière-clad divine received him at the office door one storey up. The door was teak, a huge heavy dark thing into which hasps and clasps and Judas grille and several types of locks and bolts had been let in; it would have taken a charge of dynamite to get past it, but Weaver breathed the magic password and was instantly admitted by Lore in slippers and a kind of housecoat.

Weavers was given a conducted tour of the premises. Here was Heinz Walser's mighty leather-padded Boss Swivel, and there Lore's more modest chair where she took dictation in three or four languages, and there was the Old Admirer's seat, in a graduated proximity to each other. Weaver thought he heard heavy ghostly breathing, the stertorous regular disturbance of the Old Admirer.

There was the rolltop desk, a huge safe, icons with bulging eyes, knick-knacks from travels in the Orient; a rich man's spoils mixed up with a movie mogul's bad taste; all much too purple for Weaver, who liked restraint in some things.

Lore wore a loose housecoat and nothing underneath, as Weaver ascertained when he kissed her. A bottle of good red wine was produced with a flourish and a corkscrew.

'Where?' Lore wanted to know.

The Walsers took their vacations apart and did not share a bedroom. Heinz's sleeping quarters, which Weaver was now admitted to, was a sumptuous darkly enveloping airless chamber where a bishop or even a cardinal might without losing any cast have breathed his last, so confined and airless was it.

'Christ!' breathed Weaver, backing out. 'A mausoleum. Not here.'

In the kitchen the tins of dog-food were stacked and on the floor the dog-baskets and rubber play-biscuits and rubber bones for Grete Weiser's miniature Yorkies, who may have departed in a body but had left their distinctly doggy stink behind. Then Lore showed him the housekeeper's bedroom.

'Here,' Weaver said.

It was the only room with daylight and air in it, facing west and the yards below and the pigeons cooing and fidgeting on the roof just above their head. The single bed was pushed against the wall and within the narrow confines of the room was still reflecting the last sunlight on its clean white covers already drawn back.

'But first a bath,' said Lore and in a trice had drawn a deep bath of lukewarm water, to conserve Weaver's *force*; two glasses of ruby red on the broad wooden rim of the bath into which they stepped together and submerged to the sound of a collective cooing on the roof, a throaty warbling and canoodling of amorous pigeons.

The last sunlight swam through yellow muslin curtains that blew inward as Lore on the flat of her back began taking ever deeper breaths before diving deep with eyes closed, letting go of herself; the wine glasses by the bed reflecting ruby on the ceiling, jumping and flooding along the wall.

Sated with her body Weaver saw the ceiling swimming away where the shadows of the leaves had all of a sudden begun to tremble and dance again. She had told him that the long working hours produced 'an enormous need for compensation'. Was that enormous need satisfied now? Was it part of the Boss-Perks to enjoy the favours of his beautiful and obliging private secretary? Grete had been the pander, hidden behind a curtain when the job-interviews were in progress; she had given Walser the high sign for Lore.

One could understand how murder could be done, with such a woman for accomplice, to lead the victim in, entrap the unwary, arrange the details, Weaver thought, lying on his back alongside her. Practically everything was a trap, potentially; and weapons (innocent-looking) lay everywhere to hand. An umbrella (for tripping and maiming), ammonia (for sudden blinding), heavy iron fire-dogs (for crippling), dumb-bells (for smashing), an open window (for pushing victim), wine bottle (full, as club; broken as gasher), and Luger almost certainly locked away within easy reach in the rolltop desk. The imposing safe with its hidden wealth, its secret combinations, seemed to imply a protector, a killer (Luger with safety catch on), and Lore had the key. The days of old admirers were numbered.

Pray, madam, were you ever in keep?

7

An Ominous *Litfasssäule* (The Empty Ruins)

The shuttered Italian and Spanish embassies faced the Tiergarten, that haunt of whores. Both were empty ruins now, grievous presences abandoned but not quite defunct. A charged atmosphere surrounded them; all the former hectic activity had ceased when the Red Army came. Their absolute stillness was perhaps a shocked silence; as if that time of gross splendour and nationalistic fervour could begin again any day now, resume its fierce tenure, its cruelty, its National Socialist storm.

Yet these abodes were tenantless and humbled centres of finished ambitions for *das tausendjährige Reich*, hereabouts as dead and gone as Tara or Stonehenge, the Alhambra or the megapolis of Allied and Axis dead at El Alamain. Certain smoke-blackened ruins, and perhaps they most of all, were the essential Berlin; the gutted Soviet Embassy had been left standing as a monument, as had the Memorial Church at the end of Kurfürstendamm near the Romanisch Café where Georg Grosz had tossed back schnapps and smoked rank cigars by the ice rink where Laforgue had skated, and later Nabokov (a brat in teeth-braces eyeing the pretty girls); it was not far from the Schröders' apartment on the other side of Olivaer Platz.

Lore had shown it to Weaver as if unwillingly – the Soviet shell darkened by a fire gone out a quarter of a century before; shown it

43

as if unwillingly, something that yet had to be seen, though not something a Berliner could be proud of; always she showed him the ruins of her city with this diffidence, proud yet ashamed.

Some of her political prejudices had been inherited direct from her stern Papa; casting a vote had to do with fear of Communism, and father, wife and daughter conscientiously voted CDU. ('Unsound,' Lindemann rumbled into his long-stemmed green glass of Moselle, '*most* unsound. Mistrust German politicians who come from Bavaria. Regard the wild man Strauss.')

In the cul de sac planted with lindens stood the *Litfasssäule*, facing the abandoned embassies. It was one of those manifestly Berliner constructions that are truly Berlin in the way that *pissoirs* epitomize Paris. The Axis soul had fled the twin embassies and settled here among the lindens, the tall characteristic weeds, the ivy that gripped.

On its defaced surface a patina of proclamations well weathered by Time had been destroyed back to the acid; not as the fungus of trees – a natural growth of decay – a natural dragging down; for no hand had yet removed the ordinance, a proclamation become threatening even against its own Folk. Consumed by the passage of time, by nativities wildly cast, fearfully cast, the paper this was printed on had laid down its lost propaganda life long ago, its purpose; become emblematic – sinister as the hidden pillbox in the anti-tank gun emplacement come upon at the turn of the cobbled road leading to the Jochen-Klepper-Weg, before it dipped down to the Rehweise sunken meadows; died and rotted back into its singular decayed repose.

Beauty is a projection of ugliness – the erudite Professor must have come upon this somewhere in his reading – the notion sounded vaguely French. By developing certain monstrosities we obtain the purest ornaments. The muzzle of the anti-tank gun protruding from behind its camouflage netting.

'Let's move on,' Lore suggested, 'arming' the Professor. So

they moved on arm-in-arm, the Professor pinioned to Lore's side. In the Tiergarten some wildly excited *Gastarbeiters* – Serbs or Balts by the sound of them – with their shirts off were playing a rowdy game of *Fussball*. Behind the shouting Slavs the *Siegessäule* rose up glorious and golden into a clear blue Prussian sky. '*Ach, Quatsch!*'

Time passed.

The calm grey evening clouds were also massing over the Europa-Center and the revolving Mercedes-Benz star. In their compounds in the Berlin Zoo the grey elephants stood still as boulders. Those prehistoric creatures move about in their own time. Three snow-owls on a perch dozed in a soiled cage. There were few people strolling between the compounds and the cages. Lindemann the soured lexicographer had betaken himself home to Haus Hecht in woody Dahlemdorf and sat himself at his desk, heaving a great sigh, and begun transcribing voluminous *Zeitgeist*ical-zoological notes on animals, birds and serpents into a foolscap notebook, addenda for a great novel long planned; a glass of Cognac to hand, puffing a Danemann, as Professor Weaver, his foul- and fair-weather friend, passed into the hippo compound.

The air of the place was permeated with their sluggish swampy presence, their thick cowy smell. Submerged to their great flared nostrils in the dank cement ponds fouled with their droppings, the hippos masticated slowly, eyeing Weaver.

Weaver watched that weighty avalanche of sore-looking pinkish meat and hairy gristle subside into the man-made ponds soiled with dung, until only the bulbous pachydermatous eyeballs showed, still fixed on Weaver.

A patient line of protest-marchers, demonstrating solidarity with some cause or other already as good as lost (marching it is said will soon be replacing people), was wending its way along the Bundesallee past the Dresdener Bank and Dr Wieland Weissenborn, carrying a briefcase, stood on the steps to watch them go by.

A voice in despair gasped out '*Untröstlich!*' by the pedestrian island at Weaver's side, his arm was jolted, he saw the riot police lined up grimly on either side. Along the whole Bundesallee the blocked traffic waited for the lights to go green, to rush the next lot of halts.

In police paddywagons parked out of sight on side streets the riot squads were photographing faces and taking notes as Professor Weaver stepped, with relief, into the Paris Bar where all was calm, as if in another time. He unhooked a *Die Zeit* from the stand, found an empty table, summoned a waiter to order a flagon of house red, bit the end off a cigar, becalmed himself. The newsprint was so much double Dutch to him but the layout and paucity of pictures reminded him of Smyllie's *Irish Times*. The elderly aproned waiters moved as slowly as waiters in Jammet's and the Red Bank in the 1950s, and he seemed to be home again, young again. Outside the marchers were singing.

Time ran out in a circle but the constants remained. The riot bullies were shuffling their boots, gloved fists tightening on the batons. Amerika Haus was bullet-riddled. At a table outside Alexander's two Frenchmen were coldly insulting a German waiter who stood to attention by their table. The heads and shoulders of Alsatians with redly lolling tongues protruded from open car windows, signifying their owner's opulence and how all would fight to protect it. The unwashed hippies had their baubles and trinkets set out on the wide pavements as primitive tribal artefacts in a jungle clearing.

An old and dirty train was about to leave the Zoologischer Garten terminus for Frankfurt am Main across two hundred kilometres and more of grubby GDR territory. In a fag-fouled second-class *Raucher* an official was already checking tickets. A young couple sat close together and the youth tried a feeble joke about East and West winds at the retreating back of the official who was already closing the sliding door. The windows of all the carriages of this sorry rolling-stock were sealed and many residual layers of gritty foul weather had caked themselves on the opaque

glass. Those blocked windows indicated: *Here turbidity reigneth.*
Witness the stoic calmness of those who have long given up. So
what now, *Kameraden*?

8

The End of the Polish Week

Somewhere, just out of sight,
the savages are howling.

It was agreed that they would go, but not recognize each other. Lore thought it would be *sehr komisch* to go to the Akademie der Künste masked as it were, for the final night of the Polish Week, and pretend not to recognize each other. This was decided the day before; she had received an invitation through her boss, Heinz Walser, who would not be going with Grete Weiser. 'It will not be so funny if Nancy smells a rat,' Weaver said. 'Believe you me.'

Nancy had expressed a wish to go. The neighbourly Weissenborns said they would look after Nico. 'No sweat,' said Wieland.

Nancy dressed up in her best finery, they took the U-Bahn to Breitenbachplatz and had a pizza at Il Gattopardo and from there proceeded in high style by taxi to the Academy. Nancy thought the Kuguars would be there, it being such a Polish occasion; and possibly the Borns, Franz attending in his official capacity as boss of DILDO. Weaver bought two packets of untipped Gauloises from an automatic dispenser and pocketed some pfennigs change.

When they arrived the party was already in full swing. While discarding and handing over their lightweight overcoats at the cloakroom counter and accepting the ticket the thought had crossed Weaver's mind that one or more of Lore's five admirers (oft spoken of but never seen in the flesh) might already be dancing attendance within. As indeed they were: four of them were there already!

All but the Platonic Lover, who had wisely decided to stay at home; the rest had lined themselves up to be counted: Dr Cock, the Chief Admirer, Sweaty Petersen, the most persistent, the Grey Man still hanging in, and the Old Admirer (four score years if he was a day), knowing he had no chance but still there on the fringe.

No sooner inside but Weaver saw Lore, the first face seen and recognized within the thronged concourse. Her admirers, still nameless, were clustered eagerly about her. They milled about, big, well-fed ball-eyed well-disposed pedigree hounds waiting for a kind word from the mistress. She held a small glass of neat vodka in each hand, away from her body, and was slowly rotating to give each admirer in turn a flash of her beautiful eyes, laughing the while at her own brilliance and party improvisation: look, look, vodka in each hand! the admirers agog; sweaty, oldie, greyman, cocky, all agog, all turning with her, smiling, admiring.

'Who's that?' asked Nancy.

'I do believe I know her,' said Weaver deviously, advancing boldly, calling out.

'Have we not . . .' (he called out to the brilliant twirler who had twirled closer, Maria Vivo flashing her dark Andalusian eyes, showing off her love-locks, her hips, her style) '. . . not met before, Fräulein Schröder is it not?' He waved a vague hand, not too specific.

'At Sepp Walser's, some months ago!'

The name Walser stopped her in her tracks, with not a drop spilled.

'Yus,' she said, positively vibrating.

'Like you to meet my wife Nancy.'

The admirers just melted away, vaporized; and now there were only three people in a crowded concourse.

'May I offer you a vodka? I haven't spilt a drop.'

Lore, herself always the cynosure of all admiring eyes, had a disconcerting way of prolonging eye-contact a shade longer than normal, just an *Augenblick* short of being rude; and this she did with Nancy as they shook hands. Whereupon Weaver, not a little disconcerted in *his* loyalties, now seeing his nice wife diminishing to much-reduced proportions within those tigerish pupils (he had never seen her this way before; the presence of all the admirers at once had charged her up) now slipped diplomatically away into the crowd.

A distinctly foreign (to Weaver's Irish ears) uproar came in great pulsations – the discordant baying of an Unappeasable Host – from the main reception area, long and lofty as an aircraft hangar, warm as a granary or tropical greenhouse, indicating where the wildly excited Eastern Bloc *Gast*s were congregated and living it up (a huge damp bonfire set to ignite), for the Poles had been at it for a week now, recklessly putting away ninety-proof vodka, and these were the dying hours of that long Slav debauch.

Doubtless Bogdana (Mr Cogito with collar undone) was deep in this revelry, a dancing dervish awash in sweat and vodka, and his Polish Baroness with her jet-black hair (that remoteness of hers enhanced by an unearthly Polish pallor), dancing the night away.

The kind 'Sweaty' Petersen had come forward and borne Nancy off for a drink at the far side of the great circular bar which was almost deserted, for the dancers were already assembling by the polished dance floor at the other end of the long room, Lore and Sepp Walser in his blind man's dark glasses amongst the first to take the floor as the band struck up.

Dr Cock and Petersen had the bland assured overbearing manners of English Guardsmen, two upstanding six-footers very sure of themselves; the former in a lounge suit of light blue twill, a Cambridge man; the latter already in a perfect lather of anticipant sweat, for tall swaying Nancy was rather his (the Lore) 'type'. The Grey Man in tussore hovered near, on the fringe, admiring. The Old Admirer (the sender of boxes of chocolates, perfume, cartons of cigarettes, theatre tickets, the sharer of office space, the nearly-positioned-one groaning as she moved) red in cheeks long and pendulous, sad in the eye (he had no chance against these younger bucks), with a bulbous brandy nose and those watery blue orbs, had offered Weaver a convulsive handgrip and fallen back into the crowd. After two double vodkas to get in the swing of things, Weaver had decided to beard the main enemy, the blandly assured Dr Cock, the Blue Man who seemed to be on his own at the circular bar, observing Petersen and Nancy through a row of inverted spirit measures. They were behaving most correctly.

'Dr Cock, I presume?'

Drink in hand Weaver had casually sidled up to his man and fired at point-blank range. This thrust was taken in good part; for drawing back his Guardsman's shoulders and affecting to click his heels, the good Doctor smilingly and with narrowed eyes extended a manicured hand.

'Hahn, actually. Rooster in English, I believe. Professor Henn was the Yeats authority. You must be the Irish Professor of whom Hannelore has spoken.'

(Quick beady eye-contact here, looking quickly down into his Scotch.)

'She's a most dear person and a long-standing friend of mine. Can I get you a drink?'

'Hah!' Weaver said, as though thumped on the chest. A challenge! In the smooth German gentlemanly code presented to him like a keen blade, Weaver took 'a-most-dear-person' to mean 'a-most-sweet-puss-whom-oft-have-I-shagged-silly' and the barbed rider (the 'long-standing' friend part) to infer 'and-a-jolly-

51

fine-ride-she-was-too'; intended to mean that and taken up as such. With the implied tag: 'Your-turn-comes-now-vishy-vashy-Irishman . . . but-you-yust-vate-vee-Germans-have-a-vay!'

'You have been long here in Berlin?'

'Actually not long.'

At that moment (saved by the bell) Lore found them looking into their drinks and patently at a loss for a word; she with another vodka in hand, a cigarette lit, still playing the giddy party girl Rotraut Richter who falls downstairs every night.

'What does he say?'

'He says he knows you.'

'Oh I've known Dr Hahn for *years*. We are old friends. Now who goes dancing?'

Cocking an eyebrow at the *Gast*, Dr Hahn intimated that he should offer to dance with her; but Weaver was not a dancer, so Dr Hahn offered her his arm, most correctly and politely, and swept her off to the dance floor where Sepp Walser was whirling like a top, preparatory to going off his rocker again.

Weaver found a place where he could watch the dancers and stood with gin and tonic in hand. Lore moved from the arms of Dr Cock to the Grey Man, suddenly materializing on the dance floor, from him to the Old Admirer, and they danced what looked like a polka to the beat of a Beatles' song, and then she danced away with Sepp Walser, who looked like a frightened ferret on its hind legs, miming fear-of-the-predator, his hands or little paws up; then she danced away with a stranger and Weaver lost her.

But in a little while she reappeared, left the dance, crossed to the far wall and sat recovering her breath, seated on a chair, and then she rose up and, fanning herself with a programme, crossed directly to him, as filings to a magnet, as was only fit.

'Am I making a great fool of myself?'

She was *washed with all waters*, as the Germans say; the dark eyes brilliant. She was streaming.

'Am I being extremely silly?'

And then from nowhere came Nancy like a fury to stand before them, take one quick look at each, and demand: 'Now tell me what's going on here? These two know each other . . . and I distinctly smell hanky-panky.'

Hot intemperate words were exchanged, since smooth words could not pacify, between the Weavers, and then unforgivable insults added, things better left unsaid. Shortly thereafter the party began to break up. No one had much stomach for any further merrymaking, the band had packed up and were going home. Nancy was pacing to and fro trying to recover her composure, Petersen hovering near. Looking very white in the face Lore had retired to powder her nose. On the cloakroom counter a great pile of expensive overcoats had been deposited by the attendant who had gone home. It was two o'clock in the morning of the day after the end of the Polish Week.

Weaver poked about among the overcoats in search of two cheaper models that he would recognize at once for what they were, unmistakably inferior-quality weaverishirish property – viz., one lightweight tweedledum brown tweed overcoat, unlined, £28 from Menswear of O'Connell Street, Dublin; one belted tweedledee off-white Swiss raincoat with shoulder tabs and considered (by the Weavers) the very pinnacle of fashion when purchased in higher Grafton Street for Nancy's thirty-sixth (last) birthday – but poor stuff now amid opulent Berlin loot: opera cloak of black velvet lined with lilac satin, a gorgeous matt red Dior scarf like a *muleta*, a man's long astrakhan street-coat with sable collar brought back from Smolensk.

Here the calm and assured Dr Hahn spoke confidentially and cocksurely into Weaver's ear:

'You should perhaps leave her alone . . .' (but checked himself on seeing the forbidding expression already 'dawning' on Weaver's angry face) ' . . . that is,' he amended easily, tightening a blue silk scarf about his neck to make his grey eyes bulge, 'unless you've already gone too far. Your affair entirely. Good night, Professor. Nice meeting you.'

'I fail to see,' Weaver had begun frostily, holding up an armful of coats like a feeble shield, but went no further, as Nancy came forward to be vested.

'*Gute Nacht!*'

'*GUTE Nacht!*'

'*Gut Nachtle!*'

'*Gottle . . . !*'

'*Adieu! Adieu!*'

And so the Akademie der Künste emptied and the Polish Week ended.

It was the dead hour of an ironbound Berlin winter night when Weaver and Nancy left that warmth and made their way across the forecourt covered in snow, which was falling again, and had been falling when they were squabbling within. The wind blew it off the roof ledges and whistled through the ample holes in the Henry Moore bronze nude. No lifts were being offered to mere pedestrians and no stray taxis circled the Academy as Dr Hahn's glistening black Merc glided by. The faces of the 'well-matched pair' within showed up greenish from the dashboard lights, lit up like window dummies in a boutique closed for the night, their eyes glittering but dead as buttons; the gloved and soberly hatted Doctor now deeply immersed in intimate conversation with his lovely passenger. The pair of them looked magnificently haughty and remote, preserved and secured by wealth and investment, as the big tyres crunched over the snow, the shining limousine dipping its lights and weight into the street in a gallant well-sprung lordly manner before turning sharp right and smoothly moving off, *accelerando*! From the exhaust vent a fishy steam was contemptuously ejected back at them in quickly regulated spurts. As it gathered speed, the exhaust funnelled itself out into brilliantly white curlicues. *Thanksforthenicetimeandgo*! panting out its last gasps: Unndonne-undonnemmme! in dismissive red-tongued flourishes.

Without speaking the Weavers had jointly decided to proceed forthwith in the general direction of the Charlottenburg *Rathaus* where a cruising taxi could surely be picked up. Still wordless and well muffled up, not linking, they set out.

But they had not been walking ten minutes and had reached the Spree when Weaver (who had already gone too far) sensed more than saw the imminent horror as they came up to it. A snow-covered mound seemed to move uneasily by the low embankment wall by the Spree, lit by the down-turned headlights of a parked car in a line of such snow-covered vehicles waiting for their owners to arrive.

Weaver saw confusedly what at first he took to be an ancient grey elk (escaped from the zoo?) of great decrepitude and crippled with one broken hind leg (but were there elks in Berlin Zoo?) in the process of struggling painfully to rise and falling back, moaning pitifully the while. Or again, Weaver wondered, peering, perhaps it was a tarpaulin-shrouded mound of builder's rubble buffeted by the wind (but there was no wind). It was one of those Berlin winter nights when a scarifyingly freezing Baltic cold could flay the very skin off your face.

But on advancing closer to this monstrous group of flapping and moaning things he found a fellow prone on the ground with trousers down about his knees and shirt tails flapping, being most vilely set upon by a scragger without overcoat or headcover or muffler who lay grunting on top of him while actively engaged in the gruesome business of throttling the life out of him, pressing down with all his force, hissing ferociously between his teeth.

Weaver, who had never witnessed a murder done close up, clearing his throat nervously, was all set to utter a feeble 'Hey there, you, stop that!' or the subtle 'Nice one, Ginger!' when four (four!) maddened eyes glared up at him from the snowy ground lit up; whereupon the tall one resumed his murderous attack on the fellow below him who was moaning '*Oh, oh, ohhh . . .*' presumably now *in extremis* and breathing his last.

Weaver perceived in the nick of time that what he was about to intrude upon was both intensely private and improper: two mature consenting adult males were hard at it in thirteen degrees below freezing and still falling. When you kill the lights where does the darkness go? It was like watching the secret mating rituals of exotic insects, recovered from a part of the tropical forest into which one would never penetrate, struggling before your eyes, observed through the thick plate glass of an aquarium. Two sad sodomites frantic with grief and betrayal were copulating in the snow, lit by the headlights of a parked car, a maroon Plymouth with the windscreen iced up and already turning to a hill of snow. They might have been on a stage, lit on location for a movie. Weaver averted his eyes as he would have looked away from a bloody traffic accident. Nancy (who never noticed unpleasantness) with hands to either side of her face, holding her hat and missing it all, as she would have walked through dog-turds, marched ahead over the low bridge. The sight of an illuminated yellow phone booth on the other side had suggested a call-taxi service to her.

Hot holy shit! thought Weaver, following the resolute form of his wife, so that's it, that's what – holy dogshit!

Weaver, walk on! for pity's sake walk on! For now with a sobbing cry the hatless one had flung his arms around the no doubt already stiffening corpse and seemed to be pressing frantic hard kisses on the darkly yielding lips already sunken and lifeless. A fierce heartbroken shagger now transformed, no, transmogrified into a cannibal surprised in the act of devouring his trussed-up freshly slaughtered captive taken on some distant island and dispatched not five minutes before by repeated clouts from a heavy club. One resolute blow after another until the skull cracked inwards like a split coconut; then eagerly breaking open the brain-case to see what's on for lunch, the man-eater kneeling and handling the meat, grunting with anticipation, knuckling the tenderized prime pork; what's this then, *prosciutto crudo?* popping a swiftly severed testicle into his mouth for starters. Meanwhile the other savages, *bona fide* carnivores ravenous after their long morning row, have dragged the painted war-canoes above the tide line onto the palm-fringed beach and are now joyfully capering about the fire, brandishing their primitive weapons, all with hard-ons and stinking like wart-hogs as they jig howling about the flames.

With the short hair on the back of his head beginning to rise Weaver walked on out of this circle of perdition but had not proceeded fifteen paces when he sensed the light swift feet spurning the snow and the Holy Terror was swiftly bearing down on him once again, even worse than before, now detached from his sobbing victim.

Snuffling and weeping it (he) flew past Weaver onto the low bridge, leaving a hellish stench behind. In a fever of fearful intent began to discard thin jacket, then nimbly onto the wall, looked back to where the other was, uttered a cry – '*Meecheeellle!*' – and holding his nose, dropped from the bridge and straight through the ice below, still stiffening into all its freezing components. A black hole in the frozen Spree showed where he had gone down, with bubbles rising, disturbed white churning water, and there the head and shoulders appeared, having hit bottom and come up from below with loud gaspings and splashing and sobbing, the breath knocked out of him.

Meanwhile the vilely assaulted one had risen on one knee and was pulling on trousers and buttoning up flies, waving, staggering about, then came gamely on, still calling out as if with something of moment to contribute. Whereupon Nancy, cool as you please, had left the yellow booth and came strolling over the bridge, asking: 'What's all this hullabaloo? Fishing for bass?'

'Summon the Law will you!' Weaver called histrionically. 'One of them is in the Spree!'

'One of whom?'

'One of the sodomites.'

'Don't be a bloody ass.'

The tarpaulin-heap or broken elk or ex-corpse or cannibal-bait now joined Weaver on the bridge, with decayed teeth and foul breath smelling like a charnel house, breaking wind and hiccuping, half the size of his companion, calling:

'*Güüüüüünter!*'

He hauled in a reef at his belt, pulled at his clothes, looking over to where Nancy with the utmost composure was re-entering the yellow phone booth.

'Jeessu!' (this under his breath, brows twitching, staring at the black hole below and then across to the embankment where the other was clinging to the wall and trying not to be swept away in the current, flowing strongly thereabout. More shouting of '*Güüüüüünter! Güüüüüünter!*' were echoed steadfastly from the water by '*Mɛɛeechelle!*' like two loving corncrakes across a meadow).

'Enough of this fucking farting about,' Weaver told the frantic sodomite and pulling off his lightweight overcoat felt his way down the sloping bank until he could offer the arms of tweed as a pulley to the affrighted white face down in the black stream. And presently the groping hand caught hold and Weaver took the strain, began to move up the bank, pulling. But now the smaller one, stinking of open jakes, had slid past and was awkwardly helping, pulling and cursing, and the one in the water rose up with both hands holding fast. And then the little one slipped and went in head first to a last despairing screech of '*Mɛɛeechelle!*' quite anguished, from the water. And now both of them were embracing and spluttering and being carried away. Weaver pulled out his sodden overcoat and heard a hail from the bridge and looking up saw three silhouettes: Nancy and the Law.

'Having fun down there?' she called down. 'I didn't have to

phone. The Law has arrived in force. All we need now are long poles, with hooks on them.'

The night police had torches and fur-lined leather jackets and side-arms. With the minimum of exertion and saying nothing, using Weaver's sodden overcoat as a pulley, in short order the swimmers were dragged out of the Spree. Blowing on their hands, wringing out their shirts, with teeth chattering, they asked for a cigarette.

'Grand place for a dip,' Weaver said, holding a match, watching the thin unshaven face, the insucked cheeks. But none there had a word of English.

Twenty minutes later, having taken the sodomites somewhere, the small blue police bug overtook the Weavers, *still* walking home in the snow, in the deepening cold, Weaver now sans overcoat whereas Nancy, always bucked up by adversity, seemed marvellously cheered. Going ahead a little way and drawing in to the kerb, the bug stopped, with engine idling and a window on the near side was rolled down enough for a gloved hand to appear and summon.

'Nikolassee,' Weaver said.

'Too far,' the co-driver said, his dog's eyes on Nancy. 'On duty. But vee take you to Vestkreutz. From there train to Vannsee. Okay? Hop in, chumps.' Or words to that effect.

Tipping her Boraldino and smiling an inexplicable sweet smile Nancy lowered herself into the back seat behind the driver like a great lady getting into her very own scented carriage. The interior of the police bug stank of devotion to duty.

'They're going to strip-search you in the station,' Weaver muttered, getting in, 'and I mean Police Station. Do you over. Maybe a quick gangbang with some of the heavies. Discipline you. Tell the bastards nothing.'

An excessive amount of high-proof Polish vodka had put him into a frolicsome state and he couldn't stop talking.

'Get in, and don't be such a jackass.'

'Fair cop,' Weaver said to the two broad backs in leather, the rolls of gorilla fat pushing at the nape of the neck, extending both hands for the darbies to be clapped on.

'Cuff me.' He looked at Nancy. 'I'll go quietly.'

'We won't go at all unless you shut up,' Nancy said.

'Vee take you to Vest kreutz, okay?' the co-driver said (was the driver a dummy?).

The driver now gunned the engine and nodded to show he knew what he was doing and where he was going, even if he said nothing. They were in safe hands. The Law observed the wipers clearing frost and ice from the windscreen, going *glummmm, hummm, ummm . . . gulpa . . . gulpagulpa*, thinking their own sober thoughts, perhaps turning Nancy over in their minds; from where they sat in judgement she looked like one of those tall fallen ladies you got in (what was the bugger's name?) Schnnitzzler, a dirty writer, a filthy mind. They would take her to Vest Crutch and see what happened.

When the time seemed ripe they set off, in silence. They were taciturn officers of the Law. Below identical bullet heads (for they did not remove their caps) contented rolls of fat glistened with sweat on short-cropped napes, pressed upward and held in position by the collars. Mesmerized by their silence and by these layers of cropped fat glistening with sweat, now as if frowning, now trying out an uneasy smile (the two-faced man with different faces when inverted), Weaver thought of the dead swan and Klingsor's sword (the Electric Prunes were chanting '*Kyrie, eleison*').

Weaver tried to find a smoke, slapping his pockets, but had offered his last smokes to the sodden sodomites and where were they now, and he could not smoke Nancy's brand. His drenched overcoat lay between his legs. They drove on in silence through the slanting snow.

'*Schnee*,' Weaver said under his breath, and the co-driver drew in his breath with a great shuddering sigh, like a bullock in a byre.

'*Sprakkenze Inglish?*' Weaver tried his Low Swabish, touching the driver's leather-clad shoulder, but he did not deign to reply.

'*Nein,*' his companion said. '*Nix.*'

Weaver felt a pool of water begin to form about his frozen feet, and would not be silenced.

'No accounting for tastes,' he said into his muffler (at least that was dry). 'A bracing plunge in the Forty-Foot by night in the depths of winter to clear the head. Have I not done it myself in my time? Have *you* not done it?' (elbowing Nancy). 'Remember the other sod?'

'I remember that other. sodomite,' Nancy responded in her deadest voice, a spirit medium with very bad news from That Other World.

That other world! After the Prendergast party at Otranto Place the Weavers had gone stark naked in the Forty-Foot and a flabby white lecher had pursued Weaver into the swelling tide. 'Go home you!' Weaver had barked at him as though addressing a cur, and he had paddled back and slunk out. And lusty Weaver had enjoyed Nancy's riper favours while bending over in a cement shelter smelling of seaweed and turds and incoming tide. Winky Prendergast kept open house but Nelly was rather tired of open houses and the carryings-on of her horny husband.

Visibility was down to nothing, the road surface frozen, little or no traffic at that hour, and the air inside the police bug was bad.

And not a word good or bad was exchanged – the two law-enforcers now smelling to high heaven – until they pulled up before Westkreuz Station in the swirling Schnee and with many a hearty *Gute Nacht* and *Vielen Dank* parted company. Doors were slammed and the police bug began to crawl slowly away, leaking poisonous blue exhaust.

'Grand lads,' Weaver said, drawing in a deep breath of freezing air strong as chloroform, 'even if they do give off a bit of a pong.'

But Nancy had taken to her heels already, crying back 'Come

on, *come on*! The last train for Wannsee!' as she ran towards the booking office over the tunnel.

And sure enough there came the rumble and disturbance of an approaching train, coming through the freezing air, the rumble and rattle of the last for Wannsee.

Safely aboard and Nancy had wrapped herself up like a babushka in stoic silence opposite Weaver on the bare wooden seats roasted by the heating turned on full blast, steadily observing her reflection in the glass, wrapped up in close silence.

Bitter things that could never be taken back had been said, unpalatable evidence of misconduct brought to book, it was the end of more than the Polish Week. So the Weavers rode in silence in the overheated wooden carriage through Grunewald Station and racketing on to Nikolassee, to walk home in silence, as they had set out, Weaver for his part wondering if the game was worth the candle.

9
Baron Bogdana Kuguar and the Polish Baroness Kasia

Early one grey afternoon, when least expected, the Kuguars called and the host marched out! Joint get-togethers with Weavers, Kuguars and Pflückers had not proved too fruitful and had by mutual consent been discontinued. For after politely bidding their hosts the time of day in English, the guests reverted to German and continued to speak German to each other for the rest of the evening, leaving Weaver quite in the dark as to what they were discussing with such animation, with Nancy, bored stiff, translating episodically.

So wily Weaver was all set to depart via the kitchen window as the unexpected guest (Pan Cogito) could be heard roaring masterfully for strong potions in the living-room.

'You are leaving us?'

'Look's like it.'

'Well damn you then and go,' Nancy responded with smouldering eyes. 'God is good, Jack is earning, and everything is nice in its own time. So fuck off!'

She looked daggers at her estranged bedfellow, then added an inspired afterthought: 'I hope that whore gives you some frightful disease.'

Stepping closer, lowering her voice, looking dangerous. 'A good dose of *Raptus* to shrink that over-active prick of yours.'

Weaver fell back, stunned at the virulence of this.

'Thanks . . . most kind of you I'm sure. You will entertain our guests?'

He was already on the window-ledge, like a bird, was to meet Lore in twenty minutes outside Podbielski Station, had dropped from sight. Nancy stuck her head out the window. 'And fuck you too!' she screeched haggishly.

But Weaver, silently letting himself out the gate, was already flitting away, bathed in an amber light and head down as if advancing against imminent storm. The light was near-umber, as if torn from unhappiness. *Dominations first; next them, Virtues; and Powers the third*; thus spake sapient Carey.

Nancy (what had gotten into her?) was developing new techniques of intimidation and retaliation. Weaver might be immersed in Pavese (*Among Women Only*) which he had come upon in Margot Schoeller's bookshop and raising a casual right hand for a glass might look up from the printed page to find Nancy staring at him with an intense basilisk stare (or glare) of probing and purest hatred.

Or again, encountered going through a doorway, she would make a quick unexpected lunge, with a karate hand angled at his face, Weaver throwing up his hands to protect himself; and then the cat-like counter-lunge at his unguarded privities, the gloating cry '*K'nangg!*' and then the fire in the crutch, and Weaver doubled up, gasping, holding onto the doorway. The Queen of Air sailing off upstairs, calling down 'Serves you right you dirty bugger.'

Weaver was nonplussed by the tactics deployed, and the new crudeness of the language used, and for self-protection and a quiet life took to occupying rooms other than those occupied by his wife. If she came in he would move out. They were like opposing small wooden figures in a Tyrol clock. If she came to watch television that Weaver was watching, he moved away. Then she would sail in: 'If I sit down, will you get up?'

Up stood contrary Weaver, bridling.

'I might.'

'Weaver!' (the threatening edge, the rising intonation).

Weaver (rhetorical): 'Tell me, when is this bloody nonsense going to end?'

Nancy (brightly ironic): 'Oh so you begin to see it's nonsense? You are coming to your senses?'

'I am going out,' Weaver said, and he did just that.

As he came out of Podbielski Station Lore ran across the road with her hair flying and they kissed like lovers in an old French movie, Gérard Philipe and Madeleine Robinson in *Une Si Jolie Petite Plage*, an old sepia print the colour of happiness.

Nancy, wringing her hands, her face twisted and ugly, being diabolical: 'Ah, you are leaking? Are you sober yet?'

These latter tactics (*K'nang!*) he put an abrupt end to one day, when attempted once again in the kitchen; by forcibly bringing down the heel of his fist on the top of her bowed head with such violence that two fingers were dislocated and to his amazement Weaver found the lethal Sabatier in his right hand which he instantly plunged into the breadboard and left the kitchen with fluttering heart, feeling murder in the air.

Thereafter Nancy complained of a ringing in the ears and thought to consult a doctor ('I will simply tell him that my dear husband has gone mad over another woman and likes beating me insensible') but did nothing more about it. Then her teeth were giving her trouble. She and Nico made sorties across town to visit a handsome Polish dentist who was adept at his job. Weaver was advised to go and see Dr Slobodanka Gruden.

'No thanks.'

Of course it was not always open warfare.

Drinking alone in a Spanish bar opposite their old haunts near the Hotel Bogotá Nancy had fallen into conversation with a stout sweaty oleaginous umbrella manufacturer from Bruges who tried to get her drunk enough to say '*Je't'aime*'. He was a simple soul but could neither get her drunk nor persuade her to say '*Je t'aime*', not even meaning it.

'Such a big fat wobbly *mercenary* Belgian!' cried she gaily, 'just imagine.' Mercenary was a very bad word in Nancy's vocabulary.

'Oddly enough,' said Weaver, twirling the ice, 'friend Bogdana's Baroness, quite unsolicited, said that to me at one of Born's dos. I may say it was a little embarrassing.'

'Said what to you?'

'*Je t'aime*. Is that soliciting? She seemed quite sober.'

Nancy showed her intense interest by not reavealing it.

'And what did the fierce Resistance fighter say to that affront to his Polish pride and honour?'

'He was at the other end of the room killing off the vodka supplies and not available for comment. I wouldn't care to mix it with old Bogdana – or all that pent-up Polish rage. I bet he fights dirty, probably carries a shiv.'

Weaver suspected that Bogdana rather fancied Nancy; he had called once when Weaver was away, burst his trousers and had to go home for a new pair. He returned to take Nancy and Nico out boating on Schlachtensee.

How did he burst his trousers, pray?

Nancy's reply: 'He has a pot belly.'

Was that an answer? Weaver smiled, thinking of female fickleness and their own perplexing anatomy. Perplexing for the owners. Once at dinner with the Kuguars and the Pflückers, Bogdana had leaned across the table as if to kiss Nancy on the cheek but taking hold of her nut-brown tresses began pulling her across the table until her eyes filled with tears; and nobody said a word, least of all Weaver. The host had been drinking vodka all day.

Pan Cogito became waggish in his cups, but it was a Polish waggishness that had sharp edges to it, unpredictable elements and uncomfortable fun. Weaver did not understand this wit delivered in German, French, part Polish and Yiddish. Kuguar's grandfather had spoken only English, his mother was Armenian, his father a lawyer and professor of economics. 'Hence my syncretic religion – Orthodox from my grandfather, Catholic by my father and all round evidence of Hasidic culture.' But he never spoke of the war, his time as a Polish Resistance fighter.

'How you you say Resistance in Polish?' Weaver inquired.

'*Opór, Résistance, Notstand.*'

'What is one to think of Katyn?'

'One doesn't,' Bogdana answered, blessing himself.

He had a most princely air; it came from the rough olden times.

He then joined Professor Paul Pflücker the ex-Luftwaffe liaison officer, embracing him and the pair of them were soon sitting cross-legged on the floor.

Nancy in her cups could be most amusing; inebriation seemed to release some hidden joy and she became flirtatious like a scheming tease in Restoration comedy – Mrs Bracegirdle? Only a good-looking broad could have carried it off. If booze made other women contentious and dull, it enlivened Nancy Els: she positively sparkled.

10
Mando Again!

Afflicted with nerves Mando strode by the Spree, slapping her mighty thigh, seeking a good metrical bounce. The apartment DILDO had found her in Wildpfad was close to the Grunewald and the wooded dangerous border zone where the Americans were engaged in periodic sharp-shooting at invisible Russkies in hairy headgear with earflaps, muddy combat boots uncleaned since the horrific Ukraine campaigns, armed with primitive Tommy guns, slipping unseen through the wood at all hours of the day and night.

The long silences of Berlin nights were punctuated by the *rat-tatting* of automatic weaponry – a mailed fist hammering on a heavy door that refused to open or yield. All this spurious but none the less dangerous peace-time military activity ravaged Mando's nerves, prolonged her insomnia. The sound of incoming trains reminded her that she could at any time escape to Paris. She called on the Weavers at their house in Nikolassee, she and Nancy hitting it off splendidly.

'Birds of a feather,' Weaver pronounced.

Mando had a nose for hot scandal and knew what was going on among the DILDO guests, who was having it off with whom, which husbands and wives were parting, what marriages were on the rocks, who was arriving and who departing. The English sculptor Armitage had just left, rudely advising Mando to watch her liver; Per Olaf Enquest and entourage were expected soon from Stockholm.

Apart from all that, Mr Beckett himself had arrived from Paris and was already rehearsing *Endspiel* in the Schiller-Theater Werkstatt where *two* German translators had been placed at his disposal but Mr Beckett had at once chosen Tophoven the Dutchman. He had an atelier in the Akademie der Künste and was always first to arrive by taxi for rehearsals, very punctual and polite; all who encountered him were taken with his fluent German and charmed by his modest manner; he was most self-effacing, for a great man. Mando herself had not seen him, but he was about.

'You intend to interview him?' Weaver inquired.

'Certainly!' Mando cried with her skittish high young-girl's laugh, a little innocent with all her life before her.

'He famously doesn't grant interviews,' Weaver said.

'I had a dream the other night,' Nancy cut in here, in the annoying way she had, 'about this man whose mouth was full of gold teeth. He came into the self-service in filthy white canvas shorts and in a very angry voice said that he'd ordered half a dozen Schultheiss Pils and why hadn't they arrived! The stuff had just never arrived. He was very angry, his gold teeth positively flashed. The depressed hag at the checkout *cringed*. He was roaring at her. I noticed that she had mildewed fingernails.'

Weaver looked at Mando and Mando looked back at Weaver, puzzled.

'What was this, please?'

'She had blue-mould on her fingernails.'

'Ahh.'

Sometimes in deep sleep Nancy groaned and spoke in a voice not her own, the words slurred and run together, as if she were drunk or being tortured, or having her fingernails pulled out with red-hot pincers; with head averted, breath foul, twitching all over, possessed by some dibbuk or African spook.

'Whassa-meaney-these-anti-snail-eaters? . . . whassa-alla-dis-barley-fields-an-pink-pigs-ripening-down-de-lane?'

Silence, listening, intake of foul breath; then, abrupt and clear, angry: 'Something funny's going on here and *I don't like it*!' This most vehemently.

Not long after this Mr Beckett was recognized rising sedately in the Akademie der Künste elevator or 'lift' with his steely grey hair erected like the comb of an enraged cockatoo, dressed in bottle-green cord slacks and nondescript tweed jacket.

11

A Prize for Sam

'I see Sam's got the Nobel Prize,' said a distinctly Dublin voice behind Professor Weaver's back.

Weaver's mother (RIP) had a term for such amiable buffoons: they were said to be 'consequential articles'. It was a grey Berlin day towards the end of October 1969. Weaver had been reading off the new titles in the English-*sprach* or right-hand window of Margot Schoeller's famous bookshop on the Kurfürstendamm. He now began a thoughtful circumspect half turn, to see who this remark might have been addressed to; two Dubliners were chatting with their backs to the display window, as if standing outside Eason's in O'Connell Street on a cold grey October evening with the light just dying and a dead cold air rising up off the river and their thoughts rather turning to a few quick balls of malt in, say, The Old Stand or the International opposite or O'Neill's snug around the corner, still in Suffolk Street. They had the knack, a trick peculiar to its citizens, of carrying the city around with them like a handy but empty refuse bucket that could be set down wherever they chanced to be.

Greyly and unobtrusively it had become a distinctly Dublin day in Berlin. The rank outsider, the Master of the Leopard-stown Halflengths, a dark horse if ever there was one, had come romping home at long odds, leaving the rest of the field nowhere and bankrupting all the bookies. *Throwaway* how are ye! Weaver was thinking of Wilde's *mot*: a small-size curly-brim gent's hat in a Paris shop window and below it on a handwritten card the prescription 'With this model the mouth is worn slightly open.'

In Dublin, all over Ireland today, there would be many wide-open mouths. But here and now the Berlin rush-hour traffic fidgeted for the lights to turn green; now they were inching forward, now they were off! Wasn't it Tacitus who said that speed was akin to panic? Running in the streets conveys an impression of terror, wrote gloomy Adorno.

NOBELPREIS AN
SAMUEL BECKETT

said the handwritten sign. Most likely Frau Margot herself had propped it up on the plain white jackets of the Suhrkamp uniform edition. The bulging myopic eyes of James Joyce peered out from under a ridiculously inflated motoring-cap and seemed to focus uncertainly in a hostile sort of way in Weaver's general direction. Was he among his own? A block from where the Professor stood, fabled Bleibtreustrasse crossed athwart the Ku'damm where Poldy Bloom was on the lookout for dreams of well-filled hose, plump mellow yellow smellow melons.

The small photograph of the author was inset into the top left of the plain white wrappers that made up the Suhrkamp edition. Ellmann's monumental biography, even more extensive in German, was resplendent alongside a paperback RoRoRo *Murphy* with the bold banner *Nobelpreis 1969* across its plain jacket. It occurred to Weaver that when it first appeared in 1936 from Routledge of all houses, James Joyce had been alive enough to read and enjoy it enough to quote a passage back to its author. James Joyce would have been aged fifty-nine years old when *he* passed away in Zurich without the Nobel Prize; whereas Yeats had been a year younger when he received it in 1923. Beckett in Paris was sixty-nine. The two gabby jackeens had strolled away, still talking. Weaver moved across to the left-hand or German-*sprach* display window.

And there was Sam Beckett's work in French and English with Elmar Tophoven's translations into German – said to be outstanding – with the author's own Frenchified *Watt* (dismissed by its author into Weaver's ear as not so much shit as dysentery). The great titles sang out in plainchant: *Der Namenlose*, *Erzählungen und Texte um Nichts*, *Wie es ist*; the last-named sounded like a heavy German philosophical treatise: *How It Is*. Weaver noticed for the first time, like finding a clump of mushrooms in a field supposed to be traditionally empty of mushrooms, that Joyce and Beckett had the same German publisher – Suhrkamp Verlag, and now both shared window-space at Margot Schoeller's, to be gaped at by Weaver and two Dublin jackeens.

The coast now clear, Weaver made his way past Bleibtreu-strasse and continued on by junctions where the evening whores were beginning to appear, a sure sign of falling darkness, feeling himself to be now entering familiar territory; for had not the Weaver family been put up by DILDO for a fortnight or more in the Hotel Bogotá?

Ahead of him at the level of first-storey windows a hawk planed silently across Schlüterstrasse into the gloaming sur-rounding Olivaer Platz, to beat the bushes for an evening meal, about the *Kinder* playground where Nico had amused himself with other kids in the sandpit in May. And there was the Hotel Bogotá. Was Jimmy Zucker, the Basque waiter, still serving meals in the stuffy dining-room? He had been very good to Nico; his wife was in the clothing business; the hard-working Zuckers were saving for their retirement in Zaragoza. Professor Weaver stepped briskly into the lobby.

Why of course the sulky blonde receptionist remembered the Professor and was so glad to hear they had a house rented in Nikolassee and Herr Born had been in not long ago and naturally it was no trouble at all to put through a person-to-person call to

Paris for a certain Monsieur Bickitt, whereupon the obliging Professor dug out his little pocket-book and supplied the number.

'I have it here. It's Kellermann 8311.'

The blonde receptionist called the exchange and waited. She wore a russet one-piece woollen dress that hugged her all around and left her arms bare and rounded; add to this the pushful bust of a pouter pigeon and an expressive (sulky) lower lip permanently wetted, like Arletty nude in the revolving water-barrel.

One morning, strolling into reception after breakfast, purporting to inquire for Weaver mail, he had watched this same blonde lady fairly demolish an American guest who had come down from his room to dump a holdall of soiled linen on the counter, demanding to know where it could be dry-cleaned.

'One moment please,' said she, out went the damp lower lip and heaving pouter chest, pushing across a service-sheet with dry-cleaners itemized as the retractable pen ticked off three addresses within walking distance, tic-tic-tic, then snapped shut like a cross little beak. Her aloof Berliner correctness was admirable, graven in acid; and Weaver had been lost in admiration. She put the guy in his place. Where could it be cleaned? Sloppy Joe leaning over the counter, giving her the boiled eye through his bifocals. Had he dirty ideas? She didn't care for this approach.

But she liked the handsome owner of the Hotel Bogotá. One could tell that when they stood together on his side of the counter, running the place; together they were an efficient team. Weaver had seen them lunching à deux near the window of a good restaurant on the Kurfürstendamm and had speculated whether they slept together. Was sleeping with the owner a part of the business, like running the place or demanding a rise, part of promotion as with rising starlets and the casting-couch? It was none of his business, as she would have been one of the first to tell him.

'It's ringing but no one is answering,' she said, holding the receiver out from her ear. 'What shall we do, Professor?'

'May I . . . ?' making a long arm the Professor clapped it to his left ear.

In a high flat in Paris overlooking the Santé Prison the phone continued to ring. The iambic pentameter is a heartbeat, he told himself pedantically, hearing the distant shrilling in his ear, and counted up to fifteen of them. Then, to be on the safe side, five more. The very pretty Irmgard, who had probably slept with the owner, was occupying herself with dockets and hotel files, scrupulously not listening but out of earshot some way down the counter.

'*Nada*,' the Professor said, handing her back the instrument that was still ringing, the connection still alive.

'The bird has flown. He must be in Tangier. May I order a drink?'

'But of course, Professor.'

She touched the bell.

'Is Jimmy still with you?'

'Jeemy?' She was puzzled, frowning. Was this another of the Professor's obscure jokes?

'We have no one of that name staying here.'

'Well, you had,' Weaver said. 'Jimmy Zucker in the dining-room. Our Basque waiter.'

'Ah, *Jeemy*! Yes, he's still with us.'

He had suggested tasty and economical portions of swine cutlets for Nico, pleasing both mother and son; had spoken to him in Spanish, had told Nancy of a dry-cleaner's run by Spaniards not too far away.

There was a large black-and-white print of the remote city of Bogotá on virtually every wall of the hotel and the nosy Professor had questioned the owner.

'So what's all this about Bogotá?'

The owner answered that he just loved the place and its people and the high and bracing air and he hoped to retire there in his secure old age. It was 2600 metres up in the cold drizzle of the Andean plateau; walking the streets gave you the staggers.

He had proved to be most obliging; informing the Weavers of washing facilities in the kitchen, and they could use the iron there when the girls had tidied up after lunch. Some cooking could be done there too, if Frau Weaver wished. He told them of the small playground in the square, spoke to Nico in Spanish, and this was perhaps the bond that endeared the vague Professor (who seemed to spend an inordinate amount of time chatting to his receptionist) to him – the Spanish-speaking son.

In the empty bar with Steinhäger and beer chaser before him, Weaver recalled with some amusement that his friend Lindemann had been barred from browsing in Margot Schoeller's bookshop by the lady herself. He had been brought before her when barely out of college, caught red-handed pilfering some expensive tomes.

12
Nico

Had the silver amulet worn about the neck been swallowed up and lost in his own chaotic filing system, or where had it gone? The little Piscean fish, a birthday present from Lore, had vanished. Rummaging among his papers Weaver came upon a dog-eared, well-thumbed Spanish *cuaderno*; a no less chaotic record of Nico's three months of schooling in Málaga, where subjects were jumbled together on the lined pages, Mathematics and Religious Knowledge, History and Geography, with coloured drawings of alluvial soil and a wonky Holy Family with manger and camels, oxen and the Virgin Mother with her halo and crown, long tots and spelling tests; a vigorous pell-mell sort of *Creación del mondo* in the Andalusian manner.

Also evidence of an English-speaking school he had passed dreamily through without leaving much impression, except one of extreme vagueness. He belonged to another, earlier century, and was lost in the twentieth. Weaver's heart was touched and troubled by these bright turbid Pentel drawings and the stories in their vivid colours; the purposeful scrawl of an effort towards . . . towards what exactly?

He saw his son writing laboriously, head tilted, eyes narrowed as if priming a bomb, to get down the title. 'Mi Childhook, mi

Life.' Taking the exercise book to his desk Weaver opened a page at random and read:

Wandey

mi father wos raiting and i wos pleing aut said and then i sor thet mi father wos gon the end of mai stori*

Wan Die

Wan die dei was a babun in a old haus wif a boy and the boy was feri fraitent and wan naight the boy went slouli slouli daun da maunten**

Wonday

I was walking along when i hered a noise it wos skratching like and buches began to muve and sadenly the sun began to go down and then houling noise it wos a wolf howling and scratching noise and a shape of a man and mice runing and i woked on when i so a house i began to get closer and i thought that hands came on my shoulder and skriming and i sudenly turnd and so a wolf runing after a gerl i then so nathing i went in the house and sow the gerl ded on the ground and a moving shadow in the kitchen. When i so the costume of the wolf it was a man in the citchen and then i got

* My father was writing and I was playing outside and then I saw that my father was gone, the end of my story.

** One day there was a baboon in an old house with a boy and the boy was very frightened and one night the boy went slowly slowly down the mountain.

a nighf and killed the man then i sudenly so it wos my brother ded

I wos so sory then i beried him in the house so then i preid so sorry i was and then i so some fases looking at me when i so a leter on the table it sed

'dier brother if i dy pleace bring the gerl next to me i am geting fierser and dangerras and i will give lots of love i live you with this house and the wolf skin my brother.'

i wos so sory then i heard that when one day anather leter came and sed im in AMERICA frend there it finished then i fented then i reilised that i was tricked i then went back home when my brother siting on a sher and the gerl i cudent belive my eyes.

For Margarete

wan dei there wos a smol man and hi lukt laik a rat and hi wos smol as a rat and hi went in the houl and hi kudentt kamaut andhiwos lokt in andhi wos lokt for ever and that wos the end

The Strange Kritcher

One day there lived a famaly they grew a little monster they dident now whot to do so they left him on a tree they went home and the kritcher began to grow and got wilder and wilder soon they had to go and kill him. He all ways won so they weghted for same one strong there was a baby hoo was a champ at fighting soon he had to fight the kritcher and killed him and that wos the END.

The Bird Who Got a Worm

Once upon a time there was a houke he was very hungry so he whent to a bush and then he so a worm it was turning round and round then the howk kowt the the worm it was slipy and it nearly escaped then she began to eat it then she began to eat it and then fell down ded the END.

Punch

Punch and joudy, joudy gets the beyby then she sees you get beybey now you get the beyby no you get the beyby im going to get the soseges you look after the beybey wile i get the soseges thoump were is the beybey daun sters the sosegis i got the soseges goup you giv the so sigis to me goup the end

The Famely

There wos this ophill creature he could eat people . . .

The Strange Land Where We Wance Stood

James stood on the doorway hoping to se his his lover one night when in the distance came a hevy mist heding towards his front door and between the mist his lover stood and holding a nighf slowly stabed her self and disaperd.

the following morning he went into town asking if anybody had hered his love non replide and walked of he slowly walked towards the church and there in front of him stood a little young girl saying that she was his lover and now yunger, james asked her questions and every thing she answered was write he nelt and praid the girl stood there for a while and walked on antill he could not se her he walked on and went to a s

The Werelwind

One day there was a very windy storm the parm trees were blowing back and forward the ships were frown against the rocks and smashed to peases there on the harrber people started to get in there cars and drove to safety they all manigged to get away from it except one family who did not have a car or money they had a farm from his ded mother the father he was married to Maria his wife they had two sunns but they were only 8 years old and they were twins they all ran to a cave which they had made for their children to hide in. They were all safe but they had no food for six days and at this time one of their children had died of hunger the mother had fainted and at this time the wind had stopt. John the father had come out and sow the farm was smashed to peases cars had been blown apart there on the ground lay 5,000 people ded one of his suns lay ded as well there out of rock came a 7 year old girl but she could not see. She was blind. John ran and picked her up and the first thing she said Father and John put her down and said I'm not your father but you and my sun and my wife are the only people alive at this moment momment she started to weap and pickt up a rock and was just about to kill her self when John coght her hand with the stone in [it] and she started to shout Lieve me alown do you anderstand and out came Jim out of the cave and shouted Father whots going on. Belinda the girl opened her eyes and ran to Jim and kissed him all over Jim did not understand why. Then she said I was blind a minnute a gow but when I hered your lovely voise I opend my eyes thats wright said John and walked into the cave to see if Maria his wife was all wright. Jim and Belinda sat down out side talking about their lives when out of the cave came John weeping Jim said is there something wrong and John said Maria was ded she had a hart attack. Belinda did you have a father said Jim yes I did we were both in a car and father opend my door and ditermind that I would get killed by pushing me out of the car which he did then this big jayantick werel wind. Was it a werlwind said Jim of corse it was no ather wind could do that.

Said Belinda Jim whot is your best subject motor macanicks said Jim. Whot is yours cooking Jim ran down to one of the cars which was not badly brocken down and starte[d] fixing it and then father shouted Jim look at this Jim ran round some rocks and found father nealing infront of a space cappsel.

A Story Without Beginning or End

Chapter 1 Arrival

. . . jonah hit the ground, he had landed In A forest. jonah Rolled up his Parachute and hid it in a bush, he looked at his hands they had been badly burnt he put his Right hand under his left shoulder and his left hand under his right Shoulder and ran through the grass. he stopped and listened, Suddenly a hand covered up his mouth and a machine gun was put to his face. 'Who are you' Said a young lady, in a french acsent 'my name is jonah I'm in the R.A.F.' Replied jonah.

The young lady walked in front of jonah 'It is true' said the young lady admiring jonah's medal.

The young lady Was Wearing a black jumper a brown pair of jeans, A pair of Plimsels a leather belt strapped with bullets. her hair was long and black and came down to her shoulders. her eyes were hazel Brown and her lips cherry red. 'Are you french' asked jonah, Rather puzzled. 'oui, monsieur' che Replied With a smile. 'you are admiringly beautiful' Said jonah with a close look. 'Merci' che Replied 'but now you must come with me' che said. Jonah stopped 'Where are you taking me' he asked. 'Why to our hideout' che said.

'Who's *our* hideout' asked jonah with a puzzled look.

'Let me explain' che said.

'I should jolly well think so' Said Jonah sitting on a log.

'My name is linda tennis, My father used to be a banker until the germans Invaded france, my father was killed, everyone Ran away and hid iff they could. The germans tortured my mother to the death And I am Revenging their deaths, I have friends In my hideout, now will you Please come with me'

'yes' Replied jonah 'but my hand theyve got blisters'

Suddenly there was a shot linda and jonah stood still. A german voice came out of the woods:

'hauben Krau lotze un bieren' (the voice said, meaning stop where you are, the wood is surrounded).

'It is an ambush' Said the young lady, quickly Run.

Linda Ran but jonah still stood, not knowing what to do. Linda staggered to the ground. Then there came the sound of Machine guns. 'oh my god' Said jonah covering his face. then the german voice spoke again:

'harben zi gnitze' (meaning do not try to resist).

A minute later the germans came out from behind the trees with rifles and machine guns. The leader spoke

'Get up.'

Jonah did not stirr. the leader kicked jonah on to the floor. jonah stood up in a rage and yelled 'murderer' jonah tryed to strangle the leader but was knocked out by the end of a german Rifle.

Chapter 2 Imprisonment

jonah awoke to find himself in the back of a truck with 3 germans with machine guns standing by him, jonah's hands and legs were also tied up, so that made him helpless.

'Where are we going' asked Jonah.

'Stuttgart' Replied a german.

Stuttgart was a german Imprisonment for British prisoners everyone knew the place or either had heard the name.

'hotze uf Naken irr' said one of the germans (meaning have you a cigarette).

'ja Kaultze urr laten' (meaning yes here take one) the other german Replied

The german handed an open packet of cigarettes over to the other German and then passed the packet on to the third german.

'grassias' he said (meaning, thank you).

After many hours driving the truck finally stopped, the three germans dragged jonah out, the light blinded him for a second. When jonah slowly opened his eyes he looked around. Stuttgart was a large Prisonment. On jonah's left were the generalls quarters and the ammunition hut for the sentries on the right were the sleeping huts for the prisoners and behind jonah the sentries sleeping huts and not too far from that the cooking house.

The soldiers dragged jonah into the generals hut. The general was a fat man with a desperate look he held a cane in his right hand.

'Vat is your name' he said coughing a little In Between.

'my name is jonah Mackol RAF, squadron 8.'

'zearch him' said the general.

The sentries searched jonah. they found a packet of gum a compass, a picture of his family and a knife in his Buckle.

'Do you know anything of the British Plans' Said the general.

jonah didn't Reply, then the general struck him across the face.

'Anzer me' he said the general.

'I Do not' said jonah Rubbing his cheek in a fury.

'I do not believe you' said the general. 'Put him in the concentration camp for two months' he said with a laugh.

jonah was led down corridoors, there were doors and doors on every side, the german in front of jonah stopped and unlocked a door, the german behind jonah pushed him into it. And the door was locked again. jonah looked around, the room was small but uncrowded a small bed lay in the Right hand corner and near to the barred window was a table with a chair. Jonah stood on the chair to look out of the barred window. he saw the British prisoners lining up, they all looked very weak. Suddenly one of the men flopped in-to the floor, jonah saw one of the germans kick him but the prisoner did not stir.

'Take him away' said the german.

jonah climbed down from the chair and lay on the bunk. The hot sun turned the place Into an oven. Days passed jonah becoming weaker all the time the only thing they gave him was Raw fish, Bread and water. They gave him injections trying to force him to tell the British Plans. On the last day jonah was practically dead his legs could not move he could barely move any of his body the german sentry gave the prisoners jonah to take care of. jonah felt water treacle on to his dry mouth and flow onto his neck 'thank you' said jonah very slowly and then fell uncunsious.

Chapter 4 Friends

Two days later jonah felt Better, the prisoners had taken good care of him, feeding him on meats starch and all the proteins of a good square meal. Bob one of the young men had taken more care of jonah than any of the other men. he had stole some of the food that jonah had eaten for the two days from the generals food store in Stuttgart iff you were caught stealing food the penalty was death. When jonah awoke he found four men around him 'you look Much Better today Whats your name' Said a tall man with a small moustache. jonah Rubbed his eyes. 'My name is jonah.' 'hye' said Bob smiling. Then the fellow with the small moustache spoke again:

'My name's clark stairs this is stephen mayday that is . . .

Oh that uncertain spidery precursive!

On the verso side of the last page (father kneeling in front of a space capsule) Weaver found the likeness of his own face executed by his brilliant son, in the process of losing the endgame in what looked like an exhausting game of chess, and going down to the fridge helped himself to a chilled Schultheiss beer.

13

At the Philharmonie*

Together they attended an interminable series of concerts. *Mit*:
Möhring *und* Krumme, Riemann *und* Schilling, Kunz *und*
Zentrum, Kaese *und* Wagenkneckt, Lehmann *und* Lohmann,
Herdenverhalten *und* Lebensfähigkeit, Havel *und* Havelturm,
Bleibtreu *und* Güntzel, Hecht *und* Hirschsprung, Tucher *und*
Podex, Alt-Moabit *und* Jung Krumme Lanke, Blumen *und*
Bäumen, Wald *und* Weg, Wasser *und* Wiese, Kneppen *und* Rut,
Flut *und* Schaum, Kiefer *und* Wirt, Muschi *und* Möse, Furchel *und*
Fotze, Rille *und* Nille, Dattel *und* Ding, Zähringer *und* Zille,
Erdmann *und* Waidmann, Krupp *und* Essen, Scharnhorst *und*
Gneisenau, Underberg *und* Eppert, Borgelt Schmidt *und*
Hannelore Boyken-Schein, Lübars *und* Ungeheuer Tiefkühlung
und Schockfrieren, Saubersucht *und* Tagenacht, Körper *und* Glut,
Weltschmerz *und* Langnese, Kempinski *und* Bilka, Atika *und* Volle
Pulle, Lubberhuizen *und* Elmar Engels, Bembo *und* Blickens-
dorfer, Imhof *und* Kamm, Bildung *und* Bodenbach, Bullenwinkel

---

* Cf. Ernest Bornemann's *Sex im Volksmund* for German dialect versions, muggerslang,
Rotwelsch. As: Honicke *und* Neumeier, Kantschu *und* Knie, Hinauf (Up!) *und*
Sporengeklirr, Firlefanz *und* Webstuhl, Hackfleisch *und* Zweibelfleisch, Knatternd *und*
Zischend, Rucula *und* Pepperonta, Murmel *und* Poppi. As: The Largely Accommodating
(or Roomy) Cunt, The Twitchy Cunt, The Smelly Cunt, The Warty
Cunt, The Snappy Cunt, The Electric Cunt, The Smarting Cunt, The Kitchen Cunt,
The Swimming Pool Cunt, The Flushing Cunt, etc., etc.

und Blumenstein, Kreilkampf *und* Klostenberg, Herrdoktor-peterwelter *und* Fraurosemariewelter, Gesundbrunnen *und* Nürnberg, Herbst *und* Humboldt, Ruhleben *und* Friedrichsfelde, Flut *und* Britz, Schäumen *und* Schinderhannes, Schläge *und* Esel, Fischer *und* Wollfisch, Doktor Borgelt *und* Hannelore Schmidt, Walhalla-Genossen *und* Wallhall-Wisch, Hinauf *und* Sporengeklirr, Kantschu *und* Raps, Kastrati *und* Klar, Hackfleisch (minced meat which Germans eat now as formerly they were said to eat their own children) *und* Zwiebelfisch, Jeliffe *und* Goldstein, Schnappfotze *und* Klemmfotze, Steckdose *und* Schwanzschlucker, Vogelkiste *und* Schnalle, Fickritze *und* Brunzrutsche, the delight-fully deleterious pair Bamm *und* Baff, Grete Weiser *und* Margot Schoeller, Saftpresse *und* Glitsche, Orgel *und* Loch, 'Pussi' *und* 'Punze', Kofferdeckel *und* Kitzler, Steckdose *und* Planschbecken, Gottlieb *und* Gut, Rüdesheimer *und* Kirchnerpfad, P. Podbielski* *und* B. Breitenbach, Papst Pacelli *und* Onkel Tom, Doktor Dexenheimer *und* Graacher Himmelreich, P. Pfefferbüchse *und* F. Fickritze, Fotzenwarze *und* Schnappfotze, Schmidt *und* Wessen, Martin Bier *und* Hanna Buber, Bubikopf *und* Zwicke, Weib *und* Ente, Handschuh *und* Knie, Firlefanz *und* Webstuhl, Frückstücks-stunde *und* Sägezähne, Hinauf *und* Sporengeklirr, Hölle *und* Hund, Kluger *und* Hecht, Sachs *und* Cotzias, Bullenwinkel alone; not to mention Stryshewski *und* Lebedinskij, Sichert *und* Skujin, Hellmer *und* Holstein, Fellner *und* Linz, Peek *und* Cloppenberg, Alexander Kempinski solo. As Minki. Then came the whoresons Klamps *und* Klocke, Heidi *und* Rosi von Alm with udders aquiver. Sir Delves Digby Bullpitt of the British Council with dull wife.

Also in attendance were Old Ranke and Hans Joachim Schoeps, Harry Gelink and Uta Zweisamkeit, Granzao and Grimzoo, Nachtportier and Berlinerzimmer, Mosch and Schwester-Ente, Muschi and Putsch, Maelstrom and Zitzewitz,

---

* Podbielskiallee runs parallel to Pacelliallee in Dahlem. It's the name of a count; link-ing the Schorlemerallee to Breitenbachplatz since the world began.

Schlehbaum Punze of Den Haag with the deathly-pale Dutch gynecologist and specialist on matters urinary, Dr Lena Luge in tow with Regina Whuk (of Warszawa), a sinister threesome. Then Nansen and Sporengeklirr, Peter Pan van Cack, Johannes Weissenborn Eiserner-Vorhang alone, Welchselborg and Gamaschenrittertum the lovers of Purcell ('When night her purple veil . . .'), Hinauf and Menschenkericht, lastly Schinderhannes and Schöpfungslieder trooped in. And now all was complete, all the beasts inside and the doors closed, and the compromised conductor Fürtwangler stepping on to the podium for *Götterdammerung* – a real *Fest* for music buffs (but Richard Wagner had privily revealed to Weaver a world he *did not dare* to enter).

But for years now, and thus as good as dead, not to be seen at the Philharmonic Hall were neither Rot nor Körperköpenick, nor Flotow, nor Malchow, nor for that matter

Pankow nor
Buckow nor
Rudow nor
Ostmauer nor
Westmauer nor
Krasna nor
Hacks nor
Barillet nor
Gredy nor
Rummelsberg nor
Griebnitz nor
Arxangels nor
Karlshorst nor
Schönweide nor
Lindenthaler nor

witty Wittenau following after. But for the rest, all were present and correct and ready to be numbered off and counted, as the matched beasts of the Great Ark in the days of Father Noah. And the new faces of Möbel-Hübner and Britz, Adia and Eck, all ears, arriving in excited couples, as the creatures roaring and trumpeting, boarding their floating home or zoo, lustful and panting, ripe for breeding.

The Deutschlandhalle was vast ('only fit for horse-racing,' Nancy said humorously) but Scharoun's oddly shaped Philharmonie was a veritable pasha's tent, and high Oper on Bismarckstrasse was as nowhere else. Figure Weaver and the lovely Lore Schröder there, taking their seats, opening their programme, waiting for it to begin.

The Germans have ever been gross addicts, from the stiffest of generals (say Schmundt) to the grottiest of *Gauleiters* (say Stöhr). From steel mill to ball-bearing plant they doted on operas by (let us say) Offenbach, those madly gifted pair of wops Puccini and Rossini. Not to mention Massenet, Janáček, Dallapiccola; loud performances of *La Bohème, Schwanensee*, Verdi's timeless *Otello, The Marriage of Fig*. Fischer-Dieskau singing at the Philharmonie; *Tristan und Isolde* at the Deutsche Oper.

'I know you,' Nancy sneered, bitter as quassia, 'lusting and panting after those degenerate Northern women.' And instantly poor Weaver was shrunken to the size of a worm, reduced to the proportions of a . . . pea.

14

In the *Abendland*

The stations from Wittenbergplatz to Krumme Lanke on the suburban commuters' very clean and tidy U-Bahn read like a poem by Gottfried Benn. The *Zugabfertiger* in his peaked cap and motley uniform sang out '*Alles zurück bleiben!*' (Weaver distinctly heard '*Alles verrück bleiben!*') for the pneumatically operated doors to whoooosh shut and they were off to

    Augsburger Strasse
    Spichernstrasse
    Hohenzollernplatz
    Fehrbelliner Platz
    Heidelberger Platz
    Rüdesheimer Platz
    Breitenbachplatz
    Podbielskiallee
    Dahlem-Dorf
    Thielplatz
    Oskar-Helene-Heim
    Onkle Toms Hutte
    Krumme Lanke;

thirteen stations, all with their calls of '*Alleszurückbleiben!*' the whooshing doors, the well-sprung passage from darkness into daylight. The stations were all on a decent human scale, and

Weaver's spirits (generally improved when travelling on a train) rose when he bounded up the steps past the ticket check and out onto Fischerhüttenstrasse, to the Kurgarten, the serving wench with long dark hair that was something from the Brüder Grimm, dispensing sweet smiles and Moselle in long-stemmed green goblets in equal measure. Weaver went there to hear the rising pitch of the war widows at *Kaffee und Kuchen* time, the accelerating clatter of loose dentures. It was a lift of the spirits not available at Connolly Station (once Amiens Street) nor at Daly Station (formerly Bray), nor at Ealing Broadway for that matter.

You never knew what pleasures might be found on the green U-Bahn line connecting Uhlandstrasse to the Görlitzer Bahnhof. Four beautiful Chinese girls with faces white as flour, hair black as pitch, all chittering and fluttering, with paper umbrellas, who seemed to walk on little stilts, for Weaver was close behind them as they tottered onto the Kurfürstendamm pavement, into falling rain. Weaver sometimes took trips out to the Kottbusser Tor and back again to Uhlandstrasse, or getting off at Kurfürstendamm and diving into Margot Schoeller's bookshop. The stations on this line were equally Bennish, betokening his drunken floods. As:

Wittenbergplatz
Nollendorfplatz
Kurfürstenstrasse
Möckernbrücke
Hallesches Tor
Prinzentenstrasse
Kottbusser Tor
Görlitzer Bahnhof
Schlesisches Tor.

The overland S-Bahn rolled drunkenly out of Wannsee, stopping at Nikolassee to take Weaver and Weissenborn, already the worse for wear after the beer stop, and whirled them to Grunewald, to Westkreuz, to tarty Charlottenburg, to Savigny-platz and the terminus in the Zoologischer Garten.

Once, travelling alone, smoking a cigar with his feet up on the opposite wooden seat, Weaver had been reproached by a GDR functionary, delighted to have caught one of the capitalist swine red-handed, smoking in a non-smoker with his feet up, doubly *verboten*. He pointed, he shook his head, he threw a sulphurous look; whereupon Weaver removed the stub of his Danemann, dropping it at the furious functionary's boot, on the platform, inquiring in a high affronted tone: '*Verboten?*'

Once, travelling by bus to the Egyptian Museum with Nancy, they had found themselves in a bus-load of old semi-demented freaks, who stared fearfully about, like creatures on their way to certain slaughter. The light inside the bus was that of an eerie summer's night. And Weaver remembered that this was the city pulverized by bombing. Berlin was the '*Bullenwinkel*' to the RAF and received the hardest hammering, ahead of Essen, Cologne, Duisburg and Hamburg. The service ceiling of Lancaster and Halifax bombers was 20,000 feet and from there four hundred of them (the next night it would be double that) released bombs the size of pillar boxes, packed with high explosive. No part of Berlin was to be spared. *Hereinbrechendes Feuerwerk, knatternd und zischend!*

> Wenn die Brücken, wenn die Bogen
> von der Steppe aufgesogen
> und die Burg im Sand verrint . . .

wrote crafty old Benn, puffing on his cigar.

One clear day, standing on Nikolassee Station waiting for a train to take him to Grunewald Station and Lore waiting in her Karman Ghia, Weaver had been nonplussed to see Lore, or a figure very similar, running below, and Weaver waited, Steinhäger in hand, for her to appear and wave from the end of the platform; but no, she suddenly appeared on the opposite platform and stepped into a train about to leave for Wannsee and was carried away – a spectral Lore, for the real one was awaiting him calmly in Grunewald.

One Saturday the three Weavers watched a military march-past on the Sieges Allee. Or rather it was the motorized equivalent of a cavalry trot-past. Tanks came thundering by followed by motorized units moving in creepy silence, watched by the Berliners in stony silence, feeling themselves to be overmarched. The names of Berlin suburbs were painted in white on the long steeply tilted gun barrels of the tanks, Schmargendorf and Wilmersdorf following after Lichterfelde and Zehlendorf, and then along came Nikolassee ('Oh look, that's us!'), and the guns mighty enough to lob shells over the Urals and into Red Square.

'Are they Russians or Americans?' Nico asked, pulling Weaver's hand.

'You may well ask,' Weaver said, looking down at him, and then to Nancy: 'Out of the mouths of babes and sucklings.'

'I'm not a suckling,' Nico said, removing his hand from Weaver's.

'Of course you're not, my pet,' Nancy said, taking his hand.

'Asiatic hordes,' Weaver said. 'Take a look at those slitty Mongol eyes.'

The high yaller tank crewmen were putty-coloured, American and Soviets identical, as in the length of their gunbarrels, even to the stars painted on the turrets, one red, one white; they went grinding by, staring far off into the future. The British tank crews held themselves ramrod stiff; and these were followed by French units in kepis, saluting from bicycles, as if the whole thing was a joke.

Puffing out clouds of high-quality cigar smoke, and breathing through his nose, Benn wrote:

> ... *wenn die Häuser leer geworden,*
> *wenn die Heere, wenn die Horden*
> *über unsern Gräbern sind –*

Eines lässt sich nicht vertreiben;

dieser Stätte Male bleiben

Löwen noch im Wüstensand,

wenn die Mauern niederbrechen,

werden noch die Trümmer sprechen

*von dem grossen Abendland.**

* 'When the bridges, when the arches have been swallowed by the plains, and the castle turned to sand; when the houses have been emptied, when the armies, when the hordes will be on our graves –

'One thing you cannot make vanish, the wounds of this place will remain. Lions still in the desert sand, when the walls come down, the ruins still will speak of the Great *Abendland* [the West].' 'Berlin', 1948.

15
Legends of the Living-Room

Was this the same accommodating female ('one of those *desperate* Northern women'), as Nancy, the dispossessed and disgruntled spouse, had suggested (and dismissed) in an aside of sour asperity? It was indeed. Nancy would seek out Axel Schröder's ex-directory address and forthwith dispatch a steamy missive dictated in angry German: *Deine Tochter!*

The whole unseemly affair had begun, then, as High Farce? The curtain rose jerkily on some spontaneous 'business', unrehearsed at that, taking place one warmish night in the *Berlinerzimmer* amid stout furnishings of durable dark teak of pre-war solidarity; in a mansion quite detached, Im Dol–Dahlem area, zip code Berlin 30. Good-quality furnishings, heavy hardwood dining table and matching chairs with leather seats, expensive Indian rugs with matching buff drapes, sideboard with two wine glasses, a reading lamp. The glasses hold a third of white Italian wine, mediocre quality but chilled, on this warm September night of that year in Berlin that was to break up the Weaver family, begin to break up the marriage that had lasted thirteen years and produced two male children. (Nico's elder brother Emmett, born in Johannesburg, having died in Dublin, aged three.) Nor do we recall the exact date; I think it was forgetmenot.

In the warmly lit room which appears deserted a middle-aged

couple married now some thirteen years are coupling on the carpet behind the sofa, pulled out at an angle.

SHE (archly frigid): 'Don't be so disgusting!'

HE (busy): Ooopla!'

SHE (warming): 'Pretend I'm a . . .'

Now, quite fittingly, the curtain should lower itself to embarrassed titters from the stalls and raspberries from the invisible gods, but not at all; it remains wrapped up in the flies as NANCY WEAVER crawls into view, hair dishevelled, adjusting her clothes. And was not the long arm of coincidence perhaps already reaching out towards THE OTHER WOMAN who will in due course appear as HANNELORE (LORE) SCHRÖDER, only daughter of Axel and Magda Anneliese Schröder; aged twenty-seven years and fluent in four languages, *still* living at home with her parents, renting one room, employed as private secretary to Heinz Walser the Berlin film producer (*The Search*) and lawyer specializing in film contracts, whose only son was just going mad again, around the time (late October) when Weaver first met Lore Schröder?

Now the maroon curtain is rising again to renewed tittering and raspberries. *Mise-en-scène*: *Berlinerzimmer* as before. Warm lighting. Middle-aged ruffled couple surprised at game of two-backed beast behind accommodatingly large sofa. Bum arched to receive the full charge, NANCY groans as if in the very toils of love.

SHE (weakly dreamily): 'Pretend I'm somebody else.'

HE (fiercely rutting): '*Glugglug de vendange!*'

Oh was poor Nancy Weaver fully aware of the dire consequences of such frothy apophthegms, so fraught with dangerous implications not only to her husband (just a shaky hand reaching out for wine glass a third depleted) dressed only in all-wool socks and Peek & Cloppenberg cotton shirt; to herself too; and not least to the little innocent lambkin sound asleep in the bedroom above?

This, after all, was the land of gnomes and rapacious witches, the trolls and ill-disposed evil stepmothers known to the Brüder Grimm; as faintly and unmelodiously is wafted from just across the way '*Yussalick the vons vee* . . .' For jackass Ulli Udet has joined Horst Busch in a rousing chorus, both waving brimming steins level with their flushed faces.

And not too long a time would elapse before THE WHORE (*Hure*) or OTHER WOMAN would appear in the well-heated *Sonnenraum*, up to no good, in a state of nature (warmly accommodatingly nude). The twin sets of interleading double doors dividing dining-room from living-room were fixed on rollers and heavy drapes hung from ceiling to floor, closed now for reasons of privacy and modesty. In the evenings there, in little cul de sacs, noted Randy Nab, the very hole seems to dissolve.

SHE (panting): 'Pretend I'm a . . . '

HE (eager): 'Oak before ash, in for a splash. Would it suck off a nig?'

SHE (gushing): 'Hare!'

HE (coming): 'Whore?'

'*Ich schreibe Ihnen,*' her friend Irma dictated, '*weil Ihre Tochter, die seine Hure ist* . . .'

Ach! Der Lappen, mit dem ich mir den Hintern abwischte.

I used the face-towel thoughtfully provided, the Schröder guest said. Papa Schröder fairly exploded into guffaws. '*Das Tuch, mit dem ich mir den Hintern abwische!*' Har, har, har!

Was this how it all began? Husbandly arms embracing wifely waist and the indiscreet summons winging its way to the ravening demons who were all ears in the woods around; as down the wire the message sped to the brown-skinned charmer just back from the Corsican nudist camp, now attempting to rid herself of the attentions of Sweaty Petersen (who was proving most persistent), one of at least four persistent admirers, Lore (for it was she) not half an hour away by swift Karman Ghia down the autobahn.

The *femme fatale* had appeared from out of nowhere, slipping off the prow of a yacht into the Havel, smiling her lopsided smirk, slipping out of her clothes like an eel and gliding between the blue sheets held invitingly open by a hand belonging to him who shall be nameless, occupying the divan that opened out into a daybed in the *Sonnenzimmer*, with the soundless snow falling out of the dark and the fireworks exploding.

'He was red in the face for two days with pure love,' Nancy said. 'He wouldn't leave it out of his hands. Once into his grasp its chances of survival were slim. He loved it so much he put out one of its eyes, blinded it.'

Her hand covered her mouth, beginning to smile; behind the open fan of fingers her humorous brown eyes positively twinkled with mischief.

'It was in the very articles of death as soon as Nico got a firm hold. Finally it was like a bit of rag. The end of that poor thing was awful; physically the slow-worm was unable to take it. Poor lamb, he couldn't leave it out of his hands. There's real love for you.'

'He's still wetting his bed. When will that stop?'

'Oh in time,' said Nancy airily (she rather liked to overstate things, grind down possibilities). 'All in due time you know.'

'And in the meantime?'

'Patience.'

She lay back in the deep armchair where a famous English screenwriter had reclined in expensive black boots and becoming black turtleneck sweater, not a week before, sipping chilled Schultheiss beer in lieu of the Scotch requested, in the company of the moneyman who was 'Jumping Jack' to his intimates – a fire-eating Machiavellian fellow astute and cunning in matters commercial, squatting in a cloud of expensive cigar smoke, saying little but missing nothing. They had flown in from London that morning to discuss the possibilities of adapting one of Weaver's slim *Ur*-novels; to try and put on some badly needed flesh and life, firm up its weak bones. Weaver was being closely observed by four calculating Jewish eyes and had begun to feel that it would not be shot in his lifetime, not bleeding likely, not in *their* lifetime.

Now on *Litfasssäule*s all over Berlin the second half of the DILDO Winter Readings programme at the Akademie der Künste had replaced the autumn readings. Two Austrians had read before Christmas, with Jürgen Becker of the GDR. Wolfgang Bauer, Peter Handke and Jürgen Becker were over-postered with the new names:

> Günter Blocker of the GDR,
> Bogdana Kuguar of Poland,
> Dallan Weaver of TCD and Ireland

Weaver had already been interviewed by a lady from the *Frankfurter Allgemeine Zeitung*. Walter ('Shorty') Hasenclever would be Moderator. On the morning that the Sybil Worshing interview appeared in the *FAZ*, with profile of author taken on 'chocolate side', the neighbourly Weissenborns sent across their copy with 'Congratulations!' on the front, for the edification of the Weavers, still abed. A party would be thrown in the Born apartment following the reading, scheduled for early March, close to Weaver's birthday.

16
Dreaming Women

1 *Nancy's dream*

I had a dream the other night (said Nancy). I am leaning against a boulder. It's by the sea. Small waves are coming in and furniture being washed ashore, if you please. And not just any kind of junk either but really elegant period stuff. A child is holding my hand, looking up into my face, and it's not Nico.

A high-backed chair floats in. Then another after it, both encrusted with barnacles. A feeling of wellbeing pervades all. Don't ask me why.

2 *Loretraum*

Lore was also dreaming. Hers was of climbing a hill with Weaver to the sounds of stones rattling, splashings from above and gurglings from below, coming down off a rain-sodden mountain into a flooded valley.

'We come upon a spring that gushes out,' said Lore, 'and an elephant, dripping wet, is washing itself there. As we approach it turns itself into an ape. Imagine that! What does it mean, I ask you. It means the beginning of the world, you tell me, quite soberly. In this symbolic form you say. I say, *Doch, doch*!'

'No dreams are very logical,' Weaver said, 'and yours are always zoological, my dear Schmutzig. Are there sounds in dreams?'

'In mine yes, always sounds,' Lore said.

They were dining on house red wine and Four Seasons pizzas at Il Gattopardo in the company of four Germans, two couples as suntanned as they were disgusting, gluttonish after a day's sailing on Wannsee. Atika couples to the life.

17

Traum

One week ago I had a strange but somehow great dream, said Lore. I was lying somewhere on a riverbank. And then this mysterious light between day and night with hardly any colours. Anyway . . . a calm and peaceful atmosphere. The river was not very large and surrounded by wonderfully bizarre trees.

Suddenly I noticed a little island swimming down the river, coming towards me, and on it seven or eight huge grey elephants all very quiet and looking at me.

I became afraid, but thought that it would be best to keep very quiet and not to move at all, and to make myself very small. Then the mysterious island stopped and the huge elephants moved towards me and went very slowly one after the other over me without touching me. I saw the enormous heavy bodies above me.

And in this stately way that these fantastic creatures had arrived and passed me, they disappeared again. When I woke up I felt a great admiration for the very strong Nature and its marvellous and peaceful and so powerful creatures.

18
Sortilège (The Talking Tea-Leaves)

One evening when Weaver was out about his business and Nico had finished his homework and supper and Nancy was finishing a cup of tea, Nico asked her to read the tea-leaves as Weaver's mother used to do, for their edification and amusement.

'Oh I can't do that,' Nancy said.

Weaver's acid-tongued mother, a disappointed woman, had learnt it from her mother, who had picked it up from *her* mother, who had it from *her* mother in Carrick on Shannon; seas of teas and streams of homespun received rural wisdom dating back to the latter part of the seventeenth century, with an old biddy smoking a dudeen and slobbering on the banks of Lough Bofin or Gowna, Sheelin or wherever. The Talking Tea-Leaves of Granard.

'I can't do it.'

'Why can't you? *Anybody* can do it. *I* could do it.'

'Well you do it then.'

'No, I want you to do it.'

Nico could be very persistent. Nagging.

'Okay, I'll have a go,' Nancy said, taking up the cup. Some tea-leaves stuck to the side, damp hieroglyphics signifying God knows what. She saw Emmett as a toddler crawl towards a huge breaking wave one roasting day on Hermanus beach; asleep on a mat in the shade of a fig tree with huge leaves at home in Kingwilliamstown;

crawling all over the *Warwick Castle* that carried them from East London to damp Tilbury.

He had crawled from East London via Port Elizabeth and Cape Town, St Helena and the lazy Azores to grey Tilbury docks. She peered into the cup and was about to poke the tea-leaves when Nico shouted out: 'You mustn't touch!' She peered in again. She said: 'I see a great big hippo stuffed in a museum. I see pawpaw trees. I see avocados and naartjes! I see an old black woman in a little cement room small and stinky as a dog-kennel. It's old Megs! No, it isn't, it's her mother, old Nookie!'

'Where is it?'

'It's King where I was born.'

'What else do you see?'

Nancy tilted the cup and squinted in again.

'I see fins racing through the sea. Sharks! I hear palm trees thrashing when the great winds blow. I hear baboons coughing in hidden places near a lagoon. I hear . . .'

'You *hear* things? You mustn't cheat you know.'

'Oh yes, I hear these things. I see a big ship about to leave for Cape Town. I see a little boy with his mother at the rails.'

'Is Weaver with them?'

Nancy looked down into her cup as if he might be hiding among the leaves.

'No, he is seeing them off.'

'Are they happy?'

'Yes and no.'

'Yes *or* no, they can't be both. Which are they?'

'Sad.'

'Why are they going to Cape Town if it makes them sad?'

Nancy was stumped.

'How do you know they're going to Cape Town?' she asked.

'Because you said so.'

'Okay. They stand at the rails. They wave.'

'And then?'

'Weaver waves back. They weep.'

'Is he sad? Does he weep?'

'He is *very* sad but he doesn't weep. He feels sad but doesn't wish to show it. That's it. He wants to hide the sadness. He is sad on the sly.'

'Weaver isn't sly.'

'No?'

'No.'

'If you say so, my pet. Well, they are both sad and happy at the same time and don't know why they are going to Cape Town. Does that satisfy you?'

Nico considered this, studying his mother's amused eyes. 'I don't think tea-leaves are very helpful,' he said.

You mustn't cheat with children, Nancy told herself. In the middle of the story he was already asleep. Nancy made herself a strong drink and took it into the sunroom. She thought of what her Dublin friend Patricia had told her of Irish mothers not breastfeeding their babes in the nursing-home and of all the self-deluding yarns of miracle-working cures for gouty legs and chesty coughs, of unbaptized babes insecurely buried in sod fences by the Connemara seashore, refused Christian burial in consecrated ground by ignorant and bigoted priests, then the Atlantic rushing in and washing them away. Now what sort of consoling Christianity was that? And what class of good Christians were they? A bleached-out religion for a cowed congregation, when all was said and done. Do as you are bid and ye shall be saved.

And where was Weaver in all this?

A white-legged superstitious race, she thought. Goat's milk is good for the whooping cough. Goats and donkeys strayed about the Grand Canal paths near Baggot Street bridge and an inquisitive neddy poked its bony elongated head inside the hood of Nico's pram where he slept like an angel. Weaver's mammy, living poorly, brought rice puddings for her little grandson, for his da had been partial to them as a child, still was.

Nancy saw a skinny self-willed sickly child with rickety legs and Weaver's foxy face, the daddy-to-be. She heard the click of the garden gate at Charleston Road and Nico cried out: 'Oh here come Sasha and Bart!' and up the garden path strolled the Murnanes bearing gifts, come from their high flat in Fitzwilliam Square among the nobs.

A devious and most superstitious race, Nancy thought, the Irish, devious and superstitious; with a public transport system that was a bad joke – the buses never left the Donnybrook terminus; nor did unbaptized infants make it up to Heaven.

And Weaver . . . what was he up to?

19

Hereinbrechendes Feuerwerk . . .

If it was the Berliner idea to welcome in the new year by letting off noisy fireworks, it was Lore's idea to withhold her full favours until the time was ripe; and it would be ripe when the new year was welcomed in by bursting fireworks.

'This is a lovely room. Is this where you sleep? I'll come here on New Year's Night and go to bed with you here.'

The divan in the *Sonnenraum* could be made into a three-quarter-size bed at night. Nancy was away in Wuppertal, looking for the roots of the Els or Ehls.

'Professor Weaver never kissed a girl before,' she taunted, divinely flushed.

Lore wished to make a present of herself – a present of Love – Lore Schröder gift-wrapped on New Year's Night, for the thoroughly aroused Weaver to unwrap and enjoy, when the time *was* ripe.

But if it was Weaver's bright idea to solace his existence in that drenched and brimming Prussian pussy avid to receive him (Lore nougat brown and glossy with good health, as nude in the blue sheets as she had been in the sea at Bastia), it was Nico's idea to call down from the landing: 'Do you see the fireworks?', for Weaver, cursing like a trooper, to dress himself in shirt and trousers and hurry to meet Nico already come trailing halfway down the stairs. They watched the fireworks from the master bedroom. Below, all was quiet. But the spell had been broken. The time was ripe but *Schnicksal* had determined otherwise. Weaver crept back into bed to Lore who received him into her arms and whispered: 'The fireworks were lovely. Your room is lovely. Another night, another time, dearest.'

Lett nott the sonne gou doune upon youre wrathe.

Outside it was all aglitter in the seasonal snow with the last fireworks expiring over Beskidenstrasse. Lore would have to leave early in the darkness. *Hereinbrechendes Feuerwerk, knatternd und zischend!*

'Did Elijah not ascend into Heaven in his bodily form?' groaned Weaver.

II

Fugacity of Pleasure,
Fragility of Beauty

*Das Holz muss frisch aus dem Sägewerk kommen, denn es
duftet wunderbar nach Wald.* *

Albert Speer, Spandauer Tagebuch

---

* 'The lumber must be fresh from the sawmill, for it smells wonderfully of forest.'
Spandau: The Secret Diaries

20
An Apartment in the Sky

A configuration of melting snow made patterns on the exposed side of the building where the wind had driven it. Inside the furnaces would be burning. Theirs was the end flat to the left on the top floor, the sixth, Lore said, pointing. Weaver knew where it was of course, from seeing her home.

The last touch of warm lips, the final embrace, and Lore *Schlüsselkind* now become statuesque brunette, her remarkable dark eyes fixed upon him, left the wayward Prof with snow on his furry cap. Dipping one gloved hand into her handbag she *at wance* found the Yale key, no fumbling about in the freezing night air, inserted it and unlocked the heavy street door with a practised turn of the wrist, blew a last kiss and vanished.

What happened thereafter remained a mystery. Whether she lived in moderate comfort or in outright luxury, this Weaver did not know, nor how she was received by the Schröders who would be staying in for the evening. Would a meal be prepared? No, Lore did her own cooking; she was self-sufficient, both outside and inside dependency. Papa Schröder sometimes paid for petrol or car-repair bill; the Karman Ghia had been bought second-hand.

One day, when appropriate, she would show him the flat and her room, she had promised. The entrance had no protective porch; it was a cold place to embrace in. Weaver heard that her father, stern Axel, had been the head of a chemical works and was now living in retirement. When the war was ending their troubles began, when the advance patrols of the Red Army began flitting through the woods, and their horse was shot standing between the shafts of a cart that would take them out of Berlin and into hiding. A second horse was harnessed; their housekeeper hid a valuable sapphire in a bag of flour. Disguised as villagers the Schröder family fled from Berlin. The Red Army was coming with its huge tanks; the bombing was terrible, the earth trembled. The family hid in a village while the Red Army raped and pillaged its way through Berlin. Lore was aged two, *zwei*.

She was a child in a city selected for destruction. In a way that no other city could be, it belonged to the dead. The ring was sold and they lived frugally on the proceeds until it was thought to be safe to return to Berlin. Axel Schröder went alone and found the flat as they had left it. He stood on the steps of Berlin Zoo Station and could see the end-of-the-world conflagration on Lüneburg Heath reflected in the clouds. Berlin was a ruin. Barter had become cut-throat; in black market dealings you took your life in your hands. An uncle was lost returning from conducting some business deal in Hanover, perhaps pushed from a train.

Lore was sent to school, then to dancing classes in Berna-dottestrasse not far from Podbielski U-Bahn station, where she would run to meet Professor Weaver, years later.

Axel Schröder went into retirement, though he was still in contact with the chemical works as consultant and adviser; he had his office in the apartment with filing cabinet and records. The pills that Lore took thrice a day came from the chemical works at discount.

Axel Schröder was willing himself to be old before his time; only then would he be safe, this stern-faced Prussian whom Weaver knew only from the family photographs and reports from his daughter. There was also a son in Hamburg. Axel said that he would 'prefer not to meet' Professor Weaver, being 'too old to start learning a new language'. There were no invitations to dinner.

One freezing winter day during a snowstorm Weaver found himself on the wrong U-Bahn line and being carried further and further away from the place of assignation. On a station platform in already dim light he phoned Lore's home number, a *verboten* move. Snow swirled over the station as a bass voice said 'Lore at Krumme Lanke' in a manly confidential voice into the Professor's ear. 'She wait there for you.' The receiver was then replaced.

He had an ungovernable temper. Once he had beaten her; she had stood up to him, not flinching, her Prussian will become 'hard as steel'. With eyes flashing Lore admitted: 'Inside I was on fire!' Mutti Schröder had been most properly alarmed: 'Stop it, Axel, you will kill her!' Professor Weaver tried to imagine the paterfamilias relaxed at home in carpet-slippers and smoking-jacket, puffing at a thumping big cigar, breaking wind, booming out fatuities to his admiring womenfolk, cracking Prussian jokes. He could not.

Then one evening the Schröders were dining out at Kempinski's, after *Ariadne auf Naxos* at the Deutsche Oper and would be returning late. Lore phoned Beskidenstrasse at an hour she knew Nancy and her son would be away. 'You may come now if you like. I am all alone here.'

An hour and a half later the Professor arrived dressed as for the Arctic, pressed the bell at street level and heard a disembodied female voice ask *Wer ist dort, bitte*.

The Professor cleared his throat.

'Eisenhower,' he hazarded into the spy-hole.

'You are alone, my General?' an amused voice breathed back.

'Sure thing honey, I'm all alone down here, freezing my ass off.'

'Then you may come up,' the breathy voice laughed down at him. 'Come up.'

The door-lock clicked and he entered. He ascended a nondescript shadowy stairway, climbing up by cooking smells and hum of dog, coming at last to a heavy door on the sixth floor, pressed the bell, the door opened at once and there stood Lore welcoming him in with her lopsided smile. She took his tweed overcoat (the same which had saved the sodomites from drowning in the Spree), set it on a wooden hanger which she set on the hat-stand heavy as a gallows on which hung expensive winter-wear in the way of overcoats and hats; then waited to be embraced.

'But you're cold as *ice*!'

Then taking him by the hand she led him along the corridor with rich wall-to-wall carpeting, murmuring at open bedroom doors: 'Papaschrödersroom!' then 'Mamaschrödersroom!' threw open a third door and announced triumphantly: '*My* room!'

It was a bridal chamber all in white. A good bottle of French wine was uncorked and two glasses ready on a bedside table. A mandolin and batik cloths (colour of Mediterranean fruit and tropical flowers, the colours of convalescence after fever in Weaver's distant childhood; tones of bear-brown and lemon yellow) were now brought out for him to admire. Then the wine was poured out. The winter heating was full on, and Lore very lightly dressed. Outside it was bitterly cold, a perishing Baltic wind setting its teeth into Berlin. Her bed was narrow. The wine was her own; Papa Schröder kept a stock, but if she took a bottle she would replace it. This one an excellent *appellation*.

'And now, my General,' she said playfully, 'being a good American soldier, I suppose you'd wish to rape me?'

Quick curtain here to indicate the Passage of Time.

Who wrote that the toilets of the rich flush silently? The Schröders' had a silent flusher in sumptuous rosewood. The naked General padded from room to room; all small and interleading, the windows sealed behind drawn drapes, on tables covered with knick-knacks the cut flowers in vases gave out little or no scent. The airless rooms had an unlived-in atmosphere, lifeless with all the air pumped out. The family photographs angled on ornate frames might have been of dead people (Lincoln's home with spurious household effects) in a funeral parlour, and Lore as a little girl a white and ghostly figure, the dead child in *Wuthering Heights*.

This high shrouded place was the last refuge of the Schröders. It would last their time. It seemed to the Professor (the General having crept away without a word) that they begged and longed for it to end; yet neither of them was of a great age – both in their early seventies. But it was their wish to remain hidden and anonymous.

In the neatly kept blue-and-white tiled kitchen the cooking pots and pans were tidied away and all was spick and span as if newly painted; no coarse cooking smells diminished its austere antiseptic style. Prowling about stark naked the intruder now turned the key in the door facing west, pushed it open and stood amazed.

A turbulence of heavenly buttermilk was churning and moiling about in the western sky, flooding the walkway that gave access to other kitchen doors overlooking the void (some thrown open, and from these had emerged casually dressed sixth-floor residents now luridly lit and calmly admiring the stupendous cloudscapes worthy of the brush of Kaspar David Friedrich) and the western wall lit with an unearthly incandescent glow.

The silver tops of tall lindens were buffeted by a late breeze two floors below, and further down at ground level a man well muffled up against the cold was crossing the cobbled compound in the deepening twilight. All, all attested to an invincible Germanic *Ordnung* of which the Schröder apartment in the sky (with the lovely Lore intact as a regular rent-paying tenant) was but one factor in the disposition of an obstinately German whole. Now feeling chilled he closed and relocked the white door, padded through the kitchen and on to the thick wall-to-wall carpeting of the hallway, and through the narrow dining area, past the small television room and onto the narrow balcony that projected over the street; here was an arboretum of potted plants and creepers clamouring for yet more *Lebensraum*: Mama Schröder's private grotto in the sky. Lorelove now entering naked as Eve found her Adam testing one of her father's superior cigars lifted from the cuspidor.

21

Fornication in the Ditch Called Sodom

It was an old story. They had nowhere to go, nowhere to stay. Until invited to a party at Bernadottestrasse by the Blacks, the pale American sculptor and his severe battle-axe wife with the forbidding profile of a Shawnee squaw. Weaver had thought to overstay his invitation and then plead insobriety, beg a night's lodging, being unfit to drive home. Weaver had thought to ask whether they could spend the night together there.

Professor Black seemed an amiable enough type. When they arrived the party was already in full swing, the young children already abed, or rather hanging on the banisters, looking down. There were some pot-smokers among the guests, making much of a to-do with their rolled 'joints', squatting in a circle like true savages, as was their wont, or cluttering up the stairs, chattering like monkeys in trees, except for the deep silent ones staring off.

Weaver asked if he might smoke. Why certainly. And the lovely lady? Why not?

'Every little bit helps,' Weaver said, 'draw it well into your lungs.'

Lore (the best-dressed woman in the room) did as she was told, drew it in, went cross-eyed and abruptly sat down as though her legs had given way beneath her.

'Good shit,' said a neophyte, nodding knowingly.

Weaver inhaled deeply again and this time the frontal lobes slowly collapsed and thought became soft and jumbled, as a sudden thick sea-mist might roll in over Dalkey Island, and what had stood there a moment before become obliterated. The music was of course deafening, and ineffably sad, a German version of 'Yesterday'.

Weaver had already encountered the mistress of the house passing from the kitchen into the living-room and had decided there and then that no favours were forthcoming from that quarter and he would not give it a try.

Then they were outside again, Lore and Weaver and the sculptor of disposable shapes who had just laid his right hand on the curved bodywork of the wasp-yellow car as though absent-mindedly on the thigh of its owner, while looking dreamily away with a faraway look in his eye.

'I would as lief . . .' he began, but left the rest hang in the air.

'Say no more,' said Weaver. 'Say no more. Lovely party but now time to depart. We bid you goodnight. *¡Muchas gracias!*

The host had his back to them, one limp hand raised in formal adieu, while retreating to his open door. 'Night friends. Call again.'

He went in and a great darkness fell about them. There was a silence. They were not squeezing together. The vague form of a thought was passing through Weaver's head to the effect that German rudeness (as personified within by the pot-smokers) was peculiar to itself; German rudeness excluded all others. Others did not exist, unless they were famous; an authority on things hallucinatory like O'Leary in the grave.

Lore was elaborately pulling on her gloves and as elaborately taking them off again.

'Where now?'

Silence. Silence *thickening*.

'Where now?'

'Nowhere now.'

'Nowhere,' Lore repeated, staring out of the windscreen.

Longish silence. A sigh.

'Why didn't you ask?'

'I couldn't.'

Silence.

'Why not?'

Longer silence.

'I ask: Why not?'

'I could have asked him but I couldn't ask her . . .' (pause) '. . . we couldn't spend the night there with her and the kids . . .' (conclusive pause) '. . . she wouldn't have had it.'

'She wouldn't have *had* it . . .'

'No.'

'What then?'

'Oh I don't know. Will you stop doing that?' Weaver laid his hand on her bare hand, ungloved again. 'Let's get out of here first anyway.'

'What about . . . out *there*!' Lore pointed her gloved right hand dramatically into the pitch-black night, into the very black crotch of the square they were parked in, where a night bird made a cry. She switched on the ignition and small lights glowed on the dashboard and then she drove slowly about one side of the black square and switched off the engine and killed the lights and opened and closed the driver's door and followed the now very silent and thoughtful (no doubt) Professor into a shallow ditch under some scraggy bushes near a thick-boled but also leafless tree of indeterminate breed and quickly lowered her black wool slacks and flimsies together in both hands (now ungloved) as if in the haste and privacy of her own room, following a need, or the Professor's room if it went to that (for they had not yet booked into a hotel), in the absence of his wife, before subsiding face-down on the slope of the sandy bank. Hot fat on the cooker, plumpest rump-roast a-sizzle on the back burner (funny way to cook but no accounting for tastes). *Oh Bastia!* What have we here? Is it to be sodomy in the open?

Suffice to say that what stood out between the Professor's pale shanks and quite visible in the cold night air was no human hard-on (if the term be allowed) but a hot potent goad become red-hot poker, which he intended to bury deep forthwith in the deep fat offered as licence to his most urgent lustyhood, to put it mildly, there being no time for finesse.

'Oh it's good, it's good,' groaned Lore into the leaves, 'deeper, deeper,' pulling at the grass along the verge with her bare hands.

'Dig it into me! Master me! Be brutal,' she whispered shameless into the cold earth, the dead leaves. And then, low, urgent: *'Es ist gut! . . . das ist gut, sehr gut! Tief, tiefer, am tiefsten! Liebster Schmutzy, für deine Tochter . . . diese Hure!'*

Which Weaver, intensely preoccupied, heard as the sighing of absent leaves above his head, whispering *'Esistgut! Dasistgutsehrgut! Tieferamtiefsten! Liebsterschmutzy!'* Babbling and rubbing themselves together and whispering sweet nothings, straining and groaning.

Above them the headlights of a car passing went scissoring through the grass, lit up the bare branches above like a Christmas tree and then veered away into the darkness again. They were stuck together down in the shallow loamy trench as close as rabbit and stoat. Beside himself, Weaver fastened his teeth into the nape of her neck, tasted her hot flesh, bit hair, knew her excitement, as he came like a haemorrhage, bull on beef, Jupiter on Juno, Paolo and Francesca tossed around in their whirling cloud.

With her dark loosened hair streaming out behind them and still entwined they were flying out over Berlin.

Then, their small clothes adjusted and his loving arm about her they sat on the rim of the ditch and smoked cigarettes like soldiers after combat, trying to recover some composure.

'I hurt you.'

'If you did I wanted it.'

'I wanted to roar like a bull,' Weaver admitted, heart still pounding, still ringed and anointed.

'*Doch, doch*, be quiet now.'

Silence; then that bird again.

'Maybe some vodka in that place in Mexikoplatz. What do you say? It wouldn't do us any harm,' Weaver answered his own question. 'The Hotel Bubitz.'

So they drove past Krumme Lanke Station and down Mexikoplatz way where they stepped into the overheated Yugolsav hotel and sat at a table and ordered slivovitz in firkins and Lore retired to the Ladies to put herself to rights; from whence she presently emerged looking more lovely than before and sat opposite him who was still trembling (as from fun in a forest with a felling-axe) as fiery drinks with rims of scorching ice were set before them in little chalices.

When snow lay thick on the platz the grey bulbous dome of the station recalled Russia to Weaver, who had never been there in the body.

22
Chess

Nancy's face had begun to look peculiar and squeezed-up in the mirrors (the house was full of them) and the house itself had begun to feel wobbly. He had stopped working; now all his waking hours were given to the Whore. The little silver amulet (his unlucky fish) that had lain on his desk like something shameful (semen stains) was now thrown into the garden and lost somewhere between the zinneas and the azaleas. By mistake he had once worn it in bed and she had woken to find it before her eyes and waking up had hit the ceiling. 'What's *that*? Christ! Take it *off*!' And that had perhaps been a mistake.

He had searched for it among his scattered papers on the desk, in his untidy files, in the waste-paper basket, on hands on knees on the floor; but she had already thrown it away, as far as she could pitch it, as if getting rid of a rat. It flew in an arc and vanished amid the azaleas and the zinneas. He couldn't ask about it, he hadn't the nerve; he missed it. He suspected that she had appropriated it, but said nothing. She was keeping it, she had her own reasons. The conjugal act as such was finished; the conjugal bed with one pillow and a new bedspread had one occupant now. Weaver had moved to the divan in the sunroom below.

Above his head at night the Harpy flushed the toilet again and again, to wake and upset him, to annoy. When he stayed away late into the night she was in torment; when he stayed away all night she was in absolute torment, on the very prongs. But again when he stayed at home, innocent as pie, nice as ninepence, she felt irritated, somehow he was still getting the better of her, laughing secretly, amused by her torments.

Was this the same husband whom she had seen as kind and trustworthy? No paragon of virtue to be sure, but now he was the living embodiment of duplicity, waywardness, lies. He was a congenital liar; a crafty manipulator, sneaky, shiftless, bone idle. He had no sense of . . . what was the word? Probity. He was one shifty schemer, economical with the truth; it was something he said when it suited him.

The face in the bed had grown middle-aged, then old; she seemed to be wearing a hair-net, was chap-fallen, the eyes rheumy, unfocused. The barely recognized features were crunched up, the mouth set and prim, old-maidish and virginal (Nancy Els!); thin wormyveined claws held up a book on her jutted lap as defence (it was *Middlemarch*), as Weaver peered through the glass, intimidated now and reluctant to start another row; this was a real frail old biddy in the bed.

A silence had enveloped the house. The very birds in the garden and in the woods around seemed to sing in open derision, mocking her. The grandfather clock in the living-room had stopped ticking and its pendulum hung down as a tongue from the cold face, silent evermore, of a hanged man. The bulb had blown in the welcome light above the porch and Weaver had not seen fit to replace it; silence and darkness closed around a broken marriage.

Expelled from her bed and warm favours now Weaver (after assignations ending late, in a roaring students' bar, in the Yugoslav hotel on Mexikoplatz, in the bar on Olivaer Platz that was to become Joe Schindler's, at Il Gattopardo, or even closer in the Eichhörnchen beyond the Jochen-Klepper-Weg, regularly in the Rusticano, or the Greek place or in the cheap Balkan eatery) took to walking off whatever remained of the night, by perambulating around the Schlachtensee and Krumme Lanke; knowing full well that no. 51 Beskidenstrasse was closed up like a high-security prison and every door and window double-bolted.

Idle to climb onto the balcony from a table and chair on top of it, from the patio below, and slither eel-like through a top window; this unorthodox mode of entry had been instantly blocked. Idle to expect one door to be left unlocked; her early morning salutation was delivered with chilly sang-froid that would have done credit to an executioner on the morning of execution; a tone calculated to set the condemned one's teeth on edge. 'Had a nice time?'

She had his measure.

Locked out in the dog's house the unsober Weaver sat miserable in a dew-damp deckchair on the patio and watched the sun rise behind the strange yellow tree that the Queen of the Netherlands fed with milk. For over two hours he had waited, with Time portioned out like a kind of judgement, for Nancy to rise and perform her ablutions and come downstairs with Nico and stroll through the kitchen in her peony dressing-gown and slippers, fling open the back door, having casually unlocked it, and start back in mock surprise at the spectacle of an unsober man in a deckchair, brooding.

'Oh look! We have an early morning visitor, Nico. How nice! Just look whom we have here. What a most *delightful* surprise! Have you come back to us? No more rolling about in the hay?'

Always the uncomprehending son was thrust into the firing line between husband and wife, mother and father. A sound feminine intuition had told his outraged mamma, the well-and-truly cuckolded wife, how best to twist the barbs and inflict most hurt. A certain remorse went with the wrong-doing. She knew her husband.

The throwing-down of the red duvet (their proper matrimonial covering) from the upper landing had been magnificent, a symbolic relinquishing of all conjugal rights. She looked positively regal, a Queen Boadicea in her chariot, disdainful – women after all were made for such moments.

No barrage of pine cones hurled against the bedroom windows on two sides of the house, accurate enfilading fire raking the bedroom where Nancy only pretended to sleep, or sat up with a book (at 5 a.m.!), could shift her one iota from her strict resolve. Nor did abject or angry phone calls have any effect, for after the first attempt ('Would you please let me in?') the receiver was lifted off the hook, the outraged squawk sucked back into the void, into the buzzing ether which gave back a derisive echo – 'Thou fool!' Nothing moved her; she was quietly determined to give him a hard time, the hardest possible.

The face now squeezed up with its petty hatred, its purpose and feminine scheming, its intent to hurt, appeared again at the front window above the porch, as Weaver hurried away after a quick lunch of cheese omelette thrown together by his own eager hand, for he had an assignation at Krumme Lanke Station in twenty minutes. The small hurt face of his son appeared below the mother's angry face, the mouth open to scream abuse. Nico was held between her knees and was forced to watch, had to hear it all, as the shit flew.

'Watch the Sneak run to his Whore! Wave to him, Nico! That's your own dear dadda running off! Wave, Nico, wave!'

Rage had set off a bonfire in her; she had a great talent for such abuse and deployed it to shattering effect. Weaver ran like a hare.

In the change-over of loyalties to Lore's flesh that had now become *his* food and nutriment, to Lore's life past and present and to everything that wasn't Nancy Weaver, was Weaver split in twain. For there was Nico sucking his thumb, wetting his bed, regressing to infancy, gone deathly pale, all eyes. He was unhappy at home, where the flak and shit flew, and was not doing famously at the JFK school. He wept, told his American lady teacher: 'I don't know what you want me to do.' He needed help at home;

his classwork was poor, homework non-existent. The young teacher said he needed a lot of help.

He sat on his wretched father's lap and Weaver smelt his son's troubled nature, hair stuck to his skull with sweat, his breath bad.

'Well,' Nancy asked with a face like thunder, 'what do we do? You tell me. You who are supposed to be his father. What can we do to help him? Must we divide him between us . . . cut him into two? You tell me.'

¡Dolor!

'He doesn't know where he is in school,' Weaver said, 'and that's for sure. He's caught between three languages and is most confused.'

'I know.'

'And is unhappy.'

'I know that too.'

Spanish he had picked up in his childhood, English he had learnt at home, and now came German, inflected and guttural, except when spoken by well-brought-up Berliners.

¡Oh dolor!

Again at another time and place his son had confessed: 'Her anger weakens me.' He meant his mother, not his teacher (who was never angry with him). 'I know, my pet,' Weaver said, feelingly wobbly himself, shocked by this admission as though it were somehow his own fault, laying his hand on his son's hot and troubled head.

'But one day all this will blow over and we'll all be bounding about like jack rabbits, happy as the day is long.' Having uttered these crass words of comfort he felt a total ass.

¡Oh dolorissima!

23

Schnicksal (or Love Humbled)

Wounds, many . . .

Why not spend weekends with her? Why don't you go and live with the bitch and leave us in peace? Why not go the whole hog and marry her? Why don't you just *stay away*?

As a female prisoner on the rack, 'freshly caught' as Weiland put it well tortured over a period of weeks stretching into months, might end by embracing and even kissing the very implements of torture, the rack and stocks, the water-funnel agony, begging the executioner to dispatch her, put her out of misery; so had poor Nancy been airing some such woefully plaintive exordiums known to all women down the ages.

Those who believe too intensely in their own destiny – their *Schicksal* – tend to come a cropper in the heel of the hunt, when malevolent Fate or Providence deals them a resounding backhander across the kisser. Deals out something both dirty and absurd – the *Schnicksal*.

The same, possibly, holds true of races, particularly the Germans, landed with *der Lump*, Herr Dirty Destiny. But Nancy's *Schnicksal* arrived one humid afternoon in the pleasing shape of none other than Willie ('Winky') Prendergast, scion of an illustrious house, sometime sculptor, womanizer and bon vivant, rip-roaring boy, and wild seed of the near-senile old patriot Pat ('Potty') Prendergast. Blown in as a gust of rough wind of the Calary Bog, by God.

Espoused some fourteen years now, Nancy Weaver was surely challenging her *Schicksal* by demanding so righteously, so imprudently and so often, 'Why can't we be more like the nice Prendergasts?' More like, forsooth! 'Winky never washes up.'

This was magnificent; a sure proof of his uxorious fidelity and goodness of heart was his known ability never to be seen standing upright at the kitchen sink! '*Shiksal* become *Schnicksal*.'

'You mean,' said Weaver, 'that Winky never washes *himself* up?' A plunge in the freezing Forty-Foot maybe, but no ablutions in a bath. He rarely washed, for the pores closed in due course; and in his case it seemed so, for he never washed yet gave no offence with his bodily odours.

'At least he never runs out on his wife,' Nancy said lamely.

'What do you mean? Are we talking of the same man? Prendergast never stops running out on his wife. Ask Nelly.'

Having begot half a dozen bastards in the Dublin area alone, by different women all called Mary, of married men all called Murphy, none of whom seemed aware of those large-nosed cuckoos in the tidy matrimonial nest, Winky was his own man.

'Well at least he comes back,' said Nancy, back-pedalling.

Weaver strode to the window and saw or thought he saw a manly youngish figure with blond hair plastered to his brow, smiling to himself while poking into the boot of a stripped-down DKW.

'Oh yes . . . since when?' said Weaver. 'Tell that to Nelly.'

He opened the window and looked out. The now quite familiar figure of Prendergast himself waved to him.

'Or better still, tell it to Winky. He's just coming in the gate.'

'Balls,' said Nancy rudely.

'Balls or no balls, here he comes. The man himself.'

The gate-bell sounded its tinkle. Nico, just returned from JFK school, ran to the front door, depressed the lock, opened up, and looking out recognized the visitor bounding up the path, waving an overnight bag.

'Look out,' cried Nico (generations, as genders, were Greek to him), 'here comes Winky's father!'

'Jaysus I hope not!' cried the impetuous visitor who had bounded in, throwing a quick look around to see if his terrible da was lurking there, planting a smacker on each of Nancy's rounded cheeks. 'And how's my favourite wet dream?'

Weaver embraced him in the Roman fashion.

'We were just talking about you. Nancy considers you and Nelly to be paragons of virtue, the prototypal well-matched pair. No infidelities, no buns in ovens, no peddling of arses, no cross words.'

'Nelly and I are finished,' Winky shouted. 'All washed up!'

He was carrying Nico over his head about the room, marvelling at his size.

'I never want to see the bitch again!'

'You can stay with us,' Nancy said. 'We can put you up. Can't we, Weaver?'

'What's the Trimmer up to these days?' asked Weaver. 'Still soaping steps I dare say.'

'Still soaping something. The bollicks is in Australia. He's got a Sheila. He's become a man of destiny. A fellow who would go through you for a short cut.'

As dubious a good socialist as Yves Montand, the droopy-eyed Gauloise-smoker and lecher whom he somewhat resembled, Winky was in that smooth Gallic vein; an addict of the *outré*, smoked slim cigars. His strange constant smile was like a mask of happiness, one did not know what real expression lay underneath it. His friend Toby Tyrrell, agnostic and professed socialist, had soaped the steep and narrow steps of his rented house in Glasthule, hoping that one or both of the owners – two frail old Protestant ladies – might break a leg or neck; so that he could buy the place. His socialism, like his friend's fidelity, being strictly flexible.

'Of course you can stay here,' Nancy said. 'We sup around seven. Nico has his homework. Let's take him to the Gambe Stube, Weaver. We haven't been out in *ages* – let's show our guest a good time!'

Willie told them that he had come from Bruges via Veissingen. Bruges was a grand place; he would not hear one word against it. The Belgians were boring but Bruges was a great place. Nancy arranged for Margarete to babysit, or keep an eye out. Then, having supped on babotie, drunk deep on Italian white wine, had an earful of Dublin scandal, they set out for the old Gambe Stube in Winky's wrecked car. No car key but hot-wiring, the normal process of starting a car was short-circuited; anything could happen – it could blow up. The door handles had been sawn off, you climbed in and out. It had been stripped to divert his three teenage daughters, to whom he was more like a boyfriend than a father.

Off the sunken meadows, up a short elevated driveway, crouched the Gambe Stube; their guest, who spoke German, had ordered up three double Jamesons before they sat down. His roving eye caught the Lifesaving poster tacked on one wall; in the dim light it must have looked like Kama Sutra contortions – the kiss-of-life.

'Nice place you got here,' Winky said, crossing his legs and looking pleased.

It was a kinky nightclub, low-beamed and dim-lit, frequented by sombre weepy alcoholics – Dr Weissenborn's secret port of call between Nikolassee Station and home in Beskidenstrasse. It was the kind of lowly bar that Winky himself would have frequented in Connemara while on church commissions. One of his bronze Saviours was nailed to a wooden cross above the altar of a Catholic church facing Kilkieran Bay; not gazing heavenward or even at the neck of the priest saying Mass, nor yet gaping at the congregation facing Him; no, but staring out the window.

Now he (Winky) was staring into the darkly partitioned

booths where presently amorous couples were to be seen entwined and from the tape-deck redly throbbing a male voice sang

'Gestern . . . Die Liebe war so einfach!'

Smiling an unfathomable smile while sipping his whiskey and puffing a cigar, Winky had turned violet in the magic light; his eyes and teeth fairly glowed in the darkness, for quick rounds of double Jameson work wonders on receptive systems. His amused, ravening eye accepted what it saw with calm dissimulation: the single toper crouched by the counter, the entwined lovers in the booths, the stout owner pulling a pint, the Kama Sutra contortions on the wall, the luminosity of Nancy in her white singlet exposing bursting mammae and not least the promising signals given by her phosphorescent eyes.

'If I ever do marry – which God forbid – it will be someone as unlike Nell as possible . . . it'll be someone twice as young, naturally. In a civil ceremony floating over India in a balloon and I'll knock three lovely daughters out of her and we'll live happily ever after. I never want to see Nelly again and I bet she feels the same about me.'

It was a long spiel for the taciturn Prendergast.

'Any fresh copulations?' asked Weaver.

'Oh what a tactless question,' Nancy said, lowering her eyes.

'Gestern . . . Die Sorgen weit weg'

groaned the man in the machine.

Was this love of womankind something to do with a mother lost early, Weaver wondered, twirling the measure in his glass. The youthful Winky had surprised his mother in bed with her Nazi lover, the spy parachuted in by night. He (the spy Jorgen) was transmitting coded radio messages back to Doktor Goebbels in Berlin but made the mistake of showing a jealous son how to detonate the grenades he carried about. It had happened during

133

the so-called (so Irish) Emergency, better known as World War Two. While Jorgen was busily tapping out his morse code, Winky removed the pin of a grenade and moving backward lobbed it towards the spy. It fell into a gripe, was sucked down and never seen again. Old Potty had been active as a patriot as a young man, concealing guns in irrigation drains. He had a ravenous pike's mouth, his son's big nose, but not his nature.

After beer chasers and a glass of wine for Nancy they left the Gambe Stube and the next thing Weaver was pointing out a flight of steps leading at forty-five degrees from the Rehweise towards Beskidenstrasse, saying it was a short cut, as indeed it was, but for pedestrians; but Winky had turned sharp right and the old DKW was bravely mounting, an old broken-down short-winded hunter scrambling up an earthen bank, and Winky wrestling with the driving column and saying that he hated art, particularly Irish art, supposing there was any apart from the Book of Kells. 'I hear the thud of Blake's wings of excess,' Weaver said. Nancy had closed her eyes; she was seeing perhaps the grenade lobbed through the air, the busy spy bowed down, tapping away.

Granny Inés, a patriot to her backbone, had offered a Boer agent in Brussels a plan for planting bombs disguised as lumps of coke in British troopships bound for South Africa.

Nancy had said that Winky Prendergast 'made chaos commonplace'.

So, weaving from side to side, they made their way home on a road mercifully free of any oncoming traffic, travelling on the wrong (Irish) side of the road, through the bracing night air of Berlin full of unshed rain.

Gestern . . . Die Sorgen weit weg.
Jetzt sieht es aus, als blieben sie!

Winky had known Behan the tosspot and wild Ralph Cusack the bulb man of Annamoe and philosopher Ussher ('a cod') and

Francophile Arthur Power ('another') and Patrick Kavanagh the bogman from whom he had learnt rudeness and Harry Kernoff the luckless Jew and double-barrelled ffrench Salkeld (Cecil), the father-in-law of Brendan Behan. Winky had known all these (all dead now) in that time in Dublin, a time that will never return. In his frank opinion none of them were real artists, merely 'fukken eejits'. This was confided to Weaver over a nightcap in the kitchen, during which tête-à-tête Nancy had betaken herself off to bed.

Winky told of how one night in Dublin he had called on Behan in Morehampton Road and found Beatrice alone in the kitchen and the great man himself in bed upstairs with a hangover. But he didn't fancy the notion of lecherous Winky alone with his wife in the kitchen and called down 'Come up here with you now, Bethrice, an' thrim me toenails.'

'You wouldn't want to meet him on a dark night,' Weaver said, 'not if you saw him coming. All that roaring and bawling and public display – God it was embarrassing and the bad language would strip paint. And making up to the young bowsies on their way to Tara Street baths. No doubt he had been shagged silly in Borstal. Do you know that line in the *Wake*: "I'm on to that quare fellow Behan?" Astute of Joyce, seeing Behan wasn't even born when it was written, long before *The Quare Fellow* even made the stage. Time to turn in. I'll say goodnight.'

While Winky was noisily breaking wind and emptying his full bladder, Weaver took a stroll through the *Sonnenraum* where Nancy had made up the visitor's bed with clean blue sheets and set out a jug of water with tumbler, switched on the bedside lamp and set out some light reading matter which Weaver now examined with some suspicion. For in all fairness now what was a potential cuckold to make of *The Veil of the Soul* by Poe, *London Spy* by Ned Ward, *Steaming to Bamboola* by Christopher Buckley?

Weaver was beginning to smell a rat.

Lying alongside Nancy in the commodious double bed with its

red sheets Weaver stared at the ceiling and wondered again what it was about W.P. and his life among womenfolk; was it that he venerated them, was obsessed with them, a *panty-sniffer* in Nancy's sharp formulation? His life among men was different to his life among women; different again with his three pubescent daughters, for there he was a co-equal, their friend, an innocent among innocents. These different lives of his never overlapped; the stories he told his male confrères were quite different from the yarns he spun his loves.

As a child might he not once or twice have sat on the tweedy lap of W. B. Yeats himself, who had been famously infatuated with his (Winky's) no less legendary Granny Dolores Inés Vives Accosta the Catalan beauty who was herself so wholeheartedly espoused to the Irish cause? He might have heard the great man chanting.

> It's certain that fine women eat
> A crazy salad with their meat
> Whereby the Horn of Plenty is undone

'Nice place you got here,' Weaver told the ceiling and began drifting off to sleep.

For a while peace reigned in no. 51. Then this:

Judging her estranged husband to be safely asleep, Nancy slipped from between the sheets, having espied a frass of light spilling onto the patio below, and made her way glidingly downstairs (Josette Day about to meet the Beast in Cocteau's *La Belle et la Bête*), only stopping to remove pyjama top and breezily enter the *Sonnenraum* trailing this object as a torero might the *muleta* in the bullring or *Bullenwinkel*, before executing a consummate *media véronica*, stepping lightly over the sprinkled sand recently raked by obsequious *monos* (monkeys).

The Great Fornicator was sitting up and peering at the print (not one of the tempting trio set out but *The Romantic Agony* by

Mario Praz purloined from Weaver's library) through the smudged lens of granny-glasses that made him look like the wolf in bed.

'Tell me, Sir, are you a tit man or a bum man yourself?'

The wolf, quite naked, sat up in bed, lowered the book and removed his granny-glasses the better to get an eyeful.

'Zounds, Madame, do I dream?'

Cupping her breasts (a good handful) in both hands, the better to enhance their heavy rotundity and healthy sheen, prancing Nance asked roguishly, pointing *them* at *him*: 'So?'

'I do confess, fair one, to being a tittybum man myself, I cannot help it but am made that way, defenceless before beauty.'

'And where, pray, does that leave me . . . or us?'

The G.F. had been taken aback by the unexpected arrival of a simmering and 'topless' Nance and now was for laying a circumspect hand privily onto his hidden member (taken lax all of a sudden), as Wild Bill checking his trusty Gat, to check out its reassuring presence and firmness of purpose (alas!).

'Could you not go out again and come back a shade slower. Maybe with only . . . um . . . the top on?'

'Why, certes, Spigot, I am only here for pleasuring.'

'Oh Madame!'

'Very well then. Don't you stir an *inch*. Watch this.'

Exit prancing Nance with sparkling eyes to swiftly remove offending bottoms, button up pyjama tops, pinch cheeks to bring up touch of colour to face (drained of colour in her anxiety to perform well), re-enter bottomless, to strike a saucy pose, to set bull-in- bed's heart aflutter: finger indenting right cheek, eyes cast down in mock modesty, weight thrown on one hip, supple, voluptuous, as she slowly rotated herself about, weight now rolled onto the other hip, with ripple of haunches indented with dimples. Posterior aspect: amplitude of haunch, entwined poshlusty circles (the bum proper), deep cleft.

'A goodly pair,' breathed Wolf, a little rampant (Monsieur Itch alias Sir Roger Snatch).

She levelled on him her slow voluptuous gaze. 'Sire –
Mademoiselle de Maupin or *Zazie dans le Métro* – which you 'ave?'

'Zounds, Madame, both,' breathed the Wolf (yclept Sir
Schnick), feasting his ravening eyes.

The long coltish thighs, the dimpled knees he had known of
yore (from observing her while sea-bathing), but the hairy bun
was an unexpected bonus, a *very* hair bun indeed, set upon its own
Mount of Venus, as vegetation atop fabled Tara Hill.

'Gads-bud, your ladyship's so charming!'

Standing by the bed with eyes sparkling, and feasting her eyes
on him, the powerful hairy chest rising from the blue sheets (like
Dalkey Island on a summer's day), coquettishly she took the loose
cord of her pyjama bottoms (still fastened) between thumb and
devil finger and pulled it slowly, drawing out the slip-knot to its
fullest extent and allowed the pyjama bottoms to subside of their
own accord slowly and gently down to her ankles, never taking
her eyes from his (fastened not on hers but on the operation she
was performing so delicately as if on his hidden member, for – lo
– he felt it begin to rise, as she stepped out of this encumbrance,
breathing deeply, to strike a saucy pose).

'Bravo, Madame!'

Standing by the bed with eyes sparkling, pyjama bottoms about
her heels, her toolera twosome pushed out in front (with a strong
suggestion of hardening nipple) and the toolerum twosome stuck
out behind, instant provocations, our Nance looked good enough
to eat and ready for anything in the expectation of being
everything a man could desire in the way of wellfleshedout-
womaninherprime, as indeed she was.

'Bravo . . .' softly breathed Sir Schnick-Wolffe, clapping his
hands, or pads or claws softly together, his ravening eyes fixed on
her parts. Frontal aspect: goodly face, good shoulders thrown
back, rounded belly, insucked navel, hairy bun, dimpled knees, as
so oft seen in the neighbourhood of Sandycove, a popular Dublin
seaside resort near his studio, where he rarely worked.

The frisky air was full of smeggy promises.

'My liege [low], a boon . . .'

'Nay, an hundred, Madame. I am yours to command. What [huskily] is your heart's desire?'

'My good liege, pray grant me leave to fondle your goodly parts or . . . [archly] most reverently to kiss your mighty rod. Allow me to buss that meaty member.'

'Nay, good Madame,' quoth Sir Schnick-Wolffe, laughing into his beard indulgently. 'For, zounds, methinks such fresh parleying must lead from pranks to matters more serious.'

'Why, Sir, shall I then suck your fresh manhood and have done with it?'

Zounds, did cocksman ever suffer so? The saucy wench!

'Nay, nay, good Madame, for that must put Sir Schnick most randily to ginger.'

'Oh la, la . . . I am quite breathless.'

'Nay, nay.'

'Oh good Sir . . .'

'Madame, I would speak roundly with thee. Thou art a forthright wench and I do respect and honour that in thee. But, look you Madame, you do much dis*honour* me! For, zounds, how can I be my own free self with thee (much as I should relish that) while still a loyal guest to mine goodly host your husband and bondsman, who at this moment subsideth above us in ye Master Bedroom, following hard upon our mighty wassailing? How? Would you have me dishonour him, you, and mine humble self with one *dastardly* blow?'

'Oh goodly Sir [low], would that you could deal me that one dastardly blow!'

'Nay, Madame, 'tis not mine to give.'

'Oh Sire . . . [wistfully] I have long fashioned such fancies . . . but . . . alas!'

'And I too, most gracious lady, I too [subsiding].'

Here Mario Praz thoroughly underlined and dog-eared

fell with a soft clatter to the floor.

'Tush, tush,' quoth prancing Nance (her dander up) with flashing eyes, unbuttoning and casting away her top, now dressed only in fetching black velvet choker with amber brooch about the neck, hopping into bed alongside the great steaming Bull who, suddenly surprised and embarrassed, was attempting to mask an incipient erection.

'No more of this bootless parley,' shrilled Nance, 'I do here rightfully claim my prize, oh bully boy!' and suiting the action to the words laid a gladsome be-ringed possessive right hand softly on the aforesaid risen member, which on the instant, for the nonce, hath *shrunk to nowt*!

'Oh, Sir [sobs] alas!'

'Oh, Madame!'

Whereupon Weaver, who had been listening with ears prick'd, pent up with nameless venom, rose up frowningly and stern to robe himself soberly in his scarlet dressing-gown, slip bare feet into openwork espadrilles and with throbbing member pass slowly and thoughtfully into the bathroom, his stately progress punctuated with a theatrical hacking cough worthy of a consumptive on his last legs, to urinate like a carthorse, flush twice and then again for good measure, and still coughing, make his measured way back to the master bedroom onto or more properly into which he threw himself heavily, as Ox into dark Stall.

Presently she came up again, as if butter wouldn't melt in her mouth, used the toilet circumspectly, thoughtfully brushed her teeth and combed her hair, set herself to rights before slipping back into bed again, out of which she had slipped not half an hour previously.

She stared up at the ceiling. Weaver was already staring up at it. He had not heard the low moan which would have signalled the beastly *estacado*. All had been carried out in stealthy silence. Had the lusty guest been indulging himself in *unnatural* practices with Nancy below? Weaver had listened for the crash that would announce the Great Dun Bull's charge against the *burladero* (railway sleepers actually), splintering a horn and bellowing in rage and agony. Then the awful ritual of the advance of the stout picadors with chin-straps, their lances upraised, clanking in on knacker's yard mounts scarred from previous brushes with bulls, then the flighty *banderilleros* dancing in on their toecaps in satin pumps, and the final tchuck! of the *estacado* dispatching the wretched bull (Nancy) into whose dying ear the vile torero was shouting the vilest abuse and behind him the damned band playing away high up on the stands, the terraces, what do you call 'em?

'Are we having fun?' Weaver inquired in a chummy voice.

'None of your damn business, rat. We heard the fucking waterworks. Good night.'

But it was already beginning to be daylight again, after the short Berlin night of spring advancing into summer, and the birds already twittering in the trees, in the garden. But what was this '*we*' supposed to mean? Alack-a-day!

It was not possible to score debating points against Nancy Els in matters like these; her persuasive arguments (call them arguments, not whimsy, feminine wiles) had the force of axioms tried and true, invincible in that they bypassed logic and came to their own conclusions, a narrowly prearranged goal; came home to roost. In such unequal contest the poor beggar was as nothing; he hadn't a leg to stand on. Now stiff as a board, silent as statuary, seamless as mercury, Weaver subsided, listening to the night birds without. Farewell, Love . . . Thy bayted hokes shall tangle me no more.

24

Nancy Departs (*Sperrmülltag*)

After bathing his son Weaver read him a story in bed and then went down and made himself a strong drink with gin in it and lit up a cigar and wandered into the living-room, hoping to find it unoccupied (for there was no sound in the place, the grandfather clock silent, as the kitchen clock, and the welcome light not working over the front porch and no sign of the bitch anywhere), until marching in he found her slumped in an armchair in the *Sonnenraum* staring out of the window into the garden.

'You want something?' Weaver asked, holding up his drink to the back of her head (she was watching him in the reflection from the tall double-glaze windows with an expression which he did not care much for but there you definitely are).

'Come and sit down with me here a moment because I have something serious to say to you. Will you sit down? I don't want you flitting away.'

'I am sitting down,' Weaver said, doing so behind her back.

Nancy fixed a glittery eye upon him in the reflecting window, drew a deep breath, and turned to face him.

'I am not a bad wife to you. At least I have always tried to be a faithful wife. Why are you grinning like that? I tried, I said. And *almost* always I succeeded. Why then are you being such a bad husband to me? Is it my fault that you no longer find me attractive, that you no longer can fancy me? Have you gone off me?'

Weaver stared into his drink.

'I wish you would speak more to me. What's wrong?'

She had made a momentous decision, to fly to London and stay with her friend Betty Buzzard on Primrose Hill.

'And then?' Weaver asked his gin.

'And then we will see. You must recognize that we cannot go on like this. You are becoming quite dangerous. Someone might get hurt. Someone is being hurt,' she amended meaningfully. 'I am talking about your son. I fear for Nico.'

'Well, you needn't,' Weaver said, unable to meet her eye.

'Well I do.'

'All right, if that's what you want,' said Weaver.

'It's not what I *want*,' Nancy said, 'but it's what I have decided to do. We must put some space between us. When I'm away you should think quite seriously about what *you* must do if this marriage is to go on. Because it's not going on. It's gone dead, and you killed it. You must do something about all this if your son is not to be damaged. I think you have become half mad, if you want to know, and it's that woman who has changed you. You were not like this when we came here first. I won't say any more. You know all this.'

'All right, I will.'

'You will what?'

'Think about it.'

'I think you should take weekends away with her. I don't want her in the house, in my bed. I too am going mad.'

'All right, I will,' Weaver said again.

'You do that.'

She had already packed her suitcase and arranged with Randall Loftus to fly Pan Am to London, had phoned Betty Buzzard, had spoken to Nico. It was a short holiday; she was overworked. Weaver would look after him. He must be good until she came back.

'Don't say "all right" if you don't mean it.'

'I do mean it.'

So it was arranged. It was like a zoo with all the animals gone out of it, when Nancy went away.

Weaver at first sober as a judge and then progressively less so, in the *Sonnenraum*, the *Sonnenzimmer* with a bottle of high-proof blue vodka, watched the light across the way in the Weissenborn's spare room where Nancy lay that night, preparing herself for an early flight to Lund (or so she had put it about), Weaver watching with the same intensity as Gatsby looking over the intervening sound at the green light at the end of the jetty that betokened Daisy. Although he knew that he could not expect favours from Nancy any more, nevertheless he did not wish her any harm. Guilty of generous motives, he could feel sorry for her and for himself under the same cover (he was, without further beating about the bush, now not entirely sober).

The reverse (of that he did not will her any harm) was probably not true; for if a jilted woman is merciless, how much more so is the jilted wife. They can be exceptionally cruel, when the occasion arises and the time ripe to grind the heel in.

That flatulent Tudor bitch, the first Elizabeth, thought Weaver, progressively less sober and keeping a weather eye on the light across the way, must have regarded bold Sir Walt (who had emitted a thundering great fart in court and blown himself and his retinue of drunken sailors halfway around the globe – a fart by purest accident let fly, blame it on the fine fat capons he had for breakfast with his stoups of English ale) as her one true and hairy husband in the sight of Almighty God, a husband no matter how putative off pillaging and collecting 'purchase' (i.e., robbing) for the Crown (i.e., Liz); and now by God she would have the beggar's red guts for garters. She bloody well would; he had been her man, she had made him, and he had jilted her; so off with his fucking head!

He, poor fool, had worked hard and long in their far-flung interests, travelled here, planted the flag there, strolled on beaches untrodden by white men, pressed trinkets (mirrors were popular) into the hands of savages; but all the thanks he got was that she regarded him, erring Sir Walt, with no magnanimous royal (pop) eye. He was most distinctly out of Courtly Favour.

Sir Walt with throbbing temples in bad light, feeling very sorry for himself, locked away into himself, locked into the damp Tower of London among felons, heaved up a heavy sigh, seated himself at the table, trimmed the wax candle with forefinger and thumb, drew a sheet of paper to him, sent a prayer heavenward for guidance, tried to settle his troubled mind, though sick at heart, for one last epistle to his loving wife. He was writing to her and to his son, in her safekeeping, and he could not weep, not even for himself.

He wrote steadily with a scratchy quill pen cut from the tail feathers of a cock pheasant trapped in a snare in a wet wood in Dorset on the frosty Monday after All Saints. He wanted to write: 'You must peer into the dark . . .' but wrote instead (bitterness escaping now): 'I am no more yours, nor you mine.' (Or was that Edward de Vere, Earl of Oxford?)

Weaver was now exceptionally unsober, the vodka bottle half drunk, it was going on three in the morning and he felt as if his insides (not to mention his brains) were burning. Nancy, as she had put out to the great rumour-gatherers and rumour-spreaders across the way, was off for Lund on the morrow; which probably meant (thought her husband who knew her better) that she was heading in the opposite direction, heading back to London grime and the joys of Primrose Hill, weeping on the broad shoulders of the buck-toothed but goodhearted Betty Buzzard, her port in any storm. Randall Loftus the Pan Am pilot was driving her to Tempelhof, having booked her onto an early flight. (And here the light across the way was extinguished.)

25

Nancy's True
Nature and Character Revealed

Now that Nancy had betaken herself weeping northward in a positive lather of migratory sorrowing, for the time being (and Lord love her), it behoves us to try and understand something of her character (what she was born with, her racial genes) and nature (what she had made of this); or understand at least some features of that contradictory being (a Balance perpetually on the cusp), which might profitably be examined now.

She had not always been Nancy Weaver. She was born and christened into a strict penny-pinching cold Lutheran faith as Nancy Redpath Damaris Els (or Ehls) of Wolfgang and Elsie Els in Kingwilliamstown, a small museum town in Eastern Cape Province, South Africa. Of German (father) and Welsh (mother) stock, she was by nature and inclination in turns secretive and expansive, captious and anxious, generous and tight-fisted, capricious and reliable, forward-looking and backward-gazing, lusty and puritanical, filled with self-esteem and plagued by self-doubt, forgiving and unforgiving, wonderfully cheerful and quite bleak. In other words, a thoroughly representative female type of average intelligence and education a quarter way through the last third of the twentieth century.

Characteristic saying: 'Do me up.' Or: 'Would you ever do me up?' a demand in the form of a rhetorical question. A variant: 'Am

I bleeding, [when viewed] from the back?' Bombed by heavy menses. Being by nature impetuous, she set out to correct and remedy mistakes by swiftly lunging gestures (what movie people call 'contre-plonge') that were intended to liberate her, but often succeeded in landing her even deeper in the soup or shit. 'Grow up!' to Nico, at a loss.

She had a habit of mislaying things. Earlier on in their married years this may have been yet another charming foible; but now it was another irredeemable, ineradicable fault. She lost things, and at the most awkward times. If whistles blew in a station, if a gangway was being retracted, Nancy would be there and clamouring to be let off, she needed something at the news-stand, off the dock. She ran after trains, sprinting level with the last carriage, to be hauled into the guard's van as the train was leaving the station, and Weaver leaning out of a window, having a heart attack.

Nancy's 'remedies' were scalding poultices more painful, when lovingly applied, than the thing (the fault) they sought to remedy.

'Do you still fancy me?' had become modulated into 'Do you want me any more?' And by gentle implication, the oft-heard plaint of all women everywhere always: 'Am I *showing* my years? Have I got widow's hump? Do my ears stick out? Is my bum too big? Have I crow's feet instead of beautiful eyes? Has my . . . er, have my good looks gone? Am I myself any more?'

And if Weaver had lost a harridan-witch-termagant for the time being, poor Nico had acquired something far worse in Lore: a wicked stepmother, oh God! It was not Lore's fault that she was not Nancy. Her version of wholesome food (salads) did not appeal to Nico, he couldn't eat it; or if he did, under sufferance, couldn't keep it down. Food touched by Lore's hands had become poison, Nico vomited it up, in the car. So Lore brought something from the chemist next morning that would settle his stomach; Nico took a spoonful with the gravest misgiving, reported that he was feeling better. He had been knocked out by the extreme cold on the frozen lake, and in the inn Lore had pressed him to take a sip of *Glühwein*. '*Es ist gut*,' but it wasn't at all.

'He does complain rather a lot,' she said. He was stuck to the ice, his face blue. Lore walked on the ice with her throat bared. In the restaurant Nico was ultra-polite, no thank you this, no thank you that, I don't feel like it; also he contrived to shrink several inches; misery was making him smaller and smaller, diminishing him. He wanted his mother back. He didn't say it, but everything he did conveyed it. He would not utter Lore's name. 'That woman,' his skewy stare said in the zoo, observing Lore and his father seated on a bench near the tarantulas, smiling at each other. The tarantulas slept in a brown clump on a branch; diaphanous grasshoppers (their food) hopped about in the glass cage, made their eyes bulge, their long antennae sticking out. Nico watched the grinning pair on the bench, no longer recognizing his father; the stepmother was trying to poison him.

Weaver forgot to lay in provisions and walked to the bakery in the black dark at six o'clock in the morning for bread and milk, walked back in the frozen ruts to prepare Nico's breakfast, wrap him up for school, take him to where the JFK school bus stopped, Nico the sole passenger, a small set face being carried away into black Berlin, to more misery in school. Weaver lit candles and arranged them under the pipes in the basement. The Havel lakes had frozen down to their weedy beds in a cold as extreme as permafrost and skaters appeared in the mist rising off the ice, with steaming breath coming out of their mouths like horses after a gallop. A perishing wind blew over the ice and the permafrost mist hung on the surface about the holes dug in the ice surrounded by bracken cut as markers and lone skaters floated in and out of this, materializing very upright in woollen caps with bobbins, others crouched with hands joined behind their backs, and Lore walked on the ice with her throat exposed like one of the female patients (Clavdia Cauchat!) in Herr Mann's sanatorium. Nico, on the other hand, was Oliver Twist blue with cold, pulverized by misery.

Bushes had been cut by the foresters and put about the holes in the ice as markers; the ice was frozen to a depth of six feet, the fish frozen solid into it, right down to the lake bed. Weaver and Lore linking or hand in hand walked with Nico, holding onto Weaver's left hand, went out walking on the frozen lakes.

Lore had bought her clothes in a Berlin boutique at a discount arranged by her boss Heinz Walser, couturière fashions from Paris which tended to expose her neck and emphasized her long stylish legs and classical high rump; well-cut 'beautifully understated' Paris fashion was Lore's style on the Havel, with throat exposed.

'We stop here I think,' she told Weaver.

'Why?'

'You wish to die?' she said. 'The border runs through the middle of the Havel. Go beyond this point and they shoot at you.'

'They watch us?' Nico asked, looking up at her like a small owl.

'Certainly.'

'Wow!'

Crack marksmen were hidden in the bushes on the Soviet side, their gloved fingers curved around the triggers, their eyes along telescopic sights riveted on the objects fidgeting in and out of the cross-hair sights, just dying to squeeze off a round. Their officers were studying the three figures in the middle of the frozen Havel, through their powerful binoculars that drew them into focus, pulled them closer. They saw the bared throat, muttered '*Bubi, drück mich! Bald deutsche Mutter!*' sending her *ein geiler Blick* along their steamed-up sights. '*Mein Liebster, mein Allerliebster! Ackkackkacckk, babee!*'

Nico's fingers and toes were frozen, he moved more and more slowly, he wished to be carried. Then the overheated inn, the sickening *Glühwein*, the odourless puke.

But to return to Nancy.

Again rowelling the spurs ('With sounding whip, the rowels

dyed in blood,' thought Weaver, unable to resist an apt quotation): 'Why can't we be more like the nice Prendergasts.' Or again, twisting the rowel: 'If you're so fond of her, why don't you go off and live with her, fuck off from here?' The Prendergast ménage was surely an unlikely model for connubial bliss?

Biting her lips until she drew blood, Nancy whispered: 'Excite me!' This, put like that, could be a tall order. 'Can't you walk around with it sticking out?' Or: 'I'm not excited. Can you grow another?'

Pish, pish. Stir me up. Do me do. Do me doggily. Am I freakish? This on-off erratic code of sexual signals had stumped Weaver, who had never quite got the hang of it. An old chestnut with the Weavers was the story oft told of what the Munich tailor had asked Winky: '*Auf welcher Seite tragen Sie Ihr Geschlecht, mein Herr?*' On which side do you wear your shame, sir? He ran the measure up the inside of the mighty thigh. On his shoulders he carried a light fall of dandruff, he had fetid halitosis, was related to von Bismarck. Why could she not be as she had been before? a charmer, a humorous party, a good ride, a contented woman; that was asking too much.

But lo and behold, the mists lift, and Nancy is again singing. The bathroom is in fact steamed up, and she kneels by the side of the deep Berlin bath-tub where her son's head floats beside ducks and tugs, and she sings to him '*Frère Jacques, Bruder Jacques*' in an inspired mixture of demotic French (of which she has a smattering) and German (which she is picking up as she goes along), and Nico is laughing his head off at his inspired and clever mum.

'Oh isn't it a perfect day for flying!' she had said to Weaver in Dublin airport on 27 May 1969 as they prepared to set off with high hopes for Berlin. 'Please, you must excuse him, he is so excited, flying to Berlin!' she apologizes to Mel Ferrer the Hollywood star who was sitting opposite with his long legs stretched out. And Mel seemed to understand Nico tripping over his expensive brown Hollywood brogues, at least he nodded as though he understood (for stars don't talk), sending out one of his famous quiet-manly-cleft-chinned-lopsided-but-reliable smiles (a grin really) and rustled the *Irish Press* at her, before disappearing behind it ('FF RETURNS TO GRASS ROOTS').

But Nico in the deep Berlin bath was splitting himself laughing at his mum, having quite forgotten the long tweedy legs outstretched and the brown brogues so very expensive, probably bought in Hollywood, and the first vomit outside Dunleary Station and the taxi to the airport and Mel waiting behind the *Irish Press* for him to arrive and trip over his legs, so long, having also forgotten the Bremen and Hanover stopovers and his testy father watching him and saying, 30,000 feet up in the sky between Hanover and Tempelhof, with a stiff gin before him: 'In the old times the mothers trembled for their daughters' safety and virtue, at the mercy of stray rapists in foreign places – now they must start worrying about their sons. Ignore that fellow, Nico, will you? [Nico Weaver was causing a sensation up front.] Like a good lad. Look out of the window at the clouds. Will we ever reach Berlin, do you suppose? Or are we going to fly around all night?'

But they landed safely at Tempelhof. Bertha Busse, Herr Born's remarkably plain secretary, was holding up a banner with a strange device at the concourse as they came to collect their luggage, some of it packed in pillowcases. On a piece of cardboard held aloft she had printed in her careful hand

WM WEAVER – DILDO

'You are Mr Weaver, I presume?'

'You presume correctly, madame,' Weaver said rather loudly, having gone stone deaf in the left ear, 'and this is my wife Nancy and my only son Nico, in whom I am well pleased [he was none too sober, himself], all in one piece. And you must be Fräulein Busse [for they had corresponded]!'

'Yus, I yam,' said Bertha Busse stoutly, with great goggle-eyed deep-sea-fish spectacles, dim port-holes, a suety white unhealthy complexion and lumpy legs in thick stockings, and it almost June.

'We have booked you all into the Hotel Bogotá and hope you will be quite comfortable there. None of our other guests booked in there have ever complained. It is a good hotel, Mr Weaver! Herr Born would like to see you at your leisure, whenever it is most convenient. Tomorrow mid-morning would suit him. Our office is only five minutes from the hotel.'

The taxi rank was outside. She would see them settled into the hotel, but now they must collect their baggage.

So they did that, and Bertha Busse sat in front with the driver, and explained this and that.

The Hotel Bogotá in Schlüterstrasse had a large room with five beds in it facing the street on the first floor and Nico was enchanted. 'Are we in Germany yet?' Yes, they were in Berlin, and this was the Hotel Bogotá and that there was his bed. And Herr Born would see them in the morning. But no, thank you, she would not accept a drink, it was late and they must be tired.

'*Au contraire*,' said Weaver, who seemed to be modelling himself on Ned Ward's London Spy. 'Fresh as daisies.'

Next morning Herr Born was affability itself. Suitable accommodation would soon be found somewhere in Berlin. The right house awaited them and it was only a question of finding it. It was important to find just the right place, nothing less would do. Somewhere quiet. They would find it. He had been to Margot Schoeller's bookshop and they had inquired of the Irish guest, had he arrived yet?

'So you are already famous. Berlin eagerly awaits you.'

Weaver was enthralled.

They walked to Margot Schoeller's bookshop and a lady who could only have been Margot Schoeller stood by the cash-desk but Weaver did not care to introduce himself just then, there would be opportunities later. He found a copy of one of his books between Henry Williamson's *Tarka the Otter* and Edith Wharton's *Ethan Frome*, and bought a Sunburst paperback edition of the suicide Cesare Pavese's *Among Women Only*.

So it began. That time of delight and storm, new life, remorse and pain, advance and withdrawal, Amsterdam, Munich and Palma, the snow and ice, the heat of Berlin summers, Lore; all of that. And his heart was singing.

Singing!

26

Contretemps at Torrox, Dubrovnik, Dover, Hamburg

> Everyone felt good about the fight and ate
> well. We drank sangria with fresh prawns
> and crisp fried octopus that tasted of
> lobster. Nobody talked about bullfighting.

The Dangerous Summer, Ernest Hemingway

It was the Silly Season then. That confused decade, the 1960s, when all the known world wished to be part of the Haight-Ashbury 'scene', the so-called Permissive Society. Short skirts had come back into fashion. In Spain the ailing Generalissimo was not quite dead yet, but hanging on, stricken with phlebitis.

The littoral around Torrox and Torre del Mar had been well manured with human sewage that smelled worse than pig sewage to the human nose (for the pigs we cannot speak); far worse at night than in the daytime when the sun had burnt away some of the noxious fumes. Figure the Weavers there.

They had found themselves in a sleazy sort of nightclub in the vicinity of Torrox, a tax haven a little way from Málaga, straight out of *Los Olvidados*. At that time Nancy was looking her best in sack dresses, tight-fitting slacks, short skirts showing off the tanned soubrettish legs. She had become skittish in beads and bangles; it was something in the air, a period of general sexual flaunting (a *gitano* had quaffed wine out of her high-heel red shoe).

The bar was empty but for a gangster in red braces, smoking a cigar. He was trying to look tough and dissipated, leaning against the bar counter, swallowing cheap Cognac. 'Guantanamera' came pulsing from the tape-deck; it was all the rage in Spain. A barman appeared and Weaver called their order – Felipe Segundo.

'Tell me, who's this fellow,' Nancy asked skittishly, 'this Juan Caramelo? We can't escape him. They all sing his praises. Who is he? What did he do?'

'*No se*,' said Weaver, refusing to enter into the spirit of antic frolic and badinage. 'What does it matter?'

'Of course it matters, chump.'

The gangster here cleared his throat, as if he had something to say about Juan Caramelo. The Weavers studied him. Now he was smiling into his drink while batting his long Spanish eyelashes. He wore highly polished brown boots with villainously pointed toes that cried out for spurs, a bestudded bomber jacket, Slim Jim tie (*de rigueur* in Westerns); the ostentatious red braces were worn high, a style favoured by the great torero Luis Miguel Dominguín on his bull-farm when preparing to slaughter black bulls in every Plaza de Toros. He looked more a down-at-heel matador, a second-stringer fallen on hard times, but still with a little money to throw about, bait to catch suckers, *extranjeros*. The waveringly uncertain eye-contact down the bar, the constant shifting of feet and nervous tapping of fingers, the throat-clearing as though about to utter something portentous, the cigar-puffing and general air of uneasiness, all pointed to this.

He was more the Manolete type, not to be compared with valiant Dominguí, despite the red braces (and on him they looked like hernia aids) worn to lend him courage. He was searching for an opening; he liked the look of the sassy *señora*. All foreign women were loose, particularly the bored wives.

Nancy certainly looked the part. The short one-piece woollen dress of beige became her; the long brown legs were at home in a nightclub, here. Weaver was trying to recall what Tante Isabel, the poet Lorca's sainted aunt, had told him of the taunting and jibes aimed at Manolete, master of the 'profile pass', tricked-up 'danger', playing doctored bulls with horns trimmed and so sensitive the bulls roared with pain whenever they hooked horns into the barriers, or padding on the picadors' nags. Manolete they thought had a yellow streak, calling down: Manolete, Manolete, why fight bulls, you who cannot even kill a shithouse rat? It was of course much more offensive in Spanish, Tante Isabel said.

'*Señor!*' Nancy called across to the shifty torero. '*¿Quién es Juan Caramelo?*'

Manolete came directly out his reverie, removed the reeking *puro* from between his lips to expose a sorry row of rodent's brown teeth jutting out at a curious angle. Thrusting narrow thumbs behind his fancy braces and throwing out his chest he answered in a hard, strange, panting voice: '*¿Por qué, señora? Un hombre . . . como yo. En verdad.*'

Taking up his Fundador he thought to sidle up to this agreeable pair in order to discuss this important matter; but on coming closer he found the atmosphere not all that friendly, for the *señor* was frowning into his drink in a forbidding manner. But he had more or less committed himself now (the bad bullfighter inviting the *corneada*) and sidled up to them, leering in an apologetic way, the high heels going clickety-click on the parquet floor. He deeply inhaled the rich feminine aroma that Nancy exuded, as though she were some tropical bloom. Bending forward Nancy (exposing a corsage fairly bursting with pomegranates) was offering the tip of her Celtas to the pointed flame he had gallantly flicked out for her; whereupon Weaver put down his drink with excessive deliberation and looked Manolete in the twittery eye.

'You'll be suggesting she suck you off next.'

This was bold; but Manolete knew no English.

'*¿Como?*'

'Back off, Jack. None of your shifty business here, cocksucker,' Weaver muttered darkly into his Cognac.

'*¿Como, señor? No laaike, eh?*' scratching his silk striped shirt with rasping vampire fingernail. About to lay a pacifying claw on Weaver's arm, he thought better of it.

'*No moleste, hombre.*'

Nancy laughed (they're fighting, for me!).

'Go and molest your own fucking bulls,' Weaver said. 'Finish your drink,' he told laughing Nancy. 'Let's get out of here. This fellow gets my goat.'

'*¡Hola, hombre! ¿Qué tal?*'

Cheeky! Cheeky!

Weaver was out with his ever-loving fancy-woman whom all the macho men of Andalucía were lusting after; with *faena*, *pase*, *remate*, *natural*, *media véronica*, *quite*, and full *véronica*; with valour, with sneakiness. And himself? With misgiving. All the land stank of human sewage thereabouts, beyond the waving plumes of sugar cane.

Our thoughts now fly in a north-easterly direction across some twenty degrees of latitude in Bonne's projection to a hot summer night in the old walled city of Dubrovnik during an open-air performance of Carl Orff's Carmina Burana, for Nancy's tastes in music were eclectic. She had just been misdirected to a non-existent Toilet for the Ladies on an upper landing, with some embarrassing consequences, as shall be told. This she carried off with panache. It fell out in this way.

They sat on good seats in the company of an oldtimer from Mlini named Karlovic Maria who had appeared in an old Hollywood movie under the direction of Francis X. Bushman in the days when men were male and women were feminine and stars were stars, in the olden times. She was be-ringed and heavily scented in a musky way and she thirsted after English-spoken culture as a bee for pollen. To-pee-or-not-to-pee-deass-ease-zequest-ti-yon, she intoned, making the row of seats quiver, her head thrown back, eyes closed, breathing deeply through cavernous nostrils – a bravura performance received with a sly rustling of programmes and tittering in front.

'Precisely my own problem,' said our Nancy, 'where is it?'

'Where is what, m'dare?'

'The toilet. The Ladies.'

'Uuup steers, I believe,' drawled Karlovic Maria grandly, waving her withered claw, as if she had just willed the place into existence. 'Try uup steers, m'dare.'

Nancy had a smattering of German, Karlovic Maria had unreliable French and Italian, and the ladies around them, fanning themselves with programmes and awaiting the return of a large mixed choir, were all either Serbs or Croats and thus no help at all.

'If I were you, dare,' Karlovic Maria said stoutly. 'I'd yust run uup steers and peess on the first empty landing you see.'

One of the more helpful lady programme-sellers was pointing upwards and Nancy was nodding, taking directions in a language she knew something of from her days in the Yugoslav Embassy in Holland Park, before setting off, waving back to them. She found the empty landing and was crouching down with skirt about her waist and in full flow already when, as if in response to a signal, two doors burst open on either side of her, and out of one trooped fifty powdered lady singers and from the other door fifty clean-shaven men in faultless evening dress; the entire mixed choir filed by on either side of her, fording the stream with averted eyes, and nobody offering any comment.

'I could not stop myself,' Nancy laughed. Karlovic Maria shook all over and wheezed, laying a companionable claw on Nancy's knee.

'Serbs are used to much worse than that, m'dare.'

Weaver recalled the swifts dive-bombing the pool of light that was the podium, the sheen of brass, the bare shoulders of the female singers, the dinner jackets of the males as they filed to their places again and the white-haired conductor came vainly forward to all the applause and Nancy quite composed taking her seat by Madame Karlovic Maria who was nodding and applauding and becoming mustier by the minute as the mixed choir went rampaging after the loudly emphatic thumpety-thumpety-thump godawful Orffmusik and glancing sideways he saw Nancy's well-rounded hamster cheeks set in a pleased smirk, a *contained* smile of quiet satisfaction.

Once, becalmed in Dover, having come by early train from Victoria, London, before crossing to Calais and going by train to Málaga, had not Nancy discovered that she had left her passport behind?

'You recall where you might have left it?' Weaver asked patiently.

'Yes I do. On the table beside our bed.'

'You're sure? Then I'll tell you what you can do. Phone your friend Betty, ask her to take the morning off, tell her to take a taxi to the flat and recover the passport. Then she takes it to the AA and get them to put it on the next train to Dover. Tell Betty that she will be handsomely reimbursed.'

'A brilliant idea,' Nancy said, brightening up. 'Better still. She may be at home. I'll try her there.'

Betty Buzzard was their friendly neighbour, another South African.

'Better still,' Weaver said. 'Do just that. You will find me lying insensible on the floor of the nearest bar.' And going forth he walked straight into the almost perfect bar: no music, no truculent morning boozers, a pool table, a good local brew on tap, a view of water, fresh air circulating, a landlord who was not morose – his requirements were not exacting. And when Nancy stepped into the bar two and a half hours later, waving the missing passport, she found her husband calmly practising cannonshots, with a tall glass of the local brew within easy reach.

'What else are the bloody AA for?' Nancy wanted to know.

In the good times gone when they had shared everything, even their thoughts, even the bathroom, even the bath, Nancy – adopting poses to please, playing the fancy-woman, the unbridled whore – generally ended her ablutions on her stomach, offering 'peerless globes' to the steadfast husbandly eye. It worked more often than not. Showing the tip of her tongue Nancy swayed back, all flushed from bathing, surreptitiously laying her hand on meat, asking 'If you want to do me up the backside the vaseline's right behind you.'

With her it was largely a matter of cleaning up. Marmite was 'the lady's bum'. After a token protest of wifely modesty she could succumb to anything; she was Messalina for whom all males were as grist to the mill she operated between her legs and avid buttocks. Nancy submitted with all the languid decorum of a grand lady briefing the humble gardener cap in hand in the morning at the back door before the Master was stirring.

Ah, Paddy! I want you to thoroughly weed out the onion beds today. Paddy, this morning I'd like you to prick over the camomile lawn. Paddy, have you seen the Master about yet? Are the radishes in? the loganberries sprayed? the asparagus well manured? Staunch husbandry.

Once, in a very grand hotel in Hamburg, where Weaver had given a reading under the kind auspices of the British Council, Nancy found that she was fresh out of sanitary towels (she tended to have heavy periods and went in for old-fashioned remedies). As it was two in the morning and long past the hour when chemists would be open (although across the street a blue neon light, which Weaver associated with Schultheiss Bier, was winking on and off), there seemed no solution (ELEFANTEN APOTHEKE! the sign signalled, then snapped off), and room service proved unhelpful.

On the evening before, Sir Kenneth Clark in bow tie and hush-puppies having dined very well with the *Burgermeister*, read a paper on 'Sign, Symbol, Image' in the same large conference room where Weaver had stood up and read his paper on 'The Forest as Metaphor and Place in the Works of Malaparte, Faulkner and Beckett' to a very thin gathering who listened with the keenest attention but none of them wished to ask any questions when the reading was over (*Der Zirkus* was showing at a local cinema), and now this.

'What do you expect me to do?' Weaver asked now. 'I can hardly phone up the good Dr Rosenstock at this hour, he would be long tucked up in his bed.'

'I'll try downstairs in reception,' Nancy said, and down she went in slippers and dressing-gown. What happened below scarcely bears repeating. Getting no satisfaction from 'a snotty bitch' in reception she had made her way to the very bowels of the big hotel, hoping to find a maid, but found instead a pale *sous-chef* rolling out pastry for a wedding reception on the morrow. Failing to explain her delicate predicament in a German becoming more laboured and erratic by the minute, thanks to her increasing embarrassment, she finally decided to mime her problem, opening her dressing-gown and, silently, beetroot red, pointed at her *mons veneris*. The poor man, holding a rolling pin in one hand, moved behind the table, shaking his head, fearing that he was in the presence of a nympho or worse.

Nancy had no luck that night and was reduced to plugging herself with lavatory paper of the very highest quality. A cold wind was blowing in a north-westerly direction from the Baltic. They had arrived that morning by train from Emden.

27

Baron Bogdana Kuguar
Puts the Wind Up Two *Hausfrau*s

One day when short of funds, Weaver was walking by the Paris Bar with Lore, and then rather put out of countenance to see approaching them whom but Pan Cogito and his Baroness, already making preparatory awkward gestures of greeting and sham delight.

Weaver kissed both round tight cheeks of the Baroness inclined for this homage, and introduced Lore.

'You are coming out or going in?'

'Well, neither,' Weaver said shiftily. 'Actually we are walking.'

'But you will have a drink with us?' Pan Cogito proposed.

Weaver looked at Lore and Lore at Weaver.

'Well . . .'

'Perhaps just . . .' Lore equivocated.

'. . . the one,' Weaver amended easily.

'March in then.'

So they trooped into the Paris Bar, Weaver, scraping and bowing, wondering whether he could hit Bog for a small tiding-over loan of say DM 50. Within another week another cheque would be in. They had the same paymaster in Bonn. Bog was in a sense the dark angel or hidden intermediary: for had he not been the guileless agent mediating between them and Fate they might never have met. Without Sepp Walser's misdirected phone call they would not have attended the same party. Unless Lore had known Sepp Walser they might never have met.

The Kuguars ordered coffee and brandy, Lore a glass of house red, and Weaver a draught beer and Steinhäger.

'The last time I was in here I ran into Reinhard Lettau,' Weaver said. 'You know him?'

'No.'

Bog crossed his stout Polish legs (bursting like sausage-casings) and looked around with a pleased expression, for the proximity of strong spirits always put him in a good humour. He who at first glance had seemed the very soul of afternoon sobriety was now seen to be in that pleasant state between moderate and immoderate insobriety where everything struck him, the relaxed observer of human foibles, as being highly amusing, a time of pratfalls. In particular the antics of a pair of stout *Hausfrau*s at a table near by, who were steadily putting away plates of piled *Kuchen*, seemed to engage his attention.

Bogdana watched the two *Hausfrau*s and Weaver covertly observed Bog. Here was a delicate situation that called for tact. An operation was required that Weaver was only too familiar with: The Touch, he thought to himself ruefully, 'as delicate as the turning inside-out of an eyelid', for he had at his beck and call a thesaurus of timely quotations, some more apt than others but all usable.

Bog was staring raptly-rudely at the slowly descending stiffly corseted determined no-longer-young rump that was slowly heavily yearningly descending (heavy as a heifer on a cowpat or the shadow of a helicopter on its landing pad), a great questing lump of sentient female matter. As it (the rump) was just about to meet the wide seat ready for it, Bog sprang up, with a most extraordinary smile fixed on his face, and offered one gracious hand (the right, or sword-hand) to the lady, who (in mid-air, as it were) responded for her part with an answering smile as strange frozen on her lips; while Bogdana's other hand, the left, was laid most gently and circumspectly on the stiffly corseted rump, hardly stroked before it had cleared imaginary crumbs and dust from the seat of the chair, to make all in readiness to receive her. It was a hidden gesture of extraordinary affrontery and recognized by the three who watched, and by the participant himself, now holding the hand of the subsidence, of the graciously subsiding but slightly embarrassed *Hausfrau*, with a fixed smile of gracious thanks fairly glued to her lips. Hand in hand now, however briefly, they might have been in some kind of a slow stately dance, a pavane, not a mazurka.

She was gustily breathing her thanks to him through her nose, fluttering her eyelids at him, she must have sensed he was a foreign gentleman (although he would have passed for a German). The smile fluttery, going on and off, the two hands just barely touching, Bog (the male partner very serious) with the 'ghost of a smile' on his lips, Baron Cogito as he might have led a dance with one of the kitchen staff (the cook?) in a manor house in Poland in the country before the war.

The expressions on the faces of the Baroness and Lore were sights to behold. The Baroness might have seen something vaguely similar before, when a furious husband had watched before brief words were exchanged and a duelling ground chosen, somewhere near an early morning wood in Poland. The Baroness was *alight* with pride in the Baron; in those quick glances she threw, Weaver seemed to detect cocked pistols and swords raised to lips, blood drained from faces, the caped seconds standing like statues, a surgeon at the ready; for honour had been besmirched and a wrong would have to be corrected, in a land where affronts to ladies were answered by bullets, sword-thrusts.

Lore looked as if she might rise up in her Prussian wrath (inside she was on fire) and fetch him a resounding buffet on the earhole, to teach him some manners and how to conduct himself properly with *German ladies*.

It seemed to Weaver, no participant, a mere observer, that

actions like these had been going on for a very long time in Europe and he (as a mere Irishman) had no part assigned; it was out of his ken, a code of honour that was lethal, blood speaking to blood; defending something obsolete as honour with forms of reprisal (the early morning duel) as obsolete. He thought of the German waiter standing stiffly to attention outside Kempinski's or was it Alexander's, the crimson cloth, the coffee and brandy, the cigars, the two Frenchmen cutting him up. Or the Spanish barman who had broken two dozen eggs deliberately on his kitchen floor because his hospitality had been impugned by another Spaniard; to attempt to pacify him, Weaver had laid a restraining hand on his chest and touched a trembling wall, hard as a castle in the sun: *Andalusian honour impugned! Banners! To arms!*

'May I?' Bog breathed, with outrageous impertinence.

She was a four-square Berlin *Hausfrau* in a corset of chain mail and with an amiable social manner as impregnable as chain mail. Pan Cogito the ex-Resistance hero must have recognized at once the mother of a *Wehrmacht* soldier, one of the field-grey ones who had run shouting *'Raus! Raus!'* across Poland for six long years of burning and raping and killing, a veritable orgy of destruction against all things Polish, from unborn babies (also murdered in the mothers) to grannies and all their homes burnt down. She might have bred three or more of such furies, released them to go *'Raus! Raus!'* through Poland, lining up the Jews before long ditches they had commanded them to dig, and dispatched them out of hand as if killing rats, which is what they had become in Nazi (German?) eyes, for Jews had ceased to be human. Special 'treats' were arranged for Resistance fighters captured by the NKVD, SS and Gestapo, and Bogdana Kuguar had been such a fighter, a brave one.

He must have known in his Polish blood and heart that here she was, the mother of all Polish misery, for his short hair was standing on end. Here was a Polish mastiff about to spring at the throat of his enemy. But of course Bog would not spring, he was much too much of a Polish gentleman; and the mother of his enemy (killed twenty-seven years before) was stuffing herself with rich *Kuchen*, for which she had a weakness, slowly easing herself down, rump foremost onto the spacious seat that he had so thoughtfully wiped clean for her; all was in readiness to receive that purposeful stall-fed complacent German bum.

Now he looked younger than his years or his grey hairs would admit, smiling that inexplicable fixed smile, a smile caught in the camera lens for a pose that was intended for his mother who was dead.

She was subsiding, a descending shadow, on a patch of clover already darkened by the great descending cowy shape, well uddered, soft and pendulous, she was *Die Rosi von der Alm*. And Zog, no polished Polish peasant but a rough cowhand in dirty leather jerkin tied about his middle and sweaty old hat worn back to front, for easy milking, was softly rubbing and stroking her great milky belly, urging her to a better yield. A *very* dirty sweated-into crumpled hat worn back to front to facilitate milking when pressed against Rosi's side and he could hear (with a halfwit's glad, sunny smile) the deep rumbling of milk as within a great deep Polish churn and his knowing fingers were squeezing pint after pint of creamy milk into the bucket, and he was adjusting the sweaty hat on his round peasant skull, Rosi and himself pestered (for it was high summer) by swarms of eager Polish flies.

Judging the time to be ripe now (for no one had suggested a second round), Weaver took out his yellow Spanish Bic retractable, snapped it into the firing position and swiftly scrawled on the back of the Paris Bar menu: *Temporarily embarrassed and need some of the readies*. He was about to add: *Can you do the decent?* but wrote instead: *Can you oblige?* Signed it DILDO and pushed it across towards Bog who had now turned his attention from the Great Milker Rosi (or was it Heidi?) and the smile was gone from his face. Rosi (or Heidi) with shoulders bowed and arms moving with contained power, as if breast-stroking, was wolfing into the heaped plate of *Kuchen*.

Here Bogdana was stumped. His French was fluent, his German more than adequate, he could get around in Italian, knew some Greek, but his English was poor and this seemed gibberish: what were readies? He stared at the scrawl and then into the hazel Irish eyes with his blue Polish eyes. You are *embarrassed*? Do you suppose I am *not*, old fornicator? (his glance seemed to say). He practised a calm dissimulation. For was he not being asked to subsidize (not only subscribe to) DILDO cuckoldry – *another* cuckoldry, for Weaver's was not the only one, marriages were breaking up like ice-floes in the spring all over Berlin. Were Poles open-handed like the Irish, Weaver wondered, Weaver who never had anything anyway. Certainly he (Bog) was not too happy about it. Was he already worrying about getting it back? The amount (a modest DM 50) would not bankrupt him.

Bog studied the scrawl, his hand cupped about a cigarette, but could make nothing of it, shrugging his shoulders and muttering '*Nyet*', and pushed the menu back to Weaver, who stroked the Bic through this message and tried another tack: *Sine pecunia* (how do you say 'I want . . . I need' in Latin?). *Can you lend me DM 50?* and pushed it across. Bog took out a pair of old spectacles, cleaned the lenses with a tissue, affixed them on his nose and studied this carefully.

'Ahhh,' he said, 'aahha, *now* I get it. That might be arranged,' he said in a tactful aside, but vaguely as if the matter did not greatly concern him, still staring abstractly at Rosi, who was still munching away; his thoughts were elsewhere.

So that was that. No subvention, no round. It was time to leave. Bog summoned a waiter.

They walked to the car, Bog talking torrentially. The small car looked as if it had been driven all the way from Kraków – a battered Lada.

'Where do you walk to?'

'Oh, around you know,' Weaver said. 'Around and about. The Tiergarten probably.'

'Hop in,' cried the Baroness, adjusting her motoring goggles. 'I drive at pro*digious* speed. Bogdana map-reads. We are safe.'

'We are not,' said Bog, climbing into the passenger's seat alongside the Baroness, who was puffing out her cheeks and pulling on gloves.

But they had not gone far when Bog cried out to stop.

'Stop. I must urrr-inate.'

Then he was out with a hop, skip and a jump, running for cover and already undoing his flies, had presently vanished into the high drenched bushes, for a shower had fallen while they were inside the Paris bar.

The vinyl seating at the back had gashes in it as though attacked by knives, a plaid rug was stretched over the front seat, a small memo pad (blank) was clipped to the dashboard, the Baroness was observing Weaver with an amused look in the little mirror.

Then she looked out towards the drenched bushes into which Bog had disappeared.

'My husband . . .'

'Is a dear man,' Weaver finished for her.

The Baroness laughed, stroking the plastic steering wheel with one finger of her glove. 'That was not *exactly* my thought,' she said, still holding Weaver's eye in the mirror. 'My dear husband is a madman. Sometimes I wonder what he would have been like without the horrible war. Perhaps quite dull. Another man.'

'There is always war in Poland,' Weaver said after a silence.

'That is true. Sadly true,' the Baroness agreed. 'There will always be war in Poland,' nodding.

Presently Bog appeared again, headless, carrying a huge bunch of drenched yellow-and-white laburnum before him; and this with some difficulty was forced in through the window and into the back, behind Lore.

'Drive on!'

Now they came to a roundabout and the two stout *Hausfrau*s of the Paris Bar were about to leave the pedestrian precinct and make the crossing to the island in the middle and from there across the perilous way to the far pavement, but had not counted on Bog who urged the Countess to accelerate about the roundabout and sticking his head and great bully shoulders out the window he was howling some of the more rousing staves of the Polish partisan song ('Jak nie Teraz, to Kiedy?') at the two hestitating *Hausfrau*s now marooned on the island in the middle and having misgivings about proceeding any further, because of the madman howling abuse at them in Polish or Russian, as the Baroness drove at a methodical 35 mph three and then four times about the circle. The two *Hausfrau*s now had the wind up them, for the brown Lada went around and around like a toy stuck on its circuit and the lunatic leaning out the window and making rude signs now with a hydrophobic foaming at the mouth looked and sounded demented.

'On,' Bog said, smiling a tight smile. 'We mustn't alarm them.'

Now began the struggle to catch and release the bumblebee. The pollen-glutted bee had crawled out of the drenched laburnum and propelled itself towards the windscreen and the light between Baroness Kasia and Pan Cogito, sunken into his seat and brooding, both of them staring straight ahead in catatonic trances as though speeding at 90 mph and not a steady 35 mph. A page of the blank memo pad was used to induce the bee to climb onto it and from there be released into the open through Bog's window.

And that was that.

On parting (no DM 50 denomination note slipped discreetly into Weaver's hand) the Baroness offered Lore a tiny frozen smile (the rarest of Polish orchids) and the back of her hand for Weaver to assay a gallant *Handkuss* (does one fall on one knee?) and then the Kuguars drove away in high style, with much hallooing and valedictory hand-waving out side windows. The back window was still blocked up with a great pile of drenched laburnum.

'Now what?' Lore asked. 'I cannot ask my father to lend me money.'

'And I certainly cannot beg favours of my wife.'

'No.'

'Do we get credit from Luigi of Rusticano?'

'We do not *ask*, dearest Schmutz. We do not *need* money. Let us walk through the Tiergarten.'

So they walked hand in hand, without a pfennig between them, through all the bronzed and burnished boscage of the Tiergarten.

28
An Irish Submarine in Palma Bay

Un día, un día como ningún otro,
un día como hoy . . .

When sufficiently tanked up, Bart Murnane craved not only to be
a poet – for he was that already – but an Outstanding Irish Poet (a
neat trick for a fellow born in Panama); he had to be Irish to be
that good, a second Willie Yeats. Of Irish *extraction* would not do;
it had to be the real thing, root and branch, the peerless bloodline
reaching back to quarrelsome Finn; to Con of the Hundred
Battles.

He had been expecting his first-born, Miranda, the only girl in
a family of four boys, to fly in from Dublin two days previously
but she had yet to show up. He had been drinking more or less
non-stop for two days when he took a taxi ride out to Palma
airport to meet his old Dublin amigo and his new Berlin girl who
had flown in at dusk from Tempelhof, twenty-four hours late.

Now it was the morning after.

On the evening and night before they had managed to get
through sixteen bottles of good red wine with some assistance
from a friend who had stayed for a couple of hours. Weaver had
helped Sasha stack the dead men in the yard that morning and the
count was sixteen. She had retired at two in the morning and

Lore soon after; the two amigos had stayed up smoking and drinking until the small hours.

'Talking about what? Gassing about women?'

'Not at all. The eternal verities, what else is there to talk about?'

'Oh *them*!'

It was a hot blue May day in Palma when they set out with the very best intentions on a sobering walk through the wild garlic in El Bosque de Bellver; but didn't make it past Vera's bar at the bottom of the hill on the borders of Torreno. Seeking the missing *querencia*, that unique and lovely word, just the three of them, Bart Murnane with his stout blackthorn, Lore in dark glasses like the cover of *Elle*, Weaver with his suffering liver.

He and Lore had left the chill north behind them and flown into this Southern summer, missing a charter flight that had flown off as they watched, and now the stone was warm to the touch (that impress of absolute sunshine) and abundant wild flowers were sprouting from the Mallorcan walls. From an open patio door of an apartment block a lovely love-ravaged young woman ran to the balcony rail and instead of throwing herself over the rail at Weaver's feet was leaning over, smiling at Weaver (pacing along wrapped in silence next to Lore), and called down:

'*Kann mir einer von euch sagen, welchen Tag wir heute haben – Montag oder Dienstag? Ich scheine die Übersicht verloren zu haben.*'

They had halted in midstride as she called and were now trapped as in a colour photo or freeze-framed in some (French?) movie: the bulky bad-tempered-looking man in the white cotton suit with a shock of upstanding white hair and a blackthorn stick on which he was leaning and frowning, the pale-faced brunette staring straight ahead, her inside companion gaping at the wall. Three halfwits escaped from an asylum, perhaps? He didn't reply because he didn't know, or hadn't heard? Were they perhaps dummies out for a ramble? They were not speaking.

Were they not on speaking terms? The bulky man on the outside with the mane of white hair would have made an exemplary Plantagenet; he had a dangerous glow about him, should have worn a cape and carried a cane. The fellow on her near side was dressed in autumnal shades of brown perhaps intended to merge into any background (except snow), brown corduroy trousers shiny at the knee, bushboots, a hunting-jacket the brown of mallard duck's chest and wing markings, a goatee and pointed nose that gave him an anxious foxy look, but overall the appearance of an alarmed grouse about to take wing. The brunette in the middle was simply a gorgeous dark doll, the paleness of the face suggesting a dissipated lifestyle. Why had they stopped? Why were they staring?

'*¿Digame por favor: que día es hoy?*'

No response.

(Weaver saw the living Palma walls on which the hot life-giving sun shone and the flies that crawled over it and the little insects that teemed over it and the marguerites and white and yellow roses and deep fuchsia gladioli and jasmine and tiny climbing roses and above that a railing and two female hands clasping it and a beautiful but certainly ravaged face bending down and smiling at him, her face another flower in May.)

'*Pardonnez-moi, m'sieur, mais quel jour est-il aujourd'hui?*'

No response; she might have been addressing statues.

'What day of the week is it?' she tried in English as a last resort, for this peculiar-looking but silent trio did not look in the least English.

'Why it's a blue day in May,' Weaver said at last, still staring at the wall, as if in reply to a riddle. Bart Murnane was most fluent in these three languages but for reasons of his own was saying nothing, frowning, leaning further forward on his blackthorn. Lore could speak these languages but the question had not been directed at her.

Weaver was recalling a famous still (the lifer dancing out

between the walls) from the great old movie by Abram Room, *The Ghost That Never Returns*, in Roger Manvell's Penguin film guide, the index of which he and his younger brother could visualize at will, so that a frame brought back a movie and a title (*Gösta Berling, The Atonement of*), when all days were different, and all days the same, in the depths of the summer in County Kildare, when the world was a different place.

A man, scowling alarmingly, had now appeared alongside the pretty smiling woman and put his arm about her waist, a very thin summer frock, as if protectively.

'I know you three,' the man said rudely. 'You are three characters escaped out of *Under the Volcano*.'

Which of us is the Consul? Weaver thought, minutely examining the teeming life on the wall; and the answer came promptly down, as if the rude fellow above could read his thoughts, for he was pointing at Weaver now.

'You [pointing] are the silly bugger – Hugh with the silly name.'

'Would you have said that if I had the walking-stick?' Weaver asked, as if addressing the insects.

'Oh shut up.'

'Now can we go ón?' Weaver asked the wall.

Above his head the young woman gave a silvery peal of laughter, a really lovely free laugh.

'*Hoy es miercoles . . . porque perdimos un dia*,' Lore said, as if under duress, creating a sensation above; they looked at each other in open delight and embraced.

'*C'est mercredi*,' Lore said. 'It must be Wednesday, because we lost a day in Berlin.'

*Sen*sation!

As they walked on they heard the enraptured pair fairly whooping with delight, because it was Wednesday, and going back again hand-in-hand into the Edificio Neptuno.

'Some people are easy to please,' laughed Bart Murnane, waving his blackthorn at the sky.

At the foot of the hill on the border of Torreno they came upon a certain sign which proclaimed in a coaxingly low voice: VERA'S BAR.

They came to a halt.

'Do these old eyes deceive me?' Weaver asked, blinking like a mole.

Bart Murnane ground his blackthorn as though something momentous had suddenly been decided and said:

'They do *not*. Now here's a thing and a very fine thing too. I think you'll like Vera, one of us and a very, how shall I put it? . . . *acrobatic* lady. She once worked in a circus. Her Spanish boyfriend Vincente Fango was a bullfighter of sorts. Hell, he was a *cowardly* bullfighter. Now he trains dolphins. When Vera's had a few she likes to toss him about the bar.'

'Sounds just like Weaver's kind of place,' Lore said, smiling her sunny smile, stroking her hair.

'Now *one* sobering drink couldn't kill us,' Bart Murnane suggested persuasively. 'Would it?'

'Oh I wouldn't be too sure about that,' Weaver said.

'But let's give it a whirl anyway.'

And in they marched. Lore, pale as La Belle Dame Sans Merci, smiling weakly. They would certainly see.

All days are different; all days are the same.

They walked into a pleasant bar where cured goat hung by shrimping nets from the low ceiling; seafaring mementos in the way of anchors, belaying pins, clocks and tridents were strewn about and Vera herself waiting to serve them.

'This is Vera herself,' Murnane now confirmed. 'Some friends fresh in from Berlin where it is colder than here. We need your strongest and most certain curative potion, m'dear. A potent Bloody Mary might work wonders. Three, *por favor*.'

A tall, upright, clean-shaven, fair-haired, well-scrubbed sober sailor was drinking by himself on the other side of the horseshoe-shaped bar and pretending not to hear. Off an English submarine that had put into Palma the day before, Vera imparted in a soft aside. Weaver thought: Tinder-box has drawn perceptibly closer to powder-keg. The sailor (no doubt from Liverpool or worse, swallowing his afflicted consonants and tortured vowels, spewing out scouse) would only have to open his mouth for Bart Murnane, the ardent patriot and xenophobic honorary Irishman, to explode. Considering the amount of drink already taken, the flint had been well and truly primed.

Bart Murnane was studying him over the rim of his first Bloody Mary, while talking of this and that to Weaver and Lore. Discipline and training in Her Majesty's Navy had imparted that scoured and scrubbed neatness; from the tassels of his sailor's cap down to his highly polished black boots he was a credit to the service.

'Will you just look at Paddy over there,' Bart Murnane called across, 'neat as a new pin.'

'Me?' said the submariner. 'I'm not Paddy, mate. Got the wrong man.'

'I've got the right man.'

Vera was pulling another pint of lager, saying nothing, musing on her hand that was grasping the beer-pull decorated with a fox-hunting scene in rural England; a huntsman in red with whip raised jumping a wide ditch on a bay gelding; Vera musing still on the easy flow into the glass, not looking at Bart who she knew could be difficult, in his cups.

'We're celebrating,' he called across now. 'I'll buy you this one, Paddy. This one on me.'

The tall sailor was smiling into his empty glass, uncertain of how to take this.

'Come over here and drink with us, you goddamn redheaded Irishman,' Bart Murnane called over in a good-natured way.

There was little malice in the man; a touch of wildness at times, but he was childlike in his wildness, almost cuddly, if you can imagine a cuddlesome gorilla.

The sailor had now decided how he would correctly respond: whipping off his sailor's cap he trapped it with elbow by his left side, the other hand free for the full pint measure, which he carried across without spilling a drop.

'Blimey, mate, I'm not Irish. Me mum came from Dagenham and my dad came from Bognor and I was born and grew up there. I'm not called Paddy. How could I be Irish?'

'Don't believe a word of that,' Murnane confided to Weaver. 'He's ashamed of his Irish blood. He's not from Bognor nor Dagenham, but from Dundrum. Listen to that broad Dublin accent. He's a jackeen.'

'Cor,' said the neat submariner, half closing his eyes and lowering his head, to dive back into his foaming pint with hardly a splash.

He had placed his service cap carefully on the bar counter as if it might slip off. All his movements were neat and controlled and he was trying not to look too hard at Lore, deprived as he surely had been of female company for months at a stretch on his mysterious voyages in the depths of the oceans. Mick Murnane now placed this service cap at a rakish angle on Lore's dark head.

'Can you do a hornpipe, Paddy?'

'I'm Lance Bartle,' the submariner told Lore.

'You won't be called Lance here,' Mick Murnane said. 'No Bartles allowed either. This is an all-Irish bar. We won't have it any other way. Look at those periwinkle blue eyes, that gingery hair, those freckled hands, Irish to the core.'

The embarrassed submariner tucked his hands behind his back, in case they might be cut off; his tow-coloured hair was trimmed short, he had gooseberry-coloured eyes that rarely blinked (long watches at the periscope?), pale submariner's indoor hands and he stood up very clean and neat, tightly contained within his naval uniform, the black boots polished to a high sheen. Asking to be excused he retired to the Gents, for he could not make head or tail of Bart Murnane and was uncertain whether he was being ribbed or ridiculed.

'Well . . .' Lore said, hoping that this mockery would abate, placing the service cap back where Bart Murnane had found it.

Bart Murnane made a circular motion with his hand to indicate the same again.

'Would you, ahem, be Aherne or Robartes?' Weaver asked.

Bart Murnane was smiling into his fresh Bloody Mary, before dipping his smiling lips into it.

'Isn't it St Patrick's Day again that's in it!' he said rather loudly, 'and here comes the bold Paddy again. Let me at least introduce ourselves. This lovely lady on my immediate left is Nora MacCool of Dungarvan in County Waterford. And the reprobate on my right is Professor Dallan Weaver of Trinity College in Dublin, the man who single-handed refuted the French Heideggereans over there in the Sorbonne. That's him, all modesty, standing there. Shake his hand. He had them all eating humble pie, those hop-o'-my-thumbs that call themselves French philosophers.'

'Pleased to meetcha,' said Paddy, shaking hands with a powerfully sustained man-grip.

'Do they serve drinks down below in your submarine, Paddy me boy?' Bart Murnane asked in a jovial man-to-man way.

'No problem there, squire. Newcastle Brown, Heinekens, anything you fancy in tins.'

'And I,' said Bart Murnane in a lordly way, laying the joined fingers of his right hand high on his chest, 'am Mehawl Kerry James Mulchinock of Cahirciveen in the Kingdom of Kerry. A great-grandson of the man who composed – if that is the word – "The Rose of Tralee", a bloody lovely chune.'

'I read somewhere of a man in a suit of armour found in the stomach of a shark,' Weaver said, to keep the ball rolling. 'I'd feel the same in a submarine myself. My mother had desperate claustrophobia. She couldn't go to Mass.'

'It's a sight safer than a bus, matey. You could cop it in a car or snuff it crossing the street in today's traffic. Not in this boat. You're as safe as houses down there.'

'Which would be worse: to be buried alive in the earth or drown in forty fathoms? I know water is our first element, but does that make it any easier? There were five hundred African miners buried near Johannesburg when I was there, and they were never dug out . . . any more than the crowd who went down with the *Thetis* submarine in Liverpool Bay and stayed down. Liverpool Bay is comparatively shallow I believe, but it was much too deep for the *Thetis*, stuck in the mud.'

'I read about that,' Paddy said, 'it happened just before the war broke out in 1939.'

'But is it possible,' Lore said, 'could a big shark swallow a man in armour? Is he big enough?'

'Is he *shark* enough?' Mehawl Mulchinock interposed here.

'How long did the lads in the *Thetis* last? Twelve hours? Longer? It must have seemed very long to them. Say the lights give out. They can hear their mates banging the sides with clawhammers. The airs gets foul. They lose control of their bowels . . . they're shitting and howling in the darkness. No one can help. It's Hell. Howling and shitting they go to their Maker.'

This produced a thoughtful silence.

'Talking of shitting and howling,' Weaver persisted, 'will you ever forget your man Behan? He used to beshit himself copiously and simultaneously vomit up his draught Guinness when I had the great misfortune to know him in Dublin. The Guards wouldn't lay a finger on him because he stank like a polecat. Worse. A Dublin northside drain or wherever he came from; he didn't change much really. When bounders abounded in Dublin, he was the worst.'

'Brendan Bean?' the submariner inquired.

'The very man. That's the lad. The Quare Fellow himself, Ireland's own. I used to pity him. When the Yanks take anyone to their heart, the great common heart shallow and commonplace as a bedpan, the subject is in bad trouble. Do you remember the talking jay-bird in the bar at Jury's? A very dirty *Nestbeschmutzer* which some Dublin bowsie had trained to say, in exactly the northside bowsie voice but a bit tinny and hollow: "Are-yiz-sober-yet?" He sounded like a bird that smoked sixty a day and swallowed God knows how many pints. He reminded me of Brendan.'

'I don't recall any jailbirds in Jury's,' Mehawl said, rubbing his nose, 'which one had you in mind, of the ones we knew?'

'Ticketyboo then,' said the submariner suddenly. 'See you later, alligators. I must report back.' Having swallowed the last of his lager he was preparing to cast off.

'He wants to show us over his submarine,' Lore whispered in Weaver's ear. 'He asked me to ask you. He's so proud of it. Shall we have a look, Schmutz?'

'What's this? What's all *this*?' demanded the patriot, swivelling around. 'Are we getting messages in code? Well, let me tell you, I wouldn't *set foot* on a bloody English submarine even if you paid me,' here roundly striking the wood with the palm of calloused handball champion's right hand. 'No, siree . . . the GAA wouldn't allow it,' he added in conclusive bigotry. 'So there!'

The submariner began to smile a crafty smile (entering now into the spirit of the thing) and glanced slyly at Lore.

'But she's not an English submarine, guv,' he said. 'Not on your Nelly. She's as Irish as yourself.'

'Was she blessed by the Archbishop? I daresay not.' He stood up to throw a withering look at his opponent, roaring out: 'Now we'll have none of that lowdown English trickery and conniving here! (eyeing him with a hostile unsmiling Irish eye). None of your lip, you young pup! You are among fierce Gaels here – heroes all!'

'But I'm Irish . . . struth. Amn't I your pal Paddy from . . . where am I from?' he asked Weaver.

'Buttevant.'

'I'm Paddy your butty from Buttevant. Paddy the junior

handball champion of all Ireland. *Now* do you believe me?'

'Of course she was blessed by the Archbishop,' Weaver now saw fit to add. 'What are you thinking of, man? Otherwise she wouldn't be let down the slip. Wasn't she christened the *Lily of Killarney* by McQuaid himself on Palm Sunday in Dublin docks at a sung High Mass, assisted by four bishops and a monsignor from Rome itself, and piped down into the water by the Artane Boys' Band.'

'Oh then we might chance a look over her,' the fierce patriot said seating himself and graciously conceding the point. He looked around under twitching eyebrows and fixed on smiling Lore.

'Are *you* Irish?'

Certainly I am,' said Lore, laughing into his face. 'Amn't I dark Noreen and isn't Weaver here my Irish boyfriend and amn't I the most fortunate girl in all Ireland [squeezing Weaver's arm] to have him? Of *course* I am!'

'Well then by God we'll have a look over her. Finish your drinks, lads. No, we'll take them with us. Take *my* arm [to smiling Lore], and off with the lot of us!'

So they tottered out, brimming glasses in hand, festive as a wedding reception on a long wet weekend at Kinnegad, for Mehawl to hail a passing taxi, telling the driver to take them to the Irish submarine. He continued raving in the taxi. And Weaver assured him that the driver was indeed Irish, a man from Kilcock with two sisters holy nuns, and the taxi likewise was Irish. Mehawl renamed himself Donnacha Og Macgillycuddy Glanaruddery 'Stacks' O'Mealdoon Muchinlock of Farranfore.

'Who can tell a funny Irish story?' he demanded of the back of the taxi-driver's brown leathery neck. 'Who without a single error can recite twenty verses of melodious Gaelic folkspiel? Who can sing a great sobbing Irish song?'

'Not in here please,' Weaver said, running down the window to let in fresh air, 'no diddley-diddley shit in a confined space.'

'Who can lep over twelve Guinness barrels laid end to end? Who can drink eighteen pints without pissing? Who can vault a five-bar gate in the dark? Who can hold a candle to my princely self, in all fairness now? Who is unquestionably the Daddy of Them All? *Misé!* Mehawl Donnacha Og!'

So they went bowling along through the lovely blue Palma day.

'Is this a nuclear sub, Paddy me boy? We refuse to be palmed off with anything less than a real nuke sub.'

'She's a nuke all right. We have been . . . here and there. All the way to Australia without surfacing.'

And at that point they drew up smartly alongside the black submarine moored on the quayside and flying the Union Jack, which the patriot was diplomatic enough not to see or make any comment on, busying himself with a thousand-peseta note in his fist, asking 'What's the damage?' or rather '*¿Cuánto te debo?*'

They came to the mole, fancy having run its course, and saw the snouted nuclear sub moored securely to the Palma quay with stout hawsers, the sinister dark-grey matt conning tower and hull towering up out of the water, and all the more sinister for the absence of visible weapons (down below the press-button missiles were programmed to wipe out whole cities). A sailor was stowing or coiling a warp on the narrowly exposed deck, keeping an eye on comings and goings along the mole.

'Is this by any chance the SS *Brian Boru*, coxswain, or have we got the good ship *Venus?*'

'Yep, that's me, squire. I'm Brian Boru. Welcome aboard.'

'Step aboard!' sang out Paddy from behind, urging them on. 'Onward and downward, but watch your step.'

'Watch your head here,' said the warp-coiler on the conning tower.

'Bit late for that now,' murmured Mehawl, advancing as though bearing a heavy crozier. '*Dignum et iustum est.*'

'Dignum's dead and gone below,' Weaver said, descending with a good deal of misgiving ('This thing gives me the creeps'), followed by Lore who was closely followed by mumbling Mehawl, all bowing their heads as if entering a Holy Place.

Inside the humming nuclear submarine a quasi-religious hush obtained; there appeared to be various crucial levels leading ever downwards on to even deeper passages; convolutions of whispering and murmuring pipes at their endless atomic tick-tocking, gushes of bad oily air and the murmuring of men's voices hidden away in their cramped quarters.

Going down out of the bright Mallorcan sun into its grim nuclear innards, Weaver, a sensitive soul, thought vaguely (being disturbed in spirit) of various things and times and with a feeling akin to awe and reverence (as in the presence of death); here was a lethal death-dealer over vast areas of longitude and latitude and on a gigantic scale at that.

It had the feeling of a great cathedral broken down. Weaver thought of barrel-vaulted ceilings of Hiberno-Romanesque churches lying in ruins and open to the elements, crows cawing, cattle scratching themselves on chancel arches, the steep-corbelled stone roof in bits on the grassy mound, with incised slabs and crosses depicting scriptural incidents, all these emblematic stones numbered and catalogued and crated for transportation across the ocean.

A crawling sensation came over him of being trapped (aged sixteen) in a hole in a high plantation wall leading into a forbidden (Protestant) wood near a narrow shallow-flowing river in Kildare, his home; or again, looking down (he was forty) into the darkness of the *toril* at the Málaga bullring, out of which glistening black bulls would charge, one by one, to their death at the hands of the posturing toreros; or again (now he was sixty, getting on), trapped in pitch darkness in the voluntary dark of the passage-grave at Newgrange; or again (lastly, but a year back) in Kinsale he was letting himself down into a muggy Protestant crypt in St Multose cemetery in search of a lost cat: Chupi.

And now they were going off in three different directions.

Mehawl went rampaging through the nuclear sub like Serge Blanco through the English defence.

'By God no, I wouldn't set *foot* in a bloody English submarine! The GAA wouldn't have it! Who can vault a five-bar gate? Who can puck a hurley ball the length of a field? Tell me who is *half* the man I am? Mehawl James Kerry O Mulchinock, the Bald Fox from Farranfore! *Half* the man! I'll fight any man who says he is! By Christ I'll destroy the man who says he *isn't*!'

This concluding sally was drowned out by a storm of laughter as though the patriot had found his audience somewhere below in the very bowels of the nuclear sub, having now reached the evanescent stage of inebriation where everything uttered seemed coruscatingly witty; and now Weaver, hearing the nearer murmur of voices, came upon an open door. Inside were layers of bunks on which sprawled submariners soberly writing aero-gramme letters home, smoking and drinking canned lager, studying the nudes in pornographic magazines.

'Where's the mad Irishman?' they called out, ruffling the pages and laughing.

'Ever put in at Mahon in Minorca?' Weaver asked the nearest sprawler.

'I've been there, matey, yes.'

'I suppose you can't say where you have just come from or where you are going? Mum's the word, what?'

'That's right, mate.'

In the distance, below, could be heard the moose-like belling of Mehawl, stirring up gales of laughter wherever he went.

'Are you with the mad Irishman? Are you Irish?'

'Yes,' Weaver said, 'I'm Irish. He's actually American . . . at least born in Panama. Who is your captain? Who drives this thing?'

'Captain Mahinnick.'

'A Cornishman? I know Fowey.'

'He's from St Austell.'

'You feel safe with him?'

'You could say that.'

Lore now created a sensation in the cubbyhole by appearing very flushed and excited at Weaver's shoulder (the cover-girl straight from *Penthouse* who had just thrown on some clothes) with Paddy just behind her, having shown her where the torpedoes were fired.

'Shouldn't we go?' she suggested hotly into his ear. 'I've been down in the engine-room, but I think it's time to go. Where's your friend?'

Some of the sprawlers followed Mehawl and party on deck and were for piping them ashore but officers were present on the quayside now and they settled for three rousing cheers, led by 'Paddy' Bartle who waved his cap.

Thus ended the boarding of the Irish submarine which was seen now to be named HMS *Triplex* and not the *Lily of Killarney*, but no remarks were passed. It had been a day not unfree of incident and there seemed no further need to pass any remarks. They left the three empty Bloody Mary glasses in a neat row on the conning tower, to show that they had been down below.

29

The Miraflores Docks
(Adios, Danny Boy!)

Bart legless, half-seas-over, and Bart cold sober were two different persons, two quite different propositions, as Jekyll and Hyde or the tides of Atlantic and Pacific.

At one o'clock in the afternoon of the day following the bash at Vera's and the visit to the 'Irish' submarine, he came down for lunch shaved and showered in sharply ironed yet yellowish flannels, a white Panama-style shirt with monogram BM emblazoned on the chest, shiny snakeskin boots with trim tango heels, a white silk cravat about the neck, scented with fine pomade and *savon*, and to all intents and purposes as sober as a judge.

After their return by taxi from the mole, Weaver and Lore had retired to bed; not so the bold Mehawl, who had sallied out again into the night, humming to himself, Sasha told Weaver, while helping stack more 'dead men' in the patio.

'Humming! Looking for what?'

'How should I know? Looking for trouble, most likely.'

'That man has the constitution of an alligator,' said Weaver, marvelling.

Two timid lunch-guests bowing like Orientals, a subdued local couple, joined the luncheon party presided over by Bart Murnane in the manner of a Roman Imperator (Pompey?) returned from a successful campaign.

But by three o'clock he would be back again in his bedroom, relaxed on the canopied double bed in his boxer shorts or standing on the balcony, a veritable Mussolini, where he could keep a circumspect eye on his silent boys gliding about in the semi-tropical garden below, Pawnee on the warpath or frontiersmen tracking buffalo; guarded by walls, Titus Elijah armed with a .22 rifle was in training for marksmanship in the XXI Olympiad to he held in Tokyo, was it, in 1976. Titus, the wordless one, could sniff out wild garlic in the Bosque de Bellver. This silent one had said nothing during the meal, quite the obverse of his garrulous da.

'I guess you guys heard of the Miraflores Docks.'

The cowed couple fumbled with their napkins, wiped their lips, cleared their throats, said nothing. Sasha glowed.

'In Balboa and Panama City the evening baseball games would have started about now in the parks.'

With the best will in the world, Weaver could not bring himself to believe anything he said; it all seemed some clever fantasy that he was spinning out to baffle his listeners and in baffling them amuse himself. Was he so devious?'

He gave it out that he had been born in Colón in the Canal Zone of an Irish father who had prospered. He had moved with his parents to the United States after graduating from Balboa High ('all the teachers assholes'). They had settled in Chicago, the windy city. If you wanted the wind put up you, that was the place to go; if you made it in Chicago you would make it anywhere. Bart told his paw: 'Paw, I wanna be a pote.' His hard-working father showed his calloused hands. 'Son, forgit it – that haint no trade.'

His grades had been far from great. 'Wise up, son.' His mum said: 'Folly your instincts, Bart. Don't mind yore paw.'

So Bart had quit, lit out for the territory. Thereafter he had vanished into his work. What exactly that work was, nobody knew. Then he was thought to be in Europe. A distant relative had seen him or his double walking in Paris. He was learning languages, sharpening his wits; already he had fluent Spanish, had met Picasso, knew Miró. And then he disappeared.

When he resurfaced he had acquired a mad gollywog mop of hair like one of the Three Stooges (Mo?) and a wife, a Russian Jewess from Odessa, Sasha Barathea; and was the proud if absentminded father of five fine children – Weaver could only remember the names Titus Elijah and Miranda – with an attractive tiled house in Palma de Mallorca, on regular calling terms with Miró and Graves, and settled on the Bollingen payroll for life. He had it made.

But could you believe any of this? Was it all a front, a cover? For what? For a start, the very name seemed bogus, a bad cover. Nancy was of the opinion that he was perhaps one of those CIA agents planted in Ireland, a sleeping mole. With funds from prize-money for translations from the Spanish of Borges and Cela he had purchased a small island off the coast of Donegal. It was their bolt-hole. The island was smaller than Inishbofin or Tory Island, not marked on any maps, with an Irish name that nobody could understand or translate.

Take this message, commit all to memory, swallow paper, over.

The nameless island off Donegal (paid for by Hoover via a bogus prize) was a station for monitoring the movements of Soviet subs lurking in the Rockall Deep.

They had over a long period rented out an unfurnished flat in Fitzwilliam Square, the topmost apartment of what once had been servants' quarters. The flat was within easy reach of a number of embassies and high enough for transmitting coded messages to Hoover ('The hens are laying fine . . . We've put down some good manure . . . We are mending the fences, over'). Are you following me now? And all this from the proceeds of translations from the Spanish – can we swallow that? Does a bear shit in the woods?

The Bollingen sinecure left him free to travel extensively in Europe with Herbert Read, allegedly on Bollingen business. He had a signed Picasso sketch inscribed '*Para Bart Murnane*' which had presumably been faked. He had *almost* met Señor Borges (walking with a 'vacillating tread' on Spanish soil for the first time) and had published an amusing account of this incident that had never happened. Oh he was his own man. He had it made. But . . .

So he shed his various skins as a rattler its scales. Even the innocent travels around Europe (in Lisbon, in Prague) took on a suspect tinge; and how could anybody make any kind of a decent living from translating Borges and Unamuno into English? Sasha dressed up to take dictation. The translations of bounding Cela seemed a complete fabrication; Bart had written another novel to amuse himself and one far superior to the original: *The Dirty Rascal*.

Every word he uttered might be a sort of code. The Miraflores Docks! He had acquired a family of five as the beasts of the wilds engender and breed with a fine disregard for the consequences of mating, of consanguinity, without any thought, seasonally and casually with this mate or that, with the minimum of fuss and bother, and with no obligations thereafter to his issue; as the tomcat that does not know its own kittens, and indeed might devour them, as food.

Was paternity, too, another pose, another disguise? Who was this fellow anyway? He was an enigma, a puzzler all right. He was: *intimado* of the vain Roberto Graves who lived not far off in fabled Deyá; knew also Robert Creeley (so far he had failed to write even one distinguished sentence), and had given a public poetry reading with self-seekers Ginsberg and Corso on a nudist beach outside Rome.

Once he had been a meat-delivery man for a Bronx butcher but had lost his job when the van shed its load as he was dreamily composing verse at the wheel. He was of a mischievous bent and had once persuaded the staid and proper Liam Miller of Dolmen Press that Weaver's wife was an easy lay and had only to be asked by the right man. The pair of them had him well tanked up and escorted over to Weaver's apartment in an advanced state of intoxication, where he had fallen through the doorway with a low moan on catching sight of the lovely Nancy advancing to meet him; and lay on the floor mumbling indecencies while polite conversation continued above his head.

Of course he knew Ferlinghetti ('another prize asshole') and the Beat who had climbed mountains – was it McClure? He knew shiftier characters as well, fringe people with small talent but large pretensions such as the Canadian academic tyro with terrible BO who fancied Sasha, sculpted in plastic, and sometimes 'overnighted' in the Fitzwilliam attic and made his awful presence felt in the Arts Club just around the corner. They had to fumigate the flat after his departure with reeking armpits and a final blast of halitosis. He knew, too, the very devious translator and 'friend' of Borges; he who might have been the casual arriver out of the night who had stayed long enough to father one of Sasha's preternaturally silent sons. But who could tell?

Miranda Murnane finally caught a flight from Dublin and joined them for lunch. Father Bart was unfolding his napkin and crossing his flannelled legs, demonstrating the fine quality of the snakeskin boots bought in Texas.

'Do not despair, one of the thieves was saved,' he told Weaver. 'We have secured alternative accommodation near at hand. It will be just like home.'

The alternative accommodation was indeed novel: a room within a bar. At the foot of a long flight of steps stood the Bar Mar Puig; a French-Algerian enterprise of long standing. The room was actually part of the bar, a corner of it partitioned off, the door of which had its padlock, though smoke and conversation drifted over the partition; not quite the desired *querencia*.

Islands can be difficult places to leave. The smaller the island the more difficult it is to leave it, as Weaver knew to his cost, fond of repeating 'The smaller the island the bigger the neurosis'. So another two days had elapsed before a cabin could be booked on the *Ciudad de Badajoz* sailing to Valencia, the port of gesticulating statuary and good white wine. Time enough for vodka and freshly squeezed orange juice in Mam's Bar on the seafront – 'a hangout for expats,' Sasha said. And chilled draught beer at the Estacion Maritimo where the boats from Barcelona arrive from time to time.

They walked through the bluebell wood of the Parque de Bellver below the castle with Sasha and her silent eldest son who disappeared silently into the wood and returned just as silently, offering a fishful of wild garlic to his mother. Bart Murnane was working. Said to be working; at all events he was not coming downstairs, but cloistered above.

The last image Weaver was to have of him – an image of those about to go from us forever, as seen by the pineal eye, the eye-in-the-back-of-the-head: scion of the great Murnane clan, alias Mulchinock the honorary Irishman: he was standing in his yellowing flannels, now with pointy-toed black ankle-boots very highly polished, the waist quite trim and tightly belted, the mane of white hair upstanding, a relaxed athletic pose adopted with thumbs hooked into the belt, bang in the middle of Dos de Mayo below the Murnane ancestral pile, the Casa Mirabel.

The eyes . . . ah!

The flecked grey eyes now glaring with a sort of angry benignancy, a final well-wishing and a suggestion (the merest) of a casual hand-wave just suppressed, checked. In the black high-heel boots a suggestion of cloven feet. The lips pursed by the teeth, bitten inwards, with the ghost of a smile (perchance relief at their imminent departure Berlinward), observed through the rear window of the departing taxi that was taking them to the docks.

Wave, Weaver, wave goodbye to your old amigo!

They sailed in the late afternoon from the port of Palma for Valencia across a mirror-like calm sea. The Mallorcans came aboard carrying great round loaves of peasant bread called *pan país*, the shape and size of dinner-gongs or bedpans, being a speciality of the island.

Their relief at leaving had only been matched by their joy at arriving, having like bone-heads watched their charter flight take off from Tempelhof for Palma before their very eyes. The charter company had obligingly found accommodation in a Tempelhof hotel, for they couldn't face returning to the flat.

Then, over two days and two long coach-rides, Valencia and Alicante; Cartagena, Almería to Nerja, Sodom of the Costa del Sol, as Torremolinos must be Gomorrah; and tomorrow Torrox and Nerja where the American tennis champion Tobias was waiting with fists hard as flyweight Jimmy ('The Ghost With a Hammer in Both Hands') Wilde, to fracture three of Weaver's notoriously pregnable ribs in a bout of fisticuffs one drunken night behind the church of the Madonna de las Angustias where a brothel was set up in the Plaza de los Martires.

What remained of that Spanish break was: a courtyard in Alicante where a girl (*Doppelgänger* for Lore aged eighteen, very brown-skinned in sandals) sat dreaming on the edge of a fountain that was not cascading; seen from the window of a hotel bedroom where Weaver had just put through a call to Palma before joining Lore at breakfast in the dining-room below. They would of course be most welcome again, Murnane assured him, but Miranda needed her room, it was her *querencia*, and the Irish sub had sailed or dived and good luck with Nerja and Sash sends love and yes okay right okay sure sure sure . . .

And then the Bach Mass played on the transistor (presumably by mistake) as their coach entered mountainous terrain just at sunset on a twisty road, plunging them into dark shade and then out again into brilliant sunshine, and the horns of wild goats high up, then again into shade (as if an accompaniment to the music of

Bach) and all the Spaniards quiet and subdued at last, for a change, the heads and shoulders darkly silhouettted, the old man selling broom handles asking to be let off miles from anywhere; then into the brilliant sunshine again and all at peace at last.

Wild alyssum and cistus roses bloom in the woods below the castle, with wild garlic and asphodel above Terrano.

A footnote to the foregoing: *Querencia* (Sp.), *quietudo*, hence *quietus*; the deepest purple stamens of the wild gladioli longing to be violated by a bee in May in the fastness of El Bosque de Bellver, Palma de Mallorca, in the Islas Baleares (Balearic Islands); the furiously blushing round bull's-eye (an untouched virgin?) longing to be pierced by the artfully flighted Zen arrow; the place in a raked bullring where the bull (mistakenly) feels safe and secure; a district in Madrid where the citizens thought (mistakenly) that they would be safe and secure from Franco's bombs during their Civil War; a child's 'secret place'; Miranda Murnane's bedroom.

30

The Watchers by the Stream

'Everything is something trembling on the verge of something else,' quoth Vlad the Impaler, lepidopterist extraordinaire, with his customary pernickety prescience and acumen. Illusion, froggy transilience, as the very stuff of happiness.

Perhaps not long ago, it (the river of no name) had a grand name but now as if accursed it had become the Rio Seco, the dry or driedupriverwithnoname in the cruel analogy of the barren woman, the hag.

Had not a race of dark brilliant mathematicians brought water by their astute calculations into the valley; harnessing Nature's own sportful hydraulics, even if handicapped by the notorious inability of water to flow uphill, aided and abetted by rain-bearing clouds, by the very slope of the ground, the steep incline. Before that it must have been a veritable furnace all summer long, in those summers of long ago; unendurable through August, the river having given up the ghost, become dry as the river-beds of Torre del Mar and Málaga.

There were two aqueducts, one close to the valley floor, the other close to the escarpment, both marvels of applied engineering, wide as the blade of a mattock, water eight or ten inches deep never flooding or running dry; the spouts having been turned on full cock for, say, six centuries, in order to thoroughly irrigate the whole valley from Frigiliana to Nerja, served by snowcapped Sierra Almijara.

'History's pomps are toy-like,' Weaver's philosophical amigo Ussher had written long ago, intending some disparagement – for he had been disappointed in the proportions of the Alhambra, anticipating something grander. Wrong, very wrong. The 'moros', long innured to owning nothing much in the way of property and personal possessions, loot, had developed finer notions of what are pleasing dimensions, subverting the grandiose and the pretentious; for house-bound Ussher dared not quit his library, his reference books, much less his wife; these were his securities. Behind all, like a mirage quivering, lay the desert, the parched lands.

Once in Frigiliana while waiting for *brasero* charcoal to be weighed up on the scales, Weaver had walked into the timber-yard and heard a bugle blare under crimson sunset clouds come over from Africa. Ambient air and drenched timber-yard and Guardia Civil barracks had all shivered as if drenched in blood; a silhouetted figure was blowing a brave bugle.

Weaver's brother had told him this was a definition of the colour crimson for a blind person born blind who had never seen any colours: bugle-blare (cock-crow) at the setting of the sun.

The last of the Spanish-dwelling *moros* who had lived in Frigiliana. Could not bear to tear himself away from this fortress-style eyrie stuck on the mountainside, and the aqueducts bringing fresh cold water by the back door, under the mill above, and before his eyes the plantations of lemon and the white *fincas* scattered like mushrooms over the sable and burnt-sienna earth, as if all adrift in the blue dreamlike air.

No wonder he didn't want to leave.

He could not bring himself to quit, tear himself away; for home now meant the redoubts of a medieval-like fortress meandering over a hill: *La Molineta*!

*

Once upon a lovely morning in Andalucía (and a gorgeous blue morning it was too) Weaver had taken Lore out into the *campo* by the Moorish aqueduct above Nerja (not yet quite fucked up, as it would be later), and he with a hangover that made him tumid as a tomcat. Laying down his suede (what Lore called 'veal') hunting-jacket the colour of impala, lining upwards, on the slope of the dry incline by the aqueduct overlooking the valley of the Rio Seco on the route to Frigiliana, he had her undressed in a thrice, intending to solace his existence forthwith; and was soon upon her and jettisoning himself recklessly into her (she took no precautions, believed – wrongly – that she could not conceive) there above the purling stream that had been pouring down since the days of weeping Boabdil. They were lying there minding their own business and watching a grass snake in the aqueduct – it must have fallen in while sleeping in the sun and been carried rapidly down – raise a curious speckled head, on its rapid free passage down into new territory, in a morning outside of Time.

The quotidian, oft banal, just for once in a while had been invested with its own mystery there in the dry river valley pretty well advanced on the way to being well and truly fucked up (a process first initiated and later fully developed and ruthlessly carried through by the three wily brothers of the banking family of the Plaza de los Martires, behind the church). It was a teeming morning in a happy time, for Weaver. Lore (supine) could see beyond his head what he (prone and naked on her nakedness) could not (not having eyes in the back of his head): the valley widening towards its exit (the mouth?) and narrowing percep-tibly towards its end (source or tail?) below Frigiliana. And pulsing in the bluish dreaming air, for the sides of the valley seemed, just perceptibly, to converge, but also to contract and expand, to inhale and exhale in a purposeful slow regular breathing of its mighty chest, fully braced to take in the air. In the hazy morning light, as if seen in a clear pool, Weaver and Lore reduced (*reduced?*) to waving algae. With the almost visible blue air streaming across it (the trembling pool where the images had now broken up, stirred by a passing breeze) as groaningweaver groaningly emptied himself into lovely groaninglore with mouth kissed out of shape, having been brought roughly into position to be taken with pussy already drenched in anticipation (a gentle Knight was pricking on the plaine) and all around them the myriad tickings and clickings that were the sounds of Nature at work, the birds flying and calling, the air streaming through the willows below, the quick-flowing water (cold and delicious to drink in cupped hands) in the here-and-now quickening in palpitant life. Pan was certainly not sleeping.

'Do not move,' Lore whispered, after an aeon.

'Do you like our missionary stew?' Weaver inquired fondly, the chef's eyes not six inches from the dark flashing eyes of the Bühlerhoe waitress sweating under him.

'I do, sire. Give me more, if you want to, when you like. Love me do.'

'I do. I just did.'

'I know it. I felt it. You had me. We're Hemingway characters in Spain.'

'We are?'

'This babbling.'

'Ah.'

'Yes. That's good. That's nice.'

Love, or some of her ever-roving outriders, had drawn close and they were as one on the dry herbal Spanish earth permeated with the mixed aromas of rosemary (for remembrance) and thyme; as the silver salvers carrying the remains of lobster mayonnaise and vinaigrette sauce were hardly off the groaning board before the steaming main dishes were borne triumphantly in.

Devious Marcel Proust, bedbug asthmatic, hypochondriac extraordinaire in the great seat of melancholy, an indoors-man *par excellence*, had nicely defined it (the he and the she of it, the whatness and whereabouts, in the flowers of summer, the shiny galvanized bucket, the cheating chauffeur, the stones of Venice, in mythical Balbec, in its enchantress (Albert), the mythical enchanter, man or woman, Albertine the horny thorny rose), as: *L'amour c'est le temps et l'espace rendus sensibles au cœur.*

'Time and space made perceptible to the heart.' Or love is time and space the heart can catch (apprehend, comprehend), and (so defined) is so precisely craftily Frog that we wouldn't wish to change a word of it, to clarify who does what to whom, while adroitly begging the question of who (or what) lies behind it all: time and space, love and heart, and only the last organic.

The young and ferociously gifted Sam Beckett, reputed to be randy as Guy de Maupassant (1850–93) who had two hundred conquests chalked up before he had come of age, later narrowed the terminology to: 'The one closed figure in the waste without form, and void.' But that rider was surely superfluous?

But along came Weaver in his heather-coloured homespuns (TCD 1942–5, Urinus Causa) to reduce it further still, rendered down in the pot with an almost Euclidean economy; highly compressed (as the fart *in vacuo*) into four wellnigh irreducible portmanteau words. The *fons et origo* pilfered from Shem the Penman (1882–1941) who had lifted it from the Bawdy Bard himself (1564–1616). Thus: 'Allspace in a notshall'. Or would 'allspice' be nicer still? Neater, don't you know?

And should it not be 'nutshell'? As: 'Allspice in a nutshell'.

31
Nancy Returns (Struggle and Strife)

The journey back was less arduous than the outward trip; one hop from Málaga International to Tempelhof, Lore marching in espadrilles between the lines of German vacationers going home, her resolute heels smacking the parquet floor, and all of them talking German. They arrived back the day before Nancy was due to return and Weaver hoovered the house from top to bottom, waxed the wood, set out flowers, made all in readiness for Nancy's return to the fold. To Weaver it was as the return of tertian fever for an old Calcutta hand; time to reach for the bottle. He spent the second half of the last day with Lore in the Little Squirrel. She insisted that he eat half a chicken and bought two carafes of wine to 'conserve his force', it was a little farewell party. Darkness was coming on apace when they walked through the Jochen-Klepper-Weg and down to Nikolassee Station. He waited for the last possible moment before phoning the house, now resplendent and awaiting its mistress. By then the darkness had quite abruptly descended. Weaver felt as though he had been keel-hauled through a sea of shit. His son's voice answered in his chirrupy Is-it-true-is-it-true-what-the-people-say pitch of excitement:

'Oh Weaver – you'll never guess!'

'Oh yes I would – your ma's home.'

'She is! She is! She's here! Will I put her on?'

'Do that,' Weaver tried to sound pleased.

'Well here I am again,' said Nancy's voice. 'The house like a new pin. And where, may I inquire, are you?'

'Oh not far away,' Weaver said airily. 'Mag gave the lad his supper. She has been looking after him. Is he looking well?'

'The dote's looking remarkably well, considering.'

'I'll be there in five minutes,' Weaver said, hanging up. He kissed Lore, saw her into her green racer, saw her off and walked home with a bottle of Rioja as a peace offering for Nancy. In Lund-London (Lunnonlundy or Lundlondon) she had bought books for Nico, socks for Weaver, daring underthings for herself, to inflame Weaver. Nancyfancy. 'Frillies for Raoul?'

The tentative sweetness however did not last long. Nico in bed and drinks in hand and Weaver broke the bad news: he and the whore had spent a week in Spain, leaving Nico in the safekeeping of the Weissenborns. Now wasn't that nice? Nancy went through the roof. She let loose her blood-curdling *abandon-ship* scream, calculated to stop the heart. MALLORCA! (Gomorrah!). ARTY-FARTY-MURNANE (Sodom!). You must have gone clean out of your fucking cotton-picking mind!

'Well, he had two other kids to play with,' said Weaver in a placating voice.

But in her yelling mood nothing would placate Nancy. She passed from room to room, banging doors behind her, and flames gushed from her eyes. It was back to normal again with a vengeance for the Weavers. Square one: Struggle and Strife.

'Such a shame,' Weaver told the assembled Meinhardt furniture. 'Such a pity,' shaking his head in mock disbelief. 'A nice full-bodied red Rioja turned to vinegar. It's a crying shame.'

'And who turned her into fucking vinegar, I should like to know,' Nancy shrilled passionately.

'Tcchh-tcchhk,' Weaver went with his tongue in a censorious manner calculated to annoy, 'or a lemon gone off. Spoiled fruit.'

Here Nancy hit the fan. Stir it up! Stir it up!

32

Sir Delves Digby
Bullpitt of the British Council

Weaver had put his foot in it again and this time with Sir Delves Digby Bullpitt, of all people! Mando had been most insistent that they should avail themselves of the open invitation from the British Council to join them for drinks after dinner in the Bullpitt place. But was that sufficient for a formal or *pro forma* invitation, Nancy wished to know, didn't they rather go in for formality? Not at all, Mando assured them, the Weavers would be more than welcome. Sir Delves had been *most* insistent that she should bring more DILDO guests along. It was open house and pot luck.

The British Council always gave good parties, Mando said. She had attended a number; it was quite an honour to be invited along. An address was supplied. It was miles and miles away.

The Weavers supped early, arranged for kind Margy to have Nico for the night in her place. Dressed in their best they left home in good time, took the U-Bahn, broke their journey for a drink on the way, and planned to arrive by taxi. All went well until Nancy had some trouble finding her address book. After much rummaging in handbag and turning out of pockets, she had to come to the conclusion that she must have left it at home. Weaver stared fixedly into a mirror behind the bar and a total stranger glared back with basilisk eye, one claw raising a

Steinhäger to its lips, the beer chaser neatly positioned, and then a ghastly grin spreading from ear to ear.

There was nothing for it but phone Margarete and tell her where it might be. She had the key. This was done, and the address book found by the bed, the address read out. It was still miles away. A taxi was ordered on the spot. The sullen driver admitted to being unfamiliar with the area but would see what could be done, studying a street map. They arrived two hours late and were embraced by Mando herself at the Bullpitt door.

'You have come!'

They were welcomed with smothering embraces. The Bullpitts received them with a smooth politeness just this side of rudeness. 'Ah Professor Weaver and Mrs Weaver, we are honoured indeed! Unfortunately we have already, ah, partaken, but do please join us for a drink. We are presently to have a harp recital, which should please you. Now in liquid refreshment we have everything but Guinness, I am afraid. Hahaha.'

But Weaver had already spotted the Martell.

'We have come by forced march, Sir Delves, my bearer and I, encountering many unhelpful and unfriendly natives. Hence the delay. You must please excuse – no, overlook – our inexcusable lateness. We are but the playthings of chance.'

'All is forgiven,' cried the insipid no. 2, one Meyric Mellor, springing up dutifully. 'Shall I do the needful?'

'I might chance a Martell then.'

'And the madame?'

The madame would accept a gin and tonic.

There were about two score people in the room, a mixture of Germans, Americans and English rising from the long dining-table; having dined well they had reached the brandy and coffee stage, awaiting the harpist. Mando's face was on fire. Bangles jangled like wind-chimes on a windy day, she wore knee-boots of calf the colour of bull's blood, and her complexion had darkened appreciably. She was into the Martell.

They sat about, Weaver trying to make up for lost time.

'A meeting of incompatibles,' said Meyric Mellor with a simper. Looking out of his office window near the zoo had he not seen an extraordinary sight: *elephants in the snow*!

'What's incompatible about that?' Weaver inquired truculently, anxious to prove his metal. 'Elephants in the zoo – where else would you find them, in these parts?'

'Elephants in the *snow*, please!'

'So what? Less incompatible. You are forgetting Hannibal.'

'What of him?'

'He took elephants across the Alps in winter and presumably encountered snow. I *never* see elephants without thinking of snow.'

Weaver now went among the German guests and put them completely at their ease by dismissing Beethoven (too loud) and Thomas Mann (too long) with a right and left barrel.

'Oh come now,' said a small academic with a mouthful of carious teeth, 'surely with Beethoven's Fiffth we are talking of undissphuted gwateness?'

'I'm not speaking of greatness but of undisputed loudness,' the Professor said rather too emphatically. 'Loud garish music like some ostentious military uniform too baggy at the knees. Too much toccata-toccata and general horsing about. A streak of vulgarity there.'

The Professor recommended Olivier Messiaen the Parisian church organist and composer of devotional music. 'Even when working on loud church organs he produced tranquil effects. The voice of God is practically inaudible in *Méditations sur le mystère de la Sainte Trinité*. He got the idea listening to the call of an unknown bird in Persia in the evening. Imagine the almighty racket Beethoven would unleash for this.'

The German guests were smiling tight smiles and nodding sagely.

'Someone has wisely said that Nature herself couldn't

stand another Beethoven. The question is: Can she stand one Beethoven?'

The Germans were nodding uneasily at each other.

'The composer must always be coming up against silence. I want a music closer to silence,' quoth the Irish oracle. 'Greatness is all balderdash anyway. You might as well talk of the Empyrean – the region of celestial fire or supposed abode of God and the angels. It doesn't exist. Or if it did, it's not for the likes of us.'

'Ah, Professor, you are a mystic Celt.'

'He is a mocker. A garish Beethoven, what an idea! Are there colours in music?'

'Certainly there are, colours and tones. Ever get a puck on the nose? Close your eyes. Coloured handkerchiefs waving on the dockside at the ship departing. Music is a system of farewells, Cioran thought.'

'Charming, charming.'

'We have music,' someone said, for Vernon Hoare the harpist had slipped in, a slim pale fellow in a lounge suit pushing before him a harp on a trolley. He set it up, arranged the music stand, saw that his audience was seated, and began to play a selection of delicate airs among which sparkled an exquisite Debussy *Arabesque*. Weaver fell silent, his long curved nose sniffing the potent fumes of French brandy.

When the harp recital ended the party resumed, Vernon Hoare graciously accepting a glass of white wine from the hand of his hostess, Lady Joan.

All went well, for a time.

The unexpected recital of poetry, the chanting of rhyming verse, particularly without prior warning (when discharged at point-blank range at those ill-prepared to receive it), has an unsettling effect, and can produce an embarrassed silence, as happened now. Making lapidary motions of his hands as though conducting some of his silent music, Weaver was reciting in dulcet tones

> 'When Klopstock England defied,
> Uprose terrible Blake in his pride.
> For old Nobodaddy aloft
> Farted and belched and coughed . . .'

Into the shocked silence the level voice of someone hard of hearing, who had missed the above, said in a plaintive voice: 'I am *extremely* relieved.'

Then they all began talking at once. Lady Joan rose up and began handing around After Eights. Sir Delves in dinner jacket and patent leather shoes was looking very *stürmisch* indeed with brow furrowed, but turned on a winning smile when approached by his guest of honour, the celebrated one in hush-puppies, in a rather loose-cut grey suit, who wanted to know what he thought of the damned Russian MiGs banging through the sound-barrier and breaking Berlin windows when he (Sir Kenneth) was dining with the *Bürgermeister*.

Sir Delves replied stoutly, Well, what more could you expect from the likes of — and — (naming Soviet officials in the diplomatic set). *Their* ideas of expediency would not be ours; and of course it was all done with the express purpose of embarrassing the *Bürgermeister*, and indeed had succeeded. Not forgetting Khrushchev removing one shoe and banging the heel to disrupt a UN session. *'Nyet'* had gotten so badly into their system that they couldn't think any other way. It was a rough-and-ready type of diplomacy.

'American foreign policy,' the raised and contentious voice uttered distinctly, 'just you tell me what is that! A series of loud farts in embassy corridors.'

From what he judged to be a safe distance, by the service hatch, Meyric Mellor was covertly observing the obstreperous Irish guest and keeping a tally on the brandies consumed; for if it was dangerous to offer him another, it would be doubly dangerous not to. Surely he had had enough already?

'You Germans need your masters, but I'm not one of them. Now Dev . . .'

Meyric Mellor shuddered but diplomatically managed to avoid Sir Digby's protruding parboiled blue eyes. This would have to sort itself out.

'The trooping of the colours is based on illiteracy,' the Professor was shouting into a hairy American ear. 'And parade-ground drill is intended to kill thought.' A tall willowy woman with the sylph-like name of Estelle was murmuring confidentially into Sir Kenneth Clark's inclined ear while his slitty Oriental eyes were fixed thoughtfully at a floral arrangement on the sideboard, while judiciously tasting a Scotch and splash. Now his narrowed eyes flew open to their utmost extent, for Weaver had cried out: 'Vengeance! Vengeance on the murderers of Jacques Molay! The past is irrelevant.'

He was on his way through the sound-barrier. The hostess was everywhere at once. Sir Delves was inching towards his incompetent no. 2, who was smiling a nervous temporizing smile, just waiting for the hand to be laid on his arm, the order suggested more than given: Get rid of this fellow. Get him out!

The pitch of the party was certainly rising. The guests were not mixing but huddled in a corner, bleating, hoping not to be picked out individually, as prime examples, for argument's sake. A certain type of English voice never failed to rile Weaver, and he had just heard it. It had the immediate effect of making him twice as argumentative.

'We Irish are too easily fooled,' the voice came rocketing forth (the invisible opponent was just a frozen smile out there somewhere) 'too easily bullied, if it goes to that. Geographically we are badly positioned in relation to England, as I believe Castro said of Cuba and America. We haven't a hope in hell where we are; we should have been put down somewhere off the Gulf of Mexico.'

'Heeheehee ssshh,' a sibilant whispery voice said: the sound of a snail drawing in its horns.

'Joan dearest, can you please *do* something.'

'That *idiot* Meyric!'

The terrible drunken Irishman seemed to be all over the place, glass of brandy in hand, puffing a cigar, being too familiar, throwing his weight around. This dreadful, dreadful man was disrupting her party and upsetting her guests, and now he had reached her husband who inclined his head with a sickly smile, a victim at the block, as the too-familiar arm was wrapped around his shoulders.

'D'ja understand the servant Joseph's Yorkshire dialect in *Wuthering Heights*? Can you whistle a few bars of Mozart's *King Thamos*? What do you make of Cioran's witticism: Why read Plato, if a saxophone can give you an idea of another world? *If* you read Plato.'

'Oh yes,' Sir Delves said, freeing himself.

Now the intruder put one arm familiarly about Sir Kenneth's narrow shoulders and winked at Sir Delves Digby.

'I know *you*, you old bollicks!'

Sir Kenneth took it very well. The guests still huddled in a corner. But soon they left, pointedly ignoring Weaver, effusively thanking the Bullpitts for the lovely meal, the harp recital, among them Vernon Hoare with his harp wrapped up. Nancy told Weaver that it was time to go home.

So they assembled together at the door, the last to leave, Mando and the Weavers, the last with his last glass of Martell in hand, far from sober.

'Jolly good show. We're off then?' said Sir Delves.

'We have enjoyed ourselves immensely!' Mando cried.

'Is there somewhere out there a friendly face?' Weaver asked the darkness, pretending to point a lantern.

'You must come again,' Sir Delves said, with no indication that his patience had been sorely tried, still involved in a handshake with Weaver.

'Germans shake hands too much, have you noticed? It's a

form of uncertainty with them – as Americans on first-name terms too soon.'

'You must certainly come again,' Sir Delves said, offering a cool hand to Nancy, a small tight smile. 'We need a man of his stamp in Berlin.'

'Oh do you?' said Nancy. 'How nice.'

Sir Delves and his wife Joan exchanged a close meaningful look, seeing the rumbustuous DILDO guests off the premises. A taxi had been called. They were in it, they were waving, they were away.

The Bullpitts stood amid the ruins of their party.

'Phew!' said Sir Delves, wiping his brow. 'Take a memo, Meyric. In future, no Greeks, *strictly* no Irish and underline that, twice. We've just had the very dregs of DILDO.'

Lady Joan was renderd speechless; it was as if a bomb had gone off in her lovely living-room.

Now they were in the U-Bahn hurtling through the night, Mando powdering her nose in the toilet.

'That bloody Mando and her Greek expansiveness!' Weaver cried. 'We weren't wanted there at all. Second-hand generosity! Hospitality on the cheap – Greek hospitality! She should never have invited us.'

'Well, you didn't exactly improve the shining hour by telling the German guests that Beethoven was too noisy – that went down a treat . . . like offering them sodium ampthils instead of After Eights. And bringing up military matters to Germans is like farting in their faces. By the way, I noticed that you and Mando made heavy inroads into the Cognac.'

'Oh pish pish, we only did what we could to keep the ball rolling. But never again. Greek diplomacy – cadging drinks, Sir Digby Pewter Pot! Christ Almighty take me home.'

It was to be their first and last outing since Nancy's return from London and Weaver from Málaga; it had not been a great success.

'I'll never again go out with you,' Nancy vowed. 'It was *most* humiliating.'

'Here comes Mando,' Weaver warned.

33
The Vile Nip (A Lewd Chapter)

Lore had discovered a good Japanese restaurant near Fat George's flat and she and Weaver went there sometimes, though rarely calling on Fat George.

Then one evening, returning from a meal and a carafe or two of sake at the Japanese place, feeling in a social mood they decided to call on Fat George, and found who but Willie Prendergast lying on the floor like Buddha resting his head on the palm of one hand, the right hand that 'never did a stroke of work', whatever else it did; for Winky was God's gift to women. Weaver told them of the good Japanese meal while Lore was in the kitchen arranging canapés.

Winky settled comfortably on the floor with drink to hand told Weaver that a Japanese sculptor named Takahashi-san who taught in the Free University was in the process of shooting a hard-porn movie that would end all hard-porn movies, in Sweden with a nude blonde model, Brit Unguland. This one was going right over the top.

'The red roundel of the bull's-eye bisects the Zen arrow thudding home,' sniggered Fat George, who was a bit of a reader himself, lounging on the sofa with a beer lifted to his fat lips, giving one of his fat greasy smiles.

> 'Bulls aim their horns
> And asses lift their heels,'

said Weaver, ever one for the pithy quote.

'You should see Brit's.'

'You have seen this thing?' Weaver asked.

'Takahashi-san showed us a rough-cut.'

Nude Brit rode a stallion without bridle or saddle through woody terrain; it was a nature movie gone mad, a *Wald und Wiese* to end them all. When glossy Brit – a real stunner – throws her legs over the broad twitchy back of stallion Thor and urges him forward with her knees, her thighs are already wet from the sweat of his great heaving flanks. She walks him sedately, she canters, breaks into a gallop, and every time they clear an obstacle together, Brit and snorting Thor, the fair rider cries out 'Whee Thor!'

She cries out, exulting and taunting, as a matador about to dispatch a bull; feeling the male beast power surge through her she rides him hard.

Now in a stealthy travelling-shot, cleverly cut *contre-plonge*, a shabby line of drawerless and toothless troglodytes are seen wildly masturbating themselves and drooling as Thor and Brit thunder past, while unspeakable things are happening in the woods, filmed in gauzy long-shot, as you can tell from the trembling leaves. All is explicit and shifty innuendo at the same time.

Brit is caught as it were in mid air, breasts thrust out, her mouth wide open, she is calling something out, no doubt obscene, in Swedish.

The gallops over, she rides Thor sedately into the stable yard, which appears to be deserted; the prying camera travels along a line of open stable doors and dungy drains, with a sudden suspicious lunge at a steaming midden. As Brit dismounts the camera performs a somersault in an effort to catch a close up of quivering quim, but we have the spreading bum, the mesial groove, the dishevelled blonde hair to her waist, the pouty look, the dilated nostrils. Brit is obviously mightily aroused and so is Thor. Now he is for it; now he must perform.

She walks him, calming him as he blows through his great nostrils, runs a hand over his gleaming pelt, is perhaps considering rubbing him down with a damp cloth or a handful of hay; but no, she deftly positions him over a drain, runs a low trolley under him and lies down on this, holding a plastic bag in one hand, snatched from the manger.

Now face-up and in profile she closes her swooning eyes and kisses the great prick, licks the huge trembling thing, and then manually masturbates him into the bag. The great Erection, the steamy Stallion Come, wow, mindless mind-blowing de Sadean bliss!

She gets to her feet and pours the come over herself, showering in the stallion-come, rubs it well in, excellent for the complexion. Then, ever adaptive and ready to try something new, she crawls naked and all smeared with filth into the pigsty from which all the sows have been driven, and there the Boar waits.

'Your man is grunting to himself inside on the shitty straw,' Winky laughed. 'This part is a bit much actually. Being serviced by the old boar who gets up on her when she lies down and encourages him. I am told it can be quite dangerous, messing around with a boar. It can't get the prick out. Certainly it was quite disgusting to see, as I suppose was intended. The students of this primal filth seemed to go for it.'

Mad Takahashi-san was of course highly popular with his students and lent them his beaten-up Studebaker, inviting them to his flat, pot-smoking, showing porn movies. He had shot his girlfriend dead with a rifle, an accident while cleaning it.

'You saw all this?' Weaver asked.

'A rough-cut. The film is almost ready. He's trying to raise funds through Axel Springer.'

Fat George was wheezing and laughing to himself, his lips white with beer foam.

'Who is this vile Nip? He should be castrated.'

'Just a sculptor who makes dirty movies,' Winky said.

'What does he call it? The Whole Hog?'

'It hasn't got a title yet.'

'It doesn't deserve a title.'

'That's Berlin.'

'What's Berlin?' Lore asked, coming in bearing little fishes in a dish, with rice and sliced gherkin.

'Filthy practices in a porn movie,' Weaver said.

'*Oh Quatsch!*'

'Exactly my own sentiments,' said Weaver.

'Who is for small but succulent fishes?' Lore asked, holding up the plate invitingly, at which bait Fat George rose up, Blubbery Billy Bunter.

What was it about Winky that so appealed to the ladies, Weaver wondered. Was it his known surgical quality (shades of Murphy)? His sexual secrets, the tousled manner both accommodating and threatening, as if he might get out of hand – was that it? Was Winky secretive? Yes, in a way; his secret life among women was shrouded from the eyes of other men.

Military subjects with faceless protagonists whose flesh was painted as veal featured in the canvases of Fat George and were hung about the walls, as carcasses in a butcher's shop. But, Weaver reminded himself, thinking of the *boucherie* opposite the Grand Hôtel de la Loire, first-class butchers were always clean; particularly so in summer when the flies were a nuisance. The Paris women came in and fingered the joints, discussed their choice with the expert, who allowed himself three or four Gauloises in the course of the day, smoked outside his shop, which was hosed down when he closed and opened again. It was instructive to Weaver, who was staring across, famished without food for days at a stretch, half starving. Fat George had come under the influence of Larry Rivers, who had painted *The Last But One Confederate General*. He (Fat George) was dubbing porn movies into English: *The Sex Life of the Three Musketeers*. That was Fat George, that was Berlin.

Not all the cocks that crow can command the farmyard. Winky himself was a case in point, despite his numerous conquests, he had known failure with women. No sooner into bed with his new ladylove but his *dick* flatly refused to perform, and next morning the same story, he had admitted to Weaver. Was this what the Frogs called *le fiasco*? They would have a name for it, being specialists, unlike the Irish, of whom Winky was by no means a fair representative. Once on the slopes of the Big Sugarloaf he had attempted the al fresco seduction of a pretty young strumpet from Köln. He was given every encouragement. She had a splendid pair. 'I couldn't get a grip,' Winky admitted. 'And kept slipping down the fukken mountain.' Love was not such an easy game to play. So priketh hem nature in hir corages. But what would Granny Inés have thought of such jejune cavortings, she who in her heyday had been courted by W. B. Yeats himself? The Köln strumpet (a musky teenager with bursting *pommettes*) thought him *sehr komisch*. This he confided to Weaver with his mad gollywog grin.

Ah Winky, Winky, what a mad fellow thou art!

34

In Secluded Woodland
and Thickety Retreat

In the summertime (when the living is easy) it was a very different story. For all around them were the Berlin woods made for assignations and al fresco venery. In spotless white linen slacks, Lore would not hear of sitting or lying on the nasty loamy lake verges, much less swim therein; and as for swimming nude at night (at Weaver's insistence), well forget that. There were rapists about, the woods were 'not safe'. She was too well brought up, too careful, clean.

Well, in due time, with some coaxing, all this changed, and Lore primped in her minute café-au-lait bikini on the little sandy shores of Krumme Lanke and Schlachtensee, walked through Zehlendorf Forst, Königal and Tegel, Jungfernheide, Schwanenwerder and about the Hundekehlesee or 'hound-throat lake' and followed intrepid Weaver into the fastness of the woods at night, carrying a rug, for congress in the dark, behind a bush.

The Professor (Veneris Causa) gave tutorials on the edges of the lakes, encouraging her to look into the poetry of the Earl of Rochester and the bawdy divine John Donne, randy clergyman Robert Herrick, those matchless cocksmen Smollett and Fielding, the cock-swollen fancies of *Fanny Hill*. He explained low innuendos, as, a piece of, clip, blowjob or suckoff, getting-it-up, having-it-off, drinking-your-coffee (in Swift's *Journal to Stella*), tail and (a bit of) strange, rump-roast and missionary position – the nuances and gross multiplicity of these allusions.

Not forgetting cock, dick, cod, bun, pussy, snatch, willie, pecker, cabbage stalk (!), old man, or the more formal horn and erection, the more esoteric limp-father-of-thousands (in James Joyce's *Ulysses*) or the more ingenious *reverse* missionary position as favoured by the poet Shelley and his wife whilst boating on the Thames.

Not to forget lead-in-pencil and American slang terms such as goin' down on, pay dirt, crumpet, honk, ride, ass, oats (feeling your), score (scoring butt, stinking of score), makin' out, hot piece, quick trigger, dunkin' Dickie, chokin' on chicken, playin' around, makin' it, shootin' a load, humpin', equipment, tool, butterin' parsnips, Fuller Brush Man, the old one-two, knob (*m*), struma (*f*), jelly, meatbun, quim, meat, bounce, flower, cherry, yummy snatch, pussywussy, juice time, yummyyummy, wampum.

Rod, micky, prick, member, It, nuts, rocks, organ, private parts, credentials, peashooter, Hamilton Long, willy, dingy, perform trick of loop, jig, hand-job, blow-job, getting it on, up, game of two-backed beast, dipping wick, *koinonia*, tup, congress, screw, making it, nookie, poke, turning trick, merry clip (arch.), cherry and on distaff side: fox, pussy, twat, snapper, fanny, bun. All this since hairy old Adam covered hoary old Eve, harking back to Eden Garden and the Expulsion.

'Look up cock ("the one who arouses slumberers") in the OED,' quoth Weaver.

'Oh what a dirty language is thine,' laughed Lore and emerged dripping from the Oxo-brown lake like the first day of Creation, or the one closed figure in a waste without form.

'First love, then the *farmacia*,' said the Professor (quoting Cioran the cynic), wrapping her in a blue bathtowel and beginning to dry her, rubbing her down as if she were a mare. Whistling through his teeth the while; her stableman, ostler, groom.

'*Oh Quatsch*! I will groan if yet another word in English goes

wrong, since every third or fourth word must be improper.'
Lore's wet face fairly glowed.

Now the Alsatian dog that had been enjoying a swim in Krumme Lanke came out in a state of beast-tumescence to shake itself vigorously all over a group of chattering Japanese who all laughed the same tinkling laugh.

'We have to find the terminology for all that confusion of desire – calling the loved one mouse and chick and baby.' Weaver was thinking of Lore as she walked to the bathroom of her small boxlike white apartment, a wristwatch worn as ankle bracelet suggesting slavery status; before their siesta (her euphemism for intercourse or what the Germans in their winsome way call *Schäferstündchen*, 'little-shepherd-hour') she had removed the wristwatch for Love's sake, in order to be even nuder for Weaver; one round cheek of her bum stamped with a vaccination mark, for Mama Schröder would not have her darling girl defaced in any way and had arranged it so, not on the upper arm (where it could be seen) but on the bum, where Weaver had seen it among the rashes and love-bites (his own teeth-marks), as if lashed or caned, when marked by the coarse grain of the carpet, slightly reddened where it (the bum) had taken her full weight.

Her broad buttocks were marked so by the coarse grain of the warp where she had sat and her weight had made an impress on her arse. Kneeling nude odalisque she had spilled the contents of her vanity box or jewel case onto the carpet, where she and Weaver had fallen from the daybed after a bout of passion, and was showing him her rings, brooches, medallions, lucky charms, earrings and such-like presents with more valuable pieces given at successive birthdays by Mama Schröder to her darling daughter.

But now it was riding-time again. In the open; that is, hidden in the depths of the Grunewald in the middle of the afternoon, back off a sandy horse-riding path where they had picnicked in the nude. And Lore was taking great breaths and clinging fast to Weaver who was about to ream her most villainously with the minimum of tenderness and the maximum of force and roaring loudly the while – great Jupiter discharging into his supine moaning bride. Was this what Nancy (a Christian Scientist of sorts) meant by the Charming Variations: secret love-in-the-woods, an ancient god and goddess fucking themselves silly?

Yes and no.

The stern stance, worthy of a bowsprit or figurehead or a Roman bronze nude male, enhanced the virility and vigour of that male participant and gave the other (below) a rapt femininity that nothing could dispel; for no patter of little feet could disrupt the exalted state of such tenderness masked and carried through as with the most ferocious cruelty.

Withdrawing his dagger (a well-used stubby weapon with browned bone-handle engraved with running stag and motto *Semper sursam* (Always Rising) wrought about the shaft in flowering grot, a huntsman's fancy) and wincing the while, still puffed from the kill, Weaver cleaned it by repeated thrusts into the dry earth and put it away in a leather sheath, as the still-palpitating much-tousled lovely bride sat up, divinely flushed, to light a cigarette with the most natural sang-froid imaginable.

All about them the Grunewald was crackling as if about to ignite. They had withdrawn some way from the sandy bridle-path where the remains of their nudist lunch had been wrapped up and hidden from sight and they themselves had withdrawn into a more hidden place free of undergrowth and had found a leafy depression out of sight of any horse-riders that might be passing, which seemed unlikely at this hour in the hot and enclosed wood.

Naked as Adam in the tropics and streaming with sweat, Weaver bethought him of an icy stream coming down from the Sierra Almijaras and the two mounted *guardias* on patrol with bicorn hats and rifles in pouches by their saddlebags, passing them by not seventy paces across the little stream where Lore lay stark naked, and Weaver with three fractured ribs unable to move. The *guardias* had gone by with their green capes spread over thoroughbred haunches; the two nudists ignored (unlikely) or not seen (more than unlikely), and the horsemen continuing at a walk up the narrowing valley towards La Molineta.

Now Lore, the nude slave-wench of the lower quarters, with drenched armpits and awash with perspiration between the breasts (if her breasts were melons her buttocks were big pomegranates), now stubbed out her tipped cigarette and carefully buried the 'collar' in the sand, giving Weaver a smouldering look as she rose up stretching herself; as Weaver stood up his member stood up with him, and then Lore was for giving him a taste of her pulpy lips and her tongue that tasted of wine and gherkins, saying hotly into his ear: 'Will you come again with me, Sir, into the em, em . . . you know?' And so saying, not waiting for an answer (for it was quite visible), took him by the hand and led him back into the hollow and slid down slowly upon him, matching and wedding her quivering quim to his up-raised cock and slid ever so slowly down, for the randy emissary to come again and take his German missionary stew, clasping her back and holding her to him, making sweet moan.

In the trees around, in the grass, in the heated air of summer, all was alive and stirring, as in the undergrowth some distance off and along the deserted paths blurred in a bluish-grey heat haze where no horse-riders came blowing out their cheeks. All was alive with teeming insects of summer that whirred and chirruped and pulsed and buzzed and sang and mumbled and smote scaly sides and whistled with pure joy in a great seasonal descant and chaunt of climacteric uproar, upsoaring and then subsiding.

And Lore too gave a sigh and closed herself about him, for now his prong-horned huntsman's dagger was buried to the hilt in a drenched place and her extraordinary eyes were fast closed; just the lashes twittering as if she were smiling secretly within.

They heard again a voice that sang in German, some aria from an opera. It was the coloratura practising some part while walking a hidden path. They listened; it was part of the hiddenness of the

220

Grunewald that an opera singer should use it as a rehearsal hall for the Deutsche Oper, preparing a character to go onto the stage.

'What's she singing?' Weaver kissed the heated cheek.

Lore listened, her full weight on Weaver, their blood and breath ran together, her expelled breath fanning his face. With eyes still closed and beginning to smile she said: 'It's something from . . .'

'It's not *Ramona*.'

'No . . . not *Ramona*.'

Now she opened her eyes and Weaver could look down at close range into that other world; glory be, he was most taken by this hot missionary stew.

Could it be . . . *Mazeppa*?

35
Prendergast

William Prendergast was to be the second Irishman – Weaver being the first – to receive the DILDO *stipendium*. He accepted it as a sculptor after he had verily lost faith in his own profession (*Maler*), which gave him all the more time to pursue his real interest: fecundating the ladies. Sculpting was 'fukken nonsense'; but the ladies found him irresistible and he did his level best to accommodate them all. Even the excessively homely Bertha Busse was rummaged ('Art*ists*!') and the very prim and proper Titty Born attempted.

'Tit,' he declared warmly, 'you're my meat.'

But she wasn't having any of *that*; nor was Nancy Weaver, who had rather thrown him by soliciting him before he could solicit her. Even a small dark practising Sapphist was propositioned; two of them were 'embracing madly' on a chaise-longue when he made advances to 'the little dark one underneath'. He had never seen women kissing before. Going out for beer he instructed Weaver to 'keep her amused' until he got back. But she never showed up. She had other fish to fry.

'Have you ever seen two women kissing?' Winky asked.

The Great Plant was now put to work overtime, with nightshifts thrown in; involving even Lindemann's pretty sister, Uschi.

'We are going back to the flat to discuss something,' he had informed the assembled company at the Paris Bar, 'and may be some time.'

His herdsman, major-domo or Fidus Achates 'Mad' Mick had sworn by him. When strong men flinched he (Winky) advanced to show his true mettle; he was all steel, all quiet resolution. Ten minutes of nerve was all that was required (passing nonchalantly through security checks, crossing borders with contraband) and he had it. He just stared them down and brazened through. He was a hard man, a sound man; you could depend upon him. Once Mick, much the worse for wear, having dispatched a bottle of rum, was attacked by two Wicklow mountainy men who bore him a long-standing grudge. They waited until they had him alone, footless, then set upon him, roaring abuse.

Now Mick sober had the strength of a bull; Mick well oiled was still formidable, but Mick footless was as a babe, incapable of defending himself and next to useless in a fight. But they hadn't bargained for this – Winky soberly sitting there sipping his pint. Off came the coat and he waded into them. The shirt was torn off his back but the two mountainy men fled for their lives. They hadn't bargained for another madman, and Winky in fighting trim with his dander up was like fighting ten madmen.

He had made a great impression upon Franz Born who perceived him as a true 'red-blooded Irishman', and on his (Born's) high recommendation he was voted in as the second Irish DILDO member and given a large studio near the Opera. Born thought that he understood archetypes and took to Prendergast, whereas he felt uncomfortable in the eely presence of the slippery Weaver.

The welcome party for William Prendergast was memorable. He read a come-hither gleam in Titty Born's honest brown eye (she, one of the most upstanding and correct of all the DILDO wives) and told a distinguished French critic to fuck off.

Mellowed with vodka Winky followed Titania into her kitchen

and before you could say Jack Robinson had her skirt up around her neck as she bent to remove something hot and tasty from the oven.

She was livid.

'I most certainly am not your girl nor your meat,' she told him, storming out to the guests with a plate of pies.

His louche Jacobean style of seduction (grin, ogle, pinch, proposition, pounce) did not appeal to all. The Blacks were there with five unprepossessing daughters in teeth-braces, Frau B. confiding that 'any woman can refuse penetration'. In a conspiratorial German-speaking huddle the Borns and the Kuguars discussed *Kabale und Liebe*, which they had seen together.

François Bondy, having just flown in from Paris, was kneeling behind the sofa where Peter Handke reclined; the distinguished French scholar straining his ears to catch what Handke was murmuring. Great things were expected of this Austrian *Wunderhorn*. *Die Publikumsbeschimpfung* had announced the arrival of a German-language prodigy of the finest water. Wolfgang Bauer, another Austrian dramatist from beyond the Alps, was in his shirt sleeves and could be heard distinctly. Not Handke.

Winky, at home at once, sat on the floor with his back to the wall, one arm about a pretty brunette. When asked to draw in his legs so that others could pass, he said 'Just jump over will you or fuck off?' to François Bondy, of all people, as though bullying a bullock through a hedge in Laragh.

From the hidden depths of County Wicklow with its protection rackets and organized thuggery for the Provo cause, Mad Mick had formulated his own generic term for those engaged in disreputable activities: 'Touaregs'. Was Master Winky, assuredly no friend of Provos, a . . . a Touareg? The itinerants or Travelling People called him Boss. They helped him shift a great boulder from the driveway, among the ferns. They called it 'her' and 'she', the inert granite pile was feminine and somehow shameful when exposed. They assured him they would hide it, bury it, from the eyes of the Missus, its rival. Winky spoke to them as man to man, and they in turn knew him for what he was: Lord of the Manor. They addressed him respectfully as 'Bossman'.

Had he not killed a man once, by mishap, one wintery night? Two boon companions had come down from Dublin for a booze-up; after a day of heavy drinking they were worn to a frazzle, one of them fast asleep in the middle of the path. Blinded by Winky's powerful headlights the inebriated friend may have given confused hand signals; but if he had made a haims of the hand signals it was nothing to the mess the heavy-duty Range-Rover made of his sleeping friend as Winky rode over him in slow reverse.

Exonerated in the District Court – the findings were that no negligence was involved – he felt there was blood on his hands. He was innocent but guilty. This happened in the foothills of the Wicklow mountains, into whose fastness that master of diguise Mick Collins had marched his secret army. The Prendergast domicile was a flea-ridden ancestral cottage in a hilly region of double rain shadow where rainfall seldom abated and the cattle strayed about bleeding from their udders and mooing piteously. From his sleeping-bag on the earthen floor Weaver saw the morning stars shining down the chimney and a rough-voiced man on local radio spoke with authority about bulls.

It was the drunk man's mistake, but he never got up after Winky had passed over him in the heavy Range-Rover.

III

*Injuries of
Time and Nature*

Im Gemäuer pfiff der beste Wind

Varve (Sw. formerly *hvarf*) turn, layer. A pair of thin layers of clay and silt of contrasting colour and texture which represent the deposit of a single year (summer and winter) in still water at some time in the past.

The Oxford English Dictionary

36
Prinzregentenstrasse 5

About this time Lore at last quit the parental home for a small self-contained flat on Prinzregentenstrasse. Her first act of independence had not been a dose of the clap but an unwanted pregnancy; but Lore never intended to marry and did not want a child. 'You have too many already,' she told Weaver.

An old ('old and dirty', Lore said, sniffing) Polish woman had lived at no. 5 Prinzregentenstrasse for many years and had moved out of Berlin as Lore signed the lease. The place was filthy but she had seen possibilities. The painters were sent in with a crate of beer and transformed it into a white chocolate box. Mama Schröder contributed cutlery; Lore hung her own drapes, bought a bed, had a shower installed. Papa Schröder would use her empty bedroom as his office. A new carpet was laid at No. 5 and Papa and Mama Schröder came with a bottle of champagne for the house-warming. Weaver roamed the vicinity, waiting for them to leave. Her dancing-teacher was also anxious to view the new quarters; Lore had moved fast, was installed within a week of seeing the advertisement.

When he judged the coast to be clear, Weaver phoned the new number. It was on the ground floor overlooking an area of shrubbery and the back of a block of flats in a quadrangle, but with enough space between; Lore had a small balcony for sunbathing. The controlled rent was most reasonable. It was a flat for one person. Lore's few books were arranged on the shelf behind glass: Kokoschka's autobiography, Peter Brook on the theatre, Hemingway's *Fiesta*, a birthday present from Weaver for her twenty-eighth birthday.

It was to be a move towards finding a larger flat that would be home for Lore and Weaver when Nancy and Nico left Berlin; *her* dream realized. 'You must be stern,' she said. 'You must be hard; you have to be harder than she is.' A divorce solicitor had been consulted, a man oily as a Freudian, with a wet handclasp and a damp eye. Weaver had refused to return to the office to sign documents; we make our own verbal agreements, he told Nancy.

Lore's mother had brought roses and arranged them in a vase, and the lingering scent that remained (from the sender, not the roses) was the closest Weaver had been to she whom her daughter with heartbreaking tenderness called 'Mammylein', on her new white telephone (for that had been installed too).

Lore used a special voice for her parents. Every evening about six Mammylein phoned, and Lore had this special loving voice for her. She had perhaps inherited some of her mother's nature; Weaver thought of her as both anaemic and neurasthenic. *She* had moved silently from her bed into another room, a spare bed, when loud jazz was played in the flat below, said nothing. The awfulness of war, the humiliations endured while they were in hiding, this had made her withdrawn and frightened; her nerves were scraped clean. Lore had held the receiver out and Weaver had heard the thin nervy voice of Axel's *Frau*.

Lore had spent some time in a sanatorium at Bühlerhoe in the Alps. At Harrogate she had felt homesick and lied about the state of her health in letters home. Come home, they wrote. *Not* to be in Berlin was a sickness; she must return immediately. They sent the air fare and were waiting at Tempelhof when she stepped off the Manchester flight amid 'her bunch' who all looked pale and ill when she was looking radiant (back in Berlin again!), 'positively in the bloom of health'. They were loving parents, Axel (Weaver saw him as if cast in bronze) and *Kränkelnde Mutter*, the ailing one who wore gloves in bed in order to keep her pale hands clean while reading *Christ und Welt*; and there came Papa Schröder in slippers and dressing-gown, bearing the morning breakfast tray of coffee and toast, opening the curtains, assuring Mammylein that the day was fine, all solicitude, smiling at his wife who was carefully drawing on gloves of finest chamois, a lady from a previous century, a porcelain doll. Delicate and pale Mama Schröder had quietly withdrawn herself from this raucous century; what love she had to give she gave to Axel, to Lore ensconced in her nice new flat, to the Hamburg son, and that was it.

The two red roses on the bedside table, her mother's present, were dying with their heads down. Weaver, no handyman, had painted two cupboards a splotchy green: Hooker's *No. 2*? The indicators on the Karman Ghia were not working, the door on the passenger side would not open. At least the Ristorante Rusticano had not changed, the patrons and the music were unchanged, 'their' waiter was off duty. Lore ate a good dinner and asked for a second carafe of Landwein instead of coffee. The place was half empty. Lore wore mulberry wool slacks, a white baneen jacket, a white linen scarf. Her moods flew around like a weathervane. She was going through all the humiliations attendant upon abortion procedures.

Crude as the medieval water-torture with leather funnel and a grinning fellow coming with big jugs of water, she was forcing herself to swallow four-litre bottles of Hungarian purgative, *Bitter Wasser aus der Budaer-Heilwasserquelle Medimpex*; an old doctor gave her a hard injection and told her to return in ten days 'to learn her fate'. Her dancing-teacher was rallying round and had found a place to stay in The Hague. Lore had been in contact with a Mevrouw Schlehbaum and booked herself into the Hotel Ardjdena, Den Hague, Gross Herzog 204, where she could be contacted. 'If I come back,' she said sourly. The Monday after the operation she had free; her boss was away. Her dancing-teacher had promised to look after her. She would lose a lot of blood. Her nights were disturbed with many visits to the bathroom, she wanted to trample on Weaver snoring in the camp-bed that resembled a stretcher or straitjacket. In the daytime after work she sat watching TV on Mammylein's small black-and-white set. All day on Saturday she sat before it, she who rarely looked at TV (Weaver never); but her temper did not improve. She was thinking of The Hague, the humiliations ahead; what she called 'my Conossa'.

37
Autobahn in Twilight

Not all women weep alike; some are as different as ice and fire, some are womanly weepers, others weep rarely and hard. Nancy *dissolved* into tears. Lorelove bled tears, wept blood, chewed up her pulpy lips, looked daggers – these were *German* tears. But it took a lot to make Lore cry.

But now tears that were heavy as mercury fell straight down and splashed between her boots on the bare floorboards of Winky's studio, where he swore he would never work. Fate was at play. Now that he was sculpting small hand-sized objects, sheila-na-gigs and suchlike, he was given a large studio where he could, if he wished, sculpt veritable giraffes.

Lore wept because Weaver was leaving Berlin and would not return; his promises were all lies. She wept because of something that she must explain. In the meantime she granted him her last favours but as if absent-mindedly, her thoughts far away (on the outskirts of Geneva on the autobahn at twilight), herself far away too. She was his to use or abuse as he saw fit; his pleasure would always be hers as well, but now she had little relish for it. Her heart wasn't in it; but she would oblige him anyway, leaning over the wooden bar and looking down into the shadowy well of the studio, full-bottomed with hair about her face, masked by her dark tresses, and miles away in her thoughts.

The large undraped window gave on the street two levels below and on the Opera opposite where lights showed GÜNTER GRASS: DIE VOGELSHEUCHEN spilling out though not far enough to reach into the studio which was shrouded in darkness. Passers-by if they looked in would only see a shadowy formlessness, a clump of darkness on the upper level, where Weaver for the last time enjoyed Lorelove's favours *a tergo*, as she was undressed only enough to admit him and was weeping as if something had been broken in her or something was hurting her (and it wasn't Weaver).

A shining yellow limousine glided by with a gloved driver deep in conversation with a lovely lady in furs. The figures, seen from the chest up, looked bluish in the dashboard lights; the driver with a thumping fine cigar clenched between his teeth and his jaw stuck out, the two of them in fact looking magnificently stuck up and haughty, with this stealthy *clandestine* look about them, as if up to no good; now drifting out of sight as Lore choked on her tears.

'Oh I'm being silly . . . need to blow my nose. Do me up, Weaver, be a gentleman. I'm all wept out.'

Weaver in a gentlemanly way zipped himself up and in the bare kitchen or gallery found a bottle of Smirnoff half depleted and made up two fierce Polish-Russian shots with blocks of ice as they often had in the Queer Bar run by a pederast Pole who greeted them ironically: 'How are the young lovers this evening?'

'Here – this should brace you up. I'll be back in Berlin before you know I have left. Don't fret.'

He knew it was a lie. They would never share an apartment in Berlin; he had known that when they stood together in the terrible flat in Charlottenburg.

'Fret? I do not fret. You will return if you can. But' (she touched his arm) 'I am . . . *untröstlich*, Weaver.'

Here she wept; for the very worst had happened on the eve of Weaver's departure for Munich. Her boss had been killed in a head-on collision with a lorry on the autobahn soon after leaving Geneva for the long haul to Berlin – he and Grete Weiser and the housekeeper and even the dogs. 'The Schwerins are wiped out,' in a silly accident that need never have happened. They who never travelled together; setting off at the very worst time, as darkness fell.

Weaver, not knowing what to say, said nothing but put his arm about her; for what was there to be said? So they sat together on the top step in the gloaming and sipped vodka and tasted the ice and fire and no doubt entertained (if that is the word) some considerations of those Final Things that must in time come to us all, to be recorded with all the ones who had gone before, all set down in the Great Book of Numbers.

38
A Purgative Called 'Bitter Tears'

1

> Then she crawls naked and all smeared
> with filth into the pigsty . . .

There was no disguising it. Lore was well and truly pregnant and it didn't improve her temper. Not that it showed much, it was early yet, but she suffered from morning sickness, her stomach was tight as a drum, her temper short as a woman's temper can be.

Now she had to sleep on her back, took to criticizing Weaver, the slovenly breeder. He moved like a scoundrel, hands in pockets, smoking Gauloises, or a cigar clenched between his teeth, without a good word for anybody. Smoking was prohibited in the flat, cigars definitely *verboten*, smoke got into the curtains, beer- drinking was not encouraged, for the stink was carried in from the bar. 'This flat is too small for that,' she said, 'it's too small for two people.' Shoes had to be removed on entering, as if coming into a mosque. She took to sunbathing in the little balcony below which Herr Kunoth the *Hausmeister* was morosely clipping the bushes. They went to the Japanese restaurant and Weaver was criticized for ordering the same meal thrice in a row;

could he not be a little more adventurous, a little less provincial, and must he smoke at table, and no she did not want any more sake.

'No,' Weaver said sourly. 'I like only what I like and that's hard enough to get. This will do.'

'*Oh Quatsch!*'

When friend Lindemann called he sat on the bed, rested his head and shoulders on the wall, and Weaver made *Kalte Ente* with champagne and Moselle and they drank a flagon or two of this and Lore's temper improved, and then Lindemann sloped off and Lore took a damp cloth to the mark on the wall where the unwanted guest's head had left a stain, from hair cream or sweat, *tich-tich*! After drinking much *Apfelklarer* with Lindemann at the Dahlem Annapam pub (the proprietor sound asleep in a dim corner, clutching an empty bottle of Perversiko), Weaver stayed overnight at Haus Hecht, rather than disturb Lore, only to be reproached for not phoning her, she had waited up with the telephone beside the bed. Well, ding and dong; it was a new regime.

The reign of the Cold Duck, Lindemann said in a sour aside. Lore said that she was preparing herself for an abortion and it would have to be done outside Germany, maybe in Holland, for with the 'Hollands' it was legal. Weaver got the addresses of some Munich abortionists and Dr Weissenborn knew of a scraper who lived in great splendour in Beskidenstrasse not a stone's throw from where Weaver lived. Then Lore, through her Hamburg brother, got the name of an abortionist in The Hague; she was putting herself in the hands of a certain Dr Lena Luge and a date arranged. It would be all over in two days; and no, she didn't want Weaver to accompany her; she would prefer to do this on her own. It was her fault that she had taken no precautions and it would be her funeral; she, not Weaver, would be 'under the knife'.

Weaver now slept on the floor in a sleeping-bag beside Lore's bed; slept on and off, watching the neon lights of the city blink on and off behind the blinds, listened to the sound of ambulances, the police sirens going all night; woke unrefreshed in the morning, stiff as if he had been whipped, with Lore stepping over him, on her way to wash and dress and take a mug of coffee and prepare herself for another day of new employment. The Karman Ghia was parked outside the flat; she had not far to go, to an office near the Europa-Center. She had an office to herself, no Old Admirer to pester her with unwanted attentions; her new boss was most formal, a Herr Hareng in a branch of UNESCO dealing with grants and handouts and such support as was thought fit and proper for certain poor under-developed countries, but one referred to them as Developing Countries, in a nice diplomatic finesse. She had a short lunch-break and took sandwiches and yoghurt into the Tiergarten; went back and took dictation in three or four languages, typed up letters from this very particularized data, offered the letters to be signed to Herr André Hareng, and posted them after work in the mail box at Zoologischer Garten opposite the Augustinerkeller under the bridge girders where she and Weaver had their first assignation in the snow.

Now she wanted to know how long he intended to stay? A year! Much too long. Six months? Too long. A month? Too long, she said, shaking her head. A week? Well . . . a few more days; she had a girlfriend coming to stay and needed the sleeping-bag, also needed time to prepare herself. Not a word of reproach, but how she had changed. Weaver saw clearly enough that it was time to pack and go. Lore was no longer interested in cooking meals; she could live on salads, and again complained when Weaver returned from a bar and stank up the place with beer-stinks; she threw open all the windows.

Weaver phoned a friend in Munich.

Varna said, But of course . . . When? She had enough room, it was no trouble. Next morning the air fare arrived by special delivery and shortly afterwards Varna phoned to ask whether

Weaver had booked his flight yet, and why not? So Weaver walked to the BA office hard by the DILDO office and booked a single flight one-way via Air France to Munich the next day, 4 September. Lore did not offer to drive him to Tempelhof. She was already at work when Weaver flew out. It was a relief to be getting out of Berlin and out of the small apartment that had become a trap for both of them.

Landing at Riem, he told the woman taxi-driver *Prinzregentenstrasse fünf, bitte!* lit a cigar and settled back like a pasha for the smooth ride into Munich. The *Föhn* was snapping at the huge Olympic flags that lined the way from Riem Airport into the centre of Munich. When that wind blows, everything before it becomes surreal. Nothing upsets Bavarians more than the *Föhn*, that devious Italian wind that slips in over the Alps and whistles through the Brenner, whispering Latin things into German ears. (Count Ciano had noted in his diary that the Germans were dangerous because they 'dreamed collectively'.) Be that as it may, when the *Föhn* blows, surgeons lay down their scalpels and publishers' readers cast aside typescripts, both knowing their judgement to be impaired. Remote objects, such as church spires, draw closer. Then the good citizens of Munich like nothing better than to sit for hours on window-seats or out on small balconies, to stare down into the street below, observe life passing.

In Jakob-Klar-Strasse the retired boxer takes up his position early, and there he sits all day, fortified by mugs of foaming *Bier* handed out to him by an unseen *Frau*, reduced to just a brawny arm.

A positively Latin feeling for blueness prevails: *lividus* bleaching out to the delicate washed-out blue-bleach of the Bavarian sky over the Englischen Garten, manifest in the watery but steadfast blue eyes of the citizens, in the flag, on *Volksbier* labels; it's a true Münchener blueness with a Catholic feeling to it – Mary's blue on a May altar – and in the old-style shops run by agreeable rolypoly women the *Grüss Gotts* ring out right merrily.

Preparations for the XXth Olympiad had intensified through summer, with Police Chief Schreiber's men out in waders cleansing the old Isar of a detergent overflow (*Neu! Ajax mit der Doppelbleiche!*) from a paint factory. Germans were on a cleaning bender, scrubbing and scouring; while the *Süddeutsche Zeitung* reported that athletes and politicians alike were 'fascinated' (*begeistert?*), yes absolutely fascinated, by an opening ceremony quite without 'military undertones', or any sort of manipulation along those lines. Lord Killanin, an esteemed and portly Irishman, was in charge.

Sitting back in the taxi at his leisure, Weaver was driven grandly through Munich and up to an imposing residence that he had never seen before in his life, and here the taxi came smartly to a stop and the taxi-woman called out '*Fünf!*' Where in the world had he seen this place before? It seemed vaguely familiar. He saw a strained pale face at a window addressing a crowd that stood below looking up. *He* covered them with the dark varnish of his public moralizing; *his* dark vision of themselves, their German destiny, their *Schnicksal*. He had offered it to them in the only form they could not resist. His 'ice-cathedral' formed and shaped by a hundred searchlights probing the night sky looked like *their* future in the clouds; the monster rallies, the chanting, the goose- stepping and the furled banners were intoxicating; *en masse* they believed him, and when he addressed them collectively they were as one (one person before the leader, obeying *his* vision which was so much greater and loftier than their cowardice, their smallness and fears); and the larger the crowd the more certain that this would occur. He liked to stare into their eyes, probing with his blue eyes; as he liked to address them in scores of thousands. The parade ground in Nuremberg could hold two million uniformed men; his own thinking had always been in millennia.

Part of the insane millennium-fixated thinking or dreaming went hand in hand with the closed-up notion of pure genetic breeding, which went with racist thinking, the concept of uncorrupted purity of bloodlines, provided of course they were German. Colossal losses in the field would be nullified by the almighty power of the chromosome breeding its teeming millions of new German infants, future citizens in the conquered lands to the east. No matter how many fell, the blonde German *Mutti* (Germania herself) could make up the deficit; she would make it up to the dead.

So went his thinking.

When a pure negroid (small 'n') American could run faster, jump farther and fly first over hurdles faster than any white man, that only confirmed his own conviction about racial degeneracy: those fellows had just come down out of the trees.

In that one-to-one situation he entrapped them; this was his spellbinding black magic. He wanted to be buried high up, higher than they could ever aspire to; up above his birthplace in a sarcophagus designed by Speer. But he had ended up much lower, down under the ground, deep in the *Bunker* with Eva Braun, and as he drew his last breath and put the pistol to his temple, the advance spearheads of the Red Army came sprinting in.

'Not quite the right address, I am afraid,' Weaver said. '*Momentito*.' This would never do. 'Blame the *Föhn*,' he muttered, consulting his address book and finding that he had confused base and destination, was moving in the reverse direction to the one he wished to move, was going backwards in a dream. He found the correct address: 'Jakob-Klar-Strasse, *bitte*,' he said (German numerals were beyond him). 'Schwabing.' The taxi-woman nodded, she was most patient. They moved off towards Schwabing.

'Once answer the false stroke of the night bell,' Weaver told all Munich, 'you cannot put it right, not ever.'

A note tacked to the door of the flat read

Willkommen Weaver!
Mi casa es su casa.
Back pronto. V.

The key was under the mat. The flat had recently been cleaned and the fridge stocked with *Volksbier* and white wine against Weaver's arrival. A cut-glass bowl held several packets of Disque Bleu, the bed was neatly made up, the aneroid barometer registering somewhere between *veränderlich* and *verstörung*, or something between distraction (the mind being drawn asunder) and bewilderment (the mind imploding). Weaver scribbled a note and impaled it with Varna's drawing pin.

Gone for walk.
Back in hour. W.

A few days later Weaver lunched with his publishers and raised some money against present emergencies. He went to have himself fitted for a two-piece linen suit. The elderly tailor had bad halitosis, snowdrifts of ancient dandruff lay like a light fall of snow on the beefy shoulders, and from the cavernous belly with each suspiration rose rich cloacal fumes of *terrine de canard* from which Weaver attempted to avert his face, while holding his breath. The tailor confessed to being related to Prince Otto von Bismarck, with seemly modesty (this Herr Bismarck kneeling and wheezing like a Pekinese); he whose bust stood in the Reich Chancellery until toppled and beheaded by an awkward workman of Speer's in that Valhalla of stone and marble whose bombed remains went into the Russian war-monument at Berlin-Treptow.

'You don't say!'

This fat old tailor was much out of condition, an indoors man, a big feeder, possibly afflicted with emphysema. He approached to stretch the tape about Weaver's waist and then knelt to run it up the inside of the thigh, inquiring civilly: '*Auf welcher Seite tragen Sie Ihr Geschlecht, mein Herr?*' (On which side do you wear your shame, sir? History repeating itself now as Farce); to which,

242

without thinking, the measured-up one stoutly responded '*Kann nie wissen*,' rather surprising himself.

Weaver continued to hold his breath, staring up at the ceiling, while Herr Bismarck grovelled at his feet.

'Oddly enough, Herr Bismarck, I believe you made up [ran up?] a pair of trousers for a friend of mine some time ago – a Mr William Prendergast.'

'Ahhhhh!' (this was enunciated hollowly with head to the very ground).

Had Winky not paid for them? Or offered a bouncing cheque?

In Schwabing now, in Varna's flat on Jakob-Klar-Strasse, amid framed pictures of strange viscera, the corks continued to pop, only stopping for punishing games of *Tischtennis*, singles and doubles with Volker Schlöndorff the movie man, his spouse Margarethe von Trotta and someone called Wolf, who appeared to be living with Varna.

The movie man congratulated Weaver on his whirling smash shot but was even more warmly praiseful of Ernst Lubitsch's *Madame Dubarry* showing in Munich and which he had seen a number of times. Weaver wanted to see Leni Riefenstahl's *Fest der Völker* which was on its eighth week at the Arri Cinema. Margarethe von Trotta spent some time under the table, retrieving poor shots, sulking, 'Shitshitshit!'

A certain freedom of language was *de rigueur* among the Munich fast set, among those who wished to thought 'with it'. 'Hi!' they said on meeting. '*Ciao!*' on parting. Hippy*sprach* was very much 'in'.

In Kolbergerstrasse among the publishing set they were apologizing for the mess at the Olympic Village and the killing of the Israeli weight-lifters and their trainers, as though personally responsible for the lax security. 'We are a disgrace in the eyes of the world – again.' Weaver wanted to say: 'Look, it's not your fault.'

Meanwhile the super-rat, immune to all poisons, had arrived in Rio. Six dead. Abu Daoud, where are you now?

Weaver was induced to make up a mixed foursome with Varna's ex-husband Willie Witty, who was in advertising, and his nice sweet new wife Hannelore (another Lore!) and an aged female friend over woody Chiemsee high up in the Bavarian Alps. Willie drove a large well-sprung limousine in a fast accomplished manner along narrow country roads, coming at last to the *Golfplatz*.

Germans togged out for golf are a sight to behold; they go for overkill, armed with *Golfschlägers*, two-tone golf shoes with spikes, a glove on the left hand (unless left-handed), peaked caps, sun-visors, zip-up jackets, scorecards; but since they cannot laugh at themselves (unlike the English, who play up their supposed incompetence, very tolerant with it: 'I made a right hash of it yesterday') they suffer agonies on the golf course; their own incompetence upsets and exasperates them. Germans cannot *endure* their own incompetence; a game without visible opponents disturbs them. And in golf you are your own opponent, even in matchplay, and particularly in mixed foursomes. *Accch Gott!*

Weaver spent most of the round helping to search for their strayed shots among the trees. Hannelore, peeved and flushed, poked at the bushes with her iron, hissing 'Shit! Shit! Shit!' between her teeth. Witty had been suspicious of Weaver's (former) low handicap (a Greystones 4) status ('*Nicht so gut*,' as Weaver duffed a shot) but the Wittys had lost 6 and 4 to the duffer and the hag, who wouldn't stop chatting. Between them they had lost three new golf balls, and by the eighteenth hole none were on speaking terms.

Showered and changed, with drink in hand in the bar, Weaver was told a shaggy dog German golfing story involving a grudge game between God and the Devil played in Heaven. *Accch*, a good German golfing story! Weaver had come to the conclusion that it was a game unsuited to the German temperament; and what a relief to be off the *Golfplatz*, with the lovely Hannelore scarlet in the face in pure rage. Weaver said he would return to Munich by train, and shared a carriage with an elderly couple of leathery skinned mountain hikers, man and wife in deerstalker and *Loden*, passing the *Oktoberfest* tents and stalls before drawing into the station, dead on time.

Was it the so-called Day of Mourning?

The leaves were turning. In shop windows now the signs read: '*Hallo Herbst! Du wirst chic!*' Weaver witnessed intemperance, fistfights, puking, in those lovely Ember Days. Tempers seemed to be frayed. *Tripper* and *Raptus* were on the increase, Dominguín had been gored at Bayonne (the *carnada* is always the fault of the torero). On the shallow balcony opposite, the ex-boxer pointed down into darkening Jakob-Klar-Strasse, and his wife appeared at the door to see what was going on. It was gusty *stürmisch* wind-tossed weather, followed by warm sunny days in Munich, when Weaver went walking.

In the streets, hands were constantly feeling and touching, groping and tapping, fingers parting long hair, touching noses, brows; the bearded lips rarely smiled, the looks exchanged with passers-by were just severe or merely sullen. Hands were never for one moment still, compulsively pulling and picking; plucking at the backs of leather seats, if a tear showed, pulling at it, tearing paper; restless, agitated, never still, the eyes restless.

Ach-ach! Tich-tich! We cannot stop even if we wanted to, have become voyeurs watching atrocious acts. The lies are without end because the hypotheses are also without end. In Munich the same feature films that were showing in Berlin had been released: *My Name is Nobody* (*sic*), *Little Pig-Man*. '*LIEBE*' was sprayed indiscriminately over walls. A Judas-grille opened and a baleful bloodshot eye observed in a hostile way; in the nightclub hot as a sauna Weaver advanced with Varna and Wolf to the small bar.

The tall unsober teacher Barbara König was swallowing ice-cubes and pulling faces. It had become suspect to 'think'; all adults occupy the thrilling realm of moral dilemmas (civic inertia), protesting had become a form of political drama: *Strassentheater* – dangerous blindness with a dash of singularity.

On the large screens of colour TV sets in the windows of banks the Olympic Games went on, or seemed to, in silence, in triplicate; but these were re-runs of what had happened two days before, some of it shot in slow motion, to add to the unreality. The high pole-vaulter in the briefest of shorts lifted herself again on unseen springs, hair streaming, collapsing in slow motion onto a bolster and being swallowed up by it, but flowing out with arms raised above her head, dancing with delight. The GDR female athletes were again pouring over the hundred-metre hurdles, elegant as deer bolting before a forest fire. From the rapt tormented expression of the high-jumper, seen in close-up, one knew that track events were now being broken in the head, had become cerebral activity; they did not run on grass and the pole was not made of wood. The athletes on the podium were crowned with the bays and gave clench-fist salutes as their anthem was played (but now in silence) and their flag flew on the mast.

Weaver walked through Schwabing in the direction of the Isar embankment; and coming to the river, in the cool of the evening, was taken aback to find it flowing in the wrong direction. At that moment a low-slung black limousine approaching the bridge swung left, smoothly accelerating, packed with what looked like Italian mobsters, all wearing hats. It carried CD plates and flew pennants the colours of the Irish flag, presumably a decoy.

Trams clanged around the steep corner at Max-Planck-Strasse, clinging to the wall. Shabby men were reading discarded newspapers in a small public park made private by high hedges. In a mossy fountain small white eggshells fallen from the nests above and broken in neat halves were somewhat magnified by the water and seemed to tremble in the slight magnification. Weaver stared long at these as though they had something significant to convey, something to teach him.

Buttercups grew along the grass verge on Thomas-Mann-Allee where a woman wearing gardening gloves was gathering red berries in a trug. Near the Englischen Garten Weaver encountered two sailors who inquired the way to the archery contest, one of them drawing an imaginary bow and letting fly an imaginary arrow. Weaver pointed in the general direction he thought it might be, walked on along the embankment, saw terns wading near the little weir and two brown beauties sunning themselves in bikinis near where two Americans had drowned on the previous summer. Men in shirtsleeves were out. Weaver strolled along the embankment, admiring the skyline of roofs painted by Grosz and Klee.

Two workmen in blue denim overalls sat silently at a table on which were arranged some empty beer bottles with the remains of their lunch under acacia trees buffeted by the wind; a most peaceful scene. But on Luitpoldstrasse, leading to and from the Olympic Village, the sirens never stopped wailing, the hounds baying after the fox had killed every fowl in the hen-coop. It was difficult to distinguish police from ambulance siren; destination lock-up, hospital or morgue. The call was for law and order; but what is that but disorder with the lid clamped down? The huge Israeli weight-lifters were all dead, their coaches too, blown to kingdom come with hand-grenades. The games would resume after the twenty-four hour suspension. The so-called Day of Mourning had been all hypocrisy; the motives for continuing were not too pure, for much money was involved, as well as national honour and pride. The word, no doubt, had come down from high places that on no account were the terrorists to leave German soil with hostages intact. Germany must not be made to look weak and foolish; the eyes of the world were upon Munich. 'You want your fucking jobs?' the red-faced Police Chief Schreiber asked the itchy-fingered *Sturmkommandos*. 'Go get those fuckers before they kill again!' A grainy photograph on the front page of the *Süddeutsche Zeitung* showed the scarcely politic Schreiber 'negotiating' on a balcony with a terrorist whose head was covered by a woman's body-stocking. To flee the world (the past) and dream, that was their intent; a sourceless craving now externalized, brought close. For them it would always be *Sperrmülltag*: Throwing-out Day. The heavy innocents stall-fed on T-bone steaks and pints of milk would lay down their lives in the Bavarian slaughter-house prepared for them.

Out in the Olympic Village the twenty-five hostages were still alive, but the ultimatum was running out. One hostage would be killed every two hours, beginning 15 *Uhr* (3 p.m.) Central European Time, unless the terms were agreed to, the Arab prisoners released. You free *our* Arab prisoners and we give you back your Israeli hostages. (Weaver was losing his bearings on the wrong side of the *friedensengel*, walking his shoes off, phoning up Varna and asking could she collect him in her Fiat, her 'Messerschmitt', he was lost). On which side do you wear your shame? Why bother about *Bach* if a saxophone gives you an idea of a better world? To say that Nature (History) abhors a vacuum is putting it mildly; *she will not have it*. The show must go on. Everything waits upon its gesture; life never holds still.

One handsome chain-smoking terrorist (Eddie Constantine playing Lemmy Caution) declared that *he* would have preferred death with brave comrades who had blown themselves up along with their victims; not a trace of remorse was shown, but no hypocrisy either. They were not interested in deals; they would kill if they must, human life meant nothing to them, and that included their own. Principles were involved; they were, if you wish, small keys to open big doors.

Aged Avery Brundage had flown in from the United States. The fire too had come from afar: Greece. Was this a good augury? Few were willing to predict. The American traveller Paul

Theroux would write later that the games were of interest because they 'showed a World War in pantomime'.

Weaver liked nothing better than to be walking his feet off in this city of fine *Fräuleins* (great-great-grandchildren of those so admired by Heine), stone goddesses guarding the bridges over the Isar (even if it was flowing the wrong way), spouting fountains, Greek sirens with Bavarian thighs, eyes closed against the insupportable weight they carried on their shoulders; heavy pillars pockmarked by bullets (Russian lead) fired from afar. They were the protectors of the river and its bridges across which at set intervals the villainously low-slung glistening black (tar-black) limousine with CD number plates crossed again, packed with what Weaver had supposed were Italian gangsters – they had the Mafia family look, all wore overcoats and hats – but which had turned out to be the Irish delegation with their Taoiseach, a Corkman by the name of Lynch presenting his credentials to Chancellor Brandt in his place in the country.

2

'Somebody for you,' Varna said holding out the long extension. She spent much time on the phone, drawing the extension cord after her from room to room, charged up, snickering.

'Who could that be?'

'Your Berlin girl, I guess.'

Lore, in Prinzregentenstrasse, Berlin, told Weaver in Schwabing, München, that she had had a phone call at the stroke of midnight on the day before, in the middle of the Al Fatah ultimatums. A muffled male voice, possibly Basque, not a Berlin accent, said: '*Es wird noch kommen*,' and hung up. It must come; it still must come; you have been warned. It was most creepy. It was not a friend playing a joke; it was the beginning of her Conossa.

She was packed and ready to leave for The Hague and the tender mercies of Dr Lena Luge.

Weaver (not at his best on the phone) was about to reply 'The best of luck,' but that would never do. 'Hope it goes well for you,' was hardly an improvement, after a long silence.

'I hope so too,' Lore replied after another pause and hung up.

The Freedom Angel (*Der Friedensengel*) balanced herself precariously on one foot while hopefully extending a palm branch into the blue void of air. Across the plinth an activist had squirted his message in white aerosol '*LIEBE DEINE TOTEN!*' Did it mean 'Love your dead'? The goddesses had closed their eyes. A shadow had followed Weaver into Munich, flying in on the same day. If the Black Death had entered Europe as a plague-bearing flea on the body of a rat, sophisticated international terrorism, late-twentieth-century-style, had entered Germany from the Middle East, via Riem, in the person of Muhammad Daoud, codename Abu Daoud, travelling on a forged Iraqi passport.

Twice had Weaver almost run into him, ignorant of who he was; not even Schreiber knew his identity, faked or not, his whereabouts or his secret intent.

Once, in his endless perambulations about the city, Weaver passed a restaurant near the station and a man was coming out, folding a newspaper, and it was Abu Daoud lighting up a Turkish cigarette, holding the rolled newspaper as a baton.

Once, for an hour or so in the darkness of the Arri Cinema, he and Weaver (unbeknownst to each other, Professor and Terrorist) would watch the same old shocker by Leni Riefenstahl: *Fest der Völker*. The acrid aroma of Turkish black tobacco that had wafted back three rows to tickle Weaver's nostrils came from Abu Daoud's hand-rolled Turkish cigarette; but the rolling plume of smoke that enveloped the Imperial Eagle might have come from the mouth of Hell itself, in the 1936 recruiting documentary for National Socialism and the new German Man. Wagner shows me a world I am not sure I wish to enter, Weaver thought again; for was not this same smoke curling from the cooling towers of the death camps? And there was stout Hermann Goering, the cocaine addict as large as life, shaking with helpless laughter – had he broken wind in the Presence, had the Führer himself cracked a bad joke about black-skinned men? He had laughed only once in his life, in the presence of Speer; and was now leaning forward, rubbing his cold political hands. All had been arranged for an Aryan triumph, and now one American black man – Hitler could not bring himself to utter the name Owens – was breaking all the track records right before their eyes. Hitler's own putative son, Hess, all eye-socket and protruding jaw, like Tollund Man, watched Jesse Owens, who assuredly was no Aryan man, run away with all the track events.

The cinema was full of Munich war widows who sat bolt upright, motionless in their seats in an uncanny silence. Perhaps they were thinking of Stalingrad and the doomed divisions that had been sent in, twice. The *frische Divisionen* of which their dead husbands and sons had been part. Did they study that puffy unhealthy face under the peaked cap and think, If I had gone to him and said, Enough now, this must stop. You must call our sons and husbands back; you must stop this.

But one did not speak that way to the Führer.

The cigarette-puffing Al Fatah terrorist, whose father worked in Jerusalem for the Israeli City Council, a grandfather six times over, watched Hitler and Goering, the suicides, and thought his own bitter thoughts; and Weaver, with the acrid smoke still tickling his nostrils, watched too, surrounded by silent war widows.

It was certainly creepy; those faces, the stout Field Marshal shaking with unseemingly mirth (what could amuse him?); Hitler rubbing his hands, leaning forward to watch Jesse Owens flying through the air, and Hess showing no emotion whatsoever.

It was like looking at the face of a dead man who had died

smiling at some terrible joke ('The farce is ended'), and now that smile was fixed on the dead lips, had it been a good joke or a bad one? Or it was like treading in fresh human ordure in bare feet (like walking on the cheesy face of a decomposing corpse) as had happened to Weaver when walking by Wannsee, past the bullrushes and the lovers clasped in each other's arms, watching Weaver pass, embarrassed, with eyes lowered.

Hess was still serving out his life sentence in Spandau Prison, the Russians would not let him go, for his presence there meant a toe-hold in Berlin. What was Abu Daoud making of all this, breathing black tobacco smoke into his lungs, rubbing his hot hands, trying to fathom the German mind? What was one to make of the spider in the web glistening with dew before the credits rolled? or the male athletes with convict haircuts running naked around a misty Berlin lake – maybe Schlachtensee – on that early morning of 1936? Again one was looking at dead German soldiers.

Varna's friend Ulrike Noyes, a movie director, had been granted a rare interview with Leni Riefenstahl, who was still a handsome woman, and thought to have had Nazi sympathies. She confided that 'Hitler had been a good man led astray by bad companions': Röhm the pederast, Streicher the Jew-baiter, Himmler the chicken-farmer, Goebbels the gnome and *Gauleiter* of Berlin, their philosopher Rosenberg – phew, the Valkyrie Cabbala!

When it was over the Inge-babies, the war widows, dispersed as silently as they had assembled there. Mouths set in grim lines they went their several ways, thinking of *Kaffee und Kuchen*. But leaving silently, Weaver among them; and Abu Daoud, who had lit up again, following deep in thought.

Two other such surreal pictures came to Weaver's backtrack-ing mind. In the La Rouche district of Paris a hand had chalked on a wall: '*LIBÉREZ HESS!* On a long wall near the Øster Søgade in Copenhagen another had chalked: '*ANARKI ELLER KAOS!*'

*

On 28 September Weaver was *still* walking around Munich, the unsober guest who refuses to leave, and cannot stop talking. By then, no doubt, Abu Daoud had removed himself, still travelling on a false passport under an assumed name, flying first in the wrong direction to put the pursuers off the scent, leaving behind the familiar acrid aroma.

FALSCHE SPEKULATION DER LUFTPIRATEN!

spookily whispered the inseminators of false information. Weaver, let it be here whispered, had been unfaithful to Lore with Ulrike Noyes, who had received him in bed in a sulphurous embrace. She had her nose broken at the age of seven in a refugee camp, as a consequence of her father's sentencing.

RUSS MAY BEEF UP NAVY IN MED

muttered the *New York Herald Tribune* in rapid newsspeak.

BODIES OF SLAIN ATHLETES REACH LODZ,
FLOWN FROM MUNICH!

At the Staatliches Museum Weaver walked after Varna, looking over an exhibition of early Bavarian folk art.

'Notice that art and progress come via the weaponry and not from the kitchen,' the Professor said. 'The arms of the footsoldiers – all peasant conscripts – hardly differ from their primitive work tools. War was a kind of labour for them; they were still doing what their Master ordered them to do. We can say that art and progress come from the finely decorated swords and pistols of the mounted officers. The men walk to battle, carrying their balls and chains. *Ergo* . . .'

'Stay out of the kitchen?'

'Damn right.'

One day Munich was as if dead. Or as if all the citizens had left; the shops were closed and the streets deserted. Ulrike played *Tischtennis* against Wolf who had a soft-porn library in his room. Mainly nudes a-frolic in sudsy baths. He (Wolf) was getting a hard time from Varna. Weaver and Varna played against the Schlöndorffs, Volker still full of praise for Lubitsch, and his wife *still* under the table, hitting the floor with the edge of her bat and muttering 'Shitshitshit!'

Weaver walked through Schwabing and in the windows of the banks there was a re-run in triplicate of all that had happened before.

Songstress Mireille Mathieu, who came from a poor family, was driven around the Marathon Sporthalle standing up in a white open-top Ford Capri while belting out *'Ein Platz an der Sonne fur Jung und Alt'*. Not to be outdone in vulgarity, Papst Paul VI stood precariously upright in a thing that was called *eine Prunkgondel*, a floating version of the Papst John Paul II *Popemobile*, while graciously blessing some Venetian sewage, in the form of a clotting of dead flowers and scum. To the rear of this precarious vessel stood a group of what appeared to be Roman centurions.

Varna's flat had been cleaned by the weekly cleaning woman and the rugs had their colours renewed. Framed on the walls were strange tortured viscera, possibly human, in monochrome. A single flower, richly red with streaks of sunflower yellow in its heart, hung in a small blue damask vase. Red of anther, hush of autumn, tread of panther.

That night, after much beer and Steinhäger, with pot-smoking and weeping on Varna's lap ('I am not good for either of them,' blubbered the deceiver insincerely, to Varna's intense embarrassment), Weaver had retired to his made-up bed and fell at once into a deep sleep; whereupon a strange and disconnected dream fell upon him – as one might say 'Darkness came and ate up the light' – shredding him to little bits.

It was like an old movie running at the wrong speed – something to do with sprocket holes – the characters moving in a jerky way, hamming it up and grinning at the camera, pulling faces. When the early mists rolled away there was Willie Winky carrying a plastic shopping-bag across the concourse before the Berlin Opera; his movements those of an Irish labourer crossing a mucky field in winter. His old wellingtons were sucking him back into the earth; he was come from milking, carrying a full milk can (in fact he was carrying half a dozen Schultheiss beers from the shop down the way); now coming closer and grinning at the camera and pretending to stagger, from the weight he carried. And Weaver stood at the long window in the studio and watched him cross the road.

Now the dream carried Weaver into a long room in another city, another continent. He stood in the long living-room at Bellos Guardo, home of the Rajinskis in Johannesburg, just after the Sharpeville massacre. The record player was playing one of Weaver's 78 rpms: Billie Holiday singing 'You're Mean to Me'. Luis Nkose was there and had drunk too much white wine on an empty stomach and was sweating. It was a month after Sharpeville and bloodstains of the sixty-nine killed still on the road and you could smell the blood, a sickly sweetish smell not pleasant like flowers. Nkose had been there among the crowd demonstrating against the Pass Laws at Vereeniging.

The wounds in the backs of the dead had been so terrible it was thought that dumdum bullets had been used; but these were 'tumbling bullets' fired from Sten guns without any pause between bursts. A rumour was circulating that a mob of Africans were marching from the locations on Johannesburg. Emmett, a newborn babe, was being carried by Nancy (how young she looked!) out of the nursing home run by Catholic nuns who had refused to release Emmett before Weaver had produced a cheque. And now they were being driven by Roger Amory (normally a daredevil on the road) at a stately forty miles an hour in his clapped-out DKW with silencer removed, home to the high flat on Isipingo Street which might just as well have been called Jacaranda Street for it was lined on both sides with these trees with their pretty blue bell-like flowers.

Billie Holiday was singing and sweat rolling off Nkose's black face, still and dark as teak. 'What kind of a chap is this Spengler?' Weaver in the nightmare was asking Nkose, of the colonel who was the Afrikaaner Chief of Police, the man responsible for the massacre; Nkose replied, with eyes closed and sweat rolling off his face: 'Spengler? He's a butcher. He has the face of a butcher.' And then Weaver touched Nkose's arm lightly with his fingertips and asked: 'Are you dying, Luis Nkose?'

'No, man, but I think I'm gonna be sick.'

Which he proceeded to do straightaway, sighing deeply and leaning forward over the revolving turntable and opening his mouth wide to deposit a small tidy colourless grey-white puke right on top of Billie Holiday, so that it was carried around and around, slowing her up, as Nkose wiped his lips and Weaver studied the puke (African beer mixed with white wine from the Portuguese corner store, it would have made even Colonel Spengler sick).

'I think I'll kip,' Nkose said, wiping his brow with one pale palm, and kneeling down he removed his thin jacket and folded it neatly for a pillow, lifted up a corner of the starched linen tablecloth, having also removed his shoes with two quick pulls, and disappeared for a nap under the table. But seconds later his voice called out: 'Hey, hey, hey, Weaver man, you wanna know what Spengler looks like? You just crawl in here! You'd never guess who's in here *snoozin*'! The Big Shot himself – Spengler! Can you beat that! Come an' havva look. This is good!'

Weaver removed his jacket (it seemed the proper thing to do) and kneeling down made to follow after Nkose who was now calling out: 'Wakey, wakey, baby, you ain't gotta pass for this place. We'll have to arrest you, my baas. Wakey, wakey!' Weaver drew the stiff immaculately white tablecloth aside and saw Nkose tweak the great man's toe, which was sticking out of his sock. The Colonel's highly polished jackboots were arranged side by side with strict military precision. His uniform was unbuttoned and rumpled and he was regarding Nkose with no friendly blue eye, which was then turned upon Weaver.

'Wake up, my baas,' Nkose said, striking the angry Colonel abruptly on the knee. 'Time to wake up.'

The table was draped with this cloth of finest Irish linen that stretched the length of a cricket pitch, purchased at Stuttaford's with no regard to cost by Rita von Rajinski (née Power). There on green baize, with a new deck of cards for every session, Weaver had played poker with Arno von Rajinski and Brian Crossley and Roger Amory, imbibing copious quantities of vodka, while Mrs R. (who played other, more serious games) entertained an Israeli parachutist on the couch. 'I'm sick of entertaining Africans,' Arno complained of his wife's many black friends and acquaintances; 'I shouldn't be surprised if there was one under the table.' And by God there was! Hereabouts the dream ended, with cards spilled on the green baize and all the gentlemen rising, as Rajinski cautiously lifted a corner of the cloth.

4

On 28 July 1960 the Weavers had walked across the East London docks and stepped onto the gangplank of the Union Castle seagoing liner *Warwick Castle*, carrying Emmett their first-born in an African basket; bound for Tilbury via Port Elizabeth, Cape Town, St Helena, Ascension Island, the Canaries; the preliminary odours of Spain – cooking oil gone off, rough brandy, a blast of halitosis, assailed Weaver. And then the Cape rollers, vomit on the companionway mats, the dining-room half empty, the horizon tilting in a port-hole and the Belgian Congo kids running mad about the ship, yelling *'Malade! Malade!'* And then the hasty burst of killing fire from the trembling Stens; in say forty-five seconds of indiscriminate firing, so many lives gone *phut*.

In dreams there is no time, no ages; just a seamless, timeless state of the sleeper's drifting fears. It had been a time of dire portents in Jo'burg, in Vereeniging, and the place and date, 21 March 1960, engraved on the African heart that had already endured so much. To remember it or have it evoked in a nightmare was to make that heart bleed again; and some vague intimations of this had shaken Weaver.

Weaver awoke covered not so much in a strange sweat as in *a stranger's sweat*; since time is non-existent in our nightmares, it was 'fresh' as the night some twelve years and six months before, when it had been sweated out of lean Luis Nkose on the night following the massacre at Sharpeville. The intervening months, some one hundred and fifty of them, were as nothing, a shrug of Eternity in the evenly regulated breathing of Time.

Weaver was *wrung out* by the African's sweat, and decided then and there that it was time to return home, no matter how frigid the welcome. Besides, his funds were low. He showered and dressed himself and going into the small kitchen found Varna seated before a mug of coffee with a fresh copy of the *Süddeutsche Zeitung* to hand.

'I feel as heavy as yonder elm,' Weaver said, standing at the window and peering out at the day. Below, a snappily dressed couple were offloading high-fashion clothes from the back of a red Saab and carrying these expensive items in through an open doorway into a flat. He was the Eddie Constantine type, she the blonde Melina Mercouri; they had a libidinous look about them, no doubt a 'quickie' had crossed their minds, to the strains of Procol Harum's 'A Whiter Shade of Pale' (all the rage with

McCartney's evergreen 'Yesterday' in German) groaning on the turntable, to Melina's moans and Eddie's piggish grunting.

Pretty girls came from all over Germany to model in Munich, make themselves available to the men with money, begin to make their own fortune, hooked onto the grafters, the upwardly mobile ones. It was like that.

'Old as Kunz Buntschuh the insane court jester,' Weaver said (now they had gone in and shut the door, leaving the boot of the Saab wide open). 'I had a terrible nightmare but will spare you the details.'

'Here's your coffee.'

'Time to be moving on,' Weaver said, sitting down. 'Are you up to a walk in the English Garden?'

For Varna Anders was much averse to walking; she preferred to fly her Messerschmitt about Munich, ordered in food by phone, the *Volksbier* supplies were in a nearby bar. It was not in her nature to walk.

Her nature, what was Varna's nature?

They had known each other for years; once briefly on a roof in Spain they had been intimate. Nancy had thought her an Olympic diver on vacation – and this was years before the fatal XXth Olympiad – Nancy with her uncanny knack of getting hold of the wrong end of the stick. Varna in fact translated English-language porn ('One thrust and he was in') for the German Olympia Press. But now she was studying law, having abandoned her Chinese studies. She was the New Woman, living on her nerves, independent of men, except for what she needed. She had told Weaver, always curious, a little of her past. Her German past. How she had walked through a burning Munich holding her mother's hand and leading her into the country. The terrible abattoir stench was burning flesh from the bombing; on the margin of a wood stiff with frost they had come upon a dead soldier shrivelled away to nothing. It was like the carcass of a rat hung on a gatepost by a farmer to act as a bird-scare. She became head of the family; until one evening of a warmish September day in 1947 a stranger came knocking, like a beggar – her soldier-father returned from Stalingrad with the dregs of the *Wehrmacht*, last residue of the 'fresh' divisions minced up before Stalingrad.

She had not remembered him, and now she did not want him, she was head of the family. He took to his bed, saying little, turning his face to the wall, began to waste and pine; and then one day he slipped away again. He had never spoken of the war.

Those who had been there, before Stalingrad, would never forget it. None who had fought there would ever forget it. 'I had no feeling one way or another,' she admitted. He had been too long away, too much had happened since, now it was another Germany. As far as her feelings went, her father might just as well have died in Russia. The man who came back was not her real father, nor was the man who died in his bed. It was far away like a terrible nightmare that you resist with all your will, to keep it from landing on your back, fastening its teeth into your neck, taking you with it, mincing you up. You could hear it muttering and roaring all night. It was chewing up the German soldiers and spitting them out; whole divisions got ready, were put into battle, were chewed up; two great armies chewed up twice. In 1942 the Sixth Army was wiped out. Fake horoscopes spoke of valleys of darkness which had to be passed through; a second Sixth Army was prepared and sent in, in 1944, and it in turn wiped out. Faces froze like masks. The triple-pronged attack, the breakout when it came, would flatten them, roll them back all the way to Berlin. A madman was in charge and no one could stop or divert him; not even Speer, who was close to him.

For, nightmare upon nightmare, his former ally had become his foe, and he was madder still. Battles would be fought at night using searchlights in the depths of a black ironbound winter. The madman paced the heated hall of the Berghof and spoke his thoughts aloud as the general mood became blacker and blacker; *he* felt free to do so, for those closest to him feared him most and the monsters he had created. His soldiers *ate* cold; they *ate* space, they were very far from home. Gestapo and Waffen SS took the Jews, took the civil population as weasels go for rabbits with their heads against the end of the dark burrow, and the horror comes for them in the dark; it was like that then in Soviet Russia, the worst horror had taken hold, the absolute *non-plus-ultra* nightmare.

Walking to and fro and cracking his finger-joints the madman said: '*Wir schicken ein paar frische Divisionen hin und dann klappt das*,' as if ordering an adjutant to throw more logs on the fire. Or as Papa Schröder would laughingly put it: '*Das Tuch, mit dem ich mir den Hintern (Podex) abwische*' – It is the cloth I wipe my arse end on. For Stalingrad was encircled; the strategic maps laid out on the table showed a front twenty-five miles wide by 125 miles long, stretching from Voronezh to Stalingrad and the madman was saying We'll just throw in some fresh divisions and that will correct everything. The German Army was the cloth the madman wiped his bum on.

During the battle he was unable to make decisions at his camp at Winniza, showing not the white feather but an untidy Schickelgruber streak ('They will put me in a zoo in Moscow!'). The snow burned to the touch and the faces of his soldiers turned first dark grey and then almost black. The Bavarian demagogue had badly under-estimated his Georgian rival on at least three counts: the unflinching Russian will, the Red Army (powered by the unflinching Russian will) and – the ally of the above, cruel Nature become kind, unbending a little, for the Russians were used to it, could stand it – the black teeth of the ferocious Russian winter.

On Saturday the *Süddeutsche Zeitung* obituary notices confronted pages of porno movie advertising of unrestrained lewdness: Marie Garibaldi was showing off her twat in *Amore Nudo*. While Gerd Müller, the saucy wizard of Bayern München, a man with two left feet, had scored the impossible goal (missed by

261

Wolf!); turning his back on the defender and executing a quick somersault to shoot into the net and be warmly embraced by his captain, Beckenbauer. (Only a will of iron, by standing still and facing it, could defeat the well-trained armies of the madman). But one thing was certain: the dead ones could not cavort with the nudely ripe Marie Garibaldi, who was positively *simmering with amore*.

A press photo of the big Olympic signboard carried a final sententious message ('Ask not what your country . . .') boldly signed AVERY BRUNDAGE, for all the world to see and admire. Why not BONDAGE? Why not go the whole hog and sign himself BANDAGE and have done with it? No press photo showed an Al Fatah terrorist with face hidden in some woman's stocking; the 'good' German dailies were anxious to bring life back to normal. A winter beach at Cuxhaven would do admirably. A breakwater with vista of calm sea, no one about; for caption the familiar rubric (reassuring smell of old vomit) '*Das Ende der Saison*'.

5

On 28 September there was 20 *Grad* of *Bodenfrost*. *Schwarzer September* had a little time to run yet. The cover of *Stern*, which Varna was leafing through, displayed a corn-yellow blonde in the act of unpeeling her corn-yellow T-shirt, her only article of clothing. Stamped on the nearside cheek of her arse, like a seal of prime quality stamped by a dealer or butcher on high-grade meat, affixed as guarantee, were the now familiar entwined circles of the Olympic symbol, alas now somewhat shopsoiled and sadly dishonoured, most poshlustily. '*La naturale temperature des femmes est fort humide*,' breathed Amyot in a soft Gallic aside.

'There are moments when I am able to look without any effort through the whole of creation [*Schöpfung*], which is nothing more than an immense exhaustion [*Erschöpfung*],' Varna confessed in her cut-glass voice. 'Ever feel that?' Answer came there none.

'Professor?'

'I have never felt any other way.'

'Let's go then,' said Varna rising with resolution, the coffee in the percolator finished, 'you and I, and walk in your English Garden. A little fresh air might buck us up. Do us good, eh?'

So out they sallied, the woman who never walked and the man who never stopped walking: *Der grosse Spaziergänger*.

Varna Anders liked to be courted by oldish, staid, rather helpless men of means, whom she felt free to treat like dogs or dirt. They would anticipate that, and were in circumspect attendance as a sort of counterbalance to Wolf, who sometimes got it in the neck, through no fault of his own. His attempts to watch World Cup soccer on the box were soon scotched. '*Nein! Nein!*' hissed Varna as if treading on a dog turd; and instantly the picture had died under his hand, reduced to a small anus, sucked inward, then darkness. Wolf, abject, slunk from the room.

Through the snarled-up Munich traffic Varna Anders drove her orange Fiat as a Messerschmitt through clouds, passing wrack. Fastidious by nature, or having disciplined herself to it, she was tidy in all she did; her flat was spotless, all very much in *Ordnung*, and the box set on the floor so that son Joachim had to lie on his stomach to see it. A woman came to clean once a week, bring back (bring up) the latent colours in the rugs dulled by use, by feet. She was neurasthenic, had taught herself to read Chinese, drank air; her nostrils seemed permanently pinched. She spoke of the *Föhn* wind and the effect (disturbing) it had on others but not mentioning herself, who always was all nerves. Sometimes she spent a whole day in bed; sometimes her blond son Joachim did the same, for he had inherited her nature. She had bought a small parcel of land in the country, a copse of trees off the beaten track; built a tree house for her son. She went there for emotional recharging, for repose.

Prone to a certain kind of spiritual narcosis, with which their naturally generous natures are oppressed, the Germans must *suffer themselves*. For the average Bavarian (a baleful mixture of sentimentalist and brute) it could get much worse, though Varna was far from being a typical Bavarian. She and her elderly admirer, a doctor who was permitted to approach just so close, had found some common ground in their fondness for Tuscany; the Italian nature appealed to them, as Munich had a partially Italian side to it.

Varna Anders was training to be a barrister, having abandoned the translation of pornographic books and any further progress in Chinese studies; now she was passing impossible exams, fainting – Madame de Warens confounding Voltaire, plunging her hands into freezing water, studying all night, trying to stay awake, keeping her brain active and steady. She gave poor Wolf unmitigated hell when it suited her; he was her escape valve, though less so than the copse in the country. She liked to watch him crawl, as the aspens fidgeting in the *Föhn*. When Weaver suggested a swim in the Starnbergersee she was delighted; a bird-cry (oyster-catcher? shrew?) wrung from her – *a swim*! Why not? Varna the ice-cool fighter pilot climbed into the cockpit of her Messerschmitt 109 and drove like the wind to a wooden jetty reaching out into the azure. She had a compulsion to memorize the five registration digits of all the cars she passed, and she passed them all, as the lovely hills rolled away.

American fighter jets were having practice runs on the far side and up there on a hill was a monastery that brewed good beer and they would drive there and drink it from tall mugs, sitting in the courtyard. Out there in the blue, under the waves, another madman had drowned together with his physician.

Victims and victors one did not speak of; yet every so often Varna let slip this and that. Her upbringing and past had indeed been curious; until one day a stranger stood at the door and demanded of her: '*Erinnerst Du Dich an mich?*' No, she did not remember him, never having set eyes on him before. '*Ich bin Dein*

Vater,' he said, so she stood aside for him and he stumbled in. He asked for a drink of water. Her mother came into the kitchen and screamed *'Hänschen klein*!' and sat on a chair as if her legs had been shot from under her. Hans Dieter Anders, late of the Wehrmacht's Sixth Army, twice defeated, twice annihilated, had returned from the dead, from Stalingrad, that tomb, walked back covered in snow, a zombie. Do you not recognize me? I *was* your father. His widow, gone chalk white, sat on a chair. She and her daughter stared at this shabby apparition that had come home. Her father from Mönchengladbach, long dead, pleads: *'Tu' etwas für mich'* (do something for me). But she cannot.

In a Schwabing travel agency Weaver bought himself a one-way ticket to London. With the last of his Deutschmarks he bought a babushka and books for Nico, a ball of wool for Nancy and a small fine marking-pen, an LP (Scriabin); and with the last of his strength bade Ulrike adieu (her hot kisses were as carbide burning).

And for Weaver, for *Willkommen* and goodbye, a squat and hostile security fellow in shirtsleeves rolled up and side-arms holstered, bawling *'Rausrausraus!'* at a line of chastened English passengers moving too slowly and a woman on the London flight having hysterics, laughing her head off. And then Weaver was in the air again, gin in hand and all remorse cast aside, puffing a slim cigar, his heart light as a feather, heading home.

The last of Munich was a roof of orange tiles lit by the evening sun and an incoming passenger jet landing on it or appearing to; Varna's car turning back from Riem, about to burn the tyres all the way to Jakob-Klar-Strasse and home, flashing by the huge Olympic flags that were being stolen as momentos.

Two months later a Lufthansa flight into Munich was highjacked and the three terrorists 'sprung' from three high-security prisons sixty miles apart. When interviewed they continued to chain-smoke and speak in broken English and were said to be 'of terrifying niceness'. They had the rugged good looks of B-movie actors and justified the killings at great length. Somewhere out in the brave Arab world three ravishing girls awaited their return most eagerly.

In February 1973, 'Abu Daoud', now passing himself off as a Saudi sheik, was arrested in Central Amman by a Jordanian security patrol. His forged passport showed him to be the father of six children. His 'wife' was a fifteen-year-old girl carrying a handgun and ammunition clips which, on being arrested, she dropped. She apologized profusely to 'Abu' who replied: 'No sweat. You're doin' great, kid,' in a Humphrey Bogart voice.

What was one to make of that? Soon whole jet-loads of passengers would be bombed out of the sky.

Weaver, now barely tolerated in his own home, thought of the 'stranger' intruding into Varna's life and her frosty welcome. In Berlin now, how many widows of a certain age were sadly admitting *'Mein Mann ist tot in Stalingrad.'*

39
Lore's Lost Child

Their child's life had been terminated in The Hague by the sinister lady abortionist Dr Lena Luge and little Hagen or was it Ulrike, unknown and unseen by either mother or father but flushed away, thrown out, discarded, buried shallowly in Dutch soil in the garden behind the clinic, was no more.

40

A Reading of the Cards

On a grey overcast Dublin day Weaver set out on a fateful journey northward, taking a cross-town double-decker via the Appian Way – Georgian doors all different colours – alighting at Lansdowne Road to change for a Dalkey-bound bus that would drop him near the Sandymount level-crossing. The learned philosopher's abode on Strand Road was but a stone's throw from the sea.

'I am in a deep mess with two lovely spumous ladies and know not which way to turn,' Weaver told the philosopher. 'Can you, old lecher, advise me how to proceed. I do not see my way at all.'

'H'mm, h'mm.'

'Nancy would have me leave her. Yet how could I manage in Berlin without some funding? – DILDO would not stump up again.'

'I know a woman who might be of some help.' She could foretell the future in cards; her flat was within walking distance. She would be at home; they could pay a call.

Ussher's house backed directly on Sandymount Strand and as a consequence he and his wife Emily spent much of the long winter abed with flu in their separate rooms, coughing and sniffling and sweating it out.

Arland Percy Ussher could speak German, French and Spanish

as well as Gaelic; he published slim works of a fine speculative nature that brought in little money, was co-author of *Symbolism in Grimm* with Baron von Metzrardt. He had his Fridays when seekers after wisdom called on him. The house with its cramped rooms was damp, but sometimes hot water came from the taps. Ussher laughed this off.

'We have no hot-water tank.'

'But we have, Arland,' Emily protested.

'I think not.'

A famous writer with a double-barrel name sat like a toad in one corner. The drinks tray tended to vanish after a short interval; two drinks per person was the prescribed allowance. The toad kept one eye on the drinks tray. The party trooped into the kitchen, led by the host, sniggering to himself as his wife pointed out a large boiler set on trestles above the sink.

'And tell me,' demanded Emily sternly, 'what is that?'

'That is undoubtedly a water tank,' cackled Ussher as though this was witty. He was in stitches.

'I too believe that everything is unknown,' said the tweedy toady author in his fatuous way. 'I too am against everything. I too believe that everything is an enemy. *Everything*!'

They set out on foot for the seer's place, a ten-minute brisk walk; were led into a fussily furnished room with a bed in it but no drinks tray or any evidence of bottles. The seer (a secret old love of many years) had the hazel eyes of Weaver's poor deceased mother, though not her high quavery voice. The votive offering of Spanish plonk was broached ('cracked', as Ussher would have it) and served up in plebian teacups, the seer refusing to participate. In a little while she brought out the cards, two used decks with a floral design on the backs. Ussher seated himself on the edge of the bed, a heron on a riverbank, balancing the teacup of bad wine on his knee and smiling into it in a conspiratorial way.

'No interruptions, please. None of your *bon mots*, Arland. I must concentrate. Shall we begin?'

269

Weaver closed his eyes the better to concentrate and a frail disembodied voice inquired of his birthday, birth-hour, his *vagitus* or coming-forth from Lilian (née Boyd) on that auspicious day (it was teeming rain) in early March of 1927, this while shuffling two decks of playing-cards, for Weaver heard the whisper of it, like a moth's wings. He did not know; 3.3.27 was stamped on his dog-collar, would that do? Here Ussher threw in one of his nervous barking laughs, and Weaver's eyes flew open to find the seer staring intently at him with his mother's hazel eyes.

'Silence, Arland! If you would be so good. Or leave us.' And to Weaver, her eyes still fixed on his:

'You know this is not easy for me.'

The sceptical philosopher looked suitably chastened and dipped his lips into the cracked teacup as if taking penance.

'No matter. We will go on . . . we *must* go on, tee-hee-hee,' she cackled.

She began laying out the cards in a certain order, face down on the cloth that covered the card table.

'Choose two cards, any two, and lay them face down, here.'

Before he had taken the two cards into his hands Weaver fancied that he had the utmost freedom to cheat and bamboozle but when he saw the cards, read them (eight of diamonds and two of clubs), he knew that he had had no choice; the cards had been chosen for him and forthwith it was impossible to cheat. Moreover the choice he had made had been fated, preordained. A number of things in the stuffy ill-ventilated room were disturbing; the close proximity of the seer and the odours and heat she generated (not urine and Pond's face powder), the antiseptic odour that clung to the woman's hands. More distinctly disturbing was the red bedspread on which Ussher balanced; and his (Weaver's) mother's eyes staring at him from the strange structure of this woman's face.

When courting Nancy Els some sixteen years previously, such a bedspread covered the narrow single bed that had become their marriage bed in an attic in Belsize Lane in NW3 after they had exchanged vows in the Church of St Thomas More (RC) down the lane. The one-room flat was on the top floor. In that narrow bed Emmett had been conceived.

The seer laid out the cards and studied them, breathing through her nose, intent, squinting, sighing.

'I see two women here.'

Hannelore Schröder of Prinzregentenstrasse, Berlin; Nancy Weaver of Charleston Road, Ranelagh, Dublin.

'One I take to be your wife. The other is . . . I should say tall and rather insolent. She has auburn hair.'

'Black actually,' Weaver said without thinking. Lorelove habitually fiddled with her dark brown hair that had reddish tints in it, worn down over her forehead, to enchance the fire of her dark liquid eyes.

'No matter.'

She liked to stroke the strands of it in an abstracted and very feminine way, while cogitating, or perhaps it was a subtle way of drawing attention to her rapt face? Nancy had said: 'Why pick *her*? There are hundreds of girls in Berlin and you had to pick the prettiest.' But a month later this had changed: 'Why pick her? She is a very common type here. I see hundreds of them walking about.'

'Two women,' the woman said, turning over a card and sighing. 'I see trouble.'

'Yes,' Weaver admitted as if it was his fault.

'You do not love either of them.'

Now she was looking not so much at Weaver as into him with his dead mother's afflicted hazel eyes, one slightly bloodshot.

'Nor yourself either.'

'No.'

'I see another – a little boy. He is yours I think . . . your son?'

'My son Nico.'

'Him you love. It's good you love someone, seeing you cannot love yourself.'

Time was (and had been for some time) running out in a circle, bearing the long-suffering Weaver with it, and with him the frozen philosopher seated on the edge of the red bedspread; gathering speed it was sucked out of the door, obligingly thrown open by no human agency.

The hag was clawing the tattered cards; Ussher was struggling not to laugh aloud in embarrassment; the bedspread was the colour of blood. Once famously 'stoned' in nooky Schwabing this selfsame Weaver, slippery as an eel, had shed copious crocodile tears on Varna's lap, clutching both her hands and blubbering 'Oh I'm bad news for both of them!' to her intense embarrassment. He would presently do himself in, with the narrow razor set in the hair-trimmer that he had pinched from Prendergast. The *suicidio* would be performed near the Magritte-like police telephone kiosk in the Grunewald above Schlachtensee, after swallowing half a bottle of blue vodka, preparatory to opening veins at both ankles, and averting his eyes from the flow.

But this desperate measure had gone the way of all good resolutions (namely, nowhere) and nothing much had ensued but for the dispatching of a bottle of blue Smirnoff in the sunroom at no. 51 Beskidenstrasse, Berlin 14. He had survived, and went to survey the site of his intended demise. The illuminated kiosk on the sandy ridge overlooking Slaughter Lake looked most eerie at dusk.

Walking back he heard again the stutter of high-velocity fire – the American Army patrol firing near the border of the Forbidden Ground. And then, a mockery of it, the quick drilling of a woodpecker above Weaver's head, as grains of sawdust fell, the small intent creature held on with its claws and struck faster than any hammer could strike.

And then, lo and behold, on the sandy ridge, a blonde with ponytail and long tanned legs in the briefest of red shorts, with a trug, bending down for mushrooms. He had proceeded smartly by with pounding heart, but had not gone eighty paces along the path before slowing up and turning back; as if now he were another man, intending to pass this vision again, throw a casual glance.

He saw coming towards him a hag carrying a basket of mushrooms; on passing she threw *him* a shifty look from under twitchy brows.

Now the seer was gathering together all the cards, shuffling them into shape, replaced them in their respective boxes and admitted 'feeling rather tired'. They took this as a hint to leave. 'It takes it out of you,' she said to Weaver, who thanked her for the pains she had taken.

And then they were out in the fresh air again, setting a good steady pace.

'I take it you didn't tell her anything?' asked Weaver.

'Of course not.'

'Strange.'

'It was revealing, I trust.'

'Strange beyond strange,' Weaver said. 'It was uncanny.'

'Ha.'

'That woman knows more about me than I know myself. Revealing isn't the word.'

'No tea-leaves?'

'None.'

They were walking at a swinging pace towards a hostelry in Blackrock where they proposed to imbibe some half pints of foaming black Guinness from the pumps. The sweaty curates were the lads to work the pumps, drawing off frothy half pints with good heads on them.

41

The Other Day I Was Thinking of You

The other day I was thinking of you; or rather of *Nullgrab*, that quartered city you love so much, which amounts to the same thing. When I recall *Nullgrab* I remember you, or vice versa. Go quietly, the ghosts are listening.

Is it even possible to think of somebody in the past? Are the memories of things better than the things themselves? Chateaubriand seemed to think so; and now he too belongs to that past.

I say things but I may mean times. I say things and times but I may mean persons and places, or may be just thinking of you. Your name at the end of the world. That's how it goes, how it always went, how it always will go. One replaces another in what you call *Herz* and the light goes out.

Your voice again. Your eyes in the shadows; reddish tints in your brown hair against the blue-and-white tiles of the Augustinerkeller under the dripping arches of the Bahnhof Zoo in the snow when we drank red wine and were going to a new cinema that was all red upholstery and that movie *If...* was supposed to be showing; but when we went there it wasn't because the cinema hadn't opened yet.

Or in the Rusticano patronized by English Army officers in mufti, with the waiter who always remembered us, from whom you once borrowed money to pay for one more carafe of house wine. You went out of your way to repay him next morning; you were like that, reliable, your word was your bond.

Or in the hothouse dining-room at the Yugoslav hotel with a view of the snow-clad dome that always reminded me of Russia (where I had never been) and slivovitz on the tablecloth that seemed pure Slav (rather poor) and folk music playing and outside was Mexikoplatz on which the *Schnee* lay deep. Or in the well-heated Greek place whose name for the moment escapes me, with the kind waiter who was working his way through university and recommended what was good in Greek food, and we were the only ones there with our backs to the television, Germany versus Italy (or was it Brazil?) in the World Cup, and our waiter said 'You mean to say you have never heard of Pelé?' (so it must have been Brazil) and we said no, and he laughed and said 'Then you are the only two in Berlin who haven't. What do you two do in the daytime? May I get you a drink on the house?'

So we ordered up another bottle of that peculiar Greek (you said 'Greekish') concoction retsina which in fact – unlike the real reality – improves with familiarity. We dined there on a black night of snow and ice when the Karman Ghia was frozen into a solid block and the Greek owner and our friendly waiter came out with ropes and boiling water and laughed heartily as you drove away with your scarf over your nose like a fleeing terrorist (the females were the worst).

Our night refuges.

Today is your name day. You, a true-born Gemini, as the horny Jack Kennedy of 'Eeek-bin-ein-be-leaner' fame. The Berlin brats call out in derision:

> *'Berlin, det Datum weess ick nich,*
> *Ick jlob et heesst verjiss mein nich!'*

and snotty French kids yell out:

'Je te tiens, tu me tiens
par la barbichette.
Le premier de nous deux qui rira,
aura une tapette!'

You smile (a smirk of liquid glue) your rather lopsided smile. Your Englishisms were charming to my ears. You said 'the Hollands' (the Dutch), remember our time in Michaelangelo-straat in Amsterdam; you said 'Trouts ... copulations ... intercourses,' plurals all the way. You called (nicknamed) the good Dr Hahn 'Doktor Cock', ignorant of the slangy ambiguity. You thought every second word in spoken English might have a sexual innuendo. You asked in high dudgeon: 'What do you take me for – an animal in a bux?' You were no animal in a box. 'Yus,' you said in your throaty siren's voice, 'yus.' And *'Oh Quatsch!'* It was another language of another world; you took me there. I couldn't follow you; but I followed you. You took health capsules the size of .22 bullets.

Do you recall the Isar flowing in the wrong direction and an invisible deer crashing through the undergrowth in the Englischen Garten and the geese-shit around the pond and the tattered tribes of hippies with their unstrung guitars below Minopterus and the fine clouds sailing over Munich and Varna's grand flat in Jakob-Klar-Strasse and how suddenly I went all giddy under a tree and the sky whirled above and it was the beer (*mucho*), the Moselle in long-stemmed green goblets and all the Steinhägers of the night before in Schwabing, in fabled and nooky Schwabing? Of course you do.

It was the air. The *Föhn*, the rich Bavarian day, the clouds always on the move; the trees *danced*, the earth moved and the air was all a-tremble in a way well calculated to bring on nausea. I lay on my back on a public bench but it was no good; the earth kept moving, the clouds passing more and more quickly overhead (as though I did not exist) and the leaves were positively *tittering*. And you said, '*Oh Quatsch!*' and took up my head (which had just fallen off and rolled away) and laid it on your warm thigh, still warmed by Bastia, and laid your cool hand on my heated brow. You did, and I became anchored to the earth again. The sky drew back, the leaves stopped tittering, earth and sky stopped their sickening whirling and the giddiness departed. I was with you.

Your cool hand through which sympathy flowed, your calming presence, the warmth of your classical thigh on my neck, all this confirmed that. (Once I had shown you something that you thought shameful. I opened my fist and there it was: an unspent rifle round that I'd found in undergrowth by lapping water near the Jagdschloss. 'Throw it away,' you said sharply. It was just something shameful that I had shown you once.)

Luitpoldstrasse was dug up. They were preparing an underground rail system for the Olympic Games, the killings to come. Our pillow-book was *In Wassermelonenzucker* by Richard Brautigan in the yellow Hanser Verlag paperback just published; and you translated parts back into California hip-talk in the big double bed in Varna's room (she was off in Tuscany with Wolfgang) with the drapes (oatmeal white from curtain-rod to floor) floating in to the sound of the Hindemith cello concerto, the beginning of the second movement with cello solo before the whole orchestra comes soaring back in; which had become a particular *Liebemusik* for that place and time. Your silence meant that in your dark head you were changing German words back into hip-talk.

It was in an outdoor café off Luitpoldstrasse and then we crossed the road and you bought a minute bikini the colour of *eau de Nil*, to look naked and feel more than naked.

For me it was always a giddy time with you, my dearest Schmutz, walking and linking arms in bright sunlight and the air with an earthy aroma in a very lush Bavarian spring. You suggested a siesta. You said in German it was called the little-shepherd-hour. Ach, how twinsome *der Poshlust*! You drew the long wheaten-coloured drapes and all was possible and permitted in the room become a shadowy wood and where all was possible again we removed our clothes in a winking and with them shed all inhibitions.

Afterwards we walked through the Tiergarten (having flown Lufthansa from Munich to Berlin the day before Varna returned from Tuscany) and I offered to take you in the 'sugar-bushes' and you said (rather alarmingly) 'Yus . . . why not. Yus.'

It was our day.

Now I am reading Heine again. About the lovely nixies all dressed in green. Today (Happy birthday!), stricken with longing, I was thinking of you.

42

In Some Far-Off Impossible Place

In some far-off impossible place, perchance lavender-scented Hvar in the Adriatic, in a walled town there, in a cool house rented near the harbour, the harbour of old Hvar, Lore and Weaver together, *nicht wahr*? On that small island where even the donkeys were lavender-scented and everything was blue, was there awaiting them some unimaginably perfect life?

Blooey!

Lore had not been feeling too well in Munich (the *Föhn?*), even less so in Andalucía (the *Terral?*) on the night when the alcoholic remittance man Rex Gamble came hammering on the door at two in the morning, demanding a game of chess. Lore had feared that Gamble, no friend of sobriety, might do Weaver a mischief, immobilized as he was like a mummy in bed with three fractured ribs taped up by the *practicante*, and had sent him packing. She had indeed been most curt, the first time Weaver had encountered that side of her nature.

'Oh *Quatsch!*' she said, expelling her breath. '*Genught* is *genught*. One doesn't start playing chess at two in the morning. And one doesn't play chess with fools.'

It was not so much her impatience with disorder and mess (Gamble's natural ambience) but rather an expression of her tender concern for the suffering patient, taped up and sweating.

'He's a dab hand at chess,' said Weaver. 'At least he can knock the stuffing out of me.'

'Haven't you had enough stuffing knocked out of you?' said Lore, referring to a bout of mock fisticuffs with the stringy American tennis player who had cracked three of Weaver's delicate ribs.

Lore called all men beasts, with their shameful or downright dirty fancies; nose-picking boys who refused to grow up. Betimes, seated on her throne, nude and brown after Bastia, she could be most stern.

43

Five Letters from Lindemann

Haus Hecht
Dahlemdorf
2 Dec. '72

Lieber Professor,

Terrible weather here in Berlin, neither hot nor warm, just grey days, drowning in greyish shade, all colours dirty and everybody in an offensive mood under heavy winter coats. Fatima washing her car before Haus Hecht with a sour face, car radio playing Jungle Boogie by some jerks – Zappo and his Hot Cats – trying to produce rutting noises.

Fatima longing for the sun, dreaming of St Moritz or Cortina. Once a week she goes to a stinking gym for ski-muscle training. She has a theory about her own skin, something about the smoothness of it and its brown pigments and its greed for the sun. Hates pullovers and winter clothes in the city, especially when there is no sun, feeling sticky all the time, her skin developing acne, rotting away. Has several anointings of Nivea Creme during the day.

I remember her being obsessed with some quite strange thoughts when we met first, for instance her fear of kisses, due to her being a dentist's daughter. 'All children of dentists loathe 'kissing,' she used to say then, with her father always talking about people's disgusting dirty mouths.

Her *Papi*, old Immin Kahn, is a strange, fierce-looking man with a wild life-story, a gambler of note, calling all females '*Püppchen*'; but also prone to sudden outbursts of anger, throwing knives and forks about. Or, when left by a girlfriend, walking around with a crutch and dark sunglasses. He has a hearing-aid which he switches off when people talk too much. Something of him in his daughter.

When she was much smaller I saw her with her family in the Berliner Wald – a child with long hair, black fur like an animal, years before we came together. Exotics solemnly walking around the lake, old Immin Kahn leading the way, me on a bicycle behind a tree.

Haus Hecht
Dahlemdorf
3 July '73

Mi profesor!

Sorry for not having written sooner, meant to unclench teeth first but guess I did just the opposite, spending an idle time with a blonde woman (divorcee) in her most corrupt thirties – turned out to be an especially *grässliche* experience, among other things being introduced into her snobbish wonderland, arts and thereabouts. She is working in the Neue Nationalgalerie, *Kunst*, or rather that messed up thing they call the 'scene', a nuthouse papered with money, huge sums circulating in there, spent on whatever imported vanities strike their fancy. *Vernissagen*, exhibitions, grim lectures on the 'grammar' of gleaming limousines neatly decorated with some pig's bloody entrails. Bonn and Berlin in my opinion sponsoring so many wrongdoers and exhibitionists. Conceit, elegant gossip, bombastic atmosphere of so-called *savoir-vivre*, would-be tarts and homos by the dozen, the flashy ones with their proud but none the less shrill self-accusation. Just the setting that promotes murder. Bad cut-up of life.

In Berlin now '*LIEBE*' splashed in aerosol on every second wall and American Chapel announced a 'Love Contest'. Send in a photo depicting your image of love. Don't suppose they want to see my picture. Parties crowded with multicoloured monsters and the inevitable wild Irishman who sits broodingly in a corner, casting wild glances as he is expected to do – Ireland, that evergreen land of obelisks and follies, being still very much à la mode; many young people going there to find out another of their illusory 'real things'. In each and every pub the Dubliners roar out 'Yore dhhrunkk, yore dhhrrrunkkk!' etc., most lustily.

Fatima left home some weeks ago for a boy who drives a Mercedes coupé and keeps telling her that he is a secret agent.

Last thing I remember of the Blonde Disaster is drinking in her best friend's (homo) flat in Wielandstrasse, thirty people talking at once, air full of poison, and BD introducing me to French terms I didn't understand, trios and quadros etc. and me winding up alone in *Berlinerzimmer* without any furniture in it, unless you count an artish object by a certain Votzrello or Vostelli, of pink penis in a glass case fucking a plastic brain.

Had some trouble for weeks to get rid of her, phoning me all day long, Lindemann swearing and menacing and the ruder I became the more persistent she became. Gave her at last a heavy hint of exactly how jealous an Oriental buddy of mine is, Afghanistan knives and all.

I hated that Blonde Bitch after a month's time, but couldn't quite manage to get away at once, probably out of curiosity, and later I tried my best being stone drunk all the time we spent together to avoid her false, theatrical ways in bed. But sure I am just a romantic idiot. But I know what I see in young girls, sense of beginning, not of rotting away. With Fatima gone, Liza hating me in Paris, I am fed up with the whole business at the moment.

Expect you'll raise a mocking eyebrow. Nothing has worked out too well by now, but perhaps it just seems so. Trouble is, am always a little afraid to write to you about it.

Haus Hecht
Dahlemdorf
30 Nov. '73

Mein lieber Freund,

Many old people are found in the Kurgarten now, down the way from Krumme Lanke U-Bahn station. They order *Kaffee und Kuchen*, they are addicted to this, it is somehow fashionable. It's also fashionable to laugh at them, all the old ladies who have seen so many things. But I do not wish them ill; I wish them well. I wish that they will not be run over, all the old ladies who have seen so many things.

Admittedly they give off a peculiar smell, while clicking their dentures; here is the true No Man's Land, this last haven of the mothers and widows of *Wehrmacht* heroes who fell before Stalingrad. This Kurgarten on Fischerhüttenstrasse is their last retreat, you know it well.

Two and a half months later:
I'm writing this in the Kurgarten on a warm day in Berlin, recollecting tranquilly while seated at the window, observing the exotic tree with the bean-like fruits and drinking chilled Moselle in a long-stemmed green-tinged glass as we did before here. You – or a ghost – are sitting opposite me with a good Danemann cigar going well. The young married couple are still serving, the fellow with the preoccupied air, the pretty young wife with the long hair. You are watching her taking an order in the garden.

Leiber Professor,

The reason I am writing today is that I had a dream last night in which you figured prominently. You and your wife were living in Berlin in a house located close to the Steglitz part of the Teltowkanal, the grounds adjacent to the backside of the Klinikum-Hospital, which one could see from a window.

You and your wife and me stood eating Langsee ice-cream in a bright room without any furniture. Your wife was tall, blonde and thin. You and I were arguing about your refusal to show me around the house. Your wife told me that you're only trying to hide your daughter from me. I said that I didn't know that you had a daughter. You assured me you had none. Your wife laughed and made some signs with her hands.

I left the room to walk about the house, you and your wife following me, your wife laughing all the time and gesticulating. I felt very tense. I opened a door to a room where a bunch of children of uncertain age and sex were playing a game. This room had no furniture either.

I discovered a steep staircase going down to a basement. I asked you, where does it lead to? You said, to the kitchen. . . .You produced a piece of paper from your pocket and began reading aloud. I didn't understand the words. I went down the staircase and your voice faded. I came to a corridor the walls of which were all covered with photos showing you and a girl, you wearing sunglasses. The girl reminded me of somebody I knew and longed to see. The longing became so strong that I had to sit down on the floor, feeling quite sick.

The corridor led to a door which opened after some time and a beautiful dark-haired girl appeared, approached and sat down beside me. She wore a black dress.

It was my Paris friend from Madrid. She said something in a language I didn't understand. We went upstairs and came to a garden. The house was gone. The garden went down to the canal.

You were working in the garden with enormous tools, wearing sunglasses. You didn't notice us. You were sitting there under a tree with a gun. One of those old cargo boats was going by on the canal. We swam to the boat and sat on it. We were floating down the canal, making love, when, passing the hospital, my sister Uschi looked out from one of the windows, shouting, 'It's war!'

They came towards us, right down the canal. They were firing and we were hit. Then I sat on a chair and somebody was standing behind me and repeating the sentence: 'It's your fault. You will never see her again.'

I really felt sad this morning, like you do after certain dreams. There are no cargo boats on the canal any more, they've closed it long ago.

What is one to make of all this, asks your *lieber Freund*

Martin

PS: You inquired about Bavaria. What can be said about Bavaria? Your true Bavarian was ever a lover of baggy *Lodens*, creamy *torten*, dogs of every description, mighty dangerous politics. Regard the wild man Strauss, not to mention *der Führer* himself, and everloyal Blondi. Keep out of it I say.

Haus Hecht
Dahlemdorf
12 August '75

Dear Professor,

Nothing much changes here. A scene of social life just like any other, did I hear you mutter? Vell, *ja und nein*. Depends what you mean by social, and (if it goes to that) by life. Go to; half a dozen chilled Schultheiss Pils on the way.

The ex-capital holds its own as a rude Prussian should. At times charming (Schöneberg), free and easy (the green lungs of Zehlendorf); at times repulsive (Wedding, Reinickendorf). The young are said to be returning but I could do without them. We believe that we can hear the howling of wolves. Psychopaths prowl the Grunewald in search of spooning couples, knock the lad on the head, screw the arse off the girl. That's quite normal here.

But look; some complacent elderly folk, lovers of nature and evening occupy a public bench facing into the setting sun overlooking Schlachtensee. The sun is laying down its last brilliance out towards Riemeisterfenn and the memorial stone to Polizei-Wachtmeister Fritz Gohrs killed (*Hier starb im Dienst am 20.7.1928*) when you were but one year old (hard to believe, but there you are).

The evening ducks fly in making that little skidding sound with their webbed feet on the surface, surfing in. A woman is humming to herself; a dog-bell tinkles in the wood above the gazebo. A large fierce German version of a French poodle cocks its leg against the bench which it has just suspiciously sniffed but the elderly nature-lovers pay no attention to the ensuing flood. They hear the sound of an S-Bahn train rumbling over the points or does one say sleepers.

Over there beyond the trees where the sandy ground rises up lies Kladow-over-Havel, *Da Drüben*, *Sperrgebiet* or what they (and we too) call the GDR or Forbidden Ground. You say we should expect a lion and lioness to come down and drink in the cool of the evening (so golden) any minute now. They do not appear. A long line of punts are being ferried back to the boathouse. They are tied together (does one say lashed?).

All around lies Prussia (say it again). Prussian soil; when cavalry charged it must have sounded like a drum; the earth of Germany, the heartlands lost, Brandenburg sand. The Brandenburg Gate is lost as Potsdam, both submerged under water, though still vaguely visible down there, on a clear day. You would recall those blue cloudless Berlinish days that can still occur all the year round? You do of course. Theodor Hosemann painted it: the spud-sellers by night at the Brandenburg Gate, snow on the winter trees, the lantern and the horses, the clasped hands. The whole as it were vibrating, as from the sudden heart-warming effects of a good slug of Steinhäger on a freezing day.

Ah, mein Inneres, Crimson-Rosen! Guten Tag, Monsieur Ich!

Anyway the line of punts tied or lashed together now passes a choleric red-faced swimmer who is crossing by breast-stroke in the too-close proximity of a huge Alsatian hound that is attempting to mount him *a tergo* in the water. The master is roaring and spluttering: '*Neinneinfritzy! Arschlockken! Scheissermensch Hund!*

Your '*Nullgrab*' exists for me. Always beyond itself, beside itself, tickled to death by itself, divided up against itself; set against another *Nullgrab* it cannot see, will never be permitted to see, as long as there are handguns in holsters or *Apen* in Africa (you see I am still the loyal zoo-attender at heart). So what is one to do about it?

Why, nothing, friend.

The father has eaten sour grapes and the teeth of the children are set on edge. What do they do in Lapland when the lights go out? Where was What'shisname when the lights went out? Where did Jacko put the nuts? And what remains?

Only a lurid glow in the sky. A red animal eye winking at the tip of the *Funkturm* over the Wall; no sanguine animal eye there where the Panting Quest (for the impossible) goes on and on *ad infinitum*; grown more difficult daily, more purposeful, hourly. *Nicht wahr?*

On the other side of the mirror we have the Outpost Cinema for the American 40th Army Brigade, showing movies that are the equivalent of high meat tossed to ravenous hounds before the hunt: currently *Cauldron of Blood*. I suppose skinflicks would only serve to remind them too painfully of home, and thegirltheydidn'tquitemanagetoscrew next door. With these cold crumbs of comfort I must leave you, *Meister*.

Stay well.
Hasta luego,

Martin

44

An Epistle from Lore

Prinzregentenstrasse 5

9 May '75

My dearest Schmutz,

I read somewhere: '*Im Gemäuer pfiff der beste Wind.*' Things are never as they appear at first glance and when we look closer we find strange and unfamiliar (unknown?) aspects of what we imagine we know, and of our first impressions not even the memory remains.

Such is the way with faces we imagine, of cities before we know them, or anybody in them (!), which we picture (so wrongly) in such and such a way – only to forget all our fancies at sight of the real thing. Such is the way with your *Nullgrab* (where you yourself are grievously missed by those who knew you, including myself), a spoiled city left over from another century, another history.

But perhaps one day you will find yourself again in this bracing city, half-city, in our leftover time. Drop your luggage in *Nullgrab* and never leave again; find *Liebe* again (at last!) in the arms of one ever-obliging Berlin girl (I think you know the one I mean). As did clever Dr Kafka . . . twice.

How can I go without you? How can you go without me? The

thought seeks a way out, as the prisoner in his small cell. You are here, yet not here. And I am sailing over the Havel with society people whom I do not like, and you would certainly *hate*. I am doing much swimming and diving and believe as a consequence that my breasts and bottom have got bigger, a legacy of idleness that you cannot enjoy.

When do you think to return, Sire? *Wann kommst Du?* When come you? Back to your much-depraved and ever-loving

Lorelei

PS I keep away from what you would call our old haunts, the walks about Krumme Lanke and Schlachtensee, because of too-painful memories.

PPS If you don't come, to you I then say just: '*Pfiff* off!'

45
The Long Train

Potsdam! Potsdam! cried the station sign in old *Sütterlin*, bringing to mind Chateaubriand and Malaparte the congenital liar and once again weedy Laforgue, *Mädchen in Uniform*, garrison bells, old Europe, lost time – two titled Italian ladies wait on a bridge (*Brücke*) as Curzio Malaparte strolls to meet them, smiling craftily, uniformed and pomaded. What was his real name? and what was he up to? No good for sure.

Now the same pigeons came again, racing before the train, fanning out over the loveliest of duck-egg-blue domes, as a sudden breeze again ruffled the surface of the pond and a single unarmed soldier continued to march towards the firing-range. Potsdam was passing, passing.

Here comes a fat officer, fairly bursting out of his regulation Red Army breeches, his great posterior weighing down a frail bike, so that he rides on the rims, wending his way towards some excruciatingly tedious office routine.

Then the firing-range, a pond ruffled by an early morning breeze that put up a flock of crows, sent them veering away. The portly cyclist went wobbling out of sight behind a pile of up-ended street-signs, as a slow goods-train drew in alongside, shuddering and spewing water; carrying what appeared to be tarpaulin-shrouded battle tanks with their long barrels not yet in place; but which on closer inspection turned out to be innocent agricultural machinery – bulldozers, tractors, JCBs and the like, now brought grindingly and groaningly to a slothful halt, as Weaver moved across to the other window and saw pigeons race athwart a cupola weathered to the pale green of a bird's egg.

Approaches to Berlin are sinister. You know you are approaching the site of a great calamity. In the thinning dark the watch-towers loom out of the mist. The war may have been over for a quarter of a century but these wooden towers are not empty; powerful binoculars were focused on the Mittel-Europa Express just now closing in on West Berlin, packed with degenerate Capitalist swine.

In the long express train that had come from Ostend through Belgium and all the stations with the names of First World War battlefields, the Poles were asleep, when Weaver made his way to the buffet. Unwashed and steaming the Poles slept amid mounds of baggage. The carriage for West Berlin came last. The long train was bound for Moscow on a different gauge into another time.

Passports had been checked at 6 a.m. in the dark; an hour later at sun-up, passports and identity photos had been double-checked once more against the partially awake ones; the murky wattage presenting the stiff elongated features of corpses.

A small wooden portable contraption depended from the bully neck of the Saxon *Vopo* guard who was taciturn and overly suspicious; nobody would pull a fast one on him. He checked photos against faces, studied the pages of passports, stamped a date. The toilets had been searched for desperadoes crouched like cats above the cistern; not once or twice but thrice, as if the object of their search – could it even be human? – was getting smaller and smaller as they prodded and poked, flushed, cursing. Alsatian sniffer dogs had been released under the carriages to no avail; no escapees clung there, riddled with pebbles.

A sinister fellow in a belted trenchcoat had swung himself aboard and was huggermuggering with the *Vopos* in the corridor, minutely examining one particular passport that had aroused their suspicions. The last such search and inspection would be carried out on the GDR-Berlin border, now rapidly approaching. Ahead lay the Free West, so called; behind for two hundred kilometres all was Soviet-annexed territory, stretching into the semi-darkness.

Now the murmured consultation broke up and the same burly *Vopo* came back into the carriage. In dumbshow he ordered all to rise so that the space below the seats could be formally checked, as also the luggage racks. This was done, all avoiding his eye; passports were returned and he departed with ill grace, none too pleased. He had found nothing; but he had performed his duty, he could do no more. The carriage door was closed and the black ladies, Weaver's travelling companions, turned to sleep again. Weaver unstuck himself from his seat, searched out the toilets, relieved his bladder, straightened his clothes, dashed cold water on his face, stood by the open window, smelt the Berlin woods. A thin sliver of yellow light ran along the horizon (sanies into a German bucket?) and crows flew over the fields as if in freedom, as Potsdam had drifted by on the left, as if seen underwater. As if, as if . . .

The Mittel-Europa Express began to get itself into motion again with much clanking and pissing off of steam and for anxious Weaver a moment of elation as he felt the wheels gather power again, eating up the kilometres now, and Berlin not far away.

Under full power the express passed screaming through an empty station deserted but for a female guard in uniform with peroxided hair propping up an unbecoming cap. She wore slingback shoes suggestive of Lili Marlene and the 1940s, for time had stopped on this line in the spring of 1945. She raised her right hand in a vague salute or greeting as they flew by.

On the road alongside the rail-bed two GDR youths were slicking back their Elvis hairdos of oily quiffs on the way to work. They had been born and reared into Soviet time, their occupied land teemed with soldiers in Red Army uniform, ever on the alert, trained for war. The GDR cemeteries were untended; these few millions of former German subjects could not lie easy in alien soil, the land itself was no longer theirs.

Then the racing sign in old *Sütterlin* cried out NIKOLASSEE as the express went racketing through and Weaver felt that he was indeed almost home. Come all the way back from Ostend in the warmly enveloping company of three female black medical students, one of surpassing beauty; they had travelled from Moscow to London for textbooks and clothes and were now returning, cheeking the *Vopos*, showing their white teeth. When they had passed their exams in Russian and qualified as doctors, they would return to their own homelands, to Tanganyika and Mali and Mauritania, to care for the sick in their own language. Had they liked Moscow? Certainly they had; Moscow was a great place. The trio exuded an irrepressible African energy. The carriage stank of lioness; they talked all the way. Nothing could diminish their high spirits; nothing, not even the soured Saxon *Vopos*.

Now came the Berliners from their darkened sleeping-carriages into the brightly rocking corridor flooded with sunlight, for they were now fairly rollicking along; the men in string vests engaged in methodical toilet as if in their own *Berlinerzimmers*. It was just gone eight o'clock on a thoroughly German morning and the long train from Ostend had not lost any time, pulling in again on schedule. The end carriages were beyond the platform and passengers for Berlin were obliged to step down onto the tracks and walk into West Berlin. But Lore was not there to meet him.

Descending from the arrival platform in the press of passengers eagerly pushing down to the Zoologischer Garten concourse Weaver recognized her white boots somewhat in advance of the waiting crowd below and elatedly descended to meet his fate. The Karman Ghia was in the Amerika Haus car park and the building bullet-ridden and cordoned off with police on guard. A handsome officer told Lore that they went through at their own risk; a bomb was said to be planted inside. They were searching for it.

Lore took Weaver's hand and said 'Alright then, we go together,' and hand in hand they crossed the minefield. Within minutes they would be safe within the Rusticano.

Epilogue: To the Havel Shore

Now *Dampfer Siegfried* passes *Motorschiff Vaterland*, the former outward-bound for Spandau, the latter heading in for the Wannsee landing.

On *Vaterland* the day-trippers crowd the rails, pointing binoculars, cameras, rude fingers in derision at two distant figures (men) who stand by the water's edge, both rather corpulent targets for mockery, one skimming flat stones, the other observing the wakes rushing to become one.

The two distinguished writers, one at the beginning of his career, the other well advanced, Günter Grass and Herr Max Frisch, have been discussing the mysteries of murderous fertilization in the world at large. The maggot in the sheep's head, Orizaba in the Mexican tropics and what goes on there, the snake under a stone in the scorching Sahara, the industrious weaver birds that build their communal homes on telegraph poles along the margins of the Kalahari Desert – nests of twigs and straw become heavy as haycocks, bending the poles down to the ground. India's teeming millions. The prolixity of the Russian Masters (such as Tolstoy) attempting in their free-flowing lines to match the very vastness of the steppes, and the Russian soul trapped in space. Thomas Mann's own imperious onwardflowing lines.

Max Frisch had flown in from Paris on the day before and tonight dines with Günter and Anna Grass, flying out tomorrow to Zurich, homeward-bound via Swiss Air. Grass expertly skims stones across the wrinkled surface of the Havel, the old *Fluss Flies* broadening out into a veritable Vistula before his narrowed Kirgiz or do we mean Pomeranian eyes.

Frisch (Mr Fresh?) lays a restraining hand on the younger man's muscular right arm (that of a sculptor of monumental graveyard statuary) and feels the biceps ripple and bulge. Grass with mustachio bristling throws and recoils on his heels as though he were a great cannon firing cannonballs across the quivering surface of the Havel, firing out a clever skimmer that dips and jumps eleven (eleven!) times, then twelve, then thirteen, then a feeble fourteenth before subsiding under the surface of the Havel, sinking down – a German record! whaddyaknow?

The hand laid briefly on the German's good right arm is almost feminine, always very dirty, stained from pipe tobacco. This was the hand of the architect who had designed the Zurich public *Schwimmbad* and written that curious novel *Homo Faber*. His friend Lindemann claimed that he loved people but not himself, not Frisch; and that this was only (or mostly) evident in his way of walking, of holding his head, his whole Frischian presence. The Swiss themselves dismissed him as a *Nestbeschmutzer* or soiler of the spotlessly clean Swiss nest and all the eggs laid in it. He had written to his friend Uwe Johnson: '*Von einem toten Partner auf Umwegen zu hören, man sei der Liebe nicht fähig, ich meine, das kann schon irritieren, veilleicht sogar töten.*'*

FRISCH: Almost every object is sexy. Even swans.

GRASS: Yes, thank God. All that lives is holy.

---

* The fearless Swiss Euro-surgeon who had practised open-heart surgery on himself in *Montauk*, wrote to Uwe Johnson: 'By the way, dear Uwe, you're not the only one who remarked on my sentence *what this woman has cost me* . . . To hear from a dead beloved, and through the grapevine, that one is incapable of loving, I mean: this can be irritating, can even kill you . . .'

'Even swans,' Grass affirms, firing off another projectile. With a short barking laugh he backs away from the incoming wake, for the swarthy Kashubian is some sixteen years Frisch's junior and feels himself to be the equal of anybody writing in German, and the answer to every maiden's prayer. He continues to skim stones from further up the beach. His is a smouldering presence. In the corner of the carnivore mouth the regulation spent third of an untipped Gauloise; on his feet, clogs; on the cruiserweight boxer's torso, a black turtleneck jumper above faded denim slacks; on the face, a dark scowl; in his heart, a murderous complicity. He squints, adjusts nicely his angle of throw, observing all the while through slitty Kirgiz eyes: the figure of his disgruntled Swiss friend (who is trying him out, pulling his leg, fishing for something), the grey Havel (great bodies of water intoxicate him), the pleasure-craft diminishing into the distance, their wakes becoming one, like a muscle. (It sank at once.)

A chill breeze blows over Schlachtensee and over the sunken Lancaster Bomber that lies in the mud, giving the stoutly panting exercisers goose-pimples; the water-lilies stretch out their rubbery fronds, and again comes the sound of a train entering Berlin outskirts from *Da Drüben*, maybe a troop-train carrying personnel to the US 40th Armored Division (motto: Have Guns Will Travel), or a passenger-train coming from the Alps; going over the points, the sleepers, the sound waxing and waning, coming and going, both close by and distant, but passing, passing.

With his feminine finger Frische tamps down tobacco into the bowl of his curly Swiss pipe, smiling to himself, thinking his own thoughts. Grass smokes untipped Gauloises; one could almost tell their respective prose styles from a study of their smoking habits. The phlegmatic Swiss pipe-smoker suggests a crafty (crafted?) fastidiousness, a mixture of Dr Jung (who after all never professed to cure anybody who consulted him, but would listen patiently to their story, their trouble) and a trusted physician. Günter Grass was not quite Jean Gabin but more like Fritz Busch the steelworker giving out a rousing Kurt Weill number (*'Mackie Messer'*) from *Die Dreigroschenoper*; his steaming breath visible on a frosty morning outside the Hamburg steelworks.

Even the swans ... achh! Tich-tich! Even their names came from the mocking Berlin wit of the quick-witted dead ones, Zille and Grete Weiser, the Berliner *Schnauze*.

Saftpresser and Pussi,
Punze and Pfefferbuches,

Schwanzschlucker and Vogelkiste,
Stekdose and Klemme,

Ente and Altes Haus,
Hohlweg and Bruntrutsche,

Furchel and Fotze,
Glitsche and Steckdase,

Schnappfotze and Fictnitze,
Muschi and Loch,

Rille and Alte Tasche,
Aquarium and Mülltüte,

Waschwanne and Scheunentor,
Lustzapfen and Kitzler,

Planschbecken and Ding,
Dattel and Fotzenwarze,

Rubikon and Kellerdeckel,
Schnappfotze and Eisernervorhang,

Orgel and Muse,
Klemfotze and Fictritze

Steckdose and Zwickezwickezwickezwickezwickezwicke ...

But the record has stuck at Zwicke and refuses to go on. And now they all come gobbling and beshitting themselves and twirling their short stumpy rumpy tails in that peerless and uncommonly brilliant *Doppelbleiche* way, moving awkwardly along the man-made Havel shore, swaying their great full crops.

It is all passing. It will all pass. And still nothing passes, nothing at all. (Everything has passed too soon.)

A hawk flies down Schlüterstrasse in the rain. Herr Carsten of leafy Lichterfelde lies buried in a small district cemetery, having expired in a state of insanity in woody Schöneberg's *maison de Santé*; Schöneberg being the district he despised most, now better known for its rash of stinking pizzerias. In Zehlendorf's loamy Waldfriedhof Erich Hinüber (Eric-all-over) sleeps his last sleep.

Nullgrab only half exists.

A blue evening has fallen and the early prostitutes, the early birds that catch the worms, have started parading the Kurfürstendamm pavements where traffic rages up and down. *Nullgrab* does not exist. City of Max Klante, the Skylanke brothers, Bernotat the bibliomaniac, the notorious Sass brothers. Snowbound city of Zille and Theodor Hosemann.

Now, today, this evening, the ever-jovial Doornkaat-drinker raises his glass and invites you to imbibe. Figure me there, tosspots.

Of all that remains, what residue is there, I ask you, trapped in vertiginous Time? Bahnhof's unbanishable stench. Egon the tame Komodo waran, last of the dragons, stalking down the Aquarium steps on its leash, sticking out a forked tongue so long ago. Do you hear me now?

Stir it up.

Langrishe, Go Down

Winner of the James Tait Black Memorial Prize

To the local people of Celbridge, County Kildare, the name of Langrishe spells money, position and respect. Yet long years of parsimony and neglect are telling on the old family house and its inhabitants. It is here that Imogen, youngest and most captivating of four unmarried sisters, begins her discreet, then heedless, affair with Otto Beck, the German scholar-poacher who has lived rent-free in the Langrishe farm cottage longer than any of them can remember.

'Higgins is very good at recreating the feeling of release and free flow of all senses that comes with the first bouts of physical love'
Guardian

'This carefully constructed and intelligent book . . . is ironic and witty in its juxtapositions'
New York Saturday Review

A. L. KENNEDY

Looking for the Possible Dance

'This beautiful novel is the story of Margaret and the two men in her life: her father, who brought her up, and Colin, her lover . . . A tender, moving story, punctuated by flashes of comedy and one climactic moment of appalling violence'
Literary Review

'A writer rich in the humanity and warmth that seems at a premium in these bleak times'
Salman Rushdie

'Praise the Lord and pass the orchids – a *real* writer is among us, with a beautiful first novel'
Julie Burchill

'An austere and intense talent . . . A. L. Kennedy turns pointlessness into significance'
Sunday Telegraph

'Here is the most promising of the rich new crop of Scottish writers'
Scotsman

'A novel of undeniable warmth and charm'
Jonathan Coe, *Guardian*

ITALO CALVINO

Mr Palomar

'Here, Calvino, probably Italy's leading novelist before he died, focuses a probing eye on one man's attempt to name the parts of his universe, almost as though Mr Palomar were trying to define and explain his own existence. Where the Palomar telescope points out into space, Mr Palomar points in: walking the beach, visiting the zoo, strolling in his garden. Each brief chapter reads like an exploded haiku, with Mr Palomar reading a universe into the proverbial grain of sand'
Time Out

'Calvino represents a highpoint of literary evolution; his skill is immense but retains a simian agility. As ever, his gaze is crystal-clear and his writing has the easy beauty of clarity. *Mr Palomar* is a work of cunning dialectics that goes beyond the delight in paradoxes for which Calvino is lazily praised'
New Statesman

'Like the nervous hero of *Mr Palomar* (superbly translated), Italo Calvino always had a telescope's eye for what can only be called the thingness of things. Stars and planets, birds, a loaded food counter, all take on an extra reality, as though observed for the first time in wonder by a man previously blind. Mr Calvino was a magician whose voice commanded us: listen, look, understand'
Sunday Telegraph

LAWRENCE NORFOLK

Lemprière's Dictionary

'What serpentine narration secretly connects the founding of the East India Company in 1600, a massacre of innocents at the siege of La Rochelle twenty-seven years later, and the publication of Lemprière's celebrated classical dictionary on the eve of the French Revolution? The answer is this ingeniously contrived, spell-binding fable. An extraordinary first novel'
City Limits

'It's poised, superbly inventive and ... gripping. With *Lemprière's Dictionary* the precocious author has catapulted himself into the premier league of English fiction writing'
Observer

'An extraordinary achievement ... at once a quest, a tragedy, a political thriller and a cultural meditation. It is a remarkable book'
Times Literary Supplement

'This is historical fiction of mesmerising complexity ... It is a masterpiece'
Daily Mail

'Astonishingly assured ... an engrossing and wonderfully intricate extravaganza'
London Review of Books

'A love story, and a story of fantastic adventure, it is also a hugely comic novel ... immense verve and brilliance'
Sunday Times

A Selected List of Titles Available from Minerva

☐	7493 9931 7	**An Act of Terror**	André Brink	£7.99
☐	7493 9985 6	**Rumours of Rain**	André Brink	£6.99
☐	7493 9147 2	**Explosion in a Cathedral**	Alejo Carpentier	£5.99
☐	7493 9970 8	**Afternoon Raag**	Amit Chaudhuri	£4.99
☐	7493 9705 5	**The Name of the Rose**	Umberto Eco	£6.99
☐	7493 9878 7	**The Call of the Toad**	Gunter Grass	£5.99
☐	7493 9080 8	**Balzac's Horse**	Gert Hofmann	£4.99
☐	7493 9174 X	**The Mirror Maker**	Primo Levi	£5.99
☐	7493 9792 6	**A River Sutra**	Gita Mehta	£5.99
☐	7493 9727 6	**The English Teacher**	R. K. Narayan	£5.99
☐	7493 9966 X	**Lucie's Long Voyage**	Alina Reyes	£3.99
☐	7493 9710 1	**The Makioka Sisters**	Junichirō Tanizaki	£6.99